Sam felt as if all the breath had been knocked out of him.

He counted back and realized it was a full three months since their night together.

Lila was going to have a baby. That would explain her contradictory actions, one minute flirting and the next throwing an invisible wall between them and refusing to go out with him.

Had she come to Texas and expected to avoid telling him? Anger stirred that she would hide the truth. Maybe she was going to wait until she was back in California to let him know.

She had to realize she couldn't hide it forever.

A baby. Their baby. He *would* marry her.

DEEP IN A
TEXAN'S HEART

BY
SARA ORWIG

Published in Great Britain 2013
by Mills & Boon, an imprint of Harlequin (UK) Limited,
Eton House, 18-24 Paradise Road, Richmond, Surrey TW9 1SR

© Harlequin Books S.A. 2013

Special thanks and acknowledgement to Sara Orwig for her contribution to the TEXAS CATTLEMAN'S CLUB: THE MISSING MOGUL miniseries.

ISBN: 978 0 263 90481 9
ebook ISBN: 978 1 472 00624 0

51-0813

Harlequin (UK) policy is to use papers that are natural, renewable and recyclable products and made from wood grown in sustainable forests. The logging and manufacturing processes conform to the legal environmental regulations of the country of origin.

Printed and bound in Spain
by Blackprint CPI, Barcelona

Sara Orwig lives in Oklahoma. She has a patient husband who will take her on research trips anywhere, from big cities to old forts. She is an avid collector of Western history books. With a master's degree in English, Sara has written historical romance, mainstream fiction and contemporary romance. Books are beloved treasures that take Sara to magical worlds, and she loves both reading and writing them.

Thanks to Charles Griemsman, Stacy Boyd
and Allison Carroll.

Thank you to a special group of writers: Maureen
Child, Kathie DeNosky, Tessa Radley, Yvonne Lindsay,
Jules Bennett, Janice Maynard, Sarah Anderson
and Charlene Sands.

Thanks to readers for their support,
enthusiasm and friendship.

One

When Sam Gordon idly glanced over the crowd at the annual Hacket barbecue, a head of straight auburn hair caught his attention. It could be only one person. Lila Hacket's silky hair was a unique color, a deep auburn shot through with red strands as natural as the rest of Lila. She was back in town and his pulse jumped over the prospect. Had she come home for the barbecue? Memories of Lila heated Sam's insides while the horse conversation faded, replaced by memories of holding Lila's warm, naked body against his.

The ranchers around him laughed over something Beau Hacket said, so Sam smiled, trying to pick up again on the conversation. Beau proudly pointed out his latest acquisition, a three-year-old sorrel, to the Texas Cattleman's Club members gathered beside the corral.

Standing with her back to him, Lila chatted with another group of guests. She was taller than several women around her. She wore a turquoise sundress that had narrow straps and a top that came down over her hips, hiding her tiny waist. Her feet were in high-heeled sandals and she looked luscious. Certain he would talk to her before the evening was over, Sam attempted once more to focus on those around him. Local cattle rancher Dave Firestone and gray-haired energy magnate Paul Windsor quizzed Josh, Sam's twin, on horses. Josh loved horses, one more thing Sam didn't share with his twin.

"Beau, did you get that horse around here?" Chance McDaniel asked.

"No. I drove to a sale in Cody, Wyoming. But that isn't the kind of horse you need on your dude ranch."

"My place is a working ranch, too, and I'd like to have another cutting horse," Chance replied, his green-eyed gaze roaming over the horses.

"Chance, you need some horses like the little mare I have for Cade. Something gentle even a four-year-old can ride," Gil Addison, another local rancher, added.

Sam was not involved with horses but most of the men in his circle were horsemen one way or another, from Ryan Grant, now retired from the rodeo circuit, to rancher Dave Firestone. All belonged to Royal's elite Texas Cattleman's Club and Sam saw them often enough that he didn't mind breaking away from the group.

"Y'all excuse me," Sam said. "I'll be back." He strolled away in an easy stride that belied the anticipation bubbling in him. When Lila had not returned his call the morning after their one-nighter, he had let it go. There were other women in his life. That had been three months ago—three months in which he couldn't shake her out of his thoughts.

Why was she back in town? Laughing, she moved away from the people standing around her. Determined not to lose her, Sam walked a little faster through the crowd.

It took only another minute to catch up. "Lila, welcome back."

When she turned, there was an almost imperceptible flicker in the depth of her crystal-green eyes. "Sam," she said. In spite of her smile, there was no warmth in her voice. "I hope you're enjoying the party," she said, sounding as if they were polite strangers and had never shared a night together. This was not a reaction he usually had with women.

"This is a great party, as usual. Better now that you're here. Did you come home for the barbecue?"

"No, as a matter of fact. I'm in town to set up for a movie that'll be filming on ranches here at the end of the month," she said. "It's nice to see you again. Enjoy yourself at the party." She turned slightly to greet her longtime friend Shannon Fentress, still thinking of her as Shannon Morrison, instead of Mrs. Rory Fentress since her recent marriage.

"Hi, Shannon. Just welcoming Lila back to town," he said.

"It's the first of August, just in time for her family's big annual party—who would miss this? I think all of Royal is here," Shannon said. "Lila, that barbecue is the most tempting smell ever. Too bad they can't bottle and sell it like perfume."

Lila laughed. "C'mon. We have a new chef. You can meet him. 'Course, my dad is going to supervise. Excuse us, Sam," she said sweetly, motioning to Shannon to follow her.

Sam watched them walk away, his gaze raking over Lila's back. Her cool reception had been a first for him. He didn't get that reaction from women. He frowned as he watched the slight flare of her hips, the sexy swing to her walk. As he studied her, he wanted to go out with her.

He shook his head and turned to go get a cold beer. Lila didn't take after her dad. She didn't even seem much like her mother, who was friendly, always happy to stay in her husband's shadow, to be the wife in the background. In her own quiet way, Barbara Hacket kept Beau happy, entertained constantly and had charity projects without ever showing the streak of independence Lila did—that need to get away from Royal, to have a fancy job. Lila and her brother, Hack, were light-years apart.

As if his thinking about Hack had conjured him, Sam greeted her brother as he approached. "Great party, as always, Hack."

"Dad knows how to have a barbecue. Saw you talking to my snooty sister," Hack said.

"Snooty is okay. At least your sister's kind of snooty is. It may not run deep," Sam replied, still watching Lila as she disappeared into the house with Shannon.

"Like a challenge, huh?" Hack said, rocking on his heels and hooking his thumbs over his hand-tooled belt. "Guess you're right. Chicks are easy. Sometimes it's sweeter when there's a challenge because most chicks are so eager they're boring."

Lost in thought about Lila, Sam barely heard Hack.

"My hotshot sister is home from L.A., where she thinks she's setting the world on fire with her highfalutin movie job," Hack continued. "She's living alone out there—or so she says—probably because no one will live with Miss Snooty. It gives me more money from the old man. My sister can just stay in California. It's a good place for her. Royal, on the other hand, does have the hot chicks. Think so, Sam?"

"There are fine people in Royal, Texas," Sam said, his thoughts still only partially on Hack.

"Speakin' of hot chicks, I see Anna June Wilson. If you'll excuse me," Hack said, walking away.

Sam took a deep breath, glad Hack had moved on. At seventeen, the kid was spoiled rotten by Beau. Sam had seen Hack around his dad. The kid was smart enough to keep on Beau's good side most of the time. The rest of the time, Beau bailed him out of trouble.

Sam raked his fingers through his hair and strode to the outdoor bar on the large patio. After Lila had returned to California, he'd called her. When she hadn't taken his calls, he had stopped phoning. Was she cool because he hadn't continued to pursue her? He should forget Lila Hacket. Trouble was, he hadn't been able to forget Lila.

"Dammit," he said under his breath.

"Sam Gordon, what are you doing standing by yourself?"

"Just looking for you, darlin'," he said, smiling at Sally Dee Caine, the perfect antidote for Lila. Known by every male in Maverick County, Sally Dee was fun and Sam enjoyed her in small doses. He took in her bright pink, low-cut, clinging jersey blouse and tight faded jeans. "You look good enough, Sally Dee, to make me forget about the enticing barbecue that's cooking. I might find what I want right here," he said, nuzzling her neck. Giggling, she wrapped her arm in his.

"Sam, you're usually a partying fool. C'mon, the fiddler's wound up and there's a barn filled with two-steppers dancing the time away."

"I thought you'd never ask," he said, grinning as he draped his arm across her shoulders and pulled her close against his side. While she slipped her arm around his waist, they headed toward the Hackets' big brown barn.

* * *

"Sorry if I interrupted you if you wanted to stay and talk to Sam," Shannon said as she walked beside Lila.

"No, you rescued me. I know you don't care to meet the barbecue cook. Let's head for the dining room. We can get some of Agnes's artichoke dip."

"Your parents' cook is the best in Maverick County."

"She's good, but we have a lot of good cooks around here. Also, I saw her carrying a tray of gorgeous fruit into the dining room."

"Yum. I won't argue that one. It's great to have you home. As usual, your family's barbecue is fabulous. Each year, this barbecue seems to be bigger than the year before."

"I think it is bigger. Nearly all the Texas Cattleman's Club members are here. There's an undercurrent this year, though. I hear people talking about Alex Santiago's disappearance. That mystery has some on edge."

"No one knows what happened to him and they're keeping publicity about it to a minimum, I think. Or maybe they just really don't know anything. It's odd and it's scary. No one, much less a member of the Texas Cattleman's Club, just disappears."

"Alex Santiago did."

Shannon shivered. "I hope they find him soon. I understand that he's a wealthy investor—who knows what he's involved in? What about you? You said you're on vacation for two weeks?"

"Yes. I have to be here in two weeks anyway because the studio will be shooting a picture in the area. I took two weeks off beforehand. I'm working a little, trying to select locations, but I'm taking some private time for myself."

"Your work sounds like a dream job."

"Sometimes it is. It can get hectic, but I'm learning and I like what I do."

"You have two weeks' vacation." Shannon's blue eyes focused on Lila. "Why don't you think about squeezing a little time to help plan the new child center at the Texas Cattleman's Club? We could use your professional opinion. The construction company is renovating the place, but they want the women's input about the decor and what we'd like to have for the children."

Lila laughed. "My dad would explode. You can't imagine—well, yes, you can imagine—how he feels about a child center. It almost did him in when women were voted into the club, Shannon," Lila said with a big grin.

Shannon laughed. "I love being a member of the club. I still can't get used to women, including me, belonging to the exclusive male bastion, the sacrosanct male domain for over one hundred years, the exclusive Texas Cattleman's Club." She laughed again with Lila. "I better not speak loudly—all the members are here tonight.

"I know it irritates your dad and some of the others," Shannon continued. "Your dad and a lot of the older members, but some young ones, too. The Gordon twins. Your brother has made snippy remarks."

"I told you years ago to tune Hack out. Dad spoils him until it's pitiful. I'm afraid Hack is going to turn out as narrow-minded as Dad. If you weren't such a good friend, I think Hack would make worse remarks to you. He can get really crude."

Shannon shrugged. "I do tune out your brother and the remarks are more than just snippy. He isn't going to like the child center. Doesn't matter. The construction company has already started renovation."

"That's great."

"Lila, you're perfect for the job because you're a production set designer. C'mon. Help us while you have some time."

Thinking over the request, Lila looked into Shannon's bright blue eyes beneath short, sassy blond hair. Lila had come home to rest, to talk confidentially with her mother, not to take on another job. If she accepted, though, it might keep her mind off her problems and it would be an interesting project. She would be with Shannon, a hard worker who was always fun. "You know, I'd enjoy collaborating with you and the idea is exciting. Besides, sometimes I like to shake up my dad. I'll do it, but if it gets to be too much, Shannon, I'm out."

"Fantastic and fair enough. I don't want you to participate if it's too much, but it won't be. I'd like your input."

"That sounds easy."

"It should be fun to do. Any chance you can meet me at the club Monday morning?"

"Sure. My schedule is open. As long as it's not early Monday morning."

"No, we won't meet early, because I have my ranch chores," Shannon said as they walked down a wide hall into the big dining room that had a table holding silver trays and crystal dishes of hors d'oeuvres.

"Hi, Amanda, Nathan," Lila said while Shannon echoed her greeting to the couple, who stood holding hands and had been gazing at each other until they were interrupted. Amanda and Nathan Battle, Royal's sheriff, turned to look at them. Lila felt an invisible punch in her middle when she saw them holding hands, clearly in love.

"The newlyweds," Lila said, smiling at them. "Congratulations."

"Thank you," they said in unison, then looked at each other and laughed.

"We were just taking a moment away from the crowd

to talk. The party is fantastic, Lila. Your folks know how to throw a party," Amanda said. Amanda's glow and obvious joy continued to give Lila a pang. What would it be like to be deeply in love, to have it returned? From the way Amanda looked, it seemed it would be bliss.

"We'll head out to get some barbecue," Nathan said.

"Don't go on our account," Lila told him. "We're here for some artichoke dip and then we're going outside to eat."

"Eat all you want," Nathan said, smiling and wrapping his arm around Amanda's waist as they left.

"They're so much in love I doubt if either one of them knows what was just said or even who was in here. Now, I think we were talking about getting together at the TCC Monday," Lila said.

"We were. Actually, the later the better for me. How about lunch? While we eat, I can bring you up to speed on what we plan. After lunch we can go look at the location. It's the old billiard room."

"That will be good. Lunch will be the best time for me," Lila said, crossing to the sideboard to pick up a plate and napkin.

"At three on Monday, there is a TCC meeting and I plan to attend, but you and I will be finished by then," Shannon said.

"I'll bet my dad is suffering over the thought of turning the billiard room into a child-care center." Lila laughed and Shannon joined her.

"It's time to shake them up a little," Shannon said. "Besides, they'll get a new billiard room. That renovation will be next."

"Shannon, do the Gordons have the construction contract?" Lila asked, realizing for the first time that she might see a lot of Sam.

"As a matter of fact, no, they don't."

"Why not? I'd think they would have been awarded the contract without any conversation about it," Lila said.

"I wondered about that, too. I was told they bowed out because of a 'conflict of interest,' but frankly, in my opinion, they wanted to avoid it because they hate to see the center become a reality."

"Could be. The Gordon brothers are as old-fashioned as my dad."

"Maybe they're that way because they lost their mother when they were so young. Perhaps their dad just settled into a chauvinistic manner toward women."

"Probably. Even with a mom, my dad's influence, unfortunately, is stronger on Hack than my mom's."

Lila and Shannon browsed, each selecting small bites of the pale, steaming artichoke dip and dainty bits of pineapple, strawberries and kiwi. As soon as both had tall glasses of ice water, Lila waved toward the wide hallway. "Let's go sit on the porch, where we can talk. Everyone's in the back or in the house."

They walked outside on the porch and sat in tall cushioned rocking chairs. The music was diminished, the sounds of the crowd muffled, while shadows grew longer and the sun slanted lower. "You look great, Shannon. Married life becomes you."

"You have to meet Rory. Right now he's back in Austin. My foreman is ill and I'm needed here, so I'm at the ranch."

"You're newlyweds, very happily married. What else? Bring me up to date on your life," Lila said.

Shannon shrugged. "While I'm here, it's just the same old, same old. I run the family ranch," she replied, raking her blond hair from her face with her fingers.

"I don't know how you do it," Lila said, shaking her

head. "I've never figured out how you manage the Bar None all on your own."

"Just one of the boys," Shannon replied dryly, and Lila laughed. "I'm not alone anymore, not since getting married. It's just that Rory is busy in Austin."

"Too bad you have to be apart."

Shannon shrugged. "When my foreman is back on his feet, I can go to Austin. Right now, this is a rare moment, this party, and I'm enjoying it. I've told you about me. Let's talk about you, unless you don't want to. We're good friends or I wouldn't ask—what's wrong?"

"Wrong?" Lila said while her heart missed a beat.

Shannon shrugged. "If you don't want to talk about it, I understand. I thought you might need a friend right now."

Shocked that Shannon could so easily tell that something was wrong in her life, Lila ran her fingers in a circle over her knee and debated confiding in her friend. So far her mother was the only Texan she had talked to.

"All right. It's confidential for now. Since I'll be here anyway in a couple of weeks, I came home early to rest and talk to Mom. Not my dad. Never Hack. I'm pregnant, Shannon."

"Great grief." Shannon's eyes widened. "Someone in the movie business? An actor? A star? A producer who's married?"

"Hey, wait," Lila said, laughing and feeling a lift to the worries that weighed on her only moments earlier. "Stop jumping to conclusions. A married producer? I wouldn't go out with one of those. I shouldn't have gone out with the man I did," she said, becoming somber again. "Shannon, he's local. He's here at the party."

"You don't have to say who it is. Are you going to tell him?"

"Not until I make some decisions. When he finds out, he's so old-fashioned he'll want to marry me."

"Oh, great grief. If it had to be a local, why didn't you pick someone who's open and liberal and not still thinking a woman's place is in the kitchen and bedroom?"

"Hindsight is always better."

"I'm sorry. I'm not helping. I can understand why you don't want to marry him, but if he's old-fashioned, he's going to want to marry you. Oh, boy, is he going to want to marry."

"I'm not marrying one of the locals to move back here and give up my career and my independence."

Shannon tilted her head to study her friend. "When are you breaking the news?"

"I wish it could be after I'm back in California and there's half the U.S. between us, but I'll probably tell him before I go back. Okay—absolutely between the two of us. It's—"

"Don't tell me," Shannon said, covering her ears. "I don't want to know."

Lila laughed. "You do make me feel better. I can tell you and you'll probably guess anyway."

"No. I don't need to know. I don't even want to know, because it will be easier later if someone gets to quizzing me. You know, you can keep that quiet only so long," she said, glancing over Lila. "I guess that's why you're wearing a dress that covers your middle."

"That's right. I'm three months along."

"Oh, my. How long will you stay in Texas on this movie-production business?"

"Probably till the end of the month. Sometimes it's shorter, sometimes longer, but once I start really working, I don't think I'll see the significant person often."

"Does your mom understand? Your dad isn't going to."

"She's supportive. I don't even understand what got into me."

"I think it's called hormones," Shannon remarked dryly. "And he's probably adorable because we have some good-looking, fun, great guys here."

"Oh, yes," Lila replied, thinking that was a fitting description of Sam. "As for Mom, we're close. Mom has two sides to her. The one my dad sees and others think she is, and then there's a side that's not that way at all. Mom manages to get her way with my dad. He just doesn't realize it. She'll help me."

"Good. Sorry, Lila. You've complicated your life."

"That's an understatement. Thank heavens I can leave Royal and go back to California."

Two men emerged from the front door and turned toward them. Lila recognized both of them as ranchers from a neighboring county.

"Hey, ladies," Jeff Wainwright said. "I thought I saw you two out here. You're missing the fun and a really good hoedown in the barn. Right now they're having line dancing. Want to give it a whirl?"

Impulsively, Lila accepted, thinking it would be good to move around, expend some energy and forget her pregnancy for five or ten minutes.

If only she could forget. The first sight of Sam had taken her breath. She had thought she wouldn't have any physical response to him, but she had been wrong. Worse, she had been unable to control her response. With a sparkle in his clear blue eyes, he'd stood facing her. His navy plaid Western shirt had the sleeves rolled high, revealing firm biceps. The shirt tucked into his narrow waist and the faded tight jeans showed his muscled lean frame. He looked sexy and filled with vitality—a good-looking, appealing man. She couldn't deny that part.

Also, it had felt good to tell Shannon about the pregnancy, to have a friend who knew what she was going through. And a level-headed friend, too.

In minutes Shannon was dancing with Buck McDougal while Lila danced with Jeff. Sam was on the dance floor with Piper Kindred, one of Royal's paramedics. As she turned, Lila noticed the ex-rodeo rider, Ryan Grant, on the sidelines watching Piper intently. Lila looked away, thinking about how she tried to avoid watching Sam or even looking at him, but it was impossible. He was light on his feet, sexy. It didn't matter how much appeal he had—his personality, his opinions, his most basic beliefs all were opposite from her own. He was old-fashioned and would never understand her career or her attitude.

She thought about that night with him. Her dad had seen Sam in Royal and talked him into dinner with them in town. When Sam had said he would take her home, her dad had gone ahead to the Double H, her family's ranch. She and Sam had flirted through dinner and afterward, until Sam invited her to his place for a nightcap and she accepted.

The flirting grew more intense until she was in his arms. A night of wild passion, laughter, loving, a night she had known she would always remember. Now there was no doubt. A few weeks later, she had learned she was pregnant.

Lila's thoughts came back to the present while she danced in the barn. They had gone from line dancing to a square dance and she noticed Shannon had dropped out and was gone.

They square danced, changing partners as the steps were called out to the fiddlers' music. When they called "Promenade left, promenade right," and she moved to the next dancer, she faced Sam and the look in his eyes made her heart pound. He wasn't saying a word, yet sparks flew and she felt at any second he might grab her and kiss her wildly.

She danced away from him and the moment was gone, but her heart still raced and she wondered if they would talk again or if he would ask her to dance. She gave a shake of her head as if to clear her thoughts. She needed to stay away from Sam. She didn't want him to guess that she was pregnant. She had to be mentally prepared for when he learned the truth.

Finally, she told Jeff she'd had enough dancing. As they left the barn, she glanced back and met Sam's smoldering gaze. Even with the length of the barn between them, the minute she looked into his eyes, a current spiraled, tickling her insides. Why did she have such a physical response to him? She did not want to know Sam better or go out with him again. Yet now she had not only bound her life with his indefinitely, she would have to struggle with his old-fashioned, narrow view of the world.

The tempting smells of the barbecue were beginning to have the opposite effect on her. To get away from the cooking, she crossed the yard until she saw a friend.

"Sophie," she called, catching up with her high school friend.

Sophie Beldon turned to wait, her light brown eyes friendly as she smiled. "This is a great party, Lila. Your family really knows how to do this. I think everyone in these parts looks forward to August because of your family barbecue. It's legendary."

"Thanks. They've been doing it long enough. It's good to see you. Where are you headed?"

"Some quiet corner—if there is such. I'm getting looks and people ask all sorts of questions. Some act like I have the answers and just won't say anything about Alex's disappearance."

"Sorry. That must be tough. You're his executive secretary, so everyone probably thinks you know something about him. I'm sure everyone has been shocked to hear Alex has disappeared. Still no word?"

"Nothing. What's bad—they don't know whether something's happened to him or his disappearance is something he has deliberately done. He had a quiet side where he kept things to himself. I've always thought of my boss as a man of mystery. Or it could be just circumstances where communication has failed and Alex thinks we all know where he is."

"That seems impossible. You'd hear from him, I'd think."

The blonde shrugged. "Who knows. You can't rule out any possibility, but his disappearance has some people on edge."

"Reasonably so, I'd say. You dealt with him daily. You should know the most about him," Lila said, stopping in the shade of a tall oak to the east side of the house and away from the crowd.

Long lashes framed Sophie's eyes while her brow furrowed. "I get looks from Nathan Battle, but Nathan's fair, so I'm not worried about his opinion where I'm concerned. I really don't have any idea about Alex and what's happened to him." She studied Shannon in silence a moment as if debating something. "I know I can trust you—I'm working now for Zach Lassiter. He's Alex's business partner."

"I've heard Dad talk about him. From what I hear, no one seems to know much about his past."

"Talk about a man of mystery—Zach is more mysterious than Alex was. I don't think anyone knows much about Zach. I thought if I could get close to him, I might find out something about Alex's disappearance."

A chill ran down Lila's spine. "Sophie, be careful. You have no idea what's involved in Alex's disappearance. It could be foul play. You really don't know anything about Zach Lassiter and it sounds as if no one else in Royal does. What you're doing might be dangerous."

"I'll be careful, and I don't see how Zach can suspect my true motives. It's a business. I can't keep from wondering what he knows about Alex, because they worked closely together."

Lila shook her head. "I don't think you should take such a risk. Be really careful about what you do. You're not a trained detective and you don't know anything about investigations. Does anyone else know what you're doing? Does Nathan Battle?"

"Heavens, no. You do now, so there's one person who knows. I promise, I'll be careful. I see friends headed our way."

Lila turned to see three more friends she had been close to in high school and her private conversation with Sophie ended, but as she listened to the light chatter of her friends, she still had a nagging concern about Sophie. She wished she had urged Sophie to say something to Nathan, although Nathan and Amanda had recently married, so he might not have his mind on Alex's disappearance. Still, Lila felt certain Nathan would advise Sophie to stay out of it and her friend might actually listen to him.

Later, lines formed at the long tables covered with food while servers at each end carved chunks of meat and ribs. Lila went inside to eat more fruit, passing up the steaming barbecue, knowing her dad saw to it that they cooked so much there would always be some leftovers if she wanted any later.

After dinner, fiddlers swung into music for more dancing and Lila enjoyed herself, dancing with many of the Texas Cattleman's Club members who always attended the Hacket barbecue. She danced with Ryan Grant, one of the newest members. His tangled brown hair fell over his forehead as he concentrated on dancing. He was light on his feet, which didn't surprise her, because she had danced with him before.

The next dance was with rancher and widower Gil Addison. She knew his four-year-old son, Cade, was with the other kids. Her parents always hired local nannies to watch the small kids during the barbecue. She enjoyed Gil in his quiet way and was sorry he was raising his son alone.

As soon as that dance ended, Sam's twin, Josh Gordon, politely asked her to dance. She could sense the coolness and disapproval in spite of his invitation and she knew he was one of the club members who disapproved of her independence. She suspected he had asked her to dance as an obligation to her dad, the host.

Although Josh and Sam were identical twins, Lila could tell them apart without any difficulty. Sam's hair was longer and he had a sparkle in his eyes, a more carefree attitude than his solemn brother.

As she danced with Josh, a fast number where they had no physical contact, she wondered what his reaction would be when he learned that he was going to be an uncle.

As soon as the dance ended and she had politely thanked him, Josh disappeared into the crowd. She turned to face Sam Gordon.

Two

"I think it's my turn. Will you dance with me?" he asked, taking her arm before she could answer.

"This is typical, Sam. You didn't even wait for my answer."

He grinned and released her, turning to face her. "Darlin', you can't begin to guess how eager I am to dance with you. Miss Hacket, may I have this dance?"

Knowing Sam was the one person she should avoid, she nodded her head anyway. "You're hopeless."

"No way, sugar. I just want to dance with you in the worst way," he said, taking her hand and coaxing her. "C'mon."

"In the worst way?" she teased, having fun even though she shouldn't encourage him.

"Oh, yeah," he drawled in a huskier voice as they joined the dancers on the barn's makeshift dance floor. "The very worst—down and hot as only you can do," he said.

A tingle sizzled while she laughed at the same time.

"Not on your Nelly, Sam Gordon," she tried to reply sternly, but it came out breathlessly. "I don't even know how."

"Oh, yes, you do, darlin'," he said, his blue eyes twinkling. "My memory is crystal-clear. In the privacy of my place, we've danced down and dirty before and it was a bushel of fun and sexy as hell." He moved closer. "And you haven't forgotten, either."

"If you want to keep dancing, Sam, you better get off that subject fast. You've skated onto extremely thin ice," she said, wishing she sounded more forceful and knowing she had made a big mistake in flirting with him even for mere minutes, not to mention dancing with him.

He waved his hands as if he had dropped a burning iron. "I'm off the subject of how enticing your dancing is. You look great, Lila, and I'm glad you're home."

"Thank you," she said, twisting and turning so they wouldn't have to talk, yet aware of his steady gaze following her every move. She should never have encouraged him, but he was fun to be with and she loved to dance. Thinking like that was what had gotten her into the situation she was in now.

The instant the music stopped, she turned to him. "Thanks, Sam. Mom asked me to mix with guests. I've just mingled with you, so I'm off to socialize with others," she said sweetly, and walked away before he had a chance to reply. Her back tingled because she knew he watched her and she expected him to catch up with her or take her arm to stop her.

As if pulled by a magnet, she couldn't keep from glancing over her shoulder. Sam was leaning against a post on the sidelines and he was watching her as she had suspected. She turned around quickly, but he had seen her look back at him.

As she moved through the crowd and toward the house, she fought the urge to glance over her shoulder again. Her mother had given her no such instructions, but she had partied all she wanted to for one night. She was going to her own room in the sprawling ranch house.

Standing near the bar, Sam watched Lila cross the back porch and enter the Hacket home. As puzzled as ever, he couldn't figure her. For minutes tonight, she had let down that guard and been open, friendly, more—she had flirted with him. And he thought she'd had fun dancing with him. Then it was over and the barrier was back between them. The moment the dance ended, she was gone. Why her coolness? Was it his attitude toward her job and women in the club? That seemed absurd and hadn't made that much difference their night together. He couldn't think of a thing that would cause this rift between them.

She didn't approve of his views of women and he didn't approve of her career, so he should accept the rejection and move on. Rejection was something he didn't experience often—was it that difficult for him to accept? He still wanted Lila in his arms and in his bed.

She had looked great tonight—a flush in her face that made her cheeks rosy, a sparkle in her fascinating green eyes, her long legs showing from the knees down.

The dress hid her tiny waist—a pity because he remembered exactly how narrow it was. But the top of the sundress was cut low enough to reveal lush curves that seemed even fuller than he remembered.

He inhaled and took a long drink of his cold beer, wishing he could just pour it over his head to cool down.

* * *

Monday, Lila walked into the rambling clubhouse made

of stone and dark wood. Sunshine splashed over the tall slate roof. The smell of bacon cooking wafted from the building, giving her a queasy feeling. Morning sickness had come early and had been mild. To her relief, it was beginning to disappear, and so far, today was one of the good days.

Shannon was waiting in the wide hallway. Dressed in a sleeveless navy cotton dress and heels, she didn't look as if she had spent the morning doing ranch chores with the men who worked for her, but Lila knew Shannon and what her life had been like until recently, single-handedly managing a big cattle ranch.

Shannon's smile sparkled. "Hi! I've looked forward to this since the night of the barbecue. I'm so excited over this child center." She leaned closer to Lila. "I'll warn you now—you're going to get some nasty glares from the members who do not welcome what we're doing."

"I'm getting looks at home from Dad. He grumbles and stomps off without really saying anything."

Shannon laughed as they headed toward the dining room for lunch.

Over crisp green salads, she enjoyed talking to Shannon, listening to plans about the center. "Remember they built onto the club and we have more meeting rooms now, so they moved the billiard tables to one of the meeting rooms. They'll renovate the room later, but for now they just moved out the other furniture," Shannon said.

"It wouldn't do for all those men to be without their billiard tables," Lila said with a smile.

"Right. Meanwhile, they've started on the billiard room and the room built adjoining it. They're taking out the walls that separated the rooms. We'll divide off areas for play, for eating, that sort of thing, and a special area for the babies."

"I know some great California stores for furniture, pictures, little dividers that still keep an open look and can be easily moved."

"Great. Give us a list. The women members are responsible for this. As soon as we eat, we'll go look at the rooms. I told you that we've agreed on the basic structure, which includes built-in shelves, drawers and cabinets. I'll show you all of our plans and notes."

"I'm sorry the other women couldn't join us for lunch. I would really be in good company with you, Missy Reynolds, Vanessa Woodrow and Abigail Price."

"You should join, too."

Lila shook her head. "I'm going back to California. You need members who will be active."

"Abigail's little girl, Julia, will attend the center as soon as it opens."

"It's exciting to be part of this," Lila said, enjoying seeing her friend and having something else to think about in place of the constant concerns about her pregnancy.

When they finished lunch, they went first to the door of the old billiard room. Men were sawing and hammering, and the noise made talking difficult.

Shannon just motioned for Lila to follow her and they went down the hall.

"We can go to the billiard room."

They entered the darkened room with four billiard tables, heavy brown leather furniture and coffee-colored walls. There were two small stained-glass windows. Shannon switched on an overhead light fixture made of deer antlers.

"Looks dark and sort of like pictures I've seen of hotel lobbies in the early 1900s," Lila said.

"They'll redo it, although I think there will still be dark leather furniture and I'm guessing the stained-glass windows will remain. That's not our deal and frankly, I don't care what they do with this room." They sat at a game table in the corner of the room and Shannon spread the papers in front of Lila.

"Here's a list of some child centers that have been recommended to us as the best examples. You can study them and see what ideas you come up with. We want a state-of-the-art child-care center."

"Will the center open onto a play area outside? I don't see a door anywhere."

"Great grief. No one has said a word about a playground," Shannon said, her eyes opening wide. "We may have been so busy campaigning to get a child-care center that we didn't stop to think about outside, but we definitely should have a playground. I'll send Missy a text about this. That's a necessity." She pulled out her phone, speaking into it, dictating her text.

"I don't know why we didn't think of that. We have plenty of space outside and we can have a fenced area with alarms, making it secure for the kids. We'll always have attendants to watch and cameras. We've ordered a state-of-the-art alarm system for an enormous price, but it'll be worth it and give families peace of mind."

"This center is going to be wonderful, Shannon."

"It is, but there's a faction who really opposed it and they still don't like it. Sometimes that makes me uneasy."

"These are honorable men. For all my dad's bluster, he does have a good heart. He's just old-fashioned but, in his own way, courteous to women and good to Mom."

"I'm sure you're right. I guess this thing with Alex disappearing is disconcerting. Something isn't right and you can't keep from wondering if anyone is in danger."

"Hopefully, they'll learn the truth soon or he'll return. As far as I know, there's been no demand for a ransom."

Shannon shivered. "One of Royal's citizens kidnapped—that's ghastly." She glanced at her watch. "How about meeting here again at twelve-thirty or one on Wednesday? If you can have lunch, great. If not, that's fine, too."

"Actually, one will be better."

"Good deal." Shannon's gaze ran over Lila. "Are you feeling all right?"

"Yes. Mornings are rocky, but then I'm okay the rest of the day. This center is exciting, Shannon. Maybe I'm interested because I'm thinking about children now."

"I'm excited and there's no little one on my horizon. I think it's great. It's almost time for my meeting. Wednesday, it is. Lunch again."

"Fine. I'm going to stay a few minutes here to think about this. You go ahead to your meeting."

"I'm going to see Abigail Price there. She's so excited about this center."

"Very good. Abigail was brave—the first woman to join the club. She'll be in their history whether this bunch of members likes it or not."

"Enough liked it to get her voted in," Shannon said, laughing. "See you Wednesday."

She disappeared out the door. Lila looked at the room, the billiard tables, imagining how many deals had been made over these tables and what a male domain the billiard room had been. It was time for change.

Less than five minutes later Lila walked out and saw a tall man in cowboy boots down the hall. She recognized the broad shoulders and lean frame of Sam Gordon. He stood in a doorway talking to someone and glanced her way. The minute they locked gazes, a reaction shook her. Another jump in her heartbeat accompanied a thorough awareness of him. She raised her chin as if meeting an adversary.

As she drew close, he finished talking, stepping fully into the hall and turning to wait for her to catch up with him.

"I haven't seen you here in a long time. Having lunch with your dad?"

"No, I'm not. I met with Shannon today. She asked for suggestions on planning the interior of the child-care center." Lila caught the slight frown that was gone from Sam's expression almost as fast as it had come.

"I can't imagine a child-care center in this club. What I can imagine is the reaction the founders would have had to such a thing."

"Sam, come into this century. The founders were a long time ago. You're way too young to be a fossil."

"I don't remember you accusing me of being a fossil when we danced or kissed," he said, leaning closer, "but then, there are some places, Lila, where our different opinions don't matter one whit."

"I walked into that one," she said. "The child center is going to happen, so you might as well get resigned. You don't like kids, Sam?" she asked, feeling a clash of wills with him.

"'Course I like kids, but here in the club—that's a different. This club wasn't founded to babysit a bunch of kids."

"Who was it founded to babysit?" she asked sweetly.

He leaned closer, placing his hand against the wall over her head and hemming her in. Too aware of his proximity and her pounding heartbeat, she drew in a deep breath. "It was founded as a male haven where men could relax and enjoy a drink or a cigar or the friendship of cronies without kids yelling and running through the halls."

She laughed. "Mercy me. You're beginning to sound just like my dad. If I heard you and didn't know you and couldn't see you, I'd guess you were part of his generation."

"That's not all bad, Lila. You go out with me tonight and we'll see if I'm an old-fashioned fossil," he drawled softly, his blue eyes holding fires that sparked.

Lila tingled. She had gotten on dangerous ground with him again. "Thank you, but, Sam Gordon, you and I are generations apart in our lifestyles and ways of thinking, the places where it really counts. Lust is universal. Compatibility is not. I'll see you around," she said, hurrying away, trying to ignore her racing pulse and the stab of longing to go out with him.

He was totally off-limits and she shouldn't have even stopped to talk to him, much less spent time flirting with him. They had little in common, so how could he hold such an intense appeal to her? Worse, now he was the father of her baby. For years to come she had tied her life to Sam's, unless he had no interest when he discovered the truth. She knew just how her daddy and some of the old-fashioned men who were his friends would have reacted to the situation, and that was exactly the way she expected Sam to react. He would want to marry her.

She shivered. She was not marrying, settling for a life like her mother's and living in Royal for the rest of her life. Being the "little woman" in the kitchen and his toy in the bedroom and being seen and not heard otherwise. No way was she going to become part of that scene.

She encountered Shannon in the hall. "I thought you'd be gone now," Shannon said.

"I ran into Sam and talked a minute."

"He's here for the meeting. I've never missed one since I joined the club, which irritates some of the good ol' boys," Shannon said, smiling broadly. "I'm sorry, your dad is one of them. If looks could kill, I'd be gone."

"That's dreadful, Shannon. I don't even know why you want to be a member and have to put up with that."

"There are a lot of benefits. This is the most exclusive, elegant club in this area, so it's great for private parties. I can swim, eat here, bring Rory here—you know they have the best chef and cooks for miles around. I love the dances."

Lila laughed. "Shannon, when you're here, you don't have spare time to do anything except ranch chores."

"When Rory can come and my foreman is well, I have more time. Rory does a lot. Maybe I can't resist shaking up the old boys a little," she added with a grin.

"Go to your meeting and shake them up. I'm going home to the Double H," Lila said, walking away before she ran into Sam again.

Sam relaxed in the meeting room at the Texas Cattleman's Club. He tried to focus on what was being said by Gil Addison, their president, but his thoughts kept slipping back to discovering that Lila intended to help plan the child-care center. The whole idea was repugnant to him. He looked around at the dark, rich wood, the mounted animal heads, trophies of past members and evidence of their shooting skills. The clubhouse was over one hundred years old, now, a monument to being built right and using the best materials.

The club had been a male haven. Leadership, Justice, Peace—the basic founding motto of the members. In an earlier day the club's members had banded together covertly on secret missions to save innocent lives. That wouldn't happen now with all the changes. The club was relaxing, filled with the things he liked to do—swim, dine, play billiards, exercise, just talk with friends. It was the perfect place for business lunches or dinners. Now women had moved into it and changes were coming, but the biggest alteration was a child center. Children racing through the clubhouse and scampering over the grounds would change the ambiance and the noise level would rise like a balloon in the wind. A child-care center. Beau Hacket had been bitterly opposed and Sam, as well as his twin, had lined up with Beau. There was not one positive reason to take children into the Texas Cattleman's Club, but they had been voted down.

Sam glanced across the room at the female members, clustered together, their husbands, mostly younger members. Why did they want to be part of the club? A streak of stubbornness? To ruin the club for the men? To take it over and turn it into their own club? He couldn't figure the logic, but they were not going away. Between their husbands, boyfriends and friends, they had solid backing, not only gaining membership but easily voting in the child-care center. Once they got the center, the club would become a whole different type of organization.

His gaze rested on Shannon. She was Lila's close friend and the one who had talked Lila into helping plan the child center. He liked Shannon; she was a no-nonsense person and a fine rancher. Of all the women who had joined, Shannon probably had the most right to be there because she was a rancher and toiled like the men on her ranch. She ran the place and fit in with other cattle ranchers. A stranger would never guess, because when she left the ranch, she looked all woman.

Lila would help with the center. If she lived here, she would want to join. Beau had definite ideas, but he hadn't been able to control Lila or raise her to live the way her family did. There were probably some stormy conversations at the Hacket house.

Sam tried to stop thinking about Lila except to acknowledge she was taking over too much of his thoughts.

Once again, he tried to pull his attention back to Gil, who stood relaxed, his black hair combed back and one hand holding a small card that he occasionally glanced at.

In his quiet, efficient manner, Gil had covered the business of the day and Sam had barely heard a word.

"I know some of you opposed the new child-care center, but it's been voted in and work has started. During the renovations, we'll have noise and interruptions, but we've had that before. The child-care center is going to be reality in the near future. We want a state-of-the-art center."

Annoyed, Sam thought it would partially be thanks to Lila's input. In fairness, the billiard room would be renovated into a center for kids whether Lila helped or not. The founders of the exclusive men's club would be stunned by this latest turn of events. He thought of Tex Langley, the founding father, who might not have even wanted the club if he had known how it would be changed.

As far as Sam was concerned, the club would never be the same. He attempted again to pay attention to Gil, who seemed to remain impartial, although Gil had Cade to raise by himself, so probably, he was happy to see the center open.

"Another reminder, next month Zach Lassiter will be inducted," Gil said.

Zach was another newcomer and Sam knew nothing about his past except that he had been successful with investments and he had shared an office with Alex Santiago.

Startled, Sam realized he was thinking in the past tense about Alex. What had happened to the man? It was a disturbing mystery that seemed to puzzle everyone in town.

"One last thing before we close our meeting today," Gil said in a loud voice that quieted everyone. "We all know we have a missing member, one of our newest members, Alex Santiago. Nathan has something to share with us," Gil said, turning to face Nathan Battle, who rose.

Tall, with a commanding presence, Nathan made a good sheriff. He was a law-enforcement officer the town could be proud of. The men of his family had been members of the Texas Cattleman's Club for generations and Nathan had broken away from his ranching background to become a lawman. He'd become an asset for Royal.

"This will be brief. We've turned up something. My office hasn't gone public with the news yet and we don't intend to make an official announcement at this time, but I'll tell you now—Alex's truck has been found about fifty miles from town."

There was a low rumble of remarks, with surprised looks on a few members' faces.

As soon as Nathan began to speak again, silence fell over the room.

"The truck was hidden in bushes. That may indicate foul play. At this point, we're not ruling anything out. From all indications, there's a possibility that Alex was abducted."

Another shocked ripple of noise erupted.

"Nathan, when will you go public with this? Are we to keep quiet about it?" Dave Firestone asked.

"We've been investigating and trying to find out what we can before moving the truck, but several people already know about our discovery. I'm not trying to keep our news secret from the town, but I've asked to keep it out of the media at least the rest of today. Alex was a friend and one of our members and I know there's high interest in his disappearance. At this point, that's all."

Nathan returned to his seat and Gil finished the business at hand before closing the meeting.

Shocked by the news, Sam thought about Alex Santiago, a venture capitalist and new to Royal. He'd grown up elsewhere, without Texas roots that went back generations the way so many of the other members' did. Newly engaged to Cara Windsor, Alex had just recently disappeared. Word got out slowly at first and then swept over the town. Sam glanced across the room at another member, Chance McDaniel, who used to go out with Cara. Chance sat stony-faced, staring straight ahead, a slight frown on his brow beneath his blond hair.

How bitter was Chance over Cara getting engaged to Alex? Sam had wondered about that since people began to openly question what could have happened to Alex.

Jumping to conclusions wasn't good, but it was impossible to avoid suspecting Chance, who would have a motive for getting Alex out of the way.

At the same time, Sam liked Chance and would hate to see his suspicions bear fruit. He hoped Chance wasn't involved. Finding Alex's truck abandoned and hidden was not good news.

After the meeting when Sam was leaving, he stopped in the doorway of the future billiard room. The place was dim inside with muted sounds from the club, the old billiard tables standing empty. Life was changing. Was he as backward in his thinking as Lila had accused him of being? He shook his head. He couldn't imagine little kids all over the place or that their presence would be great for the club. The TCC could have built a separate building on their property or bought some land near the club and built a separate center and everyone would have been happy. Or at least that's how he and several other members viewed it, but their idea had been killed before it ever got started.

Yesterday he'd had a business lunch and he was glad he could bring a client to the club just the way it was. Time would tell whether the child center was an asset or a liability. Turning to leave, he spotted something on a chair by the door. He walked over to pick up a small stack of papers with a long mailing tube. Shannon's name was on the mailing tube, so she had probably left everything while she attended the meeting.

As he turned to go, Lila entered and stopped. "I left some of my things in here and I came back to get them."

"I just found them. I thought they were Shannon's." He handed Lila the stack of papers and the mailing tube. His hands brushed hers only lightly, yet the touch was electric.

"Did the meeting just get out?" she asked.

"It's been a few minutes. I stopped in to look over the new billiard room."

"I'm sure you'd prefer no changes to this room, just as you prefer no changes to the original billiard room."

"You're wrong there. The room is antiquated and we'll have a new billiard room. I have nothing against little children. You don't know me half as well as you think you do. But now we can begin to remedy that. I'd like to hear all about this California job you have and why California is so much greater than Texas."

"One more big difference between us. I'll be happy to tell you why California is so great—one thing is I can be independent and on my own. That's a little difficult to do here in Royal with my dad constantly present everywhere I go."

"If that's the problem, I can take you someplace where we can enjoy the shade and your dad won't be anywhere around. We can discuss that in the bar or outside on the patio where the mist makers are keeping everyone cool. It's late in the afternoon and it's nice outside if you're in the right place. Come have a drink with me and then I'll take you to dinner. Or even more private, I can take you to my place and I'll guarantee no one will disturb you."

"Except you, Sam. You're disturbing enough," she said, and his insides tightened and heated. Her eyes sparkled and eagerness made him smile.

"Darlin', you take my breath away. You look great, Lila," he said, gazing into thickly lashed green eyes that he could look at endlessly.

"Thank you, Sam."

"C'mon. Let's get that drink. What are we waiting for?"

He could tell the moment the wall came up between them. Her expression changed only slightly, but the sparkle left her eyes and she looked as if she were on the other side of a glass wall. She shook her head.

"That's a tempting offer, Sam, but I need to head home."

As she started to move away, he touched her arm lightly. "I promise. Stay and you'll have more fun. I can take you home later if you want and bring you back tomorrow to get your car."

"Sorry, Sam. Thank you, but I need to get home. I've promised to make suggestions regarding the center for Shannon. I'll see you around," she said briskly. He dropped his hand as she gathered her things and left the room.

Puzzled, he watched her walk away. Why was she avoiding him? There were moments she had been responsive and then she had closed off as if he were a stranger. What was bothering her and what had changed between them since that weekend they had been together? Switching off the lights in the billiard room, he stepped into the hall and slowly followed, still watching her walk away.

They had a big difference in their attitudes about the

club and the child center, but he didn't think that was what was holding her back.

At a loss, he watched her go out through the front doors. Was it something he had done? Was it because she was scared to be attracted to someone from Royal and get involved when she lived in California? Not for one second did he think she had to go home to study child-care centers for Shannon. There was something else that had caused the rift.

He couldn't think of a reason. One more puzzle in his life, only this one was personal. While he wanted to get to know her better, she had made it obvious she wasn't going to let him. The only reason he persisted was that she still responded to him some of the time.

Three

Lila hurried to her car. Prickles ran across her back because Sam was behind her and she had the feeling if she turned she would see him watching her. If only she could stop flirting with him. For a moment she had wanted to just toss aside worries and go sit with him and let him cheer her up because he could. In spite of his old-fashioned notions, he entertained her.

She suspected her mother had thought the same thing about her father at some point. Sam was too much like her father for her to get close to him. Yet it was too late. She had gotten up close and intimately personal and someday she would have to let Sam know about his baby, but she wanted to be on the verge of leaving for California when that happened.

Passing mesquite and cactus, she finally curved around the drive and saw the sprawling, familiar house on the Double H ranch. The place would always be home. Pots of colorful flowers hung beneath the rafters of the wrap-around porch. Her mother had made a comfortable haven on the West Texas plains.

That night over a steaming roast with potatoes and carrots, her dad talked about his day. Momentarily, Lila wished she had been able to accept Sam's dinner offer, because it would have been far more fun than listening to her dad complain about too many things.

"In our meeting today, Nathan made an announcement. They haven't gone to the media about it yet, so it isn't public knowledge," Beau said, looking at his wife and then at Lila. "He said they found Alex Santiago's abandoned truck hidden in some bushes outside town."

"That can't be good," Barbara remarked, frowning.

"No, it sure as hell isn't," Beau replied. "They're investigating. Sounds to me like someone kidnapped Alex or worse."

"Was it random or someone who knew Alex?" Barbara shook her head. "I know no one has an answer to that question, but it's disturbing. Your friend Sophie worked for him, didn't she?"

"Works for him," Beau corrected.

"Sophie still keeps the office running. Zachary Lassiter shares the office with them, too," Lila said.

"You be careful, Beau, when you're out on the ranch alone. Until we know who or why—"

"Don't worry about me. My pistol is in the truck and I'm careful. I have my phone and most of the time I'm not out without others with me."

"One of the men disappearing is frightening. Imagine that happening here."

"Things happen everywhere, Mom," Lila said.

"You're the one who lives in a hotbed of crime in a big city," Beau remarked, helping himself to more roast beef while Lila struggled to eat a little. She had lost her appetite, but she didn't want to bring it to her dad's attention.

"We haven't talked about it, but I heard you're helping with the children's center," Beau said, focusing on her.

"Shannon asked if I would just look over the plans they have and see if I can think of anything else needed."

"A new location would be nice," Beau said, and laughed at his own joke. "It's sort of embarrassing to me to have you a part of this children's center. Actually, sort of embarrassing to the whole family."

"Beau, she's merely looking at pictures and notes to make suggestions," Barbara said sweetly. "Don't be persnickety the little time we have her home with us."

"Yep, it's good to have you here, baby. I wish you'd just get a job in Royal and stay put, marry one of the locals before you meet some Californian and he carries you away from us for good."

"If that happens, I want your room," Hack said.

"Hack, for heaven's sake," Barbara chided. "No. Lila will always have her room and you have a perfectly good room, sitting room and bath that are as large as hers."

Ignoring her brother, Lila smiled at Beau. "It's nice to be home, Dad," she said.

After dinner Beau sauntered away to watch television while their cook, Agnes, cleared the table.

"Mom, I'm going to my room. I'm worn out and I want to look over the material Shannon gave me."

"Sure, Lila. I'll come up in a little while."

In her room Lila switched on her laptop and looked up the best child-care centers in the United States to see what comprised each one. About an hour later she pulled out the plans of what already had been decided on for the TCC center.

Lila began to make notes of a few changes she would

make if it were all left to her. A light knock on the door was followed by her mother thrusting her head into the room. "Can I come in?"

"Sure. Want to look at the drawings?"

Barbara crossed the room to sit close to Lila and look at the drawings while Lila pointed out various things.

"Looks very cutting-edge. I'm glad you're helping. How are you feeling?"

"Good. I get tired, but otherwise I'm okay."

"Lila, you're going to have to decide what you'll do. I'd like you to come home to have your baby."

"I don't know, Mom. I'm thinking about it."

"Please come home. I can take care of you and the baby. Also, honey, sooner or later you'll have to tell Sam about the baby. Sam and your father."

"I know I will. I have to tell Sam face-to-face. Hindsight is really great, isn't it?"

Barbara just smiled and waited.

"I have to tell him while I'm here, but I intend to do it right before I leave for California."

"That will suffice. Although I don't think the distance between California and Texas is going to slow Sam Gordon down. Those two boys grew up with a tough rancher father. They built their own successful construction business. Lila, Sam is going to want to marry you. Having raised two children, I want you to think about it before you turn him down."

"Mom, you know what Sam Gordon wants in a wife. A woman like you. You're sweet. You humor Dad. I know you get what you want and Dad doesn't even realize that he's been manipulated—"

"I wouldn't go so far as to say that I manipulate your father."

"Of course you do," Lila said sweetly, smiling. "He

can't see it so he doesn't object. But you don't work outside home and he would have a fit if you did. I love my job. I don't want to give it up to come home and live in Royal."

"Just think it over. It's difficult to raise a child, and a single parent has a hard time."

Lila thought of Gil Addison and Cade. Sometimes Gil looked harried, while other times he had a fleeting, forlorn expression—was it the lack of a mother for Cade and a wife for him?

"If you turn him down, you better be ready for a battle. Sam Gordon doesn't strike me as the type to give up. He's eaten a lot of dinners at our house. He's a nice man, Lila."

"I know he is, Mom. That helps."

"And on the subject of announcing your pregnancy— you have to tell your father."

"I told you I will before I leave, but I want to make decisions about what I'll do. Dad will want to take over totally. And there's no doubt he'll want Sam to marry me. I can't bear to think about that one. Also, I don't want to hear Hack's smart remarks."

"I could break the news first to your dad and he will take care of your brother."

"Let me think about what I'll do," Lila said, while she wished she could go right back to California.

Barbara stood and hugged Lila. "Don't worry. I'm glad you're home. Of course, if I have to, I'll go to California when the baby is born."

"I understand."

"Whatever you do, you know I'll back you up."

Lila squeezed her mother's hand. "You're still the best mom in the whole world."

Barbara laughed. "I love you, Lila, and love having you home. I'll go see about your dad now. He was asleep when I came in here."

Lila bent over plans and pictures again. She jotted down ideas as she looked at Shannon's notes. Finally, she shoved them aside to think about Sam. How was she going to tell him?

Wednesday morning, even though she didn't want to see Sam, she couldn't keep from studying how she looked before she left the ranch. She changed twice before finally settling on a plain two-piece dress, a sleeveless green cotton one with a V neckline. Like several newly purchased dresses for the trip to Royal, the top was tailored and came to her hips with a straight skirt below it that once again hid her waist.

She didn't want to run into Sam and have him studying her figure while she was wearing something that showed her waist. She brushed her hair and clipped it up on the back of her head. After a few critical moments in front of her mirror, she was satisfied.

When she reached the club, she spread her plans on the game table in the future billiard room to study them again while waiting for Shannon.

Her cell phone interrupted her and she answered to hear Shannon's voice.

"Lila, I'm sorry. I need to cancel. We have a cow giving birth and having trouble. The vet's on his way. I am so sorry since I'm sure you're already at the club."

"Stop apologizing. Let's meet tomorrow so today you can concentrate on your cow. Same time, same place."

"Thanks a lot. Gotta run."

As Lila gathered her things, Sam entered. He usually dressed casually, but this morning he was in a navy suit and tie, a snowy dress shirt and black boots, a man who would turn female heads anywhere. Just the sight of him made her heart race.

"Good afternoon—looks as if you're leaving."

"I was going to meet Shannon, but she's called and canceled. She has a cow having difficulty giving birth, plus her foreman is sick."

"I'll bet you had planned to have lunch with Shannon. Now you don't have to miss the treat of dining here at the club. I'll take you to lunch."

"You know, I eat here plenty with my family," she said, amused because Sam knew full well she was frequently at the club when she was in town.

His grin widened. "I promise I'll hide my usual chauvinistic self and we'll have a good time."

"I'll have to admit, to hear you confess that you are fully aware of your old-fashioned, chauvinistic ways is refreshing."

"Come on. You were going to eat here with Shannon. You can eat with me. We can even talk about the children's center if you want."

"Now you're stretching your credibility. There's no way you have an interest in the child-care center, so don't even pretend you do."

"Didn't say I'd pretend. I just said we can discuss it— you talk and I'll listen. Let me take your things and we can leave them with the maître d'."

"You're persistent, Sam."

"Only when it's important—I'm interested and the best-looking woman in Royal, Texas, is back in town," he said, taking her things from her.

She shook her head, more at herself than at him, yet he was so tempting. What happened to her backbone where Sam was concerned? Right now she should be saying no firmly and walking out instead of watching him tuck her papers and plans beneath his arm and smile at her.

"I'm glad we're having lunch together," he said in a

husky voice that sounded more like an invitation to step into his bedroom. "Now tell me about the children's center," he said, taking her arm and heading toward the door.

She had to either go along to lunch with him or make an issue of refusing now. It was much easier to just go with him because his sexy voice and spellbinding eyes had sealed the deal for him.

"They're moving ahead rapidly because Shannon and the other women have coordinated with the construction company. I'm surprised Gordon Construction didn't have the bid."

"No, we're closely involved at the TCC and felt it was a conflict of interest. This is not our deal."

"Does that translate into 'We wouldn't touch the child-care center with a ten-foot pole'?"

He grinned at her. "Sugar, you do have the wrong view of me."

"Has it ever occurred to you that your *sugar* endearment is a little demeaning?"

"*Sugar?* When applied to you? Ahh, never, Lila," he said, pausing and turning to face her, making her stop. He stood too close, looked at her too intently and had his hand on her wrist, where he could easily feel her racing pulse.

"*Sugar* where you're concerned is definitely an endearment," he said softly, bending his knees to look a little more directly into her eyes. "There is absolutely nothing demeaning about it."

"It sort of has the connotation of relegating me to the kitchen and bedroom. Have you thought about that?"

"Not at all, because that is not what I'm implying. Believe me, it is a term of endearment for someone who is very special and very female and important to me," he said in that same husky tone that made her feel as if she were on the verge of melting.

"This lunch is getting personal."

"Doesn't have to," he said cheerfully, taking her arm again and heading for the dining room.

"What are you doing here today?" she asked.

"I met a client. We're going to build a clinic for him and we met this morning for coffee and to talk about what he wants and for him to sign an agreement. It was all business, but this is a good place to bring clients."

"I agree with that, and my dad has made a few deals here himself, although he usually makes them out in the open looking at land, or at barns at cattle sales," she said, thankful to be on a safe, impersonal subject that would have no impact on their lives.

They entered the dining room and she waited while Sam talked to the maître d'. As soon as the waiter had poured their water, he left menus in their hands. It took her only minutes to make a selection from the familiar menu.

"What would you like, Lila?"

"I've got my choice in mind. What are you having?" she asked, determined that Sam would not order for her, knowing from past experiences that he expected to. She decided that if she behaved as independently as possible, maybe no more lunch offers would torment her.

"My usual lunch burger. I'm a burger guy and the club's are mouthwatering," he said, "but not as much as some other mouthwatering things in life."

"So what's your favorite burger on this menu?" she asked, trying to ignore his flirting, remembering how it had felt to run her fingers through his thick light brown hair that he wore collar length.

"The Swiss mushroom—gooey and delicious. I'll even give you a bite unless that's what you're ordering."

"Of course not. You and I are poles apart in everything, and that includes lunch items," she said, smiling at him. "Let me guess—you drink iced tea with your lunch."

"You're right, but you know that from being with me when we ate lunch together on my patio after the best night of my life."

"Wow, did I bring that one on myself. Want to hear one of the best nights of my life?" she said in a sultry tone, leaning closer toward him, although the table was large enough to keep a generous space between them.

"Of course, and how I hope it's the same night I had."

"Sorry to disappoint you. It was when I learned that a movie in which I had done the setup for the scenes had used nearly all my suggestions. It was exhilarating to know they were impressed by what I'd done, actually using most of it."

"Congratulations. That's impressive."

The waiter appeared to take their orders and looked expectantly at Lila.

"I'll have the Caesar salad, no chicken, and just my water. Mr. Gordon will have the mushroom-and-Swiss burger, meat medium, with iced tea and shoestrings. Just put all this on my family check—Hacket," she said, and smiled at the waiter.

"Yes, Miss Hacket," he said, glancing at Sam. "Anything else?"

"Yes, there is something else. You put all that on my bill. I insist. I invited Miss Hacket to have lunch with me," Sam said in a commanding voice that caused their waiter to start writing in his tablet.

"Yes, sir."

"You even got how I like the meat cooked right," Sam said, looking amused.

"I figured you for the macho type who wants red in his meat," she said, certain she had annoyed him by ordering.

"Trying to get me in bad with your dad when he sees the club bill, or were you trying to show me how it feels when I order for you, the independent woman?" Sam asked.

"Not one thought crossed my mind about Dad, and I don't think your name would have shown up on the final bill to him. No, it was more to let you see how it feels to have someone order for you once you're over five years old and can read."

"Or maybe you have a chip on your shoulder about being the 'independent woman.'" He leaned across the table, taking her hand. "Well, sweetie, you can just order away. I'll remember your preference after this," he said in his husky, seductive voice while holding her hand and running his thumb back and forth across her knuckles, causing tingles. "I do not want to do one thing to make you unhappy or make you feel less than the very desirable, intelligent woman you are. Now, your danged independence is sort of like a cocklebur in my boot, but there are moments when you lose that independence and that's worth putting up with all the rest," he said, dropping back into the sexy tone that kept her heart racing.

He was causing the whole process of ordering for him to backfire, because this was not the result she had intended.

"Sam," she said, withdrawing her hand. "People will see you holding my hand and think we're a couple."

"And…that's so terrible?"

She smiled broadly, wishing she could make light of what he was saying as she extricated her hand. He leaned back, looking satisfied, as if he had just won the latest skirmish between them. Why had she let him cajole her into this lunch?

"In the first place, we're not a couple. In the second,

I don't want to have to answer a bunch of unnecessary questions."

"We could be—it's all right with me. And questions are easy. Just yes or no will cover it, I think."

"Well, maybe if you hold the hand of every woman you dine with, people would accept a flat yes or no. So you and your brother didn't want any part of the child-care center for your business?"

"That isn't exactly what I said and that's an abrupt change in our conversation."

"Yes, it is, because we were getting up close and personal. Too personal. We're at lunch at the club. Everything I do here goes straight back to Dad."

"First of all, your dad and I are good friends. Second of all, he'll be more than happy for you to socialize with club members and you know it. Besides, all we're doing is having a friendly chat over lunch. That's as harmless as it gets."

She smiled at him. "True, Sam. It is completely meaningless as well. So who's the latest woman in your life? It has to be someone I know." Lila sipped her water and glanced around the club, hoping she'd convinced Sam that she felt the lunch was harmless and meaningless to her but suspecting she had not in the least.

When the silence stretched a little too long, she glanced at him and was startled to find him sitting back, his head tilted while he studied her. There was an intent look in his eyes and she was glad the table hid the sight of her waist from him.

"There's no woman in my life now," he answered evenly. "But I'd like for there to be a very special one and I don't need to tell you who. You know full well."

"That is so impossible."

"There's nothing impossible about it."

"I've already told you. Don't you listen? We're way too opposite. We have whole opposing philosophies— very basic differences that aren't going to change for either one of us."

"Go to dinner with me tonight. I'll take you dancing and I'll prove to you that we don't have a hill of beans' worth of differences between us that matter."

"Thank you, I already have plans. What are you doing now? What are you constructing, Sam?"

"I'm attempting to develop a relationship with a very beautiful, very reluctant woman," he said, leaning toward her, but the table and their lunches kept them apart. "Only that reluctance appears to me to be just skin-deep, Lila. I'll find out why or get past it. Is there a guy in California?"

"I don't want to go into that," she replied, eating her salad. "Your burger is getting cold."

"Aha, that's a no," he said with satisfaction.

"You don't know any such thing," she said, thinking Sam had expressive eyes that could convey all sorts of emotions. Her attention shifted to his mouth, remembering his kisses, until she realized what she was doing. Her gaze flew up to meet his and saw the mocking satisfaction in the blue depths.

She turned her attention to her salad. There was no way to stop the blush she felt in her face. "This lunch is not exactly turning out like I expected."

"You want me to back off?" he asked, still sounding amused. "Tell me about this movie shoot you're getting ready for."

"It has a Western setting although it's contemporary and there are some ranches around here that should be perfect for various scenes. As much as possible, we'll get set up and ready before the cast comes."

"Makes me wish I had a ranch."

"In its own way, this is interesting country and the small towns have their own ambience."

"They have that, all right. Wait until a dust storm blows through."

"No, thanks. A dust storm isn't needed for this movie, so we'll pass on the dust."

"Can anyone come watch the filming?"

"There will be a place for the public, but to get up close and for some scenes, you'll have to have an invitation. Do you want me to get you one?"

"No, thanks. I can pass on that deal. Has anyone in this movie ever ridden a horse?"

"I'm sure they have."

"Tell me about this fascinating job you have. Just what do you do? Arrange furniture on a set?"

She laughed. "Sometimes, but a little more than that. I need to help impart the film's theme and feeling through the props that we use. The set designs create atmosphere. Location is vital. I look at sites. I oversee the right props, the art department. Sometimes we can find the props we want. Sometimes we have to make our own. It's interesting, challenging, lots of thinking on your feet, so each assignment is different because each film is different."

"I can see where that would be interesting. What about the sexy movie guys?"

"They're just people."

"You say that like you mean it. I'd think any female would be attracted."

"They're larger than life on-screen and in those stories. Away from that, they're just people like everyone else."

"I'm glad you feel that way. You like being home again?"

"Of course I do."

"If you got a job in Midland and worked there, you'd be home a lot but still away."

"I don't believe they make many movies in Midland."

"I guess they don't," he said, giving her a thoughtful look that made her want to get away from his scrutiny.

She finished all she could eat of her salad, leaving half, and she noticed Sam only ate half his burger. The waiter went straight to Sam to sign for the meal.

"Thanks for the lunch, Sam." As she stood, he did, coming around to pull out her chair. He followed her to the lobby. "I'm going home now."

"Can't talk you into dinner tonight?"

She shook her head. "Sorry, I do have plans. Thanks again for lunch," she said.

"I'll walk you to your car." He fell into step beside her, taking the plans and papers from her hand.

"Have they heard anything more about Alex?" she asked.

"Not that I know about. Nathan still hasn't let the media know about the truck, but since he told the club and other people were at the scene, I think the word has gone through a segment of the Royal population."

"I'm sure it has. Sophie is still working in his office, so I hope she's safe. I hope Nathan is keeping an eye on the office."

"I'd guess he is. Sophie should be okay. She wasn't deeply involved with Alex except through her job."

Lila paused beside a dark blue four-door car. "Thanks again."

"You have a new car?"

"Oh, no. This is just one of Dad's that I'm using while I'm here." She climbed in, then started the car. When she lowered the window, Sam folded his arms on the window's edge and bent down to talk.

"Lunch was fun. It would be a lot more fun to have dinner. I'll try again."

"Give it up, Sam. We're both better off," she said, her words becoming breathless. Now he was only inches away, his face thrust into the open window. She gazed into thickly lashed blue eyes that could immobilize her, and take her breath.

He leaned closer. "See, Lila," he said softly, "you're responding to me now. Sparks fly between us. If I felt your pulse, my guess is that it's racing," he said in a husky voice. "I'll tell you something—my pulse is racing, too. I feel what you're feeling."

"Doesn't matter, Sam," she whispered. "Nothing will come of it. Now you need to move away." He slipped his hand into the car, reaching behind her head to pull her the last few inches, and he leaned in, his mouth covering hers to kiss her.

Four

Lila's heart pounded when she drove out of the lot.

She let out her breath. Her palms were damp. She was breathless from his kiss, which had set her heart racing. Her lips tingled and a pang struck her. If only Sam didn't have old-fashioned ideas. He was fun and sometimes she couldn't resist him.

As days passed, her figure was changing—her waistline was thicker. She couldn't wear her belts fastened in the notch she had once used.

She was running the risk of Sam noticing and she had to stop accepting his invitations. How was she ever going to tell him about his baby?

Sam stood a moment, watching her drive away. He ached to hold Lila. His lips still flamed from the brief, light kiss that only made him want so much more.

Why was she avoiding him? She had gone to lunch, but

if he hadn't been persistent, she wouldn't have, and she turned him down flatly for dinner. Yet she responded to him. Her pulse had raced when he had touched her wrist. There had to be a reason for the contradictions in her.

When he was at the club now, he couldn't keep from going by the billiard room and looking for her. During lunch she had challenged him, making a pointed effort to emphasize their differences, yet at the same time she had been as responsive physically as ever. The look she'd had when he had caught her gazing at his mouth practically screamed that she wanted to kiss. So why was she refusing to go out with him?

He couldn't believe it was simply the differences in their views regarding women and the children's center. Her reasons to avoid him went deeper, but he was at a loss.

One thing he knew for sure—he wanted her in his arms. He wanted to hold and kiss her and make love for hours. Why couldn't he get her out of his system?

He returned to his office, heading down the drive to the two-story red-brick Greek Revival with stately white Corinthian columns and a broad porch flanked by well-tended beds of flowers in the front. He spent a few minutes talking to Josh and then shut himself in his big office. After half an hour he tossed down the pen he held. Why was Lila trying to avoid him? She seemed torn between responding to him and turning his every invitation down. When he had coaxed her into accepting lunch, her reluctance had been evident.

If she didn't have that other side to her, he would leave her alone and make a bigger effort to get her out of his system. As it was, he wanted to know why. And he wanted a long weekend with her where they could make love like before.

Was there a man in California?

Sam leaned back in his chair and rubbed his forehead. He didn't think so. She would be firmer in her refusals and he guessed Lila was open enough to just tell him if there was someone else. So what the hell was it? He scratched his head and sighed, standing and moving restlessly to the window.

He needed to go out with her and learn what the problem between them was or just forget her. But forgetting her was impossible. He thought about her constantly. One more night with her and maybe he could get her out of his system. Only he knew better. One night would never shake Lila out of his thoughts. He wanted unending nights.

How was he going to get even a single night with her when she was so standoffish?

He decided to go see how the latest house was progressing. He had a contract to build a seven-million-dollar mansion in Pine Valley, where he lived. He had to get out and do something to take his mind off Lila.

On Thursday, Lila showered to get ready to once again drive to Royal to meet Shannon. Tired of wearing the waist-hiding dresses, she pulled on scarlet slacks with a matching short-sleeved V-neck summer sweater. When she studied her image, she could see a small bulge. Her waist was thickening already. The clubhouse would be air-conditioned, so she pulled out a short-sleeved lightweight cardigan that matched her outfit and put it on.

This time when she looked in the mirror, she was satisfied with her image. Combing her hair, she let it fall loose. She picked up her purse, notebook and the mailing tube with the plans and drawings inside.

When she entered the present billiard room, Shannon was there along with some of the other women. Lila greeted Abby Price, Missy Reynolds and Vanessa Woodrow. In minutes they were all seated around a table, studying each other's written suggestions.

Within the hour, they moved to the dining room to continue planning over lunch. As they finished eating and lingered over iced tea, still talking about the center, Lila felt a prickle of awareness. Glancing around, she saw Sam standing in the doorway. Her heart skipped a beat when he turned to look at her. For a moment she was locked into his gaze until she realized she was staring.

With an effort she looked away, focusing again on the women at her table and trying to ignore Sam.

Moments later, when she couldn't resist glancing toward the door, he had disappeared from sight. She suspected she would see him later. He had a way of popping up when she least expected to see him.

When the women adjourned to the billiard room again, everyone shared a few final ideas. They wanted bright and colorful play areas and a separate corner for babies.

Shannon looked at her list. "We'll have security cameras and parents will be able to access a closed-circuit view of the center so they can see their child."

"We'll have security at the front door and alarms will sound if anyone opens any of the doors except the front, which has a chime if opened, but two people will be at the desk by the front door at all times," Missy added.

Later, after the others had gone, only Shannon and Lila were left. As Lila put away her notes, she paused. "I think this child-care center is going to be great. The designs we have are bright and appealing."

"Thanks for your input. The California shop you told us about where we can get pictures for the walls is wonderful."

"I'm glad all of you found it helpful. I love to go there

and see what they have when I need to get a shower gift or new-baby present."

"We're getting more support, even from some of the members who opposed this center."

"But still not the Gordons."

"Heavens, no. Both Gordons fought this like crazy. Frankly, so did your dad. Some people don't change."

"I know my dad doesn't change and Hack is going to be like him, only worse. But my mom is enthusiastic about the center. Her ladies' book club is making a donation and I think Mom made a big donation herself. Dad will never know she had a part in it," Lila said, laughing.

"Good for her. We want the best possible place for the children. We barely touched on it today, but our budget is maxed out. That's something else we'll have to tackle."

"I'm sure we can get more money."

"Lila, if we need to get together again, I'll give you a call."

"Sure, but when I go back to work, I can't meet with you."

"I understand. Soon I'll be leaving for Austin. I'm ready to see Rory," Shannon said wistfully.

"Bye, Shannon," Lila said as her friend left. Gathering the rest of her things, Lila remembered her mother was in Midland with friends and wouldn't be home until later. Her dad was with her uncle in Houston to look at a bull. She didn't want to go home and listen to Hack, or worse, have to put up with Hack and some of his friends. As Lila walked toward the door, she paused to look at the room. Half of the old billiard tables were scheduled to be removed while half would remain. Renovations would start as soon as the center was finished. The clubhouse was getting updated continually, yet still retained some of its historic parts.

"Taking a last look at this room before they start working on it?" came a deep male voice, and she turned to see Sam strolling into the room. "I just passed Shannon and she said you're through for today."

"That's right."

Sam stopped inches in front of her. He stood too close and her heartbeat raced.

"Come have a drink with me. We can sit on the terrace or we can stay in the air-conditioned bar."

Lila debated a moment.

"I take that as a definite yes," Sam said, taking her notebook from her hands. "I'll carry this."

"You're sure of yourself," she said, her gaze raking over him as he turned. His short-sleeved navy Western shirt had the top two buttons unfastened. Wearing tight jeans and boots, he looked as if he had just come from a ranch, but Lila knew Sam dressed like the ranchers most of the time, she guessed because he worked with so many of them and had grown up on a ranch.

"You don't have something else you have to do and you don't look in a hurry to head home."

"Now, how do you know all that? You're guessing," she said, smiling, knowing she was once again yielding to Sam when she should have said no and gotten away from him as quickly as possible. "I was just thinking that Mom's in Midland until later. Dad's in Houston with my uncle. My little brother will be as eager to spend time with me as I am with him," she said dryly. "Hack is at an age that is not the most adorable time."

"So I'm the lucky guy who gets your company—I knew there was a reason I came by the club. How's the children's center coming along?" Sam asked, walking around the room and looking at the racks holding cue sticks, the tables with the balls ready.

"We've got all sorts of plans and the renovation of the old billiard room is progressing faster than I dreamed possible."

"Good."

"I'm surprised to hear you say that," she said.

"It's a done deal, so I might as well accept it."

"That's a good attitude," she said, wondering how much he meant what he said.

"Do you know how to shoot pool?"

"Yes, I do."

"Want to play? I can give you some points."

"I'll play and you don't have to give me any points," she said, wondering why they constantly challenged each other.

He smiled and got cue sticks, handing her one. He racked the balls.

"You can start," he said. "Go ahead and bust them."

"Sure," she said. As she lined up her shot, she concentrated, determined to beat him.

"Many a game has been played on these tables and many a deal done while the game went on," he said when it was his turn.

"Deals have been done all over this clubhouse. It would be interesting to hear what the highest amount involved was. My guess is it was in the millions but not billions."

"I agree. I doubt if a billion-dollar deal went down here at the clubhouse, but we both might be wrong. And other kinds of deals have been done. Seductions, marriage proposals, clandestine meetings, probably divorce lawyers meeting with clients here. Wagers that involved all sorts of things. Will you wager on our game?"

He straightened to watch his shot, then looked at her before he moved to shoot again.

"Maybe. If I lose, what does it cost me?"

He shot and balls rolled away. "All right. If I win," he said, straightening to look into her eyes as she realized she should have refused the bet, "I get a kiss."

A tingle slithered to her toes. "Only a kiss," she said as if his kisses didn't set her on fire. "Okay." Instantly she knew what she wanted. "If I win, you make a contribution to the child-care center," she said, resolving to get a donation for the center and avoid a kiss that would incinerate her. "It has to be over fifty dollars."

"You're on," he replied, smiling at her.

She focused on the game and for the next few minutes they played in silence, evenly matched, but she was concentrating and trying to play her best.

And then she missed a shot. Holding her breath, she watched as he made his. In minutes the game was his.

He came around to take her cue stick and put it in the rack next to his. While her heart drummed, she watched his every move.

He turned back and his blue eyes held smoldering fires. He walked to her and slipped his arm around her waist. "To the victor…and all that," he said. His gaze lowered to her mouth and her lips tingled in anticipation.

He bent lower, slowly, tantalizingly, and then his lips brushed hers. The next time, his mouth touched hers with pressure, opening her mouth, and desire swept her. She melted against him, winding her arm around his neck, returning his kiss as his tongue went deep into her mouth. Moaning softly, she was barely aware she had made a sound.

Burning with need, she ran her fingers in his hair. Why? Why did he hold such appeal for her when they were so vastly different?

His kiss continued and time ceased to exist. She kissed him in return while she wanted the barriers between them gone. She wanted more, ached for hours of loving that they'd had once before.

When she ended the kiss, she was breathless, looking up at him as she stepped away.

"Want a second match?" he asked lightly, but his voice was hoarse and his breathing ragged.

"No, I think not."

He took her hand. "Maybe later. C'mon. We'll go to the bar and have a cool drink where we can talk."

A few minutes later they were seated in a booth in the bar among only a half-dozen members. Soft music played and a waiter appeared to take their order. "Ginger ale for me," Lila said.

"Beer, chips and *queso*," Sam ordered. "Ginger ale?" he asked when the waiter was gone.

"That's all I feel like and I have to drive back to the ranch tonight."

"No, you don't," Sam said, folding his arms on the table to lean closer. "I'll be glad to take you home. Or, even better—"

"Don't say it," she said, smiling at him. "I'm definitely going home tonight."

"But not for a while. We can have some fun before you do. How did you get this job that you like so much? Is that what you went to Hollywood to do?"

"Yes, but I started much lower and when that job came open, I applied and interviewed for it along with quite a few others." As she talked, he listened as if totally entranced. She gazed at him and thought he had the bluest eyes she had ever seen. She worked with movie stars, men who were considered by millions to be handsome and sexy, and she had never had the reaction to any of them she had by simply being near Sam. That bit of knowledge annoyed her as much as it mystified her.

They talked, laughing over things that had happened in Royal. She lost track of time, but when a pianist began to play, she glanced around in surprise and looked at her watch.

Sam's hand closed on her wrist, hiding her watch. "It's time for dinner, maybe a dance with you. It's still early. We can eat here in the bar."

He motioned to their waiter and asked for menus.

"You can't keep from taking charge, can you?"

"You surely can't object to that."

"Of course not. It's just amusing because it's ingrained in you. With a twin brother, there must have been some fights and competition. I'm guessing Josh may be as take-charge as you."

Sam gave her a look that made her realize she was right and might have touched a nerve. "We had fights plenty. Big fights. And we are competitive. But we also stood up for each other. We can work together well and the business has been a good thing."

"That's great, Sam. I don't know about any of that. Hack is younger. When he was a toddler, I thought he was so cute. He was my doll, and I helped Mom with him. Dad spoils him. Mom's aware of it and has tried to get Dad to be more firm with Hack, but he isn't. A time came when Hack was no longer a baby and not so cute. We fought like cats and dogs all the way through school until I went off to college. Now he's just a nuisance sometimes or we leave each other alone. It's sad. We've grown apart and I don't think that's going to change. The one person Hack is really nice to is Mom, but he does things behind her back that he knows she doesn't want him to do. I don't know if we'll ever be close and I can't imagine ever being in a business with Hack."

"I will have to agree with you that your little brother is one spoiled kid."

"I hope he matures and changes and begins to care about someone besides himself. Enough about him, though. Families are a big influence in our lives. I'm sorry you lost your mom when you were so young. I'm close to mine."

"Yeah. Life throws us curves. What would you like to eat?"

She studied the menu even though she was not really hungry. "I think just a spinach salad."

"You can do better than that. Let's dance and maybe you'll work up an appetite."

She went with him to the dance floor and soon they were turning to a fast beat, moving with the music. Sam was a good dancer, light on his feet, moving in a sensual way while he watched her with a steady, smoldering gaze.

Each time with him was a mistake, yet she kept accepting his invitations. Soon she'd be busy with the movie and then she'd head back to California and Sam would be a memory again. Except she had to tell him the truth. When was the time going to be right?

Twisting and turning, her feet moved in rhythm. The time was definitely not now. Not until it was almost time to go back to California. Two or three days before, so he could get some things out of his system while she was still around. Afterward she would go to California, and he would have to adjust to the idea.

They danced three fast numbers before there was a ballad. Along with the music, the piano player sang a sentimental love song. Sam wrapped her in his embrace, pulling her close to slow-dance with her.

Why did it feel so right to be in his arms? To sway with him, feel his solid muscles against her? The slow steps and being held close revved desire, making her think of lovemaking with him.

When the number ended, she looked up and saw the need mirrored in the depths of his eyes. "I want you, Lila," he whispered. "I want to make love again."

"Sam," she cautioned, shaking her head. "Let's get off the dance floor," she whispered. She felt as if all her resolve was melting away. "Now I'm ready for dinner," she said, struggling to change the subject.

She wasn't one degree more hungry than she had been before, but the dancing was too close, too personal. They were touching, hugging, making sexy moves in the fast dances. She wanted to get back to the booth with a table between them, have dinner and then drive herself home. The evening had been fun, but she needed to keep him at arm's length and end it early.

Their waiter appeared, refilling their glasses before asking what she wanted.

"The spinach salad," she said.

"Is that all? You'll be hungry before you get home," Sam said.

She shook her head. "That's all."

"I'll have the New York strip, cooked medium," Sam said.

She slid out of the booth. "Need to freshen up," she said. As she walked away, her back tingled and she felt Sam's gaze on her.

In the lobby she stopped to call home because her mother worried if she didn't know where her children were.

As wild as her brother was, he kept his mother fairly well informed about where he would be. That was one of the few considerations Hack gave anyone.

No one answered at the Double H. Lila left a message because her mother checked when she returned home.

Sam watched Lila as she crossed the room. When he'd held her close, she had felt different than last time. Her waist wasn't as tiny as he had remembered. She was still soft curves, warm, enticing. He wanted her and he wanted to talk her into staying in Pine Valley at his house tonight.

When she returned, he watched her approach the table. He stood, waiting until she was seated before he sat again. He wondered whether she really disliked all the old-time courtesies or just certain ones, like ordering for her.

She was too damned independent, yet he just couldn't get her out of his system. He thought there was only one way to do so—make love until he was totally satisfied and could walk away without looking back.

Trouble was, the lady wasn't cooperating. He wasn't getting any chances for lovemaking, but tonight he was making inroads on her resistance.

As they ate, they talked about various topics. She took dainty bites, dawdling over her salad as if she didn't really want it.

Finally they finished, and when they returned to the dance floor for a fast, pounding song, he watched her with growing desire. She had pulled off the cardigan she wore over her short-sleeved scarlet sweater. Lights had dimmed and it was darker than it had been earlier.

She danced around him, hips moving. Strobe lights flashed and the dance floor filled with other dancers, everyone gyrating to the loud music.

Lights slashed across them, flashing on her face and then plunging her into darkness. Lights showed her green eyes, her flushed cheeks, the dark auburn hair swirling out behind her when she spun around. More streaks of light cut across the V of her sweater, revealing her lush curves and creamy skin. The next flash and his gaze was on her waist and stomach. He was startled to see her tummy looked slightly rounded, not flat below her tiny waist as before. The light was gone instantly. The next flash she had turned away.

He broke into a sweat as he danced, while she looked cool, composed. He wanted her more than ever.

The dance ended with a crash of drums and then a ballad started and he pulled her into his arms to hold her close and barely move in time to the music.

They danced in silence, but this time he thought about her and felt her soft body pressed against him. He ran his hand down over her hip, back up until he reached her ribs and she caught his wrist and moved his hand to her back.

She was thicker through the middle, her stomach a bit fuller, not the flat stomach she'd had before. He thought about the cardigan she had worn throughout the hot day, yet in the air-conditioned club, it would not be unpleasant to wear.

He pictured her as she had looked at the barbecue, remembering her dress and how it had hidden her waist. So had the dresses he had seen her wear at the club. Everything until today, and even then, the cardigan hid her waist fairly well.

Sam tightened his arm to pull her closer, wondering if she felt so different or if his memory wasn't good. A weight gain? He thought of how she avoided him, usually wouldn't go out with him, turning him down. Yet at the same time, she had a response every time he was around, as if she wanted him but shouldn't.

One possibility occurred to him, sending such a shock through his body that he stopped dancing.

Five

Sam quickly regained his composure. He counted back and realized it was a full three months since their night together.

He felt as if all the breath had been knocked out of him. Lila was going to have a baby—his baby. He was as sure of it as he was that flowers would grow in the spring. That would explain her contradictory actions, one minute flirting and the next throwing an invisible wall between them and refusing to go out with him.

He would be a dad. Lila was going to have his baby. He felt weak in the knees, as if he'd had a major blow to his middle.

Had she come to Texas and expected to avoid telling him? Anger stirred that she would hide from him the truth about his baby. Maybe she was going to wait until she was back in California to let him know. She had to know she couldn't hide it forever. She obviously intended to keep the baby or she would have already done something. That thought gave him chills.

A baby. Their baby. Stunned, he danced automatically, forgetting everyone around him. He would have to marry her.

The moment that occurred to him, he felt another blow to his insides that took his breath. Get married. His first reaction was a panicky feeling of being trapped.

As quickly as he'd thought of marriage, he focused on Lila. His panicky feelings evaporated. Lila was beautiful, intelligent, sexy. Marriage to Lila, a family of his own, life couldn't get any better. She was also totally independent, the epitome of the independent woman. Lila would not want to marry—if she did, she would not have been trying to avoid him.

The dance ended and another started. Without a word, he began to dance and she followed his lead, another fast piece where they danced with space between them and he could watch her and think and adjust to his discovery.

His baby. That was a miracle. His own family—if he could ever convince her to marry him.

It astounded him and annoyed him that she wouldn't share the news with him. He wanted to sweep her up and lift her high, showering kisses on her. He was going to marry Lila. He was going to be a dad.

An old favorite started playing and he drew her into his arms for some close dancing. "This is good, Lila," he said in a husky voice, his mind wrapped up in his new discovery. "Let me take you to dinner tomorrow night."

He whirled her around and dipped, pausing. As she gazed up into his eyes, her arm tightened around his neck, making his heart pound. He wanted to kiss her full, rosy lips. He tightened his arms as she wound her fingers in the hair at the back of his head.

"Sam," she whispered.

Their gazes locked and he forgot the other dancers. He wanted her more than he ever had before. This would be good, he decided. Good, when—and if—he could talk her into marriage.

"We'll go to dinner and celebrate the new movie and talk. I'll pick you up at six," he said, slowly straightening and taking her up with him while their gazes still held.

When he looked at her mouth, she licked her lower lip. His body tensed, heated with desire. He pulled her closer to continue dancing while he looked into her green eyes. "We'll go to my place and I'll cook my special steaks. How's that?"

"Sam—"

"It's Friday night. You want to stay out at the ranch with Hack?"

She smiled. "I think on Friday night the last place Hack will be is at the Double H."

"I'll pick you up at six, darlin'. You'll have a fun evening and I can show you my new outdoor kitchen and cook you the best steak west of the Mississippi. How's that for an offer you can't refuse? I might even throw in taking you dancing later."

"You're impossible," she said, smiling.

"But oh so interested in the beautiful lady and wanting to spend an evening together. We might even shoot another game of pool with another wager. I'll give you a chance to win that donation to the child center yet."

"Even if I won, I don't think you'd keep your promise on a donation to the child-care center."

"I'm not that opposed to the little tykes. You misjudge me. You doubt my word?"

"Please, Sam, I've heard you talk and I know exactly how you feel about them. I've heard how you and your brother really campaigned against the center. An evening together—all we'll do is fuss and fight."

"Absolutely not! There will be nothing but harmony— well, maybe a challenge or two—tomorrow night."

"Why do I think that's the understatement of this century?" she asked, laughing.

"There, I made you laugh. That's the best, Lila. When you laugh, you light up and I love it. I'll have to try harder."

He fought the urge to let his eyes roam over her waist. Instead, he walked beside her, asking her if she wanted anything to drink. When she chose a glass of lemonade, he summoned a waiter and placed an order for lemonade and for another cold bottle of beer.

As she stood beside her chair, his gaze slipped over her. There was the slightest bulge to her tummy. A bulge she definitely had not had three months earlier.

While he held her chair, his fingers played across her nape. He wanted to pull her to her feet and ask her about the pregnancy, but this wasn't the time or place.

As soon as their drinks arrived, she excused herself, picked up her purse and headed for the ladies' room.

Still in shock, he watched her walk away. He would have to talk her into marriage. He was certain she had already made up her mind to be a single mom. Not with his baby, would she be. He could be determined, too, and he wasn't going to let her independence mess up their child's life.

Lila went to the ladies' room and studied her image. Thank goodness the club had the lights dimmed in the dining room, although she thought her slacks and sweater hid her figure well enough. Most men she had known were not keenly observant. Heaven knows, the men in her family weren't.

She returned to the table to face Sam, who sat across from her. He looked relaxed, yet she had the feeling he was studying her intently all through their light conversation.

"When they start shooting a movie here, it'll turn this town upside down."

"Like I said, so far there's no indication it will be in Royal. Or even in Maverick County. And if something changes and a scene is shot here, I think most people are level-headed. Sam, it's time for me to start home."

He motioned for the tab and then she picked up her purse. In the foyer, he collected her things.

"We could go out to my house," he suggested. "You can stay there and it'll save you a drive this late. Or leave your car here at the club. I'll take you home."

"It's not that late."

"If you're going to go, I insist on driving."

"Just how helpless do you think I am?" she asked, annoyed and amused at the same time.

"Not helpless at all. That's not the point. Maybe I want to be with you a little longer—ever think of that?"

"All right," she said, suspecting she would lose the argument no matter how long they debated. Sam had a stubborn lift to his chin. "I'll leave my car here and you can drive me home."

"Great." He took her arm and they walked out to his sleek black sports car. Sam held the door and she slid onto the soft leather seat.

As he walked around the car, her gaze ran over him and she thought about dancing with him when he held her close. Now she was going to dinner with him tomorrow night. Would she ever be able to stop letting him talk her into things?

He slid behind the wheel, glancing at her when he drove

away from the club. "What do you do for entertainment in California?"

"That's easy. Go to the beach. I love the ocean. It's exciting, awesome, wonderful. I walk on the beach every day. I swim a lot of the time." She turned in the seat to face him. The lights from the dash highlighted his prominent cheekbones, the bulge of his biceps.

Would he kiss her good-night? Her anticipation blossomed, spreading heat low within her.

During the drive he kept her entertained with conversation and when he circled in front of the Double H, he parked at the foot of the front steps.

He came around to walk her to the door. "It was a fun evening, Sam," she said as she crossed the porch and stopped in front of the entranceway.

"I hope so, because it was for me," he said, brushing his hand lightly on her cheek. "Do you think your family is home?"

"I'm sure my parents are and have gone to bed. It doesn't matter. I have a key so I can get in."

He smiled. "I'll see you tomorrow night at six." He walked away and she turned to go inside. For an instant, even though she knew she shouldn't, she felt a flash of disappointment that he hadn't kissed her. She could still feel the brush of his hand on her cheek, a touching caress that seemed uncharacteristic of the Sam she knew.

She had to tell him the truth about the baby, but it was important to wait until the perfect moment.

Friday evening Lila was more nervous than ever. She had changed clothes three times, finally deciding on a sleeveless blue dress. It had a straight skirt that ended above her knees. She hoped her legs would take his attention. The dress had a matching short-sleeved cardigan sweater.

She left her hair loose. She wanted him looking at her hair, her face, her legs, anywhere except her expanding middle. There was a light rap on the door and her mother entered. Dressed in casual pink slacks and a pink shirt, she reminded Lila of the mothers on sitcoms when she was a little girl. The ideal wife—in another time and another era.

"You look beautiful, Lila. Just radiant."

"I don't feel so radiant, but thank you, Mom."

"Think about it. Tonight might be a good time to tell the news to Sam," Barbara said, sitting on an upholstered blue-and-white-striped chair while she watched Lila brush her hair.

"No. I just can't do it this early in my stay. He'll hound me to pieces. I'll tell him, but in time."

"Lila, Sam's the father of your baby. I think you're too harsh on him."

Lila smiled as chimes sounded. "Here he is, and I'll be nice to him," she said, amused by her mother. "You let him in and you can talk to him a few minutes since you think he's so great."

"I'll be glad to," Barbara said, leaving the room. Lila took another long, critical look at her image in the full-length mirror and decided the dress looked fine and hid everything it needed to.

She picked up her purse and went to find Sam.

Sam stood as she entered the room.

"Come join us, Lila," her dad said. "Sam and I are talking about a golf game this weekend."

Sam barely heard Beau as his gaze swept over Lila. His heart missed a beat. She wore another sleeveless cotton dress with plain lines, yet on her the dress looked great, showing off her fabulous legs. The neckline gave a tantalizing glimpse of lush curves and her green eyes were wide, thickly lashed, holding a sexy look of approval as her gaze swept over him.

There was a current of excitement that had his nerves on edge. Tonight he wanted to know the truth and he intended to confront Lila about it.

For the next half hour they sat with her parents until Lila turned down her father's offer of drinks. Sam declined, too, rising to his feet to cross the room.

"I promised Lila dinner, so it's time we leave for Royal, but I've enjoyed seeing you both. Everyone is still talking about what a fabulous barbecue you had this year. You outdid yourselves, and the Hacket barbecue became an even bigger legend."

"It's fun to do," Barbara said, walking with them to the door.

"It was a damn fine barbecue, if I do say so myself," Beau said, smiling broadly. "Bring my baby home at a decent hour, Sam."

"Yes, sir. It's also nice to have Lila back in Texas."

"Night, Mom, Dad," she said as Sam took her arm to walk to the car. "My parents really like you, Sam."

"You have nice parents. It's another member of the family that I really want to like me," he said, flirting with her.

"He does," she said.

"I'm definitely not referring to your kid brother and you know it," he said.

"Of course I like you or I wouldn't be going out with you tonight. I consider you a very good friend of the family. The whole family."

"Well, then, I'm going to change that," he drawled in a deeper tone of voice.

"Don't make me a project."

"It might be fun, darlin'. Watch what you ask."

"You control yourself, Sam," she cautioned.

"Something that's impossible to do if I have a chance to kiss you. There's no way I can resist taking the opportunity. Maybe if we just start now, I'll get all this kissing out of my system and we can enjoy an ordinary evening."

"Nice try, but no, we're not starting with kisses. Absolutely not."

"My place tonight, later, dancing if you want," he said, holding open the door to his sports car. He looked at her shapely calves as she climbed into the car. When he looked up, he found her watching him.

They drove back to Pine Valley, the ultra-upscale gated community where he lived. Security let him enter and the gatekeeper waved to him. He glanced at Lila to see her looking outside at drives that turned into emerald lawns covered with tall trees. Occasionally there was a glimpse of a sprawling, imposing mansion set back far from the main road.

"I hear you're constructing a new home out here."

"You heard right. Actually, more than one. I like working on houses in Pine Valley. They're big, expensive, challenging. They'll be my neighbors, so I like getting to know the owners," he said. Her perfume lingered in the air, an enticing scent that smelled of spring flowers.

As they approached his mansion, she stared at it. "It's beautiful here."

"I can stretch out and enjoy myself. I have my dream home," he said. "But you've seen my home and my bedroom already."

"So I don't need to see it tonight."

He pulled over and stopped, turning to her, sliding his arm across the back of the seat. She shifted to look at him, her green eyes opening wide. Her lush lips were a tempta-

tion and he ached to draw her into his arms and kiss her.
"I'm going to find out why you're fighting me, Lila. Half
of you is at war with me or wanting to avoid me, and the
other half is sending me signals and still kissing me with
enough heat to melt solid metal."

"I don't think so," she said breathlessly, gazing at him
with seductive eyes that made his breath catch. Did she
have any clue the impact she had on him?

"You're doing it now. Your eyes say yes, your body is
responding, yet your words are holding me at arm's length.
I'm going to find out what it is that's coming between us."

"Some things are best not disturbed, Sam. If you push,
I'll disappear," she said, her words almost a whisper.

"I really am curious. I'll get an answer."

"When you do, you may wish you had left well enough
alone," she said, her voice firmer.

"Now, that's interesting because that's a threat," he
said, running his hand across her nape, feeling her smooth,
warm skin.

"Stubborn, stubborn man. I'm not threatening you. I
think you've asked me out solely because I've said no to
you a couple of times."

"More than a couple," he replied. "No, definitely not
because you've said no. I've asked you out because I want
to be with you and because some of the time you seem
to want to be with me," he said, his voice getting softer,
dropping.

"Just be careful, Sam. You're going where you don't
want to go. I said yes to tonight because we had fun together and I thought this would be another fun, light evening."

"We'll try to keep it that way," he said. Knowing he
should move away or he would kiss her, he leaned back,
then drove around to the rear of the mansion.

* * *

Lila waited in the outdoor living area overlooking the patio and the pool while Sam got a lemonade for her and a cold beer for himself. She sat on one end of a sofa covered in a colorful fabric patterned with red tulips.

She watched Sam getting their drinks. He paused to shed the navy sport coat he wore and rolled up the sleeves of the pale blue cotton shirt that was tucked into navy slacks. As always, he wore Western boots. Classical music played softly in the background. She had a pang of longing, wishing that everything was all right between them, and this was just an evening out with him.

She stopped thinking about wishes and faced the reality that soon she would have to tell him about his baby.

"This is good, Lila," he said, sitting close beside her on the sofa.

Intensely aware of him, she smiled. "It will never be really good between us, because we're from different worlds. You're part of another century, with old-fashioned ideas—"

"Old-fashioned ideas aren't always bad. I have one right now. I'll show you one that is really old-fashioned," he said softly, closing the distance between them as his gaze went to her mouth.

Sam took her lemonade from her hands and set it on the table, placing his beer beside it.

Her insides tightened and she inhaled. "Sam—" she whispered, a protest that died the instant his lips brushed hers lightly and then settled on hers to kiss her.

Carried from a world of concern to a sensual world of desire, she closed her eyes and placed her hands on his forearms. His hand slid down her back, and his other hand caressed her nape. Kissing him in return, she ran her hands across his broad shoulders, longing for more, to freely make love, to not have to deal with their opposing views of life.

When she finally leaned back, she tried to catch her breath as she looked into his blue eyes.

"I asked you out tonight because I wanted to be with you. But I had another reason, Lila. I've noticed some things and I'm curious," he said, gazing intently at her, causing her heart to beat faster. "You're pregnant, aren't you? You're carrying my baby."

Six

Her heart missed a beat and then began to pound. For a moment she couldn't get her breath and her head spun. He leaned closer, giving her a searching look.

"You're pregnant, aren't you?"

"Yes," she admitted, her head swimming. "How did you know?"

"I figured it out." He inhaled deeply. "What were you going to do? Go back to California and not tell me? Send me a text someday?"

"No, I knew I'd have to tell you," she said, gulping for air and feeling as if she might faint.

"Are you all right?" he asked, his tone changing as he brushed her hair away from her face.

"No, I'm not all right," she snapped. "This isn't the way I wanted to tell you. How long have you known?" she asked. "I think I'm going to faint."

"Put your head down," he said, and left to return in

seconds with a cold wet cloth he placed on the back of her neck.

"Lila, I don't want to upset you, but we should talk. A baby is not something you can hide for very long."

"I know that," she said, sitting up and taking the cloth to wipe her brow. She leaned back. Sam had one arm stretched on the back of the sofa and he was turned toward her, his knees touching her leg. He sat close and his gaze was still intense, as if he had never really looked at her before.

"Look, sugar, I didn't intend to make you faint," he said gently, and she thought it was so typical of him. His tone was like a squeeze to her heart, gentle, comforting, yet his endearment, *sugar,* annoyed her. How was she going to deal with him? It was the question that had plagued her since discovering her pregnancy.

"Sam, please don't call me *sugar.*"

"I meant it in a nice way. Damn, Lila, do I have to call you Ms. Hacket?"

She had to smile as she opened her eyes and looked at him. She held the wet cloth. "No, you don't ever have to call me Ms. Hacket. And yes, I'm pregnant from our night together. I'm as shocked as you must be because we took precautions."

"That wasn't so damn hard to tell me, was it?" he asked, staring solemnly at her again.

"I guess not. It's what will follow now that will be difficult. You and I are so totally different."

"Differences that are incredibly appealing to me," he said, wrapping his arms around her lightly. Nothing was going as she had expected.

They gazed into each other's eyes and her heartbeat should have been loud enough for him to hear. Below his thick brown hair, which partially fell on his wide forehead, his blue eyes were intense. Desire flared, burning brightly in their depths. He looked at her lips and her mouth went dry. Sam was too physically appealing to her. "You're my downfall, Sam Gordon," she whispered.

"Never, darlin'," he replied softly before he kissed her again. His arms tightened and he shifted her, lifting her to his lap and cradling her against his shoulder while they kissed.

His kiss was stormy, possessive, melting her as always and igniting fires of longing. She didn't want this breathless, heart-stopping reaction to his kisses. She didn't want this wild surge of passion and this burning need for more of him. While thoughts of denial streamed in her consciousness, her body responded and she wrapped her arms around him.

When she realized how hungrily she responded, she pulled back and slipped off his lap, standing and walking away, trying to get some distance between them while she regained her poise. She turned to find him watching her. He sat on the sofa, his elbows on his knees, his blue shirt open at the throat.

He came to his feet slowly and her pulse began to drum again as she watched him approach. Determination showed in his eyes, his expression, his walk, making her brace for the battle to come. His chin had a stubborn jut to it while a muscle worked in his jaw, and he had a half-lidded stare that jangled her nerves.

Placing both hands on her shoulders, he stood quietly, studying her with a piercing gaze that was even more unnerving. Silence stretched between them.

"We can work this out," she said firmly.

"Oh, yeah, we will," he said. His self-assurance set her more on edge, making her certain he had already started planning for the baby. "Let's look through my house.

Whatever happens, I'll have a nursery built because I get to see my own child."

Startled, she had never anticipated his request that was unnecessary at this time. "I'll be happy to look, but it's too early to plan a nursery."

"Maybe. Won't hurt. You can humor me on this one. It will give us a chance to get used to both of us knowing about the baby."

"I guess you're right," she replied, not caring if he wanted to start planning a nursery in his house. That was the least of her concerns. He brushed a light kiss on the corner of her mouth.

"There, that's better. I want you happy," he said, his expression serious. She hoped he really meant what he said.

"I'll try to make you happy," he said as if he could guess her thoughts.

"Of course you will," she said, wondering what he was up to because he had become reasonable and cooperative, not his usual take-charge self, not at all what she had expected. Sam and his twin, Josh, were both strong-willed men who were accustomed to getting their way, so this sudden change in tactics had her guard up more than ever.

"Sure. I'll be happy to look with you."

"Lila, this is my baby, too. Dads have rights, too," Sam said, draping his arm across her shoulders and pulling her closer beside him.

"I know you do," she said, aware of touching him, wishing he weren't so old-fashioned yet knowing that was as ingrained in him as breathing.

"I just thought perhaps you intended to return to California and spread the word that you had a baby by some guy out there."

She stopped walking to face him and shake her head. "I wouldn't do that. I've been in shock because neither of us expected this, but I planned to tell you. I was trying to get accustomed to the idea myself before letting others know."

"Others is one thing. The father—me—is another. Does your family all know?"

"Heavens, no," she blurted before she thought. "You know Dad doesn't. Nor does Hack. I can't listen to Hack and all the remarks I'll get from him. Not yet. No. My mom knows."

"There's a way to avoid having to listen to remarks from Hack and from anyone else," Sam said quietly, creating a prickle of caution in her.

"I'm not sure I want to hear this. At least not this soon."

"Sooner is better." He took her hands, holding them lightly. "Has it ever occurred to you that you might be too independent for your own good?"

She shook her head. "That's where our views of life are so different. No, I don't think I'm too independent for my own good. I don't think I'm any different from a large percentage of the women in the U.S. Did it ever occur to you that you have very old-fashioned views of women that don't even apply to most of the women you know?"

"Seems to me there are plenty of women around here who are just as I expected."

"Maybe, or maybe they're just trying to please you because you're a nice guy," she said, trying to lighten the moment and postpone discussing their future.

He smiled. "And you don't care to try to please me?"

"Sam, you and I have 'pleased' each other enough that now we have a baby between us," she said, seeing the sparkle flash in his eyes while the corner of his mouth lifted.

"I'd almost forgotten how straightforward you can be. And it was damn fun and good, I'd say. Actually, pregnancy becomes you. You have a rosy glow and look gorgeous tonight," he added huskily.

"Thank you," she replied, feeling a degree better while thinking he looked incredibly good himself in the pale blue shirt that made his eyes look even bluer.

They walked through a wide hallway to a sweeping double staircase. The graceful stairs had a black wrought-iron railing. No stretch of her imagination could envision a child running up and down the fancy stairs.

"This is a showcase house. I can't imagine a little child running through here. These stairs are not kid friendly."

"I'll have to admit, I'm with you there. Maybe I'll have this iron railing taken out. Like you, I'm adjusting to the idea of a baby in my life."

She took a deep breath and let it out slowly, trying to relax. She could feel the tension between her shoulders. She hadn't made any decisions about her future, something she had planned to do before Sam learned of her pregnancy. Now he would want to be involved in everything.

"This nursery business—you're adjusting to the news faster than I thought you would."

He grinned. "Care to make a wager on which one of us makes the most adjustments to the way of living in the next month?"

"I'm not wagering with you over anything again," she said.

"Why not? I know you liked kissing me. Matter of fact, let me show you. I can prove it," he said, a twinkle in his eye as he reached out to slip his arm around her waist. "Come here, darlin'," he drawled.

She wriggled away. "All right. I like your kisses. Just no more bets."

"Scared you'll lose again?" he asked with amusement in his eyes as he teased her. "Or are you scared because you might discover that I can change more easily than you can?"

Exasperated, she turned to him. "Oh, you would so lose that bet. I work for someone else, so I have to adapt constantly to something new. You run your own business and you, Sam Gordon, are accustomed to getting your way in life. Most of the time," she added with emphasis. One corner of his mouth lifted in a crooked grin that added to her impatience with him. "Smile all you want—there is no way on earth that you are more adaptable than I am. Something impossible to prove, so you will probably argue about it on into the sunset."

"You're getting all worked up over the wrong things. Lila, stop fighting me. Things are exciting, sexy and can be so fine between us. Go with it and see what happens. We might have something really good together if you'll give us a chance."

They stood in silence and their clash of wills was palpable.

"Come on. We'll look for a room for a nursery," Sam said. "That's what we started out to do."

She nodded and walked with him. When they reached the second-floor hall, memories came of the night she had spent with him. He stopped and turned her to face him, looking directly into her eyes.

"You're remembering our night together." Sam wound his fingers in her hair. "That night was unforgettable. It was special to me before I found out that you're pregnant from our time together. Darlin', I've never had a night like that one," he said quietly. "I remember every moment and I'm guessing you do, too. Admit you remember," he coaxed in a husky tone that strummed over her raw nerves.

His fingers in her hair made her scalp tingle. He stood too close again and his gaze immobilized her. She couldn't get her breath because all she could think about was their lovemaking. Hopelessly ensnared, she looked at his mouth. As he drew her to him, he wrapped her in his embrace.

Running her hands along his strong arms, she stood on tiptoe while he kissed her. Her heart pounded and she ached with wanting him. The few kisses they'd had already had fanned flames of desire to a raging fire. She wanted Sam, wanted his loving, wanted his fun, wanted his tenderness, in spite of knowing it was an impossible situation.

She poured her passion into her kiss, hoping if she could become satiated, she would cool and her responses to him would settle. No one person had ever stirred her the way Sam could. Of all the men on earth, why Sam? Why someone from Royal with old-fashioned beliefs? But he was a sexy man filled with excitement and more perception than she had given him credit for, because he had figured out her pregnancy.

"See, you respond to me, just as I do you," Sam said after releasing her abruptly. He combed his fingers though her hair. "You set me on fire, Lila. If you'll give us a chance, there could be all sorts of good things in our lives. The loving is fantastic between us. In truth, you can't deny it."

"It's lust, Sam. Maybe I can't deny that we're attracted, but that doesn't change some basic aspirations and principles we each have."

"A relationship between us can be more than lust. And a relationship changes everything," he argued.

He released her slightly, both breathing deeply while he gazed at her. "We can have a terrific life together," he stated. "All I want is a chance while you're here in town. Go out with me tomorrow night. Let me take you to dinner at Claire's or out of Royal. You can give me that much of a chance for us to be together. Let's see if we can't get closer to working things out between us. Will you go to dinner with me?"

"Sam—"

"Look, we need to celebrate. A baby is wonderful. Let's set the future, all these worries, aside and just celebrate the little person who will come into our world."

Suddenly, she wanted to step into his arms, hold him and have him hold her. She wanted this baby to be loved and come into a family with love. Sam's words about celebration made a knot in her throat and she was torn more than ever, discovering facets to him tonight she would have never guessed he had.

"Don't make me fall in love with you," she whispered.

"Why would that be so bad?"

"We're not alike and we'll never be able to get along."

"That's not so, Lila. We can get to know each other, darlin'. In the meantime we have tomorrow night. Let's celebrate our baby."

His words twisted her heart. She nodded, feeling the threat of tears. He made her want the celebration for the reasons he had stated and he made her want to be a couple to bring this baby into a loving family.

"Yes," she replied. Either way she answered, she would have regrets. He had just given her positive reasons to want to be with him. A celebration—never in her wildest wishes had she even considered the possibility of Sam reacting to her news in the manner he was. She wanted to be with him. At the same time, she was positive if she encouraged him, he would step into her life and take charge.

He pulled her into his arms to kiss her and, temporarily, she let go of worries about the differences. He leaned down to kiss her briefly and then just held her.

"You are fighting yourself," he whispered. "I can see it, Lila. We have a baby between us now. You can't shove that situation aside and go your damned independent way. Love between a man and woman, I think, is a foundation for a family filled with love. We have something wonderful looming in our lives if you'll just recognize and cherish it," he said.

Her heart thudded. Torn between longing for the paradise she'd had with him that one night and the realities of life with all of Sam's beliefs, she shook her head even though she wanted to hug him and forget everything else.

"Sam, let's look at this house of yours," she whispered, turning to walk away, heading blindly down the hall when she didn't know where she was going.

Catching up with her, he draped his arm across her shoulders to walk close beside her. "All right, we'll look at rooms."

His arguments tugged at her emotions. His comments carried more power to move her than she had ever expected. Sam was already formidable to deal with.

She noticed that the upstairs hall was a repeat of the downstairs in the basic decor—tall palms, framed traditional Western art on the walls. Silk-covered settees, benches, interspersed with more plants of different varieties. His house was a sales pitch for his construction business. It was beautifully furnished and he had already told her the names of the interior-decorating firms that had worked with him.

They reached the end of the hall and as he started to go through a door, she paused. "Sam, this is your room. I've seen it and you're not renovating your suite to build the nursery in with you, so there's no point in us being here."

"I thought you might want to start there and see my room again. We have memories there."

"Nice try, but no thanks. Now, where from here would you want a nursery?"

"Darlin', you're just way too much all business. Let's look at the suite closest to mine."

He led her to another suite of rooms furnished in antique George II furniture with deep blue upholstery, a thick oriental rug centered in the room on a polished oak floor.

"This is a beautiful room that's close to you."

"Close is good," he said.

"I really think you'll have to make these decisions yourself. You know how close you want a nursery."

"I want you to be happy about it and approve of it. If you lived here, where would you put the nursery and playroom?"

"You do surprise me," she admitted.

"See, there are depths to me you didn't know about," he said lightly, but his voice and his expression were serious.

"I'd say this is the perfect room."

"Then this will be the nursery." He linked her arm in his. "Let's go get some dinner and talk about some harmless, less volatile subjects and just relax a little. This has been a surprise for both of us and a shock to you tonight to realize that I've guessed the truth."

"Yes, it has," she admitted, walking beside him.

"Do you own a home in California?"

"No, a condo," she replied while they headed downstairs and outside, where he'd had a new outdoor kitchen installed. He was cheerful, keeping on harmless topics, making her laugh and relax around him as he broiled steaks and served dinner.

She could eat little, but she was having a good time with him while they avoided the topic she was certain he was thinking about as much as she.

"See, I have eight bedrooms in this place. We've already selected one for the nursery and it was quick and easy. We can agree on some things. Also, I wish you would get the decorator you want, make the decisions about the decor and all that. I don't know one thing about kids. You've already had practice with the children's center, although don't copy what you did at the club, because I don't want to feel like I'm at the club when I'm home."

"All right, I'll look into it, Sam," she said, making a commitment that would throw them together. She suspected Sam would have all sorts of requests to come that would keep them together. "We have time to plan."

He changed the subject and talked about events in Royal, harmless topics that made her laugh. Even so, she couldn't stop thinking about the baby, her pregnancy, their future and the different man she had seen in Sam earlier tonight.

It was past eleven when she stood. "Sam, I should go home now. I do get tired. It's been a fun evening, but we're both avoiding talking about the baby. I assume you plan to talk about it tomorrow night."

"I'd like to. I've made arrangements about a nursery, verified that you're pregnant. That's progress. We'll take this a bit at a time. If you have anything you feel is urgent to discuss, don't hesitate."

"I won't," she said, feeling only a degree of relief that he wasn't causing a huge problem about her pregnancy, because she was certain the issues were yet to come.

Still keeping the conversation light, flirting with her, he drove her to the Double H. As they went up the walk to the porch, he glanced at the house.

"There are lights on—are your folks waiting up?"

"Heavens, no. They both probably went to sleep an hour or so ago. They just leave lights on for me. Maybe for Hack, although heaven knows where he is. He's probably staying with a friend in Royal."

At the door, Sam turned to place his hands on her waist. "Lila, I'm thrilled beyond anything I can say."

"You astound me with your reaction when this is an unplanned baby."

"As far as I'm concerned, babies are a gift. I think it's wonderful and tomorrow night will be purely a celebration. We can shove the worries and disputes to a later date."

"I can't argue that one," she said. "Actually, I'm stunned."

"If so, maybe there's more to me than you thought. I imagine there's a lot we can discover about each other. And some things we already know are fabulous," he drawled, looking at her mouth.

She drew a deep breath and then closed her eyes as he leaned closer to kiss her, a tender kiss that lasted seconds and then transformed, becoming passionate, steamy and stirring desire.

He set her on fire with longing to make love. She clung to him, still divided emotionally by desire, shock over his responses and the wisdom to know that she couldn't live with him or accept a long-term commitment.

When she stepped away, she gasped for breath. "Thanks for taking the news in the manner you did, because it made tonight much easier for me. Thanks, too, for dinner."

He smiled and caressed her cheek. "Ah, Lila, you can't imagine how I want you. I'm glad tonight was easier for you. When we go out tomorrow, I hope to have an awesome celebration."

She smiled. "I'm still in shock over that. I don't know how I'll get one hour of sleep tonight."

"I can definitely do something about that," he drawled, lowering his voice and making her toes curl. "Come back home with me and I promise you hours of sleep—maybe a few hours from now."

She laughed and shook her head. "You're temptation, Sam Gordon. Go home. I'll see you, all too soon."

"Won't be all too soon for me, Lila. I can't wait."

"Good night, Sam." She went inside and looked out the window to see him standing by the driver's side of his car. He waved to her and she smiled again as she returned the wave.

The following day, Lila spent the morning talking to one of the men whose ranch she planned on using in the movie. It was after one o'clock when she returned to the Double H and she was tired, wanting a nap, something she had not needed in the afternoon since too far back to remember.

When she got home, everyone was away except Agnes, the cook who had worked for them since Lila was three years old. Lila sat in the kitchen eating some of Agnes's chicken salad and sliced tomatoes, talking while the older woman snapped green beans.

The doorbell chimed and Agnes dried her hands, telling Lila she would get the door. Agnes smoothed gray hair away from her face as she left the kitchen, while Lila continued eating, hearing Agnes talking to someone but giving little thought to who it could be until the cook reappeared, hidden behind a huge bouquet of mixed flowers of all various shades of blue and pink. Lila hurried to help take the giant bouquet in its beautiful crystal vase, but Agnes set it down quickly.

"For you, Miss Lila," Agnes said, smiling broadly, her blue eyes twinkling as her gaze roamed over Lila.

"Agnes, you know I'm pregnant, don't you?" Lila asked.

"I thought so." They looked at each other another moment and then Lila hugged Agnes. "Mom knows, but Dad and Hack don't."

Agnes chuckled. "I know."

"Was it that obvious?" Lila asked.

"I wondered. You've had some morning sickness and you're beginning to show just a little."

"If you're observant," Lila remarked. "Not like Dad and Hack, which is just as well. Although I'll announce it before I go back to California."

"Your mom is happy and worried. I can tell that, too." Agnes turned toward the bouquet. "They are lovely flowers. My goodness. Aren't they pretty?"

"Yes, they are," Lila said, looking at a miniature teddy bear and a dainty, tiny doll tied in the center of a beautiful big bow of pink and blue ribbon.

She had to smile as she picked up the card and withdrew it. "I am so excited. Love, Sam."

She looked at the word *love* and shook her head. He had used the endearment as casually as calling her *sugar* and with the same depth of meaning, yet the flowers were gorgeous and the card was sweet, the whole thought very nice. Never once had she anticipated the enthusiasm that he expressed over her unplanned pregnancy. She was also thankful her dad wasn't home. She would get rid of the doll and the tiny bear, which, with blue and pink flowers, would give away that a baby was expected.

In spite of her feelings about Sam's chauvinistic views, she was as pleased by his flowers as she had been by his dinner invitation.

"Those are beautiful. So very nice," Agnes said, still admiring her flowers. "Someone is happy with you and wants to impress you."

"They're very pretty and it's sweet of him. They're from Sam Gordon."

"Ah, Mr. Gordon is a nice man. He's a very sweet man," Agnes said, her voice full of approval. "One of the best guests your dad has. And a good friend of the family."

"He is that, all right," she said, thinking about how much like her dad Sam had always seemed.

"Your brother or your dad can put the flowers where you want them. That is a heavy bouquet."

"I can lift it," Lila said, amused and sure it wouldn't harm her to carry a bouquet of flowers from one room to another. "I'll wait and see where Mom would most like to have them."

"You don't carry those flowers. You want them moved, please tell me," Agnes said firmly, giving Lila such a look that Lila nodded.

"Yes, I'll tell you, Agnes. Thank you."

Smiling, Agnes returned to snapping beans while Lila continued to admire her bouquet.

In the late afternoon she showered to get ready for her dinner date. After drying her hair, she dressed in a sleeveless fitted black cotton dress that had a straight skirt. Although her waist had thickened, she was relieved to get out of the tops that covered it and to shed the sweaters she had been wearing. As she had the night before, her mother appeared before it was time for Sam.

"Lila, I saw your gorgeous bouquet and the lovely crystal vase from Sam. That was incredibly sweet of him to send those flowers. That's a magnificent bouquet and vase."

"It's sort of overwhelming, but you're right—it is thoughtful."

"The flowers are pink and blue. I'm also glad you decided to tell him."

"I didn't tell him. He guessed."

"Then Sam is an observant man. That's one place you misjudged him. Your father still doesn't have any idea about you."

"Mom, I can't deal with Dad, too, right now. I can't have both of them pressuring me to marry."

"There's no need to say anything to the rest of the family yet. You and Sam come to some decisions first."

"We're going out tonight to celebrate the news."

"That's wonderful. I hope you appreciate it and I hope you both have a wonderful evening."

"Sam has surprised me, but don't get your hopes up that we'll get together. Sam is like a protégé of Dad's. He has the same old-fashioned view of women and the world and I can't live with that. I know you have and you've been happy, but I'm different."

"Maybe so. The main thing is, just give Sam a chance. You keep an open mind. Remember, you're responsible not just for you but for your baby, too. I think it's wonderful that Sam wants to take you out to celebrate tonight."

"I'll admit, I'm happy about that, too. I'm really pleased he feels that way. When confronted with an unexpected pregnancy, not all bachelors would want to celebrate. Sam hasn't proposed, but I expect him to do so. It would go against all his beliefs to not propose," Lila said as she brushed her hair.

"Just be tolerant and think over a proposal before you turn him down."

"All right," she said, smiling, knowing she would do what she wanted and there was no way she would marry Sam and settle in Royal.

"I'll go wait," Barbara said, glancing at herself in the mirror. "I enjoy talking to him. How I wish your brother would pay attention and try to emulate Sam." Barbara sighed and got up to leave the room.

"Thanks, Mom," Lila said, grateful for her mother and the close bond they shared. She turned to her mirror to study her image. She had her hair up on her head in a fancy sterling clip.

Her black dress was longer than usual, the hem mid-calf, but with a slit on one side that revealed her leg up to midthigh when she walked.

She didn't hear the chimes, but her mother informed her of Sam's approach. With one last look in the mirror, Lila left to greet Sam.

Seven

When Lila walked into the living room, both Sam and her dad stood until she was seated. Smiling at her, Sam's gaze swept over her. Nearby on the back of the grand piano was the bouquet of flowers, looking as gorgeous as ever.

"Hi, Sam," she said, smiling at him with her heartbeat pounding faster. "My flowers are beautiful. Thank you."

"I'm glad you like them," he replied.

"Flowers are nice," Beau said. "In August in the West Texas heat, it takes an ocean of water to keep any flowers alive. Is there an occasion for these flowers?"

"Yes," Sam replied, and Lila held her breath. "I asked Lila to dinner tonight and she accepted so I thought flowers might be nice for the fancy Hollywood lady."

She smiled at him in relief. "They're very nice wherever I'm from."

"You're a Texan, honey, now and forever," Beau said. "I've been thinking about calling you, Sam. I thought I'd run into you at the club, but then each time I forgot to talk to you. I want to build another house for a new hand. I want you to do the building."

"Sure. We can talk about it anytime. I'll call you tomorrow," Sam said.

Lila listened to their conversation, participating when they changed the topic, thinking how formal and polite they were, yet the sight of Sam in a charcoal suit with a snowy shirt, his navy tie, set her pulse racing. In spite of her worries, anticipation was paramount. A celebration with Sam was too appealing for her to be filled with dread over arguments to come.

When they were in his car, he turned to her. "I have an airplane waiting. How's Dallas? I considered Claire's but thought you might prefer Dallas since maybe you'd rather keep talk down in Royal about us being a couple."

"Frankly, I would," she said, thinking about Royal's elegant restaurant but preferring the anonymity of Dallas.

"Whatever you want, darlin'," he replied. Sam drove them to the small airport where a pilot waited with Sam's private plane.

Once at the restaurant in Dallas, she sat across from Sam at a table covered in white linen. He leaned back and unfastened his coat to let it swing open. Sam always oozed self-confidence, which probably was part of his take-charge personality.

He took her hand and smiled at her. Once again, for a moment a pang rocked her while she wished life was different and Sam held fresh, contemporary views.

"What would you like to drink?"

"Ginger ale is my preference."

He smiled, candlelight highlighting his cheekbones, giving a warm tint to his tan skin. "I'll have that with you, then."

Smiling, she shook her head. "You don't need to drink ginger ale."

Before he could answer, their waiter appeared and Sam ordered two ginger ales.

"That's ridiculous. Get a glass of wine, beer, whatever you like."

"When you can drink wine, I'll drink wine. Right now, you do what is healthy and I'll join you."

Looking at the dimly lit restaurant that held a small dance floor, a fountain at one end of the room, tables centered with candles in hurricane lamps, she thought of the unbridgeable chasm between them—one that she couldn't change any more than Sam could change how he felt. There was no future for them. She had to get along with Sam since he would be in her life for many years because of one strong tie. But she didn't expect to share many nights like tonight. She looked into his eyes, and it was as if a fist squeezed her heart.

He was handsome: thickly lashed blue eyes, symmetrical features, his straight, neat brown hair, a firm jaw, his straight nose. The charcoal suit gave him a commanding appearance. White cuffs showed at his wrists with gold cufflinks catching light from the candle's flame. If only he didn't hold such outdated views of women.

He gazed back, holding her hand, his thumb running slowly back and forth over her knuckles so lightly, yet she felt his touch to her toes.

"Thank you again for the beautiful flowers."

"They're a token—hopefully, something that represents joy and wonderful expectations. Lila, I'm excited. A baby seems a miracle."

She tilted her head to study him. "You amaze me. I would never have guessed your reaction to the news that you'll be a dad. You seem opposed to children at the club and yet you turn right around and seem dazzled over the prospect of having your own baby. That's an enormous contradiction that I didn't expect."

"It's how I feel on both subjects. I am dazzled over the prospect because my own baby is a miracle. Every baby is, and that has nothing to do with kids in the TCC children's center. Our baby, Lila. That just staggers me. I'm restraining myself—I want to whoop and holler and I can't stop grinning when I think about it. I can't whoop and holler here, and we'll have to toast the event with ginger ale, but I'm so excited I'm babbling."

He grinned broadly, a happy smile that made her heart thud, and she couldn't resist smiling at him in return. Startling her, he moved the candle out of the way, leaned across the table to draw her closer and kissed her hard. After the first startled second, she returned his kiss. She was oblivious to their surroundings as she kissed him. Joy tinged with a sadness filled her.

Finally, he sat back in his chair. "I'm thrilled beyond words."

"I'm glad but still shocked. Your past never gave a hint that you would react this way. You voted against women joining the Texas Cattleman's Club, and against the child-care center. If you could vote again tomorrow, you'd still vote that way, wouldn't you?"

"I think so. I don't expect our baby to be in a child-care center. Before, I never thought about the children's center in terms of myself. I've told you why I voted like I did. The club was started as a male haven. I don't see why the ladies don't have their own club. And they do have some clubs in Royal and men aren't trying to crash them. Actually, that's insignificant and tonight I'd like to stay off the subject because I want this night to be a celebration of our baby. That's the most important thing in my life right now."

"I can't argue with you on that one."

He glanced toward the dance floor. "There are some couples dancing. Let's join them."

He stood, still holding her hand, and she rose to go with him. As soon as they were on the dance floor, he wrapped her into his arms to dance. She was close against him, moving slowly with him. As always, the dance became sensual, stirring desire. The piano player sang the romantic lyrics that she knew by memory. This night with Sam would remain a memory forever.

Beautiful flowers, this dinner, his attitude about the baby, no proposal, a joyful celebration tonight—he amazed her in all those things.

They danced slowly and returned to their table when the song ended. As he held her chair and seated her, he caressed her nape, a feathery brush of his fingers that made her tingle.

Their drinks had been served, and Sam picked up his glass of the bubbly clear liquid. "Here's to our baby, Lila, and to you, my baby's mother."

"Thank you, Sam." Smiling at him, she lifted her glass. She raised it to touch his lightly before taking a sip of the ginger ale.

She raised her glass again. "Here's to you, Sam, for your understanding, for not rushing into an instant plan, especially for not proposing the minute you heard the news."

"A proposal would be so terrible, Lila?" He waved his hand. "Don't even answer. I told you that tonight is a celebration—one of the happiest occasions of my life. I don't want any controversy, even in fun. Let's stay off the thin-ice topics tonight."

"Once again, I won't argue with you. This is a wonderful evening, Sam."

He gave her such a warm look she wondered whether he had mistaken that as an invitation to seduction. "Great," he said, lifting his glass to her. They both took another drink and set down their glasses.

He took her hand, holding it gently and running his thumb over the back of her hand and her wrist, light brushes that she should have been able to ignore but couldn't. He was doing everything right and it was beginning to unnerve her.

"Have you made any plans regarding our baby?" Sam asked.

"Not really. I've just been getting accustomed to the idea. I've let them know at work and I'll take time off. My mom knows. I told Shannon and of course, my California doctor knows."

"You don't have a doctor in Royal?"

"I have my family doctor, but not anyone I've seen about this."

"I think you should see a doctor here or in Midland— I'll take you to Midland if you prefer. You never know when you might need one, and for the sake of the baby, I think you should have a record established with a doctor you want. If there's an emergency, you don't want to meet a new doctor for the first time."

"I suppose you make sense and I should," she said.

"I'd feel better about it, both for your sake and the baby's."

She nodded. "All right, Sam. You win this one."

"I'm not trying to fight with you, Lila. I really want what's best for you and our baby."

"I have to admit, you surprise me more and more.

You're not doing anything the way I expected. You have won the Most Unpredictable Man title over this."

He smiled in return and raised his glass of ginger ale in a toast. She touched her glass to his and sipped, laughing as she set it down.

"Have you thought of any names?"

"I'm debating about later and whether or not I want to know if I'll have a boy or a girl. At this point, no, I'm not thinking about names. It's too early."

"Do I get input?"

"Yes. I don't promise to let you name our baby, but I'm willing to listen."

"Good. When you decide to go public, let me know. I'd like to tell Josh. With our dad gone, we're basically all the family we have. There are cousins and aunts and uncles, but no one who lives out this way and none we're close to."

"I will soon, but not quite yet. I have to make some decisions first and I really would rather everyone in Royal know about the baby after I've gone back to California."

"Whatever you want," he said. "You said your mom knows—how does she feel about it? This will be her first grandchild."

"I think she's excited and she's supportive, but this is new to her. I'm guessing her real excitement will come when she holds her grandbaby in her arms."

"I imagine you're right, there."

"She likes you very much, so you have an advocate."

"Do I need an advocate?"

"Not really, at this point. She also thinks the flowers are beautiful."

"Flowers, taking you to dinner—those are things that I can do. What I feel like doing is dancing down Main Street and through the TCC, shouting to everyone I see that I am going to become a dad. Don't worry, I won't really do it yet. I might not be able to control myself when this baby comes into the world. We have a miracle, Lila."

"You sound convincing, as if you really mean that."

"I mean it with my whole heart," he said, his sincere tone and blue-eyed gaze giving emphasis to his words. "This is the most fabulous thing in my life."

"I'm repeating myself, but I never, ever for one second expected you to react the way you have."

"See, you don't know me all that well. But you will," he added softly, his voice holding sensual promises. "In truth, I've been a little astounded myself at how I feel. I've never given little kids a thought, because I'm never around them. We didn't have younger siblings. They just haven't been part of my life and I never would have guessed I'd feel this way, but this is my baby, Lila. I'm thrilled."

Growing solemn, she studied him. He might turn out to be far more of a problem than she had dreamed if he was locked into wanting his baby in his life. This was not something she had factored in when she had thought about Sam's reaction to the news. He had been so opposed to the child-care center that she had never imagined he would be thrilled to become a dad. And he was becoming far more appealing to her—something that could prove her undoing.

The waiter arrived to take their orders and she withdrew her hand from Sam's. As she ordered the grilled salmon, Sam waited, looking mildly amused, and she was certain it was because she had insisted on ordering for herself. He probably had ordered for every other woman he had ever taken out from the moment he had started dating.

Next, she listened while he ordered a prime rib.

"Thank you for letting me place my order," she said as soon as they were alone.

"There's no way I want to infringe on your independence in stuff like ordering dinner. That's not one of life's real issues."

"It is rather well known that leopards don't change their spots, so that was a leap for you."

"I can adapt and I can definitely try to please you," he said in a huskier voice. "That's what I most like to do." He took her hand again. "I would like to spend hours tonight, darlin', just trying to pleasure you," he said softly. His tone conveyed far more than his words and she tingled when she heard his thick, husky drawl.

"Sam, maybe I've underestimated you. You want to spend hours together tonight—that just makes my heart race," she replied in her own sultry tone, unable to resist flirting with him and letting go of worries for a while.

His blue eyes darkened and he inhaled deeply, taking her hand and placing a light kiss on her palm. He held her hand, resting his on the table. "Now, that, Lila, makes me want to chuck dinner and head for a private place where I can 'pleasure' you for hours."

"But we'll do what's sensible and sit and talk about our future," she said with great innocence, still having fun flirting with him. "But I do feel better, Sam, that you're being positive," she stated.

"A simple compliment that I will definitely reply to before this evening is over," he said softly, his voice becoming velvet, having the same effect as a caress.

"I think it's time we change the subject."

"For now, maybe, but we'll continue the conversation later back at my place."

"Back at your place? Sam, your self-confidence overwhelms me. Brace yourself—back at your place might not happen tonight."

"If it doesn't, it doesn't. We'll see," he said with all the certainty in his statement that he would have had if she had flatly accepted. His confident smile indicated what he expected to do when they returned to Royal.

"So you worked in your office today or in Pine Valley where you're building?" she asked, knowing she should stop flirting and keep space between them because she did not want a seduction scene later in the night.

"I have four houses right now that are under construction, and I spent time at one first and then another. Two are in Pine Valley. I was at my office and at the club. At the club, all the men can talk about is Alex Santiago's disappearance. As far as I know, there's still no word on Alex."

"The few times I've seen Nathan, he looks preoccupied, as if he's worried," Lila said, withdrawing her hand from Sam's.

"The last two times I've been at the club, rumors have been going around that Chance may have had something to do with Alex's disappearance."

"Why would Chance do anything to harm Alex?"

"A woman is why," Sam replied. "Cara Windsor. Chance dated her and then she fell in love with Alex."

"Chance doesn't seem like the type to harm someone, but I don't know him that well."

"I agree with you. I know one thing—the last conversation I had with Alex, which was shortly before his disappearance, was interrupted by Dave Firestone, who was mad as hell. I left, so I didn't hear what the heated exchange was about, but they were angry with each other."

"That doesn't sound so good. Have you told Nathan?"

"No, but I'm thinking maybe I should, with all the rumors flying about Chance."

"I'd think so. It might be important. It would be terrible for them to focus on the wrong person," she said, thinking more about Sam than the rumors.

Salads appeared and they paused in the conversation until the waiter had gone.

While they ate, Sam kept her entertained. She ate lightly, declining a dessert. Sam was showing his best side, handsome, charming, doing all the right things.

They danced until ten and then flew back to Royal. "Come by my house, Lila. It's not too late and we can sit and talk."

"Sam—"

"We'll talk. I'll take you home whenever you want. C'mon. Better sitting with me than going home and sitting up with Hack."

"My brother," she said, shaking her head and smiling. "This summer, you'll always win with that argument. Okay, briefly."

The moment she agreed, Sam changed course to drive them to his home in Pine Valley.

When they reached his house, Sam directed her to the kitchen. "We'll get something to drink while we talk. You're limited in your drinks. Want another ginger ale, milk, hot chocolate? I have a veritable grocery store here. What would you like?"

"Actually, hot chocolate sounds the best," she said.

"Lila, this is good tonight because I want us to get to know each other. I know a lot about your family from being friends with your folks, although I see far less of your mother than your dad."

While he talked, he removed his charcoal jacket and tie, rolled up his sleeves. He unbuttoned the top buttons of his shirt. When he reached the third button, he glanced at her to catch her watching him. Blushing, she turned away, wishing she had done something besides stare at him as he made himself comfortable.

"You can unbutton all you want, too," he said.

His words ended her embarrassment and tension. She smiled at him. "Thanks for the offer," she remarked dryly. "I think I'll keep it together."

He walked over to her. "I know one thing that can go and I hope you don't object." He removed the sterling clip holding her hair. Auburn locks tumbled to her shoulders. He placed the clip on a small table and then combed his fingers through her hair while they gazed into each other's eyes. "You know this is the way I like your hair—down, falling free. Your hair is gorgeous, Lila."

"Thank you," she whispered, looking at his mouth while he stood so close. Her breath caught as she looked into his eyes.

She expected him to kiss her, anticipated his kiss and then was surprised when he turned away. "Hot chocolate it is," he said.

She tried to ignore the flash of disappointment. He was doing what she wanted, so she should be relieved they hadn't kissed.

As soon as he had their drinks, they strolled to the adjoining living area that overlooked the patio and sparkling blue pool. She sat in a corner of a sofa and he sat beside her, closer than she had expected. There was a table beside her and one in front of the sofa, so they had places to set their drinks.

"Tonight has been fun. I'm excited, Lila. This is my first child. How could I possibly keep from being excited?"

She had to laugh at him. "You have six months to go. Some of that excitement may wear off."

"I think it may grow instead of diminishing."

"If it grows much more, I think you really will be dancing around town." She smiled at him. "I've had fun tonight, Sam. It's been enjoyable, surprising, but the problems will come."

"We can weather them," he said.

"Your supreme self-confidence is always with you."

"How much do you know about babies, Lila?"

"Nothing. I was around Hack, but I was a kid myself, albeit a bigger kid than Hack. I'm reading about parenting and I'll take a class."

"Oh, yes. I should take a class in being a dad and we probably should go together to a class on childbirth."

"I'll be in California, remember?"

"You'll come back to Texas to have your baby, won't you? I'd think your mom would want you to."

"She's already talking and making plans as if I'd agreed to do so, but I haven't."

"It would be really nice to have a Texas birthplace."

She laughed. "You get a gold star tonight for tact," she said, unable to keep from noticing the open throat of his shirt, which revealed his chest and the thick mat of curly light brown chest hair that Lila knew from memory.

"Whatever you decide. I know I don't have any influence on that one." He set down his drink and crossed the room to pick up his coat and rummage in the pocket. He held out a package wrapped in shiny blue paper and tied with a big pink silk bow. "For you, darlin'."

Surprised, she glanced at the small package and then looked at him.

"Go ahead, Lila. It's a present for you."

"Sam, you don't need to get me presents and flowers."

"I don't need to. I want to," he said as she opened the box. He sat down again beside her.

She placed the paper and bow on the coffee table and opened the box to see a gold heart-shaped necklace covered in diamonds.

"This is gorgeous," she said.

"Open it."

"It opens? It's a locket?" She pulled it open and a tiny folded paper fell out. She picked it up to unfold it and read tiny print: "For our baby's picture. Sam."

"Sam, that is so sweet. I'm touched by this and I'll treasure it." When she snapped the locket shut, she turned it over. The smooth back was gold with the current date inscribed. "You have today's date," she said, glancing at him.

"That's to remember the night we celebrated our little one's arrival."

Impulsively, she threw her arms around his neck to kiss him lightly. "Thank you. It's beautiful and that is just so sweet of you. Put it on me, Sam."

He took it from her and set it in the box on the table. "I will put it on you, but not right this minute. Come here, darlin'," he said, lifting her to his lap. "Ah, Lila, I've been wanting to bring you home with me and do this since you walked into the front room at the Double H hours ago."

Her heartbeat raced while she looked up at him. His mouth was only inches away and the look in his blue eyes conveyed his intentions. As longing pulsed with each heartbeat, she wrapped her arms around his neck.

"I'm already caught in a tangled situation that I can't control. May as well be hanged for a sheep as a goat, as the old saying goes," she whispered.

His attention was on her mouth and she raised her lips to his. His kiss was possessive, seductive, fanning the flames of desire that already consumed her. She loved being in his arms, being held by him, kissed by him, returning his kisses.

How was she going to say no to him and keep him at arm's length? At the moment, she didn't want to, which was what had placed her in this situation. Why did they have this magic chemistry between them that she had never found with any other man?

Running her fingers in his hair, she moaned softly, longing for so much more from him, wanting another night of loving. She pressed more tightly against him, kissing him with the same passion with which he kissed her.

She barely felt his fingers moving on her, but soon cool air brushed her shoulders and the top of her dress fell to her waist. Sam leaned back to gaze at her with half-lidded eyes while he removed her lacy black bra. As he caressed her, she shifted up her skirt to sit astride him.

Placing her hands on either side of his face, she leaned forward to kiss him, pouring her desire, her feelings for him, into her kiss. Every move was a mistake, but at this point she didn't care. She had had a wonderful time with him. He had hidden all the take-charge, chauvinistic, arrogant ways he had. Not once in the evening had he demonstrated any of them in a manner that had annoyed her. She hadn't seen them at all. And without those ways, he was delightful, appealing, incredibly sexy.

"Sam, you don't fight fair. You can be the most irresistible man."

"I don't want to fight you at all," he whispered while his tongue followed the curve of her ear, sending tingles in its wake.

He leaned back to look at her, cupping her breasts in his hands. "You're the most beautiful woman on earth, Lila. Each time I see you, you dazzle me and I want you in my arms," he whispered before leaning forward to trail kisses over her soft breasts.

His words enticed her as much as his kisses. She couldn't possibly believe him, but his declarations still carried a thrill of pleasure.

"This has already been lonely and difficult in some

ways, Sam," she whispered. "I want your kisses tonight, your arms around me, your reassurances," she admitted, knowing there would be some really tough decisions and moments ahead.

"You don't have to be lonely and have a difficult time," he whispered between showering kisses over her. He raised his head to look into her eyes. "Lila, that's your own doing and your own choice. I will do anything for you, darlin'," he promised softly. "I'll guarantee you won't be lonely and you won't be alone having our baby."

The thrill of his promise was as devastating as his kisses. His mouth was firm on hers. Kissing her passionately, he made her ache for him and moan in pleasure.

Tugging his shirt out of his slacks, her fingers twisted free his buttons until she could push his shirt off his shoulders to toss it away. Running her hands over his chest, feeling as if she couldn't get enough of him this night, she kissed along his throat, moving down while he caressed her breasts.

Her need built, burning like flames licking over her. She stepped off him, standing beside the sofa to pull him to his feet. He stood, towering over her even though she was tall. Her heart pounded with fiery longing and another shock: that he was causing her to fall in love with him.

When he swept her into his arms to kiss her, she locked her arms around his neck. Carrying her through the room into the hall to a downstairs bedroom, he set her on her feet and held her away from him to push her dress over her hips and let it fall in a soft pile around her ankles. "Lila, you take my breath," he whispered. "You're beautiful, darlin'."

Lila kicked off her shoes while he continued to look at her in a long, slow perusal that made her quiver and sent her temperature soaring.

"Sam," she whispered, fumbling with his belt to unbuckle it and pull it off. Wanting him with all her being, she unfastened his slacks, pushing away his briefs to free him.

She stood gazing at him as thoroughly as he studied her and then she knelt to stroke and kiss him.

Threading his fingers in her hair, he groaned. Her fingers drifted down his muscled legs, feeling the crisp, short hairs. Suddenly he slipped his hands beneath her arms to pull her up, wrapping her in a tight embrace while he kissed her hard, his tongue going deep.

Her heart raced. Heat pooled low inside her, a yearning for him that filled her. Tomorrow ceased to exist and yesterday had already passed. There was only the present with his kisses and caresses and endearments. For now, that was what she craved and wanted to give to him in turn. Another night of love between them that might mean something in her memories when this was no longer possible.

He picked her up to place her on the bed and began to shower kisses lightly below her ear, along her throat, moving down over her, caressing her, as if every inch of her was important to him, whispering endearments between his kisses.

"Darlin', you're gorgeous. Ah, baby, you're perfection, the most beautiful woman ever. Love, you can't ever know what you do to me."

His whispered words could make her feel as if she were the most desirable woman on earth, and how could she resist that? She knew he could not mean all of them, exaggerations in the throes of passion, but she liked having his hands and mouth on her, his words reflecting his desire.

"Sam, let's make love. Come here," she whispered, pulling him to her.

He moved between her legs, pausing to look at her. It gave her a chance to view him. He looked strong, virile, handsome. She caressed his muscled thighs and then tugged lightly on him.

"Come here," she whispered.

As he lowered himself, he held his weight off her slightly while he entered her with deliberate slowness.

Gasping with need, she arched beneath him and wrapped her arms around him.

"Put your legs around me, darlin'," he whispered.

She did as he wanted, holding him tightly, moving beneath him while he teased and increased the sweet torment until she was thrashing with need. "Love me," she pleaded.

Finally, he thrust deeply and moved, rocking with her as desire built swiftly. He pumped faster and she cried out with pleasure.

"My darling," she whispered, clinging tightly to him.

"Ah, love," he ground out the words as they soared together and then she crashed.

"Lila, my love," he gasped, thrusting deeply, shuddering with effort as he climaxed and finally lowered his weight and slowed. He gasped for breath as much as she. Blissfully, she ran her hands over him.

"Sam, that was perfect. Better than before. Everything was so wonderful tonight."

"I want to make love all night. If I could do what I want, really, we would stay in this room for the next week, maybe longer."

She scattered light kisses on his cheek and forehead until he rolled over, taking her with him. Their legs were entangled and he held her close against him as he brushed her long hair away from her face. She was damp, still breathing as hard as he.

"This is marvelous," she whispered, half hoping he

didn't even hear her. She didn't need to give him more encouragement, because difficulties lay ahead and their lovemaking would not do one thing to help avoid them.

He kissed her softly, trailing his fingers over her shoulder, along her throat and then combing them through her hair. "Darlin', I want you in my arms."

"As far as I'm concerned, tonight is a time to forget the difficulties and problems."

"I'll agree with that. Tonight is fabulous. It's far from over."

"Maybe," she whispered, running her hand over his shoulder, feeling his muscles. While she snuggled against him, she ran her fingers over his shoulder again. "Where do we go from here, Sam?" she whispered, not really wanting an answer at this time. She was willing to give the night over to lovemaking and set their problems aside temporarily.

"We'll go shower after a while. Right now, let me hold you close in my arms."

"No argument here," she said, rising on her elbow to kiss his jaw and throat. "You're a handsome man and at the moment, we're a mutual-admiration twosome."

"Twosome sounds good, darlin'. Really good to me." He pulled her closer against him. "Lila, it can be so fine between us. If we'll each just give a little."

"That's a dream, but with all my heart I hope you're right," she said.

"Just try. If we both just try and aim for that as our goal, we should be able to achieve it," he whispered. "We can compromise."

"Are you going to take your own advice?"

He chuckled. "You're a hard woman sometimes."

"I believe being hard belongs to you," she said, teasing him, and he smiled, kissing her forehead. She could feel his heartbeat against her. He was warm, solid muscle.

He held her close and they talked for a while before he carried her to his shower.

As she dressed, she turned to him. "Now, come put my beautiful new locket on me."

"Sure thing," he said, taking it from her and fastening it around her neck while she held her hair out of his way. He brushed light kisses on her nape and she turned to him.

"Thank you for the locket and for being so marvelous about everything."

"You're welcome, darlin'."

"Sam, I should go home."

"I guess you're right. Go out with me again. The TCC has a singer tomorrow night and the chef will have a lobster special."

"All right," she said, knowing she was sinking deeper into later complications with him. "Actually, it'll be our farewell, I imagine. I start back to work on Wednesday of next week and then I'll be too busy for anything else."

"That doesn't sound good. You're not overworked, are you?"

"I'm just busy. I'll take care of myself."

"Then we definitely go out tomorrow night. I have something special in mind."

"Now I'm curious," she said. "For now, though, I should get home."

After the drive to the ranch, she faced Sam at her doorstep. He had his hands lightly on her waist. "Lila, this has been another one-of-the-best-nights-of-my-life evening. I can't wait until tonight. It seems forever until I'll see you again."

She laughed. "Sam, you'll get through the day without me."

"Not easily. I'll pick you up at six. I have something at the house, too, I want to show you, but tonight wasn't the night. Tonight was purely celebration."

"I'm getting really curious," she said, wondering what he had planned and guessing she was in for another surprise with one of his gifts.

His arms circled her waist and he pulled her close and the kiss changed from casual to passionate.

When she stepped away, she tried to catch her breath. "I had a wonderful evening, as you know. Thank you for dinner, for my beautiful locket and thank you again for the flowers and for being so—" she paused, trying to think of something that would describe what he had done "—cooperative in your reactions."

"I don't think you really know me," he said. His expression changed as he smiled. "But you will," he said, and she had to smile in return.

"I can believe that one," she said. "Good night, Sam." She stepped inside and in minutes heard him drive away.

Switching off the lights left on for her, she tiptoed to her room. Instead of facing Sam and getting the arguments over and done, she had gone out and had a wonderful time and accomplished nothing as far as her future was concerned. Their next dinner she would talk to him about the future and their baby. Also, he had something to give her—some delightful, touching or sweet present that would make getting serious with him more difficult.

Just hours from now, she would be with Sam. Her heart beat faster in anticipation and she shook her head. She was already a little bit in love with him. She hoped it truly was a little bit, because none of their deepest feelings and individual beliefs would change. If he continued reacting as he had so far, she would fall more in love with him. Time would tell on that. Falling in love with Sam would be disastrous because somewhere inside that handsome, sexy, charming exterior was the male chauvinist, the take-charge character she had always known, and he would come out sooner or later.

In the meantime, excitement bubbled in her over the prospect of being with him tomorrow night.

It wasn't even twenty-four hours until they would be together.

That night, she dressed in a sleeveless red dress that ended above her knees. She wore high-heeled red sandals. This would probably be the last evening she would spend with Sam, because she would be too busy once she started work. It was just as well. When her job here ended, she would return to California—maybe until after the baby was born.

Sam was in a navy cotton shirt and navy slacks, and as soon as he picked her up, they drove to his home in Pine Valley. "Let's go have one of your delicious ginger ales. I want to talk to you and I have something for you. Then we have reservations at the club—the TCC has a great singer tonight and a chef's special of lobster and steak. If that doesn't appeal to you, we can eat at my place. I was going to do this the other way around, but I think we'll stop here first."

"Fine," she answered as she stepped out of the car, curious about the surprise. "Thank you for the gorgeous flowers that arrived today," she said, thinking of the latest bouquet, a far more traditional arrangement of mixed flowers with huge red, yellow and white roses mixed in with tall, colorful gladiolas, tiger lilies and other assorted flowers. "You've impressed my family. Even Hack didn't have any of his usual smart remarks."

"I'm glad to hear that."

"I haven't shown Dad or Hack my locket yet, because Dad will have a million questions and he'll think we're serious. I'll show him after I tell him he is going to become a grandfather."

"You know how to deal with your dad, darlin'. You and Hack both do."

"In spite of my morning sickness and seeing each other every day and living in the same house, neither Dad nor Hack has caught on that I'm pregnant."

"Hack doesn't surprise me. You're probably wallpaper to him and he doesn't even see you. Hack's got teenage-kid things on his mind. Your dad—that's different. Sometimes we see what we want to see."

Startled, she was surprised by Sam's answer. "You might be right."

"Let's have a drink." At the bar in a family room, Sam got two ginger ales. He motioned toward the sofa and followed her to sit close, facing her. "All I've been able to think about today is you."

She had no intention of telling him she could say the same. "That will pass," she replied, smiling at him.

He raised his ginger ale. "Another toast to making memories and having a baby. Or making a baby and having memories," he said, smiling at her.

Laughing, she touched his glass with hers and sipped while watching him. He set his glass on a table and then took hers, and she wondered again what he had planned.

Taking her hand in his, he gazed at her with an earnest look on his face. "You're special, Lila, and this baby of ours is incredibly special to me."

"Sam, I'm touched."

"I was going to do this another way," he said, "take you somewhere fabulous, but at the last minute, I wanted to be just the two of us."

Puzzled, she received another shock when, still holding her hand, he knelt on one knee in front of her.

"Lila, will you marry me?"

Eight

Even though she had expected a proposal from him the moment he learned of her pregnancy, she stared in surprise. Since he had not proposed right away, she had begun to accept that he wouldn't. Her heart began to pound. "Sam, for heaven's sake." She stood to walk away from him, turning to face him when there was more space between them.

He got up and started toward her, but when she held up her hand, he stopped.

"When you didn't propose at the first opportunity, I stopped worrying about it."

"There's no reason to worry. I mean it. I want to marry you."

"I'm sure you do. I appreciate your offer very much. I have to say no. You've been wonderful, but I can't marry you."

He frowned as if it had never occurred to him that she might turn him down.

As he crossed the room to her, she locked her fingers

together. She didn't want him coaxing, seducing, charming or doing anything else to win her over. He could weave a spell, but when marriage was at stake, she had no intention of succumbing.

He touched her closed fists, which were locked together. "Your hands are freezing," he declared, frowning. "Why can't you marry me?" he asked.

"We can settle this one quickly. We have vastly different philosophies of life. You don't want a wife who works outside the home. Correct?"

"No, I don't. Why would you want to if you have a baby to take care of, a mansion to tend, all the charities you want to run—"

"Stop right there," she interrupted. "It's okay for your wife to run charities, which takes hours away from home and sometimes can be as much work as a regular job, but it's not all right for your wife to be gainfully employed?"

"A charity is less stringent, less demanding and, most of the time, a hell of a lot shorter lasting and you know it, Lila," he replied. His blue eyes had darkened to the color of a stormy sky and she suspected a big storm was on her horizon with him.

"I don't know that all charities are shorter lasting. I've seen my mother work like crazy on charities. I intend to keep my job and my career. There is no way you would be happy with that, because it means I will be in California."

"I don't think you're considering our baby and I don't think you're being the least bit sensible about this."

"*Me* not being sensible?" she asked, staring at him. "That remark sounds like the Sam Gordon I know. Also, there's a far bigger reason, Sam, actually the biggest and most important reason of all—you and I are definitely not in love."

"Lila, we're wonderful together. It's been fantastic. I've

told you that several times and frankly, you've said the same back to me and acted as if you were happy to be in my company. What we have between us is good enough for me and you're important enough for me to say I love you."

"Please. Don't do that now. You've never said those words to me before. Don't say them now. I have no intention of marrying without love."

Silence stretched between them. "Lila, look. I think true love will come. I feel something for you, that's certain. I want to be with you. We have a lot that's good going on between us. Other than our views of a woman's place in life, we're compatible."

"Oh, Sam, if you only stopped to listen to yourself—'a woman's place in life.' Great heavens, come into this century."

"You're so damned independent. You want to go off to California and raise our baby on your own so you can work and live as you please."

"That kind of covers it," she said, her anger growing.

"You'll struggle with being a single parent, cut our baby out of knowing, really knowing, his or her blood father, just to pursue a career. A child is forever, while a career, a job, is the most fleeting thing. Why tear up your life over a job?"

"I'm not going to argue the merits of my job with you. I want my career. Period. End of discussion."

"If you have to work, there are jobs here in Royal."

"Please. How many production-designer jobs are there?"

"Okay, so no damned movie jobs. But interesting jobs nonetheless. And you know I like being with you. I think you're messing two lives up so you can prove your so-called independence that will get you nothing. Maybe some heartaches."

She walked away from him. "We're not in love and that's the most basic reason. I don't want to marry because it will be convenient." She hurt as she turned to face him again with more distance between them. "Sam, I want love. Real love. You and I don't have that between us, and don't try to tell me you love me."

"I won't," he replied solemnly. "We could give love a chance to develop between us. Has that ever occurred to you?"

"Maybe, but if we do, we'll have to give it a chance while we're single because I won't marry in the hope that love will come."

"Are you thinking about this baby?"

"Of course I am. Do you think a child is happy with parents in a loveless marriage who married for the wrong reasons?" Hurting, she stared at Sam. He was so handsome, so appealing to her, but also so old-fashioned. She couldn't cope with that every day of her life. They were poles apart and she couldn't see how either one could change.

"I would try to make you happy, Lila," he said.

"I know you would, but it wouldn't work. You want a wife who has a certain lifestyle, who will be a wife like my mom is for my dad. You don't want to live in California and I don't want to live in Royal, because I have a career in California. We're not in love. I always come back to that because that's the big one," she said firmly, but her words seemed to ring hollow. The past few days with him had made her care more for him, but the feelings should pass because they wanted different things out of life. Each time she reminded herself there was no love between them, she had a fluttery feeling, as if she knew better than what she stated. She wasn't in love with this chauvinistic, stubborn man. She could not be in love with him.

"Sam, love can overcome all sorts of obstacles and if we were deeply in love, we would try to work things out. But we're not. You're not in love with me. You didn't even pursue seeing me after your first few calls."

"You didn't return them. I don't go where I'm not wanted."

"That's understandable, and that's all past now, anyway. You're like my dad. I am not like my mother. We don't have a future together. Face that and let's work from that point. We can work out dividing our time. Loads of couples do that."

"Doesn't make it good," he said.

"I want a marriage filled with love and someone who will support me in what I really want to do. I imagine you want that, too. Did your parents love each other?"

"As far as I know. I was so young when Mom died that I might not have noticed if they weren't happy. Actually, Dad seemed torn up when he lost her and I imagine they did love each other. I never had anything to indicate otherwise."

"Don't you want a marriage filled with love?"

"Yes, I do," he replied solemnly.

"There you are," she said with a note of finality. "Now be realistic and let's work from there. The flowers are beautiful, but stop sending them and trying to conjure up something that doesn't exist. I'll share our baby. I know this is your baby, too."

"It's going to be more difficult to work out."

"That's probably true, but marrying just to make it easy to deal with raising our baby isn't my idea of something good."

"I imagine plenty of people have married for that reason, married for the sake of a baby. I'd even guess that a lot of those marriages have worked out well and the parents have fallen in love."

"I'm not taking that chance and going into that kind of union. Or a marriage where we battle constantly over my career."

His eyes narrowed and he crossed the room to her. With a drumming heartbeat, she watched him approach. "This has to count for something," he said, wrapping his arms around her and kissing her.

At first she doubled her fists and held them back to avoid touching him. All thoughts fled and she became aware of only his kiss, what she had dreamed about, like the kisses last night, steamy kisses that melted and seduced and banished differences.

She knew what he was trying to prove—that she responded to him. Her arms circled his neck and she kissed him in return in spite of knowing her response would only encourage him to argue further.

All thought processes ceased because she was submerged in sensation. She clung to him, returning his kisses as he leaned over her and then, still kissing her, picked her up to carry her to a sofa, where he sat and cradled her against his shoulder as he kissed her.

She stopped kissing him, gazing into his eyes, feeling her heart pound because she wanted him, wanted his loving, wanted his kisses. Instead, she slipped off his lap and moved to a nearby chair to sit facing him.

"We can still spend the evening together and talk about the future and what you will do," he said quietly. "Just think about getting married. Don't say no quite so fast. That isn't asking too much, is it?"

"No, it's not," she answered. His light brown hair was

a tangle from their past moments. It fell in disarray on his forehead and gave him a disheveled but sexy look.

"Good. Don't cut me out of your life, either, just because I proposed and you turned me down. We're going to have to find some common ground because of our baby."

"I know we will and I won't cut you out of my life," she said, feeling a pang because in a lot of ways she liked Sam. How deeply did that liking go? She would return to California. How much would she see him and how would they work out sharing a baby when they lived so far apart?

"If you would prefer a quiet evening here instead of going to the TCC, I'll cook steaks. I promised you a special place—"

"I've really lost my appetite and would just as soon go home. At the moment, I feel we're at an impasse."

"You need to eat something, Lila. And we can at least talk about sharing this child and how we're going to do so."

She rubbed her head. "Sam, we have six more months before the baby is due. We have a lot of time to think this through and tonight is not a good time for me."

He reached out to take her hand. "I'll take you home if you'll feel better, although I'd prefer you eat something."

"I'm okay. Even that first year, I can't imagine what we'll do because a baby is too little to pass back and forth between us."

"I'll think about it, Lila. You're right about the baby being too small, too young, for him—or her—to be away from you, so I'll have to adapt some way. I'll think about that. Later we can work it out."

"Thank you for being reasonable about it," she said, relieved that he seemed to be willing to cooperate.

"We have the next eighteen or twenty years where we will be involved with each other."

"That's sort of mind-boggling," she said, aware of him seated close beside her.

Still holding her hand, he spread her fingers out over his as he turned his palm up. Her long, slender fingers were smaller than his, her hand smaller.

"Lila, have you seriously thought about being a single parent?"

"Yes, I have. I expected to be a single parent from the first moment I learned I was pregnant," she said.

"I wish you'd been here and I'd been with you," he said solemnly.

"Sorry, Sam. Things are not working out the way you want them to work out."

"So when you go back to California, can I fly out and see where you live?"

"Of course. But do you really see any point in that?"

"If we're sharing a child, I do. I want to know where my child will be."

She gazed into his blue eyes and could feel the clash of wills and the tension crackling in the air between them. She had never expected them to agree. How could she adjust to dealing with him constantly? He was strong-willed, forceful and accustomed to getting what he wanted. He was also charming, considerate and caring. It was that side of him that was her undoing.

"Yes, you can fly out and see where I live. I'll show you around. I think you'll hate every bit of it. You've grown up here and this is your world. You're so like my dad."

"Thank you. I like your dad and think a lot of him," Sam stated.

"I love my dad, but we have vastly different views on life. He's set in his ways, old-fashioned, chauvinistic, sometimes a little narrow-minded. My family did come to see me once, and after two days they packed and came back home and have not been to California since. Too many people, too much traffic, a big city—all sorts of things that you don't have to put up with in Royal. I expect you'll react like my dad."

"We'll see. I want to be with you when our baby is born," Sam said quietly.

"Let's wait, Sam. What happens if I fall in love with someone before then? Or if you do?"

"I'm not going to fall in love with anyone before that time. Somehow I'm guessing you're not going to, either. You haven't answered my question," he said.

"That's one I want to think about. I imagine the answer will be yes. At least you can come to the hospital. I don't know who I want in the room with me other than the medical people. We'll discuss it later."

"I can wait," he said. "You know your dad will come after me like a tornado sweeping across the prairie when he learns about your pregnancy. He'll want me to marry you and when I tell him I've already proposed and you turned me down, what do you think he'll do?"

"He'll try to get me to marry you every which way he can, but I'm an adult and I learned long ago how to say no to my dad. I'm an adult, and I'm free to do what I want. I'm not worried about Dad. He's a lot of bluster where Hack and I are concerned. He dotes on us. Once he's a grandfather, he'll be so taken with his first grandchild, he won't care what I do."

"I'm not sure I agree with you there."

"Also, he has a chivalrous attitude toward females that keeps him from losing it with me the way he occasionally does with Hack."

"I'm sorry he'll pressure you. No one should be pressured into marriage."

"That's reassuring to hear you say," she said, studying

him and thinking it was contradictions like that opinion that kept her drawn to him. "So the subject won't continue to come up between us?"

He turned to look at her, giving her that intense look he could get. "No, it won't," he said as if he had just made a decision about proposing again. "But while you're here in Royal, I want to continue seeing you and going out with you. We have a good time, Lila."

"I don't see any future in seeing each other socially, just more heartache. Besides, I'll be working starting Wednesday and won't have time."

"Scared you'll fall in love with me?" he asked, watching her closely.

"No, I'm not scared," she said. "Well, maybe a little." She rose. "I really would prefer to go home."

He stood, facing her in silence, and again she could feel a tangible clash. "We'll get through this some way. I still want to be with you. I would if you weren't pregnant."

"Sam, you can be so old-fashioned and then turn right around and be so sensible or so much fun or so sexy."

"That's about the best thing you've said tonight."

"At the moment, I think you might as well take me home."

"Sure you don't want to go back to passionate kisses and hot sex?"

She had to smile.

"That's better," he said, touching her chin. "Come on, home it is." He took her hand and they headed to his car.

As they made the drive, he talked, sounding as cheerful as if nothing had happened to ruin his evening. Thankfully, he no longer brought up the subject of marriage or the baby.

"You know there's the annual end-of-summer party at the TCC coming up the end of the month. Let me take you. It'll be right before you leave for California. It's the last Saturday night you'll be here and the party is fun."

"All right, Sam. You talked me into it. We have a date."

"Good deal, darlin'. How's the children's center coming?" he asked, interrupting her thoughts about the party.

"I think it is going to be great. They're moving right along with the construction. They are working extra hours so they can get this done soon, which is exciting," she said, relieved to talk about something less personal or volatile. "They're far enough along that they are having an inspection of the alarm system tomorrow morning. Also, I'll have one last meeting with Shannon before I go to work and Shannon goes back to Austin. It'll be up to the other ladies to see it finished."

"So the children's center will open ahead of schedule?"

"I don't know, because funds are getting tight. When did you become so interested in the progress of the children's center?"

He shrugged. "Just asking because you're interested."

"Abigail keeps up with the schedule. Anytime, now, we're getting furniture and supplies ordered for the center. I've enjoyed working on it. It seems impossible to think I'll have a child who'll be there sometimes."

"*We* will have a child who will be there sometimes," he corrected. "And yes, I can't imagine that one. I can't imagine any kids running around the club, but they're going to before long."

"And you still don't approve, do you?"

He kept his attention on his driving while he paused before he answered. "I still don't. But for your sake, and our baby's sake, I'll probably accept it once it's a done deal. I have no choice."

"At least you're honest. That's right, too, you don't have a choice," she remarked, watching him. The time would come when he would pressure her more to do what he wanted, yet maybe she was misjudging him again. She lapsed into silence as he drove, her thoughts on him. Her feelings for him were growing. She couldn't make love with him without getting emotionally entangled. Even after that first night, she had thought about him far more than she had expected she would. But it was this other side to him that made such a difference to her. The past couple of days and the way he had been positive and supportive had caused her to begin to care about him and let down her guard.

Even so, his basic feelings about marriage and about the baby had surfaced and finally, he had acted exactly as she had expected and proposed.

The porch lights were on when they arrived at the Double H. Sam parked in the shadows on the drive beneath a tall oak and when she stepped out, she turned to face him. "Sorry I couldn't say yes, and I regret how the evening turned out, but I really don't have an appetite. I'll get something here soon."

"Take care of yourself and don't worry. Don't get sick over this."

"I won't."

"Lila, let me know when you want to go out and talk."

She nodded. "All right, I will. It might not be on this trip," she said, feeling as though she was saying goodbye to him in a way—the physical side of their relationship had to stop and it would be easier to walk away now with his views on marriage in the open.

"We can go out and stay off the subject of the future. Just be together."

"I don't see any point," she said, feeling sad. Even though this was what she had expected from the first, it pained her. "The more we go out, the more likely we are to fall in love and I think that might make everything worse, because you're not going to change being an old-fashioned-type guy and I'm not going to change my career," she said.

"Not even to give your baby a daddy who's there all the time?"

"No, I'm not, because I might be happy for a while, but babies grow up and go off to school and then I would be miserable without a career. Better to break this off right now than later because love isn't the total solution."

"Lila, that's a logical answer, but we can go out and just have a good time," he said, wrapping his arm around her waist. "Can't I be more entertaining than you sitting home night after night while you're here? Tonight was less than great for you. I'll go to the TCC on the way home and have a steak. I wish you'd come with me."

"Sorry, not tonight."

"Let me make this night up to you. Darlin', go out with me. I'll pick you up at six again tomorrow and take you somewhere that will make you forget your worries."

Before she could answer, he leaned down to kiss her. His kiss banished her worries. All thinking stopped as she held him and returned his kiss, running her hand across his broad shoulder and then down his back to wrap her arm around his waist, feeling certain she was kissing him goodbye.

He tightened his arms around her, leaning over her to kiss her passionately as if there had not been any argument or discord between them.

When he released her, they both were breathing raggedly. "Will you go out with me tomorrow night?"

"No, I won't, in spite of wanting to kiss you," she whispered, aware every hour spent with him made saying no much more difficult. "We can think about how we'll share our baby, but beyond that, I don't see any reason to go out together."

He put his arm lightly around her waist to walk to the house. "Don't go in and worry, darlin'. Things will work out."

"You're the supreme optimist, Sam."

"It's more fun than being a pessimist—easier, too, because you don't worry as much."

"I don't see either one of us giving up our basic beliefs and hopes and dreams. You want a wife like my mom and I want a career, independence and my California life. Just keep that in mind when you get optimistic and want us to get together," she said as they crossed her wide porch to the front door.

"There is nothing to take your mind off troubles like energetic, sexy dances, some hot kisses and lots of laughs, so if you change your mind about going out, just call me. I don't care what hour it is. I'll drop everything and we'll go."

"I'll bear that offer in mind," she said, hurting, sure they were growing more apart by the minute.

He faced her at the door. "Lila, don't set yourself up for loneliness and heartbreak. We'll work out everything, darlin'. Go to bed and don't worry." Leaning down, he brushed a light kiss on her mouth. He paused to look into her eyes and she saw a flicker in the depths of his and knew that he would kiss her again. His gaze lowered to her mouth and she couldn't get her breath. In spite of the differences between them, she longed to kiss him. He leaned closer, wrapping his arms around her to draw her up against him while his mouth pressed firmly, kissing her passionately.

When he released her, she opened her eyes to find him

watching her. She inhaled deeply. "Your kisses are sinful," she whispered.

"I sort of thought it was your kisses that were so wickedly enticing. Maybe I should try again to see if I'm right."

She stepped back quickly. "Go on to the TCC, Sam, and enjoy your steak. Good night." She hurried into the house and closed the door.

The house was silent, empty downstairs. She was certain her folks were asleep. Moving automatically, she went to her room to get ready for bed while her thoughts were on Sam and his proposal.

She couldn't marry him. There was just no way and it was asking for trouble to go out with him even one more time. But she had already promised to go to the end-of-summer party. He had a way of being cheerful and getting what he wanted. And his farewell with telling her to not worry—how could anyone involved in their situation avoid worrying? Sam was an optimist—and turned a deaf ear when anyone said no to what he wanted. He would soon see she meant it. She hurt and she wanted to get back to her busy life in California, where she could forget Royal, Texas and Sam Gordon. However much in love she was with Sam, she had only to think of his view of women and she could get over all warm feelings for him. Sam Gordon was not the man for her for the rest of her life.

Making an effort to shake Sam out of her thoughts, she focused on the child-care center and Monday's inspection. Another step closer to the finished product. The center had thick walls, insulation, an intercom, closed-circuit cameras, alarm buttons... All sorts of gadgets to keep the children safe in their new center. They needed more money, but she felt sure the club members who supported the children's center would be generous with additional funds.

After taking a warm shower and getting ready for bed,

she wandered around her room, pausing at her dresser to open the box from Sam. Light sparkled on the diamonds as she picked up the necklace.

Shaking her head, she returned the locket to the box. Sam was a combination of opposing qualities, some so appealing to her, others not enticing at all. She finally sat in the dark to gaze out the window at the backyard. Lights were on at various spots among the trees and the pool was a glimmering aqua jewel with the pool lights on. What would she do about Sam and how could she deal with him on a long-term basis?

She had no answers except the one certainty—she did not want to marry him. His unexpected behavior over learning about the pregnancy had changed some of her views of him. He wanted this baby beyond her wildest imaginings. His lovemaking had captured more of her heart than before. She knew she was in love with him, but how deep did it run?

He had so many good things about him—he could be kind, gentle, understanding, amazing in his attitude about the baby, fun, sexier than anyone she had ever known, optimistic and confident. She had a wonderful time with him always, until they got on the subject of her career and the other side of him popped up—chauvinistic, old-fashioned, stubborn. A take-charge, commanding man who didn't know how to accept not getting his way. Sometimes Sam's charming qualities outweighed the ones she didn't like—not just sometimes, most of the time.

She had to admit, she had some strong feelings for him and in too many ways she liked him a lot. What scared her most—Sam was turning into a true friend. If she really had a problem, she could tell him and trust him. Friendship: the strongest base for love.

"Sam," she whispered. "Sam Gordon, my friend, my

lover, father of my child. You already have my heart." She
didn't want him to, but she ached so badly she suspected
he did, almost completely, but not quite enough to give up
her independence, her career, the way of life she wanted.

Finally she climbed into bed to dream about Sam and
being in his arms.

Monday morning she dressed in designer jeans with
a bright red shirt that covered her waist to hide her pregnancy. How much easier this would be away from Royal.

Her cell phone rang. When she answered, she heard
Shannon.

"Lila, Amanda Battle called me a few minutes ago because Nathan got a call from Gil Addison. There was an
inspection scheduled today for the alarm system for the
new center."

"Yes, I remember. We're moving right along."

"The inspection failed. After they got to checking on
it, they said someone had tampered with it."

Nine

A chill turned Lila to ice. Her first thought was Sam. He had been so totally opposed to the child-care center and still opposed it. Sam had been at the club late Sunday night. In addition to his opposition, he was in construction and a member of the TCC. He would know how to get into the alarm system. He was a take-charge person accustomed to getting his way. Could Sam have been the one?

She doubled her fist against her heart because she hurt over the thought that Sam might do such a thing. It would be a betrayal of trust, besides being unlawful.

"Do they have a clue who did it?" She closed her eyes, hoping she would not hear Sam's name.

"Not that I know about. Nathan's over there looking into it. Nathan is a smart man. He'll catch who did this. They've already said it had to be a TCC member because no one else would have access to that room or the center's alarm system unless it was the staff, and they aren't at the club on weekend nights except for the security guard."

"There are a lot of members who opposed the center, including my dad. My dad would never willfully destroy part of the club just to cause trouble. Dad is law-abiding. You'd think all the TCC members would be," Lila said.

"I'm sure. It's terrible because friends will be accusing friends. The vandalism goes against all the club stands for," Lila said, thinking again of Sam and Josh Gordon. "My folks can account for their whereabouts last night. They went to bed early and were here asleep when I got home."

"Don't worry, Lila. I don't think anyone will accuse your dad, and definitely not your mom. I don't have a worry where she's concerned and I don't think it was a woman. This seems more like the work of one of the men who is bitter over women being allowed in and now, the last straw, having a child-care center."

"I agree. It'll be someone in that group. I hope Nathan finds him.

"Shannon, my dad, Sam and Josh Gordon, all of those men who fought so bitterly, they empowered the person who did this. That fight and the hard feelings afterward may be what pushed someone into this," she said, thinking Sam couldn't have done it. Basically, she thought he was really a good person, just had old-fashioned ways. Her first fears about him were gone.

"I imagine you're right. The person who did it is probably friends with those who opposed the center and thinks he was doing them all a favor. I'll see you later this morning. Are you still meeting with that rancher about the filming?"

"Bob Milton. Not until one o'clock. That won't interfere with us. About the alarm, do you wonder what else the person might do?"

"We may have more vandalism with the children's center."

"Between this and Alex's puzzling disappearance, some bad things are happening. And this last event means someone intends to prevent the center from opening."

"I hate to leave Royal with a disaster hitting the children's center, but Rory and I have plans. Anyway, I'll see you at eleven at the club. Bye, Lila."

Lila set her cell phone on the dresser and rubbed her forehead.

For the short time she had thought Sam might have sabotaged the alarm, she had more hurt than anger. There could only be one reason that the result was hurt. She had fallen in love with him.

Feeling forlorn and unhappy, she covered her face. She was in love and it was impossible. His attitude about the baby and her pregnancy had amazed her and won her heart, yet she was still torn, now more than ever, over his old-fashioned views, his determination to marry even though he wasn't in love with her.

A TCC member had vandalized the alarm—that went against all the club stood for. Who could have done such a thing? Her doubts about Sam were gone. He wouldn't do that any more than her dad would. But she still felt their arguments and bitter feelings had given resolve to whoever did it. The vandal may have thought the others would be supportive if he ever got caught.

In a way they couldn't foresee, with their bitter fight over the center, those men had inadvertently contributed to what had happened.

This just brought back into focus Sam's views and old-fashioned ways.

She had no control over her heart. She loved Sam and she was going to have to get over it. Moving mindlessly, she headed toward the kitchen.

She found her mother still in her blue velvet robe, lingering over her coffee. Her mom's stylish bob was neatly combed. Except for a slight frown, she looked her usual serene self.

"Hi. I guess you've heard the news about the TCC," Lila said, pouring a glass of orange juice.

"Yes, and I can't believe it. Even your dad, who definitely opposes the child-care center, was shocked and upset. It worries him most that it has to be a TCC member."

"I'm sure that will be a big concern to a lot of them. For a few minutes I wondered about Sam."

"Sam would never do something like that," Barbara said, and Lila shook her head.

"I don't think he would, but some TCC member did this. Sam was bitterly against the center but says he's not opposed to it any longer."

"Sam's a good man, Lila."

"I know he is. I need to get ready. I'm meeting Shannon at the club."

Lila went back to her room and stood there thinking about the failed inspection. She couldn't stand worrying about it all day.

As she drove into town, she was angry that one of the men would stoop to trying to sabotage the efforts to get a child-care center open in the club. She barely glanced at the familiar surroundings.

As she crossed the parking lot, Sam climbed out of his car and turned to greet her.

He wore a dark brown suit and a lighter brown tie and as always, the sight of him affected her physically, giving her heart a jump. He looked handsome, cheerful, friendly, a side of him that conflicted with his determination, self-will and authoritative manner.

"Have you heard about the child-care center?" she asked without preamble.

His eyes narrowed a fraction as he placed his hands on his hips, pushing open his coat. "Yes, I have. Too bad, but that can be fixed without a major setback. It's a temporary interference."

Taking a deep breath, she watched him intently. "I know you have opposed the center from the beginning and argued to keep it from being accepted. You, my dad, a lot of others. The bitter campaign may have given this person the feeling he had the support of all of you."

Sam's blue eyes became glacial as he placed his hands on her shoulders. "Damn, Lila, when we argued against having the center, that was just democracy. I've opposed women in the club. I've opposed the children's center. But there is no way in hell I would condone a criminal act."

She gazed into his eyes and saw the anger. She was beginning to learn that Sam did not hide his emotions. His face was expressive, and he made no effort to keep people from learning how he felt. And right now he looked like a man telling the truth.

"You know, they say it has to be a club member," she said.

"I know, and that's depressing. I would have thought all the members were above that sort of thing."

She knew he wouldn't destroy property. Sam was smart enough, too, to know it wouldn't stop the center from opening.

"Lila, let me take you to dinner tonight. I've missed seeing you," he said.

Regret filled her as she shook her head. "Thank you, but there's just no point in pursuing a relationship. You have your views and your ways. You're an old-fashioned man with ideas about women and what you'd want in a wife. Our lives don't fit together. Thanks, anyway. I'm meeting Shannon." She walked past him.

He caught up and held the door for her.

"Maybe you don't know me as well as you think you do, Lila."

"I know what's important to me. Bye."

She walked away and he let her go. Her back prickled, but she didn't glance around.

Sam walked into one of the empty lounges and closed the door. He wanted a moment to think about Lila. Looking out the window without really seeing anything, he thought about Lila's accusations of being chauvinistic, old-fashioned, even more about her earlier declarations that he didn't love her.

Why couldn't she see that love could develop between them? He wanted to be with her. He wanted her in his bed every night. If she would move back to Royal, move in with him, marry him, he was certain love would come.

He shook his head. She would never move back to Royal. He had no doubts about that. The minute she had gone to college, she never looked back. Was she right? Were the differences between them too great?

How important was she to him? That was the question.

Restless, Sam stood and walked to the window. He had sent flowers, taken Lila out, but he hadn't realized that the gulf between them might be permanent.

He wasn't in love and she definitely wasn't, but they were good together. The sex was fabulous and now they had a baby on the way. With or without love, they should get married, but she would never change her mind or settle for the life he would want his wife to have.

If she felt that way, pretty flowers or dinners out would not change her mind. It had to be a lot deeper than that.

Was he making a mistake, being too old-fashioned

in wanting to get married? Was it a mistake to marry without love? He had been so sure love would come, but what if he was wrong? Was he trying to tie himself into a relationship that would make them both unhappy? He didn't want a wife who was an ambitious career woman. He didn't want a wife who lived in California while he lived in Texas.

He didn't see how love could come without really getting to know each other. And with Lila, that would mean a long-term relationship, which wasn't going to happen with him in Royal and her in California. In two days she would be working and he wouldn't see her. In a few weeks she would go to California and he probably wouldn't see her until Christmas, if then.

He clenched his fists and thought about their baby. A baby needed a family. Maybe it was an old-fashioned notion, but he felt that with his whole being.

He was going to have to let go. Lila would share their baby, but he needed to face reality. Lila wasn't the woman for him. She didn't want to change and he didn't want to change. The differences between them were huge.

His decision brought him no peace. He hurt and he missed her. "You'll get over this," he said aloud to himself, knotting his fists and taking a deep breath. "Forget her."

How long would it take to get over her? How long would it be before she didn't occupy his thoughts through his waking hours? With a baby on the way, it seemed impossible to think he could forget her. She was going to be the mother of his child. However long it took, he was going to have to let her go.

When the movie people arrived Wednesday morning and Lila vanished from his life, Sam told himself it was for the best. Twice he couldn't resist calling her. Most of her work was in surrounding counties and the only contact he had with her was a brief snatch of conversation.

The second time when she answered her phone, she sounded breathless. "Sam, I really can't talk. They're ready to shoot a scene and they had a quick huddle about it and decided they wanted the child in the scene, so I have to find a child's bed, either an old-time wooden one or iron, preferably iron."

"Can I get it for you?" he said, heading toward the parking lot and his car in case she said yes.

"There's one store outside of Royal—Buttons & Bows, sort of a flea market. They're looking through their stuff and will call me back. There's one on the highway to Midland I'm going to look at. I'm sorry I can't talk, but someone is driving me and I'm calling places. I'll get back with you later."

"Sure, Lila," he said, knowing she would not and he would not call her again.

A week later, his first reaction was surprise when she called him at his office. His heart skipped a beat at the sound of her voice and he gripped his cell phone tightly as if he could hang on to her.

"Sam, sorry to interrupt your business day. I have a request. The director would like to meet you and I wondered if we could possibly come by your office briefly this afternoon? We should be finished by six—would that be too late?"

His pulse jumped and all he could think about was seeing Lila. "Whatever time you want will be fine. My appointments were earlier, so I'm free. Josh isn't here this afternoon."

"Doesn't matter. Roddy just wants to meet you because of the hotel in Amarillo that you built."

"Would you rather take him to the TCC?"

"Not really. I think he will enjoy seeing your office," she said, talking faster than usual, and he suspected she would end the conversation soon and get back to work. "He isn't friendly with strangers, but he was impressed by the hotel you built in Amarillo because on his first trip to Texas he stayed there. His name is Rodman Parkeson. He's a little brisk and abrupt—I'm warning you now. He's thinking about building a new house in California and I think he wants to talk to you about construction. We won't take much of your time."

"You can have all my time you want, Lila," Sam said, unable to keep a hoarse note out of his voice. "I've missed you." He was telling himself to let go, yet wanted her badly.

"Thank you," she replied briskly, making him wonder if she was with other people or really didn't care. "See you around six."

She was gone and he missed her. He didn't want her going back to California soon. He thought about the end-of-summer party at the TCC—that would be his last time with her, perhaps for a long time. He rubbed his forehead, hating to think about her leaving Texas yet telling himself it was for the best. When would he stop hurting over her?

He got up, moving chairs slightly in his office, pausing to look around and think how it would appear to a stranger. The dark oak walls still appealed to him and his hand-carved walnut desk was free of clutter. He wandered through the reception area and outside, standing on the porch.

The redbrick Greek Revival building was on a large shady lot. He and Josh had built it to look like a gracious Southern mansion, but it was a practical office that met their needs. The front porch had rocking chairs and the yard held beds of multicolored flowers. A redbrick walk ran from the parking lot to the front door.

Behind the office were the workings of the construction company with steel sheds for lumber, metal buildings for equipment. There was a garage for trucks and another building for the machinery.

The day seemed twice as long as usual, but finally at six his phone rang and Lila said they were on the office porch.

Sam strode out the front door, taking a deep breath at the sight of her. With her hair twisted and pinned up behind her head, she looked more businesslike. She wore navy slacks and a sleeveless matching blouse with navy pumps. All his intentions to forget her and get over her vanished. He wanted to wrap his arms around her and kiss her. Instead, he offered his hand. "Lila," he said, gazing into her wide green eyes, which told him nothing about her feelings.

Her hand was warm, dainty, and he hated to release her. "Sam, I want you to meet Roddy Parkeson. Roddy, meet Sam Gordon, half owner of Gordon Construction."

With an effort, Sam tore his attention from Lila to extend his hand to a stocky man with thick curly brown hair streaked with gray. His dark brown eyes were sharp and alert. He gripped Sam's hand briefly in a solid, quick handshake. "I'm happy to meet you," he said, looking around. "This office is as fantastic as your hotel. I was enjoying myself looking at this porch. This is marvelous—a beautiful addition to the town."

"Thank you. Feel free to look all you want. If you'd like, I'll show you inside."

"I'd like that. My dad was in construction and I worked in it off and on when I was a kid," Roddy said while Sam held the door for Lila and Roddy and they entered the cool lobby. Sam guessed the director to be in his forties, and he was short enough that Sam could easily see the top of his head. Roddy's nose was crooked as if broken sometime in his past and Sam noticed thick hands that looked as rough as some of the local cowboys'.

"My dad was hired to work in the film business, so that's where I've always been, but I can recognize sound construction and I know the kind of architecture and buildings that I like," he continued as Sam directed them to his office. "That hotel you built in Amarillo was excellent. And this is a fantastic office. I'm from L.A., but I had a great-aunt who lived in Natchez, Mississippi. How I loved those homes."

Sam nodded, wondering whether he had heard Lila correctly when she had said Rodman Parkeson was brisk and abrupt. He had talked constantly since being introduced. Sam looked at Lila, who smiled faintly. As Roddy circled the room talking about construction and looking at crown molding and the hardwood floor, Lila leaned close and whispered, "You're a hit."

Sam didn't answer. He crossed the room and tried to focus on Roddy's conversation, finding it difficult to take his gaze away from Lila.

Roddy spent an hour looking at the Gordon office and sitting on the porch talking to Sam and Lila.

"If you have time, Roddy, we could drive out to my home. I can grill some dinner and show you my house if you want to look at more construction, or we can just sit and talk over Texas steaks."

"Texas steaks and your home would be great," Roddy said, standing.

The evening was enjoyable while at the same time frustrating because Sam wanted Lila to himself. When they finally headed for her car, they stood on the drive talking

for another twenty minutes before Roddy walked around
to the passenger side and climbed inside.

"You were really a big hit with him. He doesn't usually
talk to strangers or take time like this when he's away on
a job. Thanks, Sam, for all your hospitality."

"A nice guy," Sam said. "We still have a date for the
end-of-the-summer party."

"Yes, we do. Night, Sam, and thanks again."

He opened the door for her and closed it when she was
seated. Stepping back, he watched them drive away. "So
much for trying to forget her," he said under his breath. If
he married her, this was the way his life would be—watching her drive away to go back to her career. He didn't want
that life, but he couldn't stop wanting her.

"Dammit," he said, kicking a pebble with the toe of
his boot.

To his relief, finally the last Thursday of August came.
As suddenly as the film people had come, they left Texas
to return to California. Lila would fly out Monday morning and be gone. Each time he thought of her leaving
Texas, his insides clutched. He hurt, and the knowledge
that he needed to get over it didn't diminish the feeling
of loss.

Sam called Lila to ask her to dinner Thursday night.
"Lila, I've had time to think about all you've said and
I've had a chance to see how demanding your career is. I
think we need to talk."

Ten

Lila's heart missed a beat. Sam's voice was solemn, different from his usual cheerful self. "Then it will be a good thing to talk," she said, wondering if he finally had realized marriage would never work.

"I'll pick you up at seven," he said and then was gone.

She replaced the phone and felt a squeeze to her heart. At the same time, she nodded. "Finally, Sam," she whispered.

She dressed carefully, a simple sleeveless navy dress that fastened beneath her chin and had a straight skirt that went to midcalf. A conservative dress she usually wore to work. She had the feeling that Sam might be ready to tell her goodbye, which should make her feel relieved instead of empty and dreading the dinner with him.

When she stepped into the living room to wait for Sam, her mother walked by, saw her and came into the room. "It'll be nice to see Sam again."

Lila ran her finger along a table. "Mom, I think this is goodbye for us."

"Lila, it won't be goodbye. You are going to be parents, and for years Sam will be part of your life."

"Not a major part," she said.

"Think carefully, honey. Sam is a fine person."

"I know. And he wants a wife just like you. I'm not that woman. Speaking of," she said, seeing Sam drive up. "I'll go on out. I might as well get this over with."

"Lila, make sure you don't want Sam to be a major part of your life. Be very sure of what you're doing."

"I'm really sure," she said, knowing this was definitely for the best. "The hurt will go away," she whispered. She walked out to get into his car, hoping to get seated before he was really out, but he had already walked around and he held open the passenger door. Her heart thudded at the sight of him. He looked more handsome than ever in his charcoal suit, white dress shirt and red tie. Her determination to tell him goodbye made her hurt even more. One look at Sam's face and she knew it would be goodbye tonight. He had a somber expression she had never seen, a hard, angry look.

"I have reservations at Willow Hollow. I thought we might see fewer people we know and have fewer interruptions."

"That's fine," she replied, relieved they weren't staying in Royal where they would see friends all through the evening. Willow Hollow was in a neighboring county and was an excellent restaurant, but she had lost her appetite again, which had been happening more and more, lately. He closed the car door and she watched him walk around and climb in.

"Are you resting up a little from the work?" he asked after they were on the highway.

"I suppose. That and packing up to get ready to return to California on Monday."

How polite they were with each other. She felt a rift between them as if Sam had put a wall around himself, which was totally unlike him. She should have felt intensely relieved, but so far the feeling hadn't happened.

"I got a call today from Roddy."

"Oh, really? Did he have a construction question?"

"Sort of. He offered me a job and suggested I think about moving my business to California."

Shocked, she stared at Sam and then she laughed and shook her head. "Roddy can be so cold to people he doesn't know. He was bowled over by your work. What a compliment, Sam. I know you have no interest—what kind of job did he offer you?"

"He wants me to build his new home," Sam said, smiling for the first time that evening.

"Oh, for heaven's sake! I knew he had talked about having a home built, but he lives in a very nice mansion. I bet he wants you to build him some kind of Georgian or Colonial or Greek Revival, something like his great-aunt's house or one of those in Mississippi."

"You're right. I thanked him. The offer was flattering and he also has a film project he wanted to hire me to do. He made a big sales pitch, which was very flattering."

"Roddy? I can't imagine. He's used to ordering people around and pushing them into doing things. What kind of sales pitch?"

"How great my construction company would be in L.A."

"That's probably true. Have you told Josh?"

"I will. He'll just give me one of his looks and go on to the next thing on the agenda."

"I'm surprised, but that's very complimentary. Wow. You really impressed Roddy. He does know construction. His dad had a successful business."

"Roddy is a nice man."

She laughed and shook her head. "He must really want you to build his house. He could hire you anyway and you could work on his house from Texas."

"Actually, he talked about that, but I don't think that would work. I'm not into flying back and forth."

She thought about their baby and wondered how they would ever work out sharing a child. That sobering thought made her forget Roddy and ride in silence until they were at the restaurant.

She was barely aware of the linen-covered tables, the dahlias in crystal vases on each table, the candlelight and soft music. All she could see was the handsome man across from her, the father of her baby, the man she was somewhat in love with. For the first time, his smile and the sparkle in his blue eyes were gone.

She ordered tomato basil soup. He ordered his usual steak and as soon as they were alone, he took her hand. "I've thought over all you've said. I've thought about our future," he said, and her heart dropped. "What may be most important, I stood on the sidelines as the movie was filming. While I didn't see you at work, I learned a little about your job and your hours. I finally listened and thought about all you've said to me and I have to agree with you. You're right, Lila," he said.

These were words she had thought she wanted to hear, so why did they cut like a knife to her heart?

"We're not wildly, deeply in love with each other," he continued in a somber tone.

His declaration hurt more than everything else. She had said the same thing to him, but when he said it, the words stung badly. A knot came in her throat and she tried to fight back tears, aggravated at herself for reacting this way when he was merely echoing her own sentiments.

"I want a wife who is home with my children. Maybe that is old-fashioned and chauvinistic, but that's the way I am. A lot of people don't have a choice, but I'm fortunate to have been successful enough that my wife can afford to do that and that's what I want. Call it selfish—I can't see it that way. You want to work and pursue a career. You're very ambitious, very independent and you don't need me and the kind of man I am in your life."

She looked down and tried to control her emotions. She needed to answer him. He was silent, and she was certain he waited for her agreement, but she was scared if she met his gaze or tried to answer him, she would burst into tears. What was the matter with her?

Knotting her hands in her lap, she looked up. "I'm glad you realize that, Sam. We're friends and we both like each other, but it isn't real love. This is the sensible thing and we'll work out life for our baby."

"After the first year, I'd like equal time. Actually, with your folks in Royal and with me being close friends with them, I think they'll be happy for me to have our baby a lot of the time."

"Half?" she said, frowning. She had never imagined having to give up her baby half the time. "We'll work it out," she said with a long sigh. Sam could be exactly right about her folks. "I'm glad you see this," she said, barely able to get out the words and looking down at her fingers locked together in her lap. "We will work it all out. We still have some time before this baby's birth."

"When will you tell the rest of your family? I want to be ready for your dad."

"I'm telling him before I get on the plane Monday. I can't live with him otherwise."

She looked up and Sam frowned slightly. "You don't look happy. I just did what you've wanted all along."

"I do want that. We were never meant for each other. It's just a hard decision and I like you. We've had a great time together and you're a friend."

He gazed at her solemnly and said, "I hope to hell we're not making a big mistake."

"Think about my career and you'll get back on track."

He looked away and inhaled deeply. When he turned back to face her, he looked more composed. "You're right. All I have to do is think about how you've been working fourteen or so hours each day lately. That brings me back to reality."

They became silent as the waitstaff delivered their dinners. After several sips of her soup, she felt she couldn't get down another bite. She looked at Sam to see he wasn't eating either.

"Isn't your steak all right?"

"The steak is fine. I've lost my appetite. We're being sensible, Lila, but all I really want to do is take you to bed with me."

"If you're not going to eat and I'm not going to eat, I think we should just go home. We've said what we needed to and it's time to move on," she declared flatly, hurting more than ever over his last statement. She wanted to be in his arms, she wanted his kisses and lovemaking, to flirt with him, but this was the only way and they weren't making a mistake. She would get over him. She had to.

On the way home they talked about inconsequential things and the whole time she tried to avoid thinking about the evening or what he had said. In a few days she would return to California and they wouldn't talk, maybe until Thanksgiving. It was finally over with him except to work out custody. Half the time. He wanted custody and he might be right about her parents wanting their grandchild in Royal often. Thinking what a muddle she had made of her life, she rubbed her forehead. For a moment she half expected Sam to reach over and touch her, to reassure her the way he had before, but he concentrated on driving and rode in silence.

At the ranch he walked her to the door. "Goodbye, Lila. I know it isn't really goodbye, but in a way it is. We'll share a baby but not much else. I will work with you, but sooner or later we can start going through our lawyers. I'll marry someday and have a family I can be a daddy for all the time and a wife who's there for me and our kids. You'll have your life. I'll still be a dad for our baby, too. I won't give up on my child even if we are halfway across the country from each other."

"I know you won't," she whispered, fighting tears more than ever. "We'd better cancel the date for Saturday night."

"Sure. Seems pointless now."

"Goodbye, Sam." She hurried inside.

To her relief, no one was around. She rushed to her room and closed the door. The tears came and she couldn't understand her reaction. Sam had finally agreed with her, done just what she wanted, so why did it hurt so badly and seem so incredibly wrong? She had a wonderful career she loved and she couldn't come back and settle in Royal, marry Sam and only do volunteer work, but at the moment California loomed as a lonely place. Once she was back in her own home and could walk on the beach and see the ocean, when she was back in the routine of work, back with her friends, she would feel differently.

"Sam," she whispered. "If only you weren't so old-fashioned…."

* * *

Friday morning she waited to go to breakfast until she knew her dad would be out of the house and more than likely her brother would still be asleep. Her mother was still in the kitchen and turned to study her. "I take it you and Sam won't be going out tonight."

"No. He finally has realized we aren't suited for marriage."

"I'm sorry, Lila. Want to go shopping? What would you like to eat?"

"I have a lunch appointment today, Mom, but thanks. Maybe tomorrow morning. I'm not really hungry."

"Eat something, Lila, so you don't get sick. You'll feel better. You can go with us to the TCC tomorrow to the end-of-summer party. You won't go with Sam now, will you?"

"No, I won't."

"It's a fun evening and you'll enjoy it. They'll have an open house in the new child-care center with tours for those who are interested."

Lila thought about the previous night and how little she and Sam had even talked to each other. She poured orange juice and got a muffin, picking up the paper and sitting at the table to try to eat a little and to try to stop thinking about Sam. Did he give her any thought or had he picked up and gone on with his life?

Sam showered and shaved, getting dressed for the day. In the midmorning he had an appointment at the TCC. This afternoon he had a house to look at. He hadn't slept and he still thought about Lila and missed her, but he expected that to diminish. He felt a pang and tried to think about her job, her damnable career that he couldn't deal with.

He was scheduled to meet with a client at the TCC and they would talk about business over lunch. He had reserved a meeting room and ordered lunch brought in so they could keep working in privacy without interruption.

Sam talked to his secretary and left, driving the short distance to the Texas Cattleman's Club.

He was meeting Tom Devlin, another TCC member. With his thoughts on Lila, Sam parked at the club and stepped into the cool front. He saw one of the signs that carried the TCC motto and had hung near the entrance for as long as he could remember.

Some member wasn't true to the motto, Leadership, Justice, Peace, or was it misguided loyalty that had caused someone to tamper with the alarm system in the children's center? Had the person thought they would be doing a favor by delaying the center from opening?

The alarm system had already been repaired. The center would hold an open house the night of the party, so the tampering really had no long-term effect. Someone was shortsighted or maybe just angry enough to want to cause trouble even when it did not stop progress.

As Sam passed the dining room, he glanced inside. All his breath left him as he gazed across the busy room and saw Lila having coffee with a man Sam didn't know. He felt as if a fist had punched him in the middle. The man was in boots, slacks and a Western shirt. A broad-brimmed Western hat was on an empty chair. The man laughed at something Lila said and Sam felt another twist to his insides.

Who was she seeing? The man was a stranger, but Lila had to be having a wonderful time with him. In minutes, Lila laughed. Sam realized how he was staring and moved out of the doorway, stepping down the hall, wanting to go back and look at them again. She was bound to go out with other men, but he hadn't expected it this soon. He hadn't expected her to date while she was carrying his baby.

Who was the man? How serious was she? It had to be a casual meeting.

Sam went to his appointment and for the first half hour tried to concentrate but could not focus on what Tom was saying. He tried all through the appointment and it finally finished. As soon as Sam was alone, he gathered papers and put them in a briefcase. As he left, he walked past the center, the billiard room and the dining room, but Lila was nowhere to be seen.

"Hi, Sam," Beau Hacket said, shaking hands with Sam. "You've sent Lila a lot of flowers this summer. Rather impressive."

Sam didn't care to discuss his and Lila's relationship with Beau. "I thought I saw her here earlier."

"Oh, yeah. Earlier she had lunch with some friends and then she met with one of those ranchers to thank him for allowing the film company to shoot part of the movie on his ranch. It was Bob Milton. No telling where Lila is now. She does her own thing."

Relief swamped Sam and he let out his breath. Suddenly the day had brightened and he could think about something besides Lila. He talked a few more minutes to Beau.

"I was sorry to hear about the alarm system failing the inspection. I think it upset Lila," Sam said, beginning to decide that Beau knew little about his daughter at this point.

"I'm sure it would, but her heart is in California and that job of hers. And she knew the alarm would be fixed and pass inspection. Frankly, I don't think it was a smart thing to do, but what's worrisome is it had to be one of us. That's what's bad."

"I agree."

"Probably all of us who voted against the center are suspects. I've already talked to Nathan, and I think he is talking to each member. There's no way to know everyone who voted against the center."

"You're right. I hope they catch the culprit quickly. It's good to see you, Beau."

"Good to see you, Sam," he said as they shook hands again.

Sam walked away feeling enormously better, in euphoria until he was in his car and then he sat still with shock. To hurt so badly and be as upset as he had been over seeing Lila with another man, how strong were his feelings for her? Had he already fallen in love with her and hadn't realized his own feelings?

Stunned, he sat in the parking lot staring into space again while the question consumed him. Was he already deeply in love with Lila? If he was, could he let her go out of his life? Could he let another man try to win her heart and take her away forever? If he truly and deeply loved her, how could he win her heart? How much would he have to change his life—and could he change?

Deep in thought, questioning his own emotions, he replayed the morning. His thoughts skipped to the times they were together and their lovemaking.

He had already realized that he had never dated another woman like her. She could excite him more, entertain him more, be a friend. He just plain enjoyed being with her. He had wanted her in his bed at night—every night—since that first time together, but he had tried to cool down that wish.

Was he in love and hadn't even realized it?

And if in love with her, how could he let her go?

Lila was absolutely the epitome of the independent

woman. Could he adjust to her need for a career? How would he ever convince her he loved her? He couldn't win her over with flowers or diamonds or proposals. How could he let her know that he would support her projects as well as his own?

He thought about Roddy's sales pitch to move his business to California. It had seemed absurd at first, but then Roddy had wanted him to build a mansion and work on a movie project. If he moved to Los Angeles, he would have contacts through Roddy. Could he leave Royal? How deep did his love run for Lila? Was it deep enough to change his whole way of life and his most basic beliefs?

In love with Lila. How had she captured his heart? One night of lust should not make him fall in love with her. Yet it had. From the first, looking back, he loved her. He had never been able to get her out of his thoughts after that first night.

Astounded by his own reactions, he continued to sit in his parked car while he thought about his feelings for Lila.

He loved her—now if he could just convince her that he did. And change her opinion of him, because she would never fall in love with him as long as she saw him as old-fashioned and chauvinistic.

How could he alter Lila's view of him? The question plagued him and he had no answer.

He pulled out his phone to call her. The minute he heard her voice, his grip tightened on his phone. "Lila, it's Sam. If you're free, I still want to take you to the TCC end-of-summer party. We shouldn't part the way we did and I need to see you."

Eleven

When Saturday arrived, eager anticipation hummed in Sam as he dressed. He would be with her again. He wouldn't think about her leaving on Monday.

The party was at the TCC and it was casual with the pool open. There would be swimming, dancing, food, contests, games and billiards. They were showing the new child-care center and Gil had announcements. The end-of-summer party had always been fun, with plenty of things for kids so whole families could attend.

Hurrying because he was anxious to see Lila, Sam walked to the door of the Double H to pick her up. Afterward, he intended to talk her into staying the night at his place.

He rang the bell, expecting to see Mrs. Hacket, who usually welcomed him.

Instead, the door swung open and Lila stood there gazing solemnly at him. The sight of her made his heart pound.

* * *

Lila faced Sam and opened the door, inviting him in. In jeans, boots and a short-sleeved Western shirt, he looked handsome, breathtaking, and longing squeezed her heart. She wanted to walk into his arms and forget all their differences, but she couldn't.

Instead, she greeted him and kept her distance. "I'm ready to go, Sam. Mom and Dad are still inside and Mom is running late. She said for us to go on ahead."

"I won't argue that one," he said, taking Lila's arm as she called goodbye to her parents, closing the door behind her.

He held her hands, still facing her and blocking her way. "You look gorgeous tonight. Thursday night was no way to part. Lila, all I want to do is pull you into my arms and kiss you."

A thrill rocked her even when she didn't want it to. "Sam, I thought we had settled all this," she said, wondering if going to the party with him was going to be a mistake. She would leave Monday for California and she didn't plan to return to Royal until Thanksgiving. By then she hoped all the longing and desire she felt for Sam would be gone. They had no future and she was determined to reconcile herself to that.

Walking to his car, he took her hand. The August sun was still high as Sam drove away from the Hacket ranch.

"You're quiet tonight," he said, taking her hand to place it on his thigh as he drove.

His thigh was muscled, firm, warm through the denim. She looked at Sam's profile and thought about telling him goodbye. She thought about her doctor's visit. She wasn't ready to break that news to Sam. On highly personal matters, it seemed easier to postpone revealing anything to him. Especially news she was struggling to cope with herself. He might try to stop her from flying out Monday and she had to get back to her job.

"You're quiet tonight, Lila."

"It's been busy for two weeks. It's nice to sit and relax."

"After the party we can go to my place and I'll help you relax," he said, glancing at her with a smile.

She shook her head. "Sorry, Sam. After the party I need to go home."

"We haven't really had a chance to talk a lot or make plans."

"We don't need to plan yet. We'll get to plans later when it's not so emotional between us. We both agreed to back off."

He nodded and a muscle worked in his jaw.

"Sam, we would never really be happy together. You saw a little of what my job is like—the demands on my time."

"Yes, I did. Tonight let's forget jobs and futures." He glanced at her as he drove. "Okay?"

"Yes." When she started to move her hand from his thigh, he placed it right back.

"I want you touching me. I've been counting the hours until tonight."

"You have so many women following you around, you can't be counting hours until you're with me."

"Oh, yes, I have, and I think you exaggerate. Besides, I shooed them away because I only have eyes for one redhead with big green eyes. A redhead whose kisses set me on fire," he added in a husky tone.

"We basically said goodbye Thursday night. Stop flirting. Habit that it is—stop. Don't make me regret coming with you."

"I'm resourceful, darlin'. Tonight I have all kinds of plans."

She studied him, wondering what he had planned. When they drove into the club's parking lot, there were already a lot of cars. A valet took Sam's key while Sam linked his arm through hers and they entered the club.

"I wish Shannon could be here tonight, but she's gone back to Austin. The other women will be here. I haven't seen the center for two weeks now."

"Come on. We'll look where our baby will be sometime," he said.

Our baby—Sam was playing on her emotions and she didn't know which was worse, the frosty silence they'd had Thursday night or his flirting and touching, because all of it tore her up.

They walked down the hall and turned into what had once been the billiard room. Lila gasped. "Would you look at this. My goodness," she said, looking around a room with colorful walls and bright colors on small chairs and tables. She glanced at built-in shelves and cabinets. In one corner were two deep sinks secured to the wall at a child's level. "Look, the sinks are in the paint area." Unopened boxes were stacked in various parts of the room. On the opposite wall from where she was standing, she saw a new wide door, plus two new big windows with a view of where the new playground would go. Late-afternoon sunlight streamed through both windows.

Other members and guests walked through the center, greeted by some of the women members.

"They have the door to the outside," Lila noticed.

"That's all. The playground hasn't been started," Sam said, looking through a window.

"This is wonderful in here." She smiled at him. "I guess I'm more excited about it than you."

"I think it's great and they're a little ahead of schedule.

They need to raise more money to finish—Gil will talk about that briefly tonight."

"I hope they can. Surely they'll be able to with this group, unless too many oppose it still."

Sam merely smiled at her and she wondered if he hoped they had difficulty raising the money.

"I'm so impressed." She turned to walk back through the center while Sam followed her into the hall, switching off lights and leaving open the door.

"I hear music somewhere. Let's go dance," he said.

In minutes they were dancing to a fast number and she moved around Sam, glad to let go and have fun, relieved to dance after a grueling two weeks and the emotional upheaval of Thursday night.

She watched Sam dance, twisting his narrow hips, making sexy moves, and she remembered his long legs entangled with hers after loving. She ached with wanting him. She loved him, but she intended to get over her feelings for him.

She watched him, moved with him. Desire simmered, heating her, making her think about lovemaking.

Later, in a slow dance, Sam held her close. "I missed you these past two weeks. I don't want you to go off like that again."

"Sorry, but we've settled all this. We go our separate ways and we'll both be happier and better off. You'll see," she said, wishing she could feel certain that's what would happen.

"I wish I could keep you here," he said.

Startled, she looked up at him and shook her head. "That's out of the question. I go back to my California life."

"This is good, Lila," he said softly, slow-dancing with her, holding her against him, and for a few minutes she closed her eyes and stopped thinking about when they would part.

As they danced in the large ballroom, the music stopped. Gil Addison called for order. "Welcome," he said, and received applause and cheers in return.

He motioned for quiet. "This is our end-of-summer party, although I don't think the weather knows it's the end of summer in Royal because it's still mighty hot. We have a big evening planned with games, hot dogs, burgers and prizes." He paused for applause and cheers. "And lots of cold beer and dancing." There was more applause.

"As all of you know, I'm sure, we've voted in a new child-care center, which has progressed nicely." He waited again while applause rose until he waved his hand and quiet resumed.

"We recently had a break-in and the alarm system was tampered with, causing a temporary setback in meeting the construction deadline. So far, no word on the identity of the person who tampered with the system, which brings me to an announcement. That catastrophe had not been budgeted. Also, a playground was suggested and voted in earlier this month. We need to raise funds for all of this. Any donations will be happily accepted. You can leave them in the office, with the staff or give them to me."

"Gil," Sam called out, startling Lila. "I want to make a donation." He looked down at her. "C'mon, honey. Come with me, because I'm doing this for you," he whispered.

Surprised, she let him take her hand and she followed as they went up steps and crossed the small stage to Gil.

Sam pulled a piece of paper out of his pocket. "I want to make a donation for the child-care center."

"Sam Gordon is making the first donation for the center," Gil announced, waving Sam's check as the audience cheered and applauded. Raising his hand for quiet, Gil glanced down to read Sam's check. Wide-eyed, he looked at Sam. "You're sure?" he asked in a hushed tone.

"Very," Sam replied, smiling at Lila, and her curiosity grew while she braced for another of Sam's surprises.

Gil looked at the crowd and waved the check. "Folks, we have a generous donor who heartily supports the Texas Cattleman's Club's new child-care center. Sam Gordon donates one million dollars for the child-care center," Gil yelled, and the crowd broke into thunderous applause and cheers.

Stunned, Lila stared at him. "Sam…" she said.

"That's for you, Lila," he said quietly, while the noise of the crowd nearly drowned out what he said to her. She stared at him as people jostled her. They swarmed around him to shake his hand and Lila got separated from him. She stepped back out of the way as people continued thanking him for his generous donation.

Smiling and laughing, he shook their hands. Some people hung back in silence on the fringe of the crowd, some bunching in small groups, and she recognized them and realized it was the men who had opposed the center so strongly, although she didn't see her dad in any of the groups and then he was there beside her with her mother at his side.

"That was a confounded-big donation Sam made to-night," Beau said. "Mom said she thinks Sam did that to please you." Beau had to raise his voice because of all the people nearby clustered around Sam who were still talking to him.

"Lila, what's going on with you two?" her father shouted over the noise. "Sam sends truckloads of flowers and makes this whopping donation to a cause he doesn't even like—"

"Isn't it great?" she asked, laughing and looking at

her mother, who hugged her. "Dad, you're going to be a grandfather. We can talk about it tomorrow when I'm home."

"I'm what?" Beau said, blinking and staring open-mouthed in one of the rare moments in her life when her father was speechless. He glanced at Barbara, who smiled and nodded. She leaned forward to hug Lila again and whisper in her ear.

"You picked a crazy time to tell him. Right now he can't say much of anything to you and it'll give him time to adjust to the idea a little. I don't mind fielding questions."

"Thanks, Mom."

"Be good to Sam. You have one million reasons to, for the sake of the child-care center and the children who will be in it. And for your own good."

"I'm flabbergasted. In a lifetime, I would never have guessed Sam Gordon would do any such thing."

"Nor would I, but I told you, Sam's a good man. Lila, for a million, he has to be crazy in love," she said in Lila's ear because the noise around them was still chaotic.

Lila stared at her mother and then turned to hug her dad, who squinted at her. "Damnation. I'm going to be a grandfather?" he shouted.

"That's right," she said loudly, smiling broadly. "You may be glad for this center someday. Now, I need to go speak to Sam."

"Lila," Beau snapped, beginning to pull himself together. His face flushed and he narrowed his eyes. "Lila—" he began again, but before he could say another word, she laughed, waved at him and moved through the crowd. The band began to play again and she glanced up to see Sam looking her way. People were still shaking his hand and talking to him.

Finally, he was there in front of her. Before she could

hug him or thank him, he grabbed her arm. "Let's go," he said, and moved ahead to lead the way to the nearest door.

In minutes they were in the car, driving toward Pine Valley. She unfastened her seat belt to hug Sam's neck.

"Hey, Lila," he said, laughing and pulling over to the curb.

"Thank you, Sam Gordon. I'm speechless and awed and sorry I ever doubted you."

"Buckle up again and we'll talk when we're in a better place."

She sat back and fastened her seat belt. "Sam, that is the most wonderful thing. I'm thrilled and I know everyone who wants the center is, also. That will pay off the debt on the center and do the things we still need to have done."

"I did that for you, Lila. The money should take care of everything, and what's left can go for more supplies for the kids. Whatever they need."

"I can't believe you did that."

"We'll talk about my reasons when we get to my place."

"I'll warn you now—in that crowd I finally told my dad that I'm pregnant."

"You what?" Sam snapped, frowning and glancing at her. "Maybe I better pull over again."

"No, you keep driving. I want to get to your house. As for Dad, I didn't tell him who the father is. Not yet."

"He can figure that one out. He's probably gone home to get his shotgun."

She smiled, feeling better, but she was beginning to face reality again and in spite of his donation, she would still tell Sam goodbye tonight. "Actually, for one of the rare moments in my life, my dad was speechless. I told him in that crowd and he just stared at me with his mouth hanging open. Mom thought it was funny. She said she would answer his questions."

"Your mom is a good sport."

"Yes, she is, to put up with my dad all these years."

"I can't believe you did that. He'll know now why I've sent you so many flowers."

"Oh, yes, he will, but he can't really do anything about it."

"Damn, Lila, what a time to tell him. He's probably looking for me now."

"I thought it the perfect time to tell him. He was very impressed by your donation, and Mom told him you did that for me, so he was trying to absorb that bit of information."

Sam shook his head as he drove. The drive to his house seemed interminable, but eventually they arrived and soon she walked into an empty hallway while Sam switched on lights.

"Finally," she said, wrapping her arms around his neck and standing on tiptoe. "You did that for me," she said. "Sam, thank you." She looked into his blue eyes and saw desire as he looked at her mouth.

"Lila, I've wanted you more than you can possibly imagine," he whispered, and leaned down to kiss her.

The moment his lips touched hers, all thought fled. She forgot the donation, her resolutions about getting over her feelings for Sam and everything else that evening. Sam wrapped an arm tightly around her waist and pulled her close against him, leaning over so she had to cling to him.

Her hips thrust against him. She hugged him tightly, kissing him with all the pent-up longing that seemed to burst into flames within her. Excitement made her tremble as she held him and kissed him.

Desire enveloped her, sweeping away thought, logic— everything except a need to hold and love him. She began to twist free the buttons on his shirt, her fingers fumbling the task in her haste. She felt his hands on her clothes and then cool air on her bare shoulders.

As they shed clothes, he walked her backward along the hall. Finally, he picked her up and carried her to a downstairs bedroom, setting her on her feet and switching on a small lamp that shed a pale glow on them. She kicked off her shoes as he did the same and then she reached for him, walking into his arms. He held her away a moment to look at her before he began to shower kisses over her, his hands caressing her.

She moaned softly with pleasure, trailing her fingers over his hard muscles, tangling them in his chest hair. "Sam, I want you."

He framed her face with his hands and she opened her eyes to look at him, starting to lean forward to kiss him again, but he stopped her.

"Lila, I want to say this when you know it's not in a moment of passion where I'm not thinking about what I'm telling you," he whispered. "I'm focused, coherent and absolutely certain. Darlin', I love you. I need you in my life."

His words were another stunning surprise. Searching his face, she gazed into his wide eyes, which held desire and tenderness, a look that melted her heart. "Oh, Sam," she whispered.

"I love you, darlin'," he repeated.

"Oh, my love," she whispered. "What will we do?" she asked, wanting his love yet knowing it would complicate their lives and a future together was impossible. "I can't, Sam—"

He silenced her, kissing her passionately while his hands roamed over her, caressing her, stirring desire. Clinging to him, she kissed him, pouring out all the love she felt for him.

"We'll love again, long and slow, but this time, Lila, I

can't wait," he whispered, and picked her up. Looking into his eyes, she wrapped her long legs around him while he lowered her to his thick rod, entering her slowly.

Gasping with pleasure and need, Lila held him tightly, closing her eyes and drowning in sensation. He eased slowly into her and then his thrusts were faster. Clinging to his broad shoulders, wrapped around him and still not close enough, she moved with him as need built swiftly.

"I love you, Sam," she whispered without thinking about it, immersed totally in awareness of his body with hers, driven to seek satisfaction.

She moved faster, finally crying out with a release that carried her into blinding rapture.

"Ahh, Sam. I love you," she whispered again, scattering light kisses on his face. She held him tightly until finally he set her on her feet and then kissed her gently as he held her in his arms.

Sam carried her to a bathroom and they showered together between long kisses. After they had dried, he disappeared and came back with two robes, handing a white one to her while he pulled on a navy.

He picked her up to walk to a sofa in a family area and sat with her on his lap. She gazed into his incredible blue eyes and kissed him softly. "I love you, Sam."

"Lila, that's the very best news of all. I love you, too, darlin'. I made that donation for you, Lila. I voted against the children's center and I didn't want it, but I wouldn't do anything to stop it. If you want it, darlin', then I suppose I want it."

"That's the sweetest thing I ever heard. You don't have to want something because I do and the donation was the most wonderful gift," she said, laughing and hugging him. "I'm still shocked."

"Lila, will you marry me?" he asked.

Her smile faded as she looked into his eyes while having a dull ache in her heart. "Some things haven't changed. I don't want to give up my career and come back to Royal. I love you with all my heart, but I can't do that. At least not at this point in my life. I may change my mind later."

He kissed her lightly and then looked into her eyes. "You don't have to come back to Royal. We'll work something out. I'd rather have part of you than none of you."

"You'll live in Royal and I'll live in California? Do you really think that will work?"

"I'm working on it, Lila," he said, suddenly becoming solemn. "I've thought about Roddy's talk. He wants to hire me to build his house. He would have contacts. He said he had a film project he would like to hire me for. That's a big start. I can open a branch in L.A."

She felt as if she couldn't breathe and her head spun. "You would do that for me?" she asked, staring at him. "You do love me," she whispered.

"Yes, I do. And yes, I would do that for you. I want to be with you. I have money invested and saved up and we inherited Dad's money—"

Flinging her arms around his neck, she let out a shriek that stopped his words. Smiling, he brushed her hair away from her face. "Lila, you're part of my life. I just want to be with you. Darlin', you captured my heart completely."

Tears of joy filled her eyes. "Sam, that is the most wonderful thing you could say or do." She showered kisses on his face, running her hands across his shoulders. "What about your brother?"

"I don't think we'll take him with us," Sam replied with a twinkle in his eyes.

"You know what I mean. What about leaving Josh?"

"Josh can run the business here. We each go our own ways and we can fly back and forth whenever we want because we each have our own plane. There's no problem there for me. If one develops, I'll tell you. But, darlin', I want to be where you want to be."

She kissed him and then leaned back. "I love you, love you, love you," she said between kisses. "I'm so happy. Yes, I'll marry you."

"You will?" he asked, grinning suddenly. "Wahoo!" he threw back his head and yelled, making her laugh. "Darlin', I'm the happiest man on earth at this moment. Hooray!" he shouted. He stood up to take a step away and stopped abruptly. He placed one hand on her waist and reached into the pocket of his robe. "Hold out your hand. I have something for you."

"Sam, is my life going to be just one big surprise after another? What are you doing now?"

"Hold out your hand, darlin'," he said. When she did, he placed a tiny package in her hand. It was blue tissue paper tied with a pink silk ribbon.

"What on earth, Sam?" She was curious because if it had been jewelry, she would have expected a box, but it was too tiny for anything else. She untied the bow and pushed open the tissue paper to find a ring with dazzling diamonds surrounding an emerald-cut stone. He picked it up to hold it out to her.

"This is the tiniest token of what I feel for you. It represents my love and my commitment to you and to our family together. It's forever, Lila. I love you with all my being."

"Sam, that is the sweetest thing," she said, getting a knot in her throat and feeling tears of joy forming. "I love you so much. I tried to avoid you and I just never could. From that first night, you captured my heart."

He drew her to him to kiss her. She closed her fist over the ring and put her arm around his neck to return his kiss, wanting him again and loving him more than she would have thought possible.

After a long kiss, she looked up. "Now I have something for you—some news that will give you something else to shout about," she said, smiling at him.

"What's that?" he asked. "I don't think anything could possibly be as important as the fact that we're in love, we're getting married and we're having a baby."

"Oh, yes, there is something, Sam. You talked me into seeing a doctor in Royal, but you never asked me about my appointment."

Sam's smile faded away. "I never saw you that week. You're all right, aren't you?" he asked.

"I'm quite all right. You were partially correct when you said that we're in love and we're getting married. But we're not having a baby, exactly."

Sam frowned. "Lila," he said in a threatening voice. "How can you not have a baby exactly?"

Laughing, she gazed up at him. "Sam, we're having two babies—twin girls."

He blinked and stared at her a moment and then he stepped back and jumped in the air, throwing up his arms while he let out a yell loud enough to make her put her hands over her ears while she laughed. "Wahoo!" he yelled again. "If you weren't pregnant, I'd pick you up and spin you around with me."

"Don't you dare," she said, laughing at him as she spoke.

"Twin girls. Lila, that's the most fantastic news. I have to call Josh right now and tell him."

"Come here, Sam, and don't be ridiculous. He's still at the party at the club."

"I don't care where he is. You've told your dad that

you're pregnant, so I think I need to call and ask him for your hand in marriage."

"Now, there's my old-fashioned lover popping out finally," she said.

"Oh, yes. You also have an old-fashioned dad—I believe you've informed me of that a few dozen times. I'm definitely calling him to ask for your hand in marriage. I should have before I proposed, but I'm not so traditional about everything. I'd go see him first, but I think I'd better place a call. I'll just have him paged at the party."

"Paged? Sam, this will be all over Royal by the time you get off the phone."

He grinned, hugging her. "Yes, it will, darlin'. I can't wait for everyone to know. Twins. Ahh, Lila, I love you so. It's going to be wonderful, darlin'."

"I think so, too," she said, smiling at him. He kissed her again and then took her hand.

"Let's go to the kitchen and I'll get that hot chocolate. Then I'll make my calls. I can put the phone on speaker if you'd like to hear what's said."

Smiling, she shook her head. "Thanks, I'll pass on that one. This is a man-to-man thing in both cases. I may be glad I'll fly out of here Monday."

As she sat in Sam's kitchen and sipped hot chocolate, she listened to him call her dad on his cell phone and ask for permission to marry her. Thinking Sam's call was ridiculous but sweet, she smiled at him. Finally, Sam ended his call.

"He is overjoyed and I'm guessing enormously relieved to find that we are getting married. Now I'm going to page Josh and tell him. This will shake up his world a bit."

"Not too much. They're your twins, not his."

She listened as Sam had his brother paged and she covered her face. If she didn't go to church tomorrow, she wouldn't see anyone except her family before she flew to California and when she came back again, she and Sam would be old news.

"Josh, Sam. Yeah, I'm okay," he said. "Keep your shirt on. You can go back to the party in a few minutes. I have news." There was a pause before he continued. "It can't wait until tomorrow. I asked Lila to marry me and she said yes."

She guessed Josh said congratulations and was probably still scratching his head over why Sam couldn't wait until tomorrow to tell him.

"I want you to be best man when we marry." She smiled again at Sam, because he was probably already planning their wedding.

"Yeah, there's something else. You're going to be an uncle."

She heard another loud yell, surprising her because Josh had always seemed more serious and controlled than Sam. Words poured out, but she couldn't understand what Josh was saying. "That's right, twin girls. Yeah, we'll celebrate."

Lila listened to one side of the conversation a few more minutes and then Sam finished his call. "He's excited. So is your dad."

"I'm surprised at two bachelors being so thrilled over becoming a dad and an uncle. Especially two bachelors who fought the child-care center."

"That was a whole different thing, and maybe Josh and I are ready for some family in our lives. I know I am," he said, leaning close to kiss her lightly. "Next time, sugar, I want to be the first to know—after you, of course. I forgot I wasn't supposed to call you *sugar,* but you know it's because I love you."

"You can call me whatever you want," she said, smiling at him and then looking at her ring. "This is a gorgeous ring. I love it."

"And I love you. I can't tell you enough." He moved his chair and reached out to pick her up and place her on his lap. "This is so good, Lila. You've made me happy beyond my wildest dreams. I'm the happiest man on earth. Two little girls. Our twin daughters. We'll be doubly blessed."

"I think so. I'm overjoyed and you're not so old-fashioned after all, I guess. Since it's twins, I might even think about cutting back a little on my work. Working at home or something while they're babies. The doctor told me to think about maternity leave, too, before I have them."

"Good. Lila, love, not in my wildest dreams did I expect this. It's the most awesome thing to happen to me."

He wrapped her in his arms and pulled her close to kiss her. She held him tightly, knowing he was the love of her life, now and always. With Sam, her future would be filled with joy and love and a precious family.

* * * * *

The level of desire in his blood climbed a few notches higher.

Alarm bells were ringing in his head. Sexual attraction was usually accompanied by danger of some sort. Every girl he even pecked on the cheek was immediately investigated by the media as a future princess. There was no question of having sex with them unless the utmost secrecy was maintained. His military background helped in matters of subterfuge, but the fact remained that usually when he wanted to kiss, or sleep with, a beautiful and intriguing woman, he had to tell himself no.

On the rare occasions when the stars aligned and he managed to secure total privacy, the moment was loaded and often quite magical. He'd even managed several actual relationships over the years, and had had the good luck to adore women who'd proved utterly discreet.

And here he was again, at the moment where he knew exactly what he wanted to do—climb every mountain in order to kiss Ariella Winthrop.

It was never as easy as that.

AFFAIRS OF STATE

BY
JENNIFER LEWIS

MILLS & BOON

Published in Great Britain 2013
by Mills & Boon, an imprint of Harlequin (UK) Limited,
Eton House, 18-24 Paradise Road, Richmond, Surrey TW9 1SR

© Harlequin Books S.A. 2013

Special thanks and acknowledgement to Jennifer Lewis for her contribution to the DAUGHTERS OF POWER: THE CAPITAL miniseries.

ISBN: 978 0 263 90481 9
ebook ISBN: 978 1 472 00625 7

51-0813

Printed and bound in Spain
by Blackprint CPI, Barcelona

Jennifer Lewis has been dreaming up stories for as long as she can remember and is thrilled to be able to share them with readers. She has lived on both sides of the Atlantic and worked in media and the arts before she grew bold enough to put pen to paper. She would love to hear from readers at jen@jenlewis.com. Visit her website at www.jenlewis.com.

For Charles Griemsman, editor extraordinaire, and the authors in this series who were such a pleasure to work with: Barbara Dunlop, Michelle Celmer, Robyn Grady, Rachel Bailey and Andrea Laurence.

One

"The prince is staring right at you."

"Maybe he needs a refill." Ariella Winthrop sent a text requesting another round of the salmon and caviar. The gala event that Ariella had planned was a fund-raiser for a local hospital and nearly six hundred guests were milling around the ballroom. "I'll send a server his way."

"You haven't even looked at him." Her glamorous friend Francesca Crowe was an invited guest at the party. With her long dark hair in a shiny sheet down her back and her voluptuous body encased in an expensive beaded dress, Francesca fit right in with the crowd of billionaires and their buddies. It was often awkward when friends came to Ariella's events and wanted to chat and hang out while she needed to attend to the details. Luckily, Francesca was the kind of person she could be blunt with.

"I'm busy working." She responded to another text from her staff about a spill near the main entrance. "And I'm sure you're imagining things." She didn't glance up at the prince. Hopefully he wasn't still looking at her. She was starting to feel self-conscious.

"Maybe he's as intrigued as everyone else by the mysterious love child of the United States president."

"I'll pretend I didn't hear that. And I'm going off the idea of meeting President Morrow on your husband's TV network." Francesca would know she was kidding, but her heart clutched as she thought about it. Everyone was talking about her and her famous father and she'd never even met the guy.

"Go on. Look. He's gorgeous." Her friend's conspiratorial tone, and the fact that she'd ignored her comment about the TV special entirely, made Ariella glance up in spite of herself.

Her eyes locked with a tall man halfway across the room. His short-cropped dirty blond hair contrasted with his black tuxedo. A jolt of energy charged through the air as he started walking toward her. "Uh-oh, he's coming this way."

"I told you he was looking at you." Francesca smiled and stared right at him. "And he doesn't need champagne, either. Look, his glass is full."

"I wonder what's wrong." Her pulse quickened and she plastered on her most helpful smile as he approached. It was never easy to know if you should introduce yourself in these situations. She was working at the event, not attending as a guest, so was it a breach of etiquette to greet a prince? She wished her business partner, Scarlet, was here. With her background as a D.C. socialite, she knew just how to handle these dilemmas.

Before she could collect her thoughts he stood right in front of her. He held out his hand, so she shook it. His handshake was predictably firm and authoritative. "Ms. Winthrop, Simon Worth."

He knew her name? Her brain scrambled. He must have read the media stories like everyone else. "Pleased to meet you." His eyes fixed on hers with startling intensity. A dark honey color, they seemed to see right past her studied professional façade to the woman beneath.

"I'm impressed." His voice was deep, with a masculine gruffness that stirred something inside her. Oh dear. There was nothing good about being attracted to a royal guest. Still it was kind of him to compliment her.

"Oh, thank you. That's sweet of you." It wasn't often that guests thanked the party planner personally. Or even noticed that she was alive. "We do enjoy hosting these fund-raisers."

He'd let go of her hand, but his gaze still held her like a deer in a rifle sight. Humor sparkled in his golden eyes. "Not your party planning skills, though I'm sure those are impressive, too. I admire how well you've handled the blazing spotlight of press attention on your personal life."

"Oh." She felt her cheeks heat, which was unusual for her. This man was having an unsettling effect on her sanity. "I suppose it helps that I don't have much of a personal life. I'm all work all the time so they haven't found a lot to write about." Now she was babbling, which made her feel even more hot and bothered. "And it's easy to stay detached when I genuinely have no idea what they're talking about half the time."

"I know how you feel." He smiled. "I've had cameras poked in my face since before I could speak. I finally realized that if there isn't a good story, they'll just make one up and hope you play into their hands by making a fuss over it."

She smiled. "So it is better to put your hands over your ears and hope that they go away?"

"Pretty much." He had a sexy dimple in his left cheek. He was taller than she'd expected. And more strapping, too. His tuxedo stretched across broad shoulders and his elegant white shirt collar framed the sturdy neck of an athlete. "It helps if you travel a lot, then they have trouble keeping up."

"I'll have to plan more parties abroad." He was easy to talk to. Which was weird. Especially with this unsettling attraction clawing at her insides. "I did one in Paris a couple of months ago, and we have one coming up in Russia, so it should prove quite easy once I get the hang of it."

He laughed. "There you go. I travel to Africa a lot now that I'm ex-military. It's quite easy to lose photographers out in the bush."

She chuckled at the image. "What do you do in Africa?" She was genuinely curious. Surely Britain didn't have colonies there anymore?

"I run an organization called World Connect that brings technology and education to remote areas. The staff is all local so we spend a lot of time recruiting in the local villages and helping them get things off the ground."

"That must be very rewarding." Gosh, he was adorable. A prince who actually cared about something other than entertaining himself? There weren't too many of those around.

"I thought I wouldn't know what to do with myself once I left the service, but I'm busier and happier than ever. I'm hoping to drum up some donations while I'm in D.C. That's another challenge that keeps me on my toes. Perhaps you can help me with that?"

"You mean, plan a fund-raiser?" Scarlet would be thrilled if she enticed another royal onto their roster of clients. They attracted other clients the way a sparkling tiara attracted glances.

"Why not?" He'd drawn so close to her that she could almost feel his body heat. "Would you join me for tea tomorrow?"

Her brain screeched to a halt. Something about his body language told her he wanted more than tea. He had a reputation for boyish charm, and although she couldn't remember reading about any romantic scandals in the papers, the last thing she needed was to give the tabloids more fuel for their gossip furnaces. "I'm afraid I have an appointment tomorrow." She stepped backward slightly.

Instead of looking angry or annoyed, he tilted his head and smiled. "Of course. You're busy. How about breakfast? That's got to be the quietest meal for a party planner."

She swallowed. Every cell in her body was telling her to run screaming from the room. He was dangerously good-looking and must have years of experience seducing women in far less vulnerable emotional states than herself. But he was a prince, so in her line of work she couldn't afford to offend him. At least not here, in public. Planning a fund-raiser for his charity would be great for DC Affairs, so Scarlet would kill her if she turned him down. And really, what could happen during breakfast? "That sounds fine."

"My driver will pick you up at your house. It will be discreet, trust me."

"Oh." Somehow that sounded more worrying than ever. If the meeting was to be all business, why would they need discretion? But she managed a shaky smile. "My address is—"

"Don't worry. He'll find you." He gave a slight nod, like an ancient courtier, and backed away a step or two before disappearing into the crowd of well-dressed partygoers.

She wanted to sag against a wall with relief. Unfortunately she wasn't near a wall, and her phone was buzzing.

"Well, well, well." Francesca's voice startled her.

"I'd forgotten you were there."

"I could tell. You forgot to introduce me to your royal friend. Very hot. And I thought his older brother was supposed to be the good-looking one."

"His older brother is the heir to the throne."

"Just think, if the USA was a monarchy like England, you'd be next in line to the throne." Francesca looked at her thoughtfully. "Your dad is the president, and you're his only child."

"Who he didn't even know existed until a few weeks ago." She tried to stay focused on her job. "And I still haven't actually met him in person." That part was beginning to hurt more and more.

"Liam's in negotiations with the White House press office about the date for the reunion special. Ted Morrow's on board with doing it. I'm sure he wants to meet you, too." Francesca squeezed her arm gently.

"Or not. I was an accident, after all." She glanced around the room, packed with wealthy movers and shakers. "It's hardly a reunion when we've never met before. We really shouldn't be talking about this here. Someone could be listening. And I'm supposed to be working. Don't you have bigwigs to schmooze with?"

"That's my husband's department. I wish I could be a fly on the croissants tomorrow morning."

"I wish I could have found an excuse not to go." Her heart rate quickened at the thought of meeting Prince Simon for breakfast. They couldn't talk business for the entire meal. What kind of small talk did you make with a prince?

"Are you crazy? He's utterly delish."

"It would be easier if he wasn't. The last thing I need is to embark on a scandalous affair with a prince." Ariella exhaled as butterflies swirled in her stomach. "Not that he'd be at all interested, of course, but just when I think things can't get any crazier, they do."

"Um, I think someone's throwing up into the gilded lilies." She gestured discretely at a young woman in a strapless gown bending over a waist-high urn of brass blooms.

Ariella lifted her phone. "See what I mean?"

The long black Mercedes sedan parked outside her Georgetown apartment may not have had "By Appointment to His Majesty" stenciled on the outside, but it wasn't much more subtle. The uniformed chauffeur who rang the bell looked like a throwback to another era. Ariella dashed for the backseat hoping there were no photographers lurking about.

She didn't ask where they were going, and the driver didn't say a word, so she watched in surprise, then confusion, then more than a little alarm as the car took her right out of the city and into a leafy suburb. When the suburbs gave way to large horse farms she leaned forward and asked the question she should have posed before she got into the car. "Where are you taking me?"

"Sutter's Way, madam. We're nearly there." She swallowed and sat back. Sutter's Way was a beautiful old mansion, built by the Hearst family at the height of their wealth and influence. She'd seen paintings from its collection in her art history class at Georgetown University but she had no idea who owned it now.

At last the car passed through a tall wrought iron gate, crunched along a gravel driveway and pulled up in front of the elegant brick house. When she got out, her heels sank into the gravel and she brushed wrinkles from the

skirt of the demure and unsexy navy dress she'd chosen
for the occasion.

Simon bounded down the steps and strode toward her.
"Sorry about the long drive but I thought you'd appreciate the privacy." She braced for a hug or kiss, then chastised herself when he gave her a firm handshake. Her head
must be getting very large these days if she expected royalty to kiss her.

He was even better looking in an open-necked shirt and
khakis. His skin was tanned and his hair looked wind-
blown. Not that it made any difference to her. He was just
a potential client, and an influential one, at that. "I am becoming paranoid about the press lately. They seem to pop
out in the strangest places. I don't know what they hope
they'll find me doing." *Kissing a British prince, perhaps.*

She swallowed. Her imagination seemed to be running
away with her. Simon probably just wanted ideas about
how to attract high rollers who would donate money to
his charity.

He gestured for her to go in. "I've learned the hard way
that photographers really do follow you everywhere, so it's
best to try to stick with activities you don't mind seeing
under a splashy headline." His grin was infectious.

"Is that why I'm afraid to even change my hairstyle?"

"Don't let them scare you. That gives them power over
you and you certainly don't want that. From what I've seen,
you handle them like a pro."

"Maybe it's in the blood." Her private thought flew off
her tongue and almost made her halt in her tracks. Lately
she'd been thinking a lot about the man who sired her.
He faced the press every day with good humor and never
seemed ruffled. It was so odd to think that they shared
the same DNA.

"No doubt. I'm sure your father is very impressed."

"My father is…was a nice man called Dale Winthrop. He's the dad who raised me. I still can't get used to people calling President Morrow my father. If it wasn't for sleazy journalists breaking the law in search of a story, he wouldn't even know I existed."

They went into a sunlit room where an elegant and delicious-smelling breakfast was spread out on a creamy tablecloth. He pulled out her chair, which gave her an odd sensation of being…cared for. Very weird.

"Help yourself. The house is ours for now. Even the staff have been sent packing so you don't have to worry about eavesdroppers."

"That's fantastic." She reached for a scone, not sure what else to do.

"So you have the press to thank for learning about your parentage. Maybe they're not so bad after all." His honey-colored eyes shone with warmth.

"Not bad? It's been a nightmare. I was a peaceful person living a quiet life—punctuated by spectacular parties—before this whole thing exploded." She cut her scone and buttered it.

"I'm impressed that you haven't taken a big movie deal or written a tell-all exposé."

"Maybe I would tell all if I knew anything to tell." She laughed. How could a foreign prince be so easy to talk to? She felt more relaxed discussing this whole mess with Simon than with her actual friends. "The situation surprised me as much as anyone. I always knew I was adopted but I never had the slightest interest in finding my biological parents."

"How do your adoptive parents feel about all this?" He leaned forward.

Her chest contracted. "They died four years ago. A plane crash on their way to a friend's anniversary party."

She still couldn't really talk about it without getting emotional.

"I'm so sorry." Concern filled his handsome face. "Do you think they would have wanted you to get to know your birth parents?"

She frowned and stared at him. "You know what? I think they would." She sighed. "If only they were still here I could ask them for advice. My mom was a genius at knowing the right thing to do in a tricky situation. Whenever I run into a snarl at work I always ask myself what she would do."

"It sounds like a great opportunity to welcome two new parents into your life. Not to replace the ones who raised you, of course, no one could ever do that, but to help fill the gap they left behind."

His compassion touched her. And she knew his own mother had died suddenly and tragically, when he was only a boy, so he wasn't just making this stuff up. "You're sweet to think of that, but so far neither of them seems to want a relationship with me."

"You haven't met them?" He looked shocked.

She shook her head quietly. "The president's office hasn't even made an official statement about me, though they've stopped denying that I could be his daughter since the DNA test results became public." She let out a heavy sigh. "And my mother… Can I swear you to secrecy?"

"Of course." His serious expression reassured her.

"My real mother refuses to come out of hiding. She wrote to me privately, which I appreciate, but mostly to say that she wants to keep quiet about the whole situation. Weirdly enough, she lives in Ireland now."

"Does she?" He brightened. "You'll have to come to our side of the Atlantic for a visit."

"She certainly didn't invite me." Her freshly baked

scone was cooling in her fingers. Her appetite seemed to have shriveled. "And I can't say I blame her. Who'd want to be plunged into this whole mess?"

"She can hardly bow out now when she's the one who had the affair with the president in the first place. Though I suppose he wasn't the president, then."

"No, he was just a tall handsome high school senior in a letter jacket. I've seen the photos on the news like everyone else." She smiled sadly. "She told me in her letter that she kept quiet about her pregnancy because he was going off to college and she didn't want to spoil what she knew would be a brilliant career."

"She was right about his prospects, that's for sure." He poured her some fragrant coffee. "And maybe she needs time to get used to the situation. I bet she's secretly dying to meet you."

"I'm quickly learning not to have expectations about people. They're likely to be turned on their head just when I least expect it."

"You can't get paranoid, though. That doesn't help. I try to assume that everyone has the best intentions until they prove otherwise." His expression made her laugh. It suggested they often proved otherwise but he wasn't losing sleep over it.

She didn't know what to think about Simon's intentions. She had a strong feeling that he didn't invite her here to plan a party, but there was no way she could come out and ask him. Maybe he really did just want to give her a pep talk on how to deal with her unwelcome celebrity.

"So I should try to approach everyone as a potential new friend, even if they're trying to take a picture of me buying bagels in the supermarket?"

"If you can. At the very least they won't get a really bad picture of you and you won't get in trouble for smashing their camera." He managed to be mischievous and deeply serious at the same time, which was doing something strange to her insides.

"Ever since your older brother got married the papers keep speculating about your love life, but I haven't seen any stories about it. How do you keep your personal life out of the papers?" Uh-oh, now she was asking him about his love life, in a roundabout way. She regretted the question, but also burned with curiosity to see how he'd answer. Was he involved with anyone?

"I have privacy." He gestured at their elegant surroundings. "I just have to be cunning to get it." His eyes shone. They were the color of neat whiskey, and were starting to have a similarly intoxicating effect on her. He had a light stubble on his cheeks, not dark, but enough to add texture under his cheekbones and she wondered what it would feel like to touch it. This was the private Simon the public didn't see, and he'd invited her into his exclusive world.

Her breathing had quickened and she realized she was still holding her uneaten scone in her hand. She put it down and had a sip of orange juice instead. That had the bracing effect she needed. "I guess I need to get more cunning, too. It must help to have friends with large estates." She smiled. "It looks like it has a beautiful garden."

"Do you want to see it? I can tell you're not exactly ravenous."

"I'd love a walk." Adrenaline and relief surged through her. Anything to dissipate the nervous tension building in her muscles. "Maybe I'll be hungrier after some fresh air."

"I already went for a run this morning. Just me and two Secret Service agents pounding the picturesque streets." He stood and helped pull out her chair as she stood. Again she was touched by his thoughtfulness. She'd expect a prince to be more…supercilious.

"Where are the agents now?"

"Outside, checking the perimeter. They'll keep a discreet distance from us."

"Oh." She glanced around, half expecting to see one lurking in the corner. Simon opened a pair of French doors and they stepped out onto a slate patio with a view over a formal rose garden. The heady scent of rose petals filled the air. "You picked the perfect time to invite me here. They're all in bloom."

"It's June. The magic moment."

He smiled and they walked down some wide steps to the borders of roses. They were the fragrant heirloom roses, with soft white, delicate yellow and big fluffy pale pink heads, so different from the gaudy unscented blooms she sometimes dealt with for parties. She drank in their scent and felt her blood pressure drop. "How gorgeous. It must take an army of gardeners to keep them so perfect."

"No doubt."

She glanced up at him, instantly reminded of how tall he was. Six-two, at least. His broad shoulders strained against the cloth of his shirt as he bent over a spray of double pink blossoms. He pulled something from his pocket and snipped off a stem, then stripped the thorns.

"You carry a knife?"

"Boy Scout training." He offered her the posy. Their fingers brushed and she felt a sizzle of energy pass between them before she accepted it and buried her nose in it. How could she be attracted to a British prince, of all people? Wasn't her life crazy and embarrassing enough already? Surely she could at least develop a crush on a prince from some obscure and far-flung nation that no one had heard of, not one of her nation's closest allies.

"You're very quiet." His soft voice tickled her ear.

"Thinking too much, as usual." She looked up. The

morning sun played on the hard planes of his face and illuminated the golden sparkle of her eyes.

"That's not always a good idea." A smile tugged at the corner of his mouth. "Maybe we'd better keep walking." His hand touched the base of her spine, sending a thick shiver of arousal darting through her. Things just got worse and worse!

She walked quickly, first to lose his hand, and then to outpace her own imagination, which already toyed with the idea of kissing him.

"I think I've been working too hard lately." That must be why the simple touch of a handsome man could send her loopy.

"Then you need to take a break." He made it sound so easy.

"It's not as if I can just step off the carousel and spend a few weeks in the islands."

"Not without the entire press corps following you." His wry glance made her chuckle. "You have to be crafty about it when you're in the public eye. You don't want to be caught topless in Vegas."

She laughed aloud. "I don't think there's much danger of that. Oddly enough, I've never been there."

"No quickie weddings in your past?"

"No, thank goodness. Otherwise my former husband would probably be preparing a tell-all biography about me."

He slowed. "Is that a risk? Do you have people from your past who could reveal things you don't want to be made public?" Was he tactfully inquiring about her romantic history?

"No." She said it fast and loud. "I guess that's something to be grateful for. My past is very plain vanilla. I was a bit embarrassed by how unexciting my life has been up to this point, but now it's a huge relief."

"But a little dull." She glanced at him as he lifted a brow slightly. As if he wanted to tempt her into sin.

"Sometimes dull is good."

"Even in the party planning business?"

"Oh, yes. Believe me, dull and tasteful goes a long way, especially when there are scandals swirling like tornadoes all around you."

"Hmm. Sounds like a waste to me. If you're going to have a party you might as well make it a live one. I suppose I feel the same way about life. Sometimes it drives the family mad that I can't just plod around opening supermarkets and smashing bottles against ships, but I have to climb mountains and trek across deserts. Turning my adventures into fund-raising activities gives them an air of legitimacy, but frankly I'd be doing it anyway, simply because I enjoy it. Maybe you need an adventure." His voice brightened.

"Oh, no." Adrenaline shot through her. "No. Adventure is definitely the last thing I need. Really, I'm a dull and boring person. Happiest with a cup of herbal tea and a glossy magazine." That should stop him in his tracks. And maybe she was trying to convince herself that she wasn't experiencing a surge of excitement just from walking close to this man.

"I don't believe a word of it." He touched the small of her back again—just for a split second—as they descended a short flight of stone stairs. Again her skin prickled as if he'd touched it right through her clothes. An odd sensation was unfurling in the pit of her belly. One she hadn't felt in a very long time.

"Trust me," she pleaded, as her body threatened to succumb to far more excitement than she needed. "All I really want is my ordinary, quiet life back."

"Well." He stopped and took her hands. Her fingers tingled and her breath caught in her lungs. "That is most certainly not going to happen."

Two

It took every ounce of self-control he possessed for Simon not to press his lips to Ariella's soft pink ones. But he managed. Years of royal training, accompanied by thinly veiled threats from older members of the family, had taught him to handle these situations with his brain rather than other more primitive and enthusiastic parts of his body.

He didn't want to blow it. Scare her off. Something deep in his gut told him that Ariella Winthrop was no ordinary woman. He trusted his gut in the line of fire and on the face of a sheer cliff. It rarely steered him wrong.

Something about Ariella sent excitement coursing through him. He couldn't explain it, or even put his finger on the feeling; it was just a hunch that meeting her could change the course of his entire life.

He even managed to let go of her hands, reluctantly, and turn toward the rhododendron border as a distraction. "The reality is that your life has changed forever."

He glanced back, and was relieved to see her following closely. "Whether you like it or not, you're public property now." It made him feel close to her. They shared a bond and his years of hard experience could help her negotiate the minefield of a life lived on the pages of the daily papers.

"But I'm still the same person I've been all along. People can't expect me to suddenly welcome the entire world into my private life."

"You're not the same, though. You didn't know the president was your father, did you?"

"I was as surprised as he was. I'd never have guessed it in a million years. Now people are even saying I look like him. It seems insane to me. I don't feel in the least bit related to him."

Simon surveyed her strikingly pretty face. She had elegant, classical features, highlighted by the sparkle of warmth from her people-oriented personality. "You do look rather like him. You both have striking bone structure, and something about your eyes seems familiar."

She let out an exasperated sigh. "You're just imagining it. Or trying to make me feel better, and it's not working. Yes, I'd like to meet him, since we do share the same genes, but I'm sure I'll never have the same feelings for him as I do for the man who actually raised me."

"Of course not." He frowned. Her moss-green eyes were filled with concern. "No one expects you to do that."

"I feel like they do." she protested. "Journalists keep talking to me as if I must be happy to have President Morrow as my father. He's so popular and successful that I must be dying to claim his revered family tree as my own. I couldn't care less. I'd rather be descended from some nice man whom I could actually meet and get to know, not some almighty, carved-from-stone figure that everyone bows down to. It's exasperating."

He chuckled. "Maybe he isn't as carved in stone as you think. Sometimes people expect members of the royal family to behave like granite statues, but believe me, we have feelings, too. It can be very inconvenient." Like right now, when he longed to take this troubled and lovely woman in his arms and give her a big bear hug.

Once again he restrained himself. He'd learned to do a pretty passable impression of a granite statue when the occasion called for it.

"I don't think the press wants me to be a granite statue. I think they'd like to see me go right to pieces. The way they've been hounding me and peppering me with questions, it feels like they're just waiting for me to say the wrong thing or break down sobbing. They must be exasperated that I'm so dull I couldn't give them a good story even if I wanted to." The morning breeze whipped her dark dress against her body. The soft fabric hugged contours that would bring a weaker man to his knees. If only he wasn't a gentleman.

"You're anything but dull."

"Why are we talking about me? That's a dull topic if there ever was one." Her eyes flashed something that warned him off. "Didn't you invite me here to help you plan a party?"

He frowned. Had he used that as an excuse? He just wanted to get to know her better. It was a good idea, though. He'd like to raise awareness of World Connect in the US and gain some new donors. "Do you think you could help me put together a fund-raiser for World Connect? We've never done one on this side of the Atlantic before."

"Absolutely." Her face lit up and he could almost feel her lungs fill with relief. "We organize gala events all the time. We can pretty much print out a guest list of people who like to support worthy causes. Happily there are a lot of them in D.C."

"They sound ideal. And I wouldn't turn up my nose at people who want to donate for the tax benefits, either."

She grinned. "They're often the most generous ones. What kind of venue did you have in mind?"

He tried to look like he'd put some thought into it. "Somewhere...big." It was hard to think at all with those big green eyes staring so hopefully at him. "I'm sure you could come up with a good place."

"The Smithsonian might work. There are a lot of possibilities. I can make some phone calls once you pick a date."

"A date?" He drew in a breath. "What would you suggest?" A date far off into the future might be good, so he'd have plenty of excuses to get together with her for brainstorming and planning.

"Summers aren't ideal because a lot of people go away to the beach. I'd recommend the fall or winter. Something about the short days makes people want to get dressed up in their sparkliest outfits and stay out late."

"November or December, then. You can choose a date that works for the venue." Perfect. Five or six months of meetings with Ariella should be enough time for...

For what? What exactly did he intend to do with her?

For once he wasn't sure. All he knew is that he wanted to be close to her. To hear her voice. To touch her...

"My partner, Scarlet, keeps a master list of venues and cultivates relationships with the people who run them. We should talk to her. It's important to find out what else is going on that week, too. You don't want two similar events taking place on the same night, or even back to back."

"Of course not." He jerked back his hand, which was heading toward hers. He needed to keep himself in check or she'd send her partner to meet with him. "I'll rely entirely on your expertise. I usually raise money for our endeavors by ringing people up and asking them for money."

"Does that work well?" Humor danced in her eyes.

"Surprisingly, it does."

"That sounds a lot less expensive than throwing parties."

"But think of all the fun I miss out on. And hardly anyone in the US has heard of World Connect, so I need to get the word out."

She stopped walking. "I have an idea."

"Yes?"

"How about an outdoor concert?"

"In the dead of winter?" Was he following the conversation? He might have lost track when he just got lost in the way her navy dress hugged her hips.

"No!" She laughed. "You could do it in September or October. The weather's usually lovely then and we've pulled festivals together quicker than that. You could get a much larger and more diverse crowd and make the same money by selling more tickets."

"I love it. World Connect is about inclusion, so the more people who can come and hear about it, the better."

"If the bands are enthusiastic enough they might even perform for free, so all the profits would go to World Connect." He could see her getting excited, which had a strange effect on his own adrenaline. "A good friend of mine is a music agent so I'm sure she can hook me up with some interesting performers."

"And how about some musicians from Africa? I could talk to some friends over there and see who would be interested. Already the world is coming together. I'm so glad I convinced you to come here today." Again his fingers itched to seize hers. Again he shoved them into his pockets. They'd walked past the rhododendrons and out onto a lawn that circled around the tennis court. "I can't believe I lucked into meeting you."

"You hardly lucked into it." She shot him a teasing smile that sent heat right to his groin. "You came right up to me."

"I like to make things happen, not sit around waiting for them to happen."

"I guess that's the best way to live your life. I'm going to adopt that attitude from now on."

"Just keep on being yourself and don't worry about the press or anyone else. Don't let the bastards grind you down."

A smile tugged at her mouth. "I bet you wouldn't say that in front of the press."

"True. So more accurately, you have to be yourself, but not put every aspect on public display. I won't lie, it's a delicate balance, but I can already see that you're more than capable of doing it."

She shrugged her slim shoulders. "I don't really have any choice."

"In some ways, I think that makes it easier." He slid his arm around her shoulders, which sent a delicious sensation of warmth flooding through his torso.

He instantly regretted the rash move when she sprang forward toward a herb border. He shook his head in frustration at himself. He could see that beneath her calm and controlled demeanor she was nervous and skittish as a startled filly. It hadn't been easy to persuade her to come here and he didn't want to add to her anxiety by being yet another person who wanted a piece of her.

Her scent filled his nostrils, delicate and feminine, like their lush floral surroundings. "A garden is the perfect backdrop for you." The sunlight sparkled in her dark hair and lit up her eyes. Even the bird on a nearby tree branch seemed transfixed by her beauty, still and unblinking, head cocked.

"I don't know why. I haven't spent much time in gardens."

"You grew up in the city?"

"Nope, in a tiny town in Montana, but my parents didn't have a garden like this. It was a smooth clipped lawn with a fence and a doghouse. No camellias to bury your nose in or arbors to stand gracefully under."

"The president's from Montana, isn't he?"

"Yes, that's how the journalists found me. They went there to do a story on his childhood and decided to tap the phone of a former White House maid who lived in his town. She inadvertently revealed that my mother—his high school sweetheart—had become pregnant and never told him."

Anger surged inside him. He knew the story already. Who didn't? It had been setting headlines on fire for months. And since he was here to sign a treaty between the United States and the United Kingdom to punish those who used technology to violate other people's privacy, it was his business to know the more intimate details. "Have you been following the story in the press? Angelica Pierce, the ANS journalist who did the illegal wiretapping is going to prison, last I heard. She's expected to get a two- to five-year sentence."

"I know. Everyone seems to think I should be thrilled about it, but I feel sorry for her. It turned out that Graham Boyle, the former head of ANS, was her biological father and had denied all knowledge of her for years. I'm not sure if she was trying to impress him or ruin him with her illegal antics, but it certainly was a cry for help. I did hear that she and her father have started writing to each other now that they're both behind bars. Hopefully they'll have a better relationship once they've both served their sentences."

"Now that's a family situation that makes almost anything seem normal by comparison, even discovering that your father is president."

"I suppose you're right. And I did have a ridiculously normal childhood." The sun sparkled in her hair. She looked so fresh and pretty out in the sunlight. None of the newspaper images did her justice.

"Did you like growing up in Montana?"

"Sure. I didn't know anything different. I thought everyone could bike to the store with their dog in the handlebar basket, or fish in a river all day long on Sunday. Sometimes I miss the simple life."

"Really?" She was relaxing a little.

"Only for a moment, though." She flashed a slightly mischievous smile. "I do love the hustle and bustle of D.C. I guess when it comes right down to it, I'm a people person rather than a hiking in the wilderness person."

"Why can't you be both?"

"I suppose I could. But in the last three or four years I've been so madly busy I can barely sleep in on the weekends, let alone commune with nature."

"Time management is an important part of life in the spotlight."

"There you go again! I refuse to believe that the rest of my life will be lived in a spotlight." She hadn't tensed. She was teasing him.

He shrugged. "Who knows? Maybe the president will get voted out of office in three years and everyone will forget all about you."

"Hey, that's my dad you're talking about!"

He laughed. "See? You feel attached to him already."

"I admit I have been thinking a lot about meeting him, and my mother. I'm nervous, though."

He shrugged. "What have you got to lose?"

"What if I hate them?"

A smile tugged at his mouth. "Then you hate them. That's hardly worse than not knowing them at all."

"I wonder." She inhaled deeply, and started walking across the lawn. He kept pace with her, trying to tug his eyes from the seductive swishing movement of her slim hips beneath her dress. She swung suddenly to face him. "What if I adore them and they don't like me?"

"That'll never happen."

"How do you know?"

"Because you're the kind of daughter any parent would be thrilled to have. The universe seems to be pushing them toward you. Take a chance, live dangerously."

"That sounds like your kind of motto rather than mine." She touched the delicate red petal of a hibiscus in a tall clay pot. "My life is spent reducing the chances that something can go wrong and trying to be as cautious and well prepared as possible. I suppose that is an occupational hazard."

"Time for a change, then." He said it softly. She was so afraid of stepping outside the boundaries of the life she'd made for herself. Too worried about her reputation and the media and what the future might hold. He'd like to shift her focus to much more interesting things like the feel of their lips touching or their hands on each others' skin.

The urge to kiss her was growing stronger each second. He wasn't quite sure what would have happened if it wasn't for all the discipline he'd developed during his royal upbringing and honed in his army training. Even her thoughtful gaze was driving him half mad.

But the way she'd leaped away from him like he'd stung

her warned him to slow right down. He'd have to go very slowly and carefully with Ariella.

"Maybe you're right." Her words surprised him.

"You're going to meet them?"

"I'm scheduled to have a televised 'reunion' with my father on ANS, but I'm not as sure about my mother. She's in a trickier position than me, really. My mom abandoned me and failed to tell the man who fathered me that I existed. She has good reason to stay hidden in some ways." Her eyes flashed with emotion. "I'm sure a lot of people would criticize her choices, regardless of why she made them."

She inhaled, that mysterious expression in her eyes growing deeper. "And my father didn't even know he was a father. He's been rolling merrily through life with no ties and no responsibilities except to his constituents and his country, and now he's discovered that he had a child all along but he's missed the whole experience. I'd be pretty cheesed off if I was him."

"I wonder if they loved each other." He still wasn't entirely sure his own parents had. There were so many forces rushing them together, only to tear them apart again.

"All the salacious media stories made it sound like they did. Puppy love."

"Perhaps you can bring them back together?"

"You're worse than the *National Enquirer!* Either that or you're a hopeless romantic."

"I suspect it's the latter."

She lifted her chin, watching him. Probably deciding that his professed romanticism was simply a cunning ploy to get up her skirt. His unfortunate reputation as a ladies' man sometimes preceded him. "How come you're not in a relationship? Your brother dated the same woman his entire adult life and now they're married."

He shrugged. "I haven't been as lucky as him."

"Or maybe you've just been too busy scaling mountains." She lifted one of her delicate dark brows.

He chuckled. "That, too. There aren't too many lovely, intelligent women at the top of mountains."

"Obviously you've been scaling the wrong ones." She turned and strode off again, but this time her movement had a teasing air. She wanted him to follow her, and knew that he would.

The level of desire in his blood climbed a few notches. He followed her into a square herb garden, with gravel paths bisecting geometrical beds of fragrant lavender and sage and oregano. She bent over a tall rosemary plant and buried her nose in its needles.

Of course his attention snapped immediately to the way her dress hugged the delicious curve of her behind and the graceful way she stood on one leg and extended the other slightly behind her as she leaned forward.

Alarm bells were ringing in his head. Sexual attraction was usually accompanied by danger of some sort. Every girl he even pecked on the cheek was immediately investigated by the media as a future princess. There was no question of having sex with them unless the utmost secrecy was maintained. His military background helped in matters of subterfuge, but the fact remained that usually when he wanted to kiss—or sleep with—a beautiful and intriguing woman, he had to tell himself no.

On the rare occasions when the stars aligned and he managed to secure total privacy, the moment was loaded and often quite magical. He'd even managed several actual relationships over the years, and had had the good luck to adore women who'd proved utterly discreet.

And here he was again, at the moment where he knew exactly what he wanted to do—climb every mountain in order to kiss Ariella Winthrop.

It was never as easy as that.

"You look more relaxed." Her entire demeanor had softened.

She looked up at him with a flirtatious sparkle in her eye. "I feel much better. I'm not sure why."

"Talking to me, of course. And breathing some fresh air doesn't hurt, either. You should come visit Whist Castle. It's my home in England where I go to get away from it all." And the perfect location for a secluded tryst.

Her eyes widened. "Oh, no. I couldn't." Then she laughed. "Of course. You're just being polite. People do tell me I take everything too seriously."

"I most certainly was not being polite. It would give us plenty of time to plan the fund-raiser for World Connect. In fact I might have to insist."

"And how exactly will you do that?" She crossed her arms over her chest. Which drew attention to the way her nipples pushed against the soft fabric of her dress.

"Perhaps I'll have the palace guards bundle you into a plane. It's primitive and high-tech at the same time."

"That may work in Europe, but you can't just shove American citizens into planes. We've started wars with less provocation than that." A smile danced around the corners of her mouth.

He pressed a finger to his lips. "Hmm. I suppose you're right. And you are the daughter of the president. I'll have to resort to more cunning means. A hand-engraved invitation, perhaps."

"I'm afraid I'm the queen of hand-engraved invitations. I've probably stuffed more than a million of those into envelopes at this point. You'll need a lot more than that to impress me."

He stepped forward, uncrossed her arms and took one

of her hands. Her fingers were cool, but heated inside his. "What exactly would it take?"

Heat pulsed between them for a solid second. He watched her pupils dilate and her lips part slightly. Then she snatched her hand back and hurried down the brick path. "I'm afraid I couldn't possibly come right now. We have a lot of events going on and I'm booked almost solid."

Now she was trying to run away from him. Could she know that only made him more eager and determined? He walked slowly, knowing that to stalk any creature you need calm and patience, so you don't spook it and lose your chance altogether. "My loss. I quite understand, though. I'm sure we can plan the fund-raiser over lunches and dinners here in D.C. Speaking of which, perhaps we can get back to breakfast? I suspect those brioche are holding up well and we can fumble a fresh pot of coffee together."

"That sounds perfect."

"Where have you been? I was trying to reach you all morning." Scarlet's voice exploded out of Ariella's phone as she collapsed onto her living room sofa. She'd only just arrived home from her morning with Simon and felt very topsy-turvy. "We have to make a decision on the courses for the DiVosta dinner by four this afternoon so they can source the lobster and crab."

Ariella drew in a silent breath, glad her friend and business partner couldn't see her right now. She was flushed and her eyes were glassy with overexcitement. "I'm sorry. I got…swept away." That was the truth, at least. "I thought they decided on the stone crab."

"They want you to make the final choice."

"Then I've just made it." She sat up. Gosh, she had so much to do. "Did the tablecloths arrive from Bali yet? I keep phoning DHL and they never seem to know what I'm talking about."

"Yup, they're here. And worth the wait, as they're absolutely stunning. Maybe I'll have one turned into a dress afterward. I ordered the cases of Dom Perignon to be delivered to the venue. Their butler swears he'll lock it all up for me so it won't be drunk before the event. Hey, are you still there?"

"Um, yeah. I'm here." Her thoughts wouldn't seem to cooperate. They kept filling up with visions of Simon's handsome and deliciously determined face. Could she really not tell the person she saw every day about her royal adventure? "I just had breakfast with Simon Worth."

"Breakfast? It's nearly three." Trust Scarlet to breeze right over the part about the prince. Raised in D.C.'s most elite circles, she was hard to impress.

"We had a lot to talk about."

"Francesca told me he approached you at last night's event." She sounded intrigued. "And you do have a lot in common. Both descended from heads of state, both lost their mother tragically young and both lamentably still single. Quick, tell me everything and I'll still have time to call about the stone crabs by four."

She laughed. "There isn't that much to tell. You pretty much summed it up. Except the single part. We didn't talk about that."

"But you did kiss."

"Not even a peck." She was a little disappointed about that. She'd braced herself for a decorous kiss when his driver dropped her off—the prince had accompanied her in the backseat, where they were hidden by tinted windows—but he'd simply held her hands for a moment, looked into her eyes and said goodbye. "He wanted to give me a pep talk. I think he's going back to England later this week. He was in D.C. to sign some international pact to stop journalists from using illegal means to dig into our business."

"He must be madly in love with you."

"Are you nuts?" The idea of Simon even lusting after her did something strange to her stomach. At first she hadn't been sure, but by the time he dropped her home she was feeling some pretty heady chemistry. Unless it was all in her head. "Why would he be interested in me?"

"Because you're brilliant, beautiful and fascinating. And now that your daddy is a head of state you're eligible to be a royal bride. Wow. Just think, DC Affairs' first royal wedding! Can we have it on the White House lawn? I think everything should be silver and ivory, with little royal crests engraved on the glasses."

"Your imagination is really running away with you. Being madly in love must be messing with your mind as none of that is even the slightest bit likely to happen."

"You're right. I'd imagine Simon would need to get married in England. A royal procession in the mall down to Buckingham Palace. You in yards of lace and tulle…"

"Stop! Now. I command you." Part of her wanted to laugh. The rest was horrified by how easily Scarlet's crazy vision came to life in her head. She must be losing her mind from all the stress she was under lately.

"Regally imperious already, I see."

"I think I have enough problems in my life without starting an affair with a prince."

"I don't know." Scarlet sighed. "That's the kind of problem most women would be happy to have."

"I don't think so. Sure, the idea of living in a castle and dressing in designer clothes and eating banquets all day might sound nice…."

"Don't forget the pet unicorn."

"But the reality of being a modern royal is very different. It's all smiling at opening ceremonies and photographers trying to get an unflattering picture of you in a bikini."

"Sad but true. And the queen is rather forbidding. I'm not sure I'd want her as my in-law."

"See? Being a royal bride is too much hassle. At the end of the president's time in office he'll go off to monitor elections in Turkmenistan and I'll slip quietly back into obscurity and maybe get myself a friendly cat for company." She realized she was pacing around her small apartment like a caged lion. She forced herself to sit on the sofa again.

"Only eight years to go." She laughed suddenly. "You're not going to believe this. Or maybe you are. This headline just popped up on my screen: *Prince Simon to extend fundraising trip in D.C.* I told you he's besotted."

Ariella realized she'd sprung to her feet again. "He totally is not. He wants to plan a fund-raiser for his charity, World Connect."

"Fabulous! I can't wait to add his name to our client list."

"I knew you'd say that." She smiled. Then frowned. "I mentioned doing an outdoor concert, and soon, so it'll be a lot of work."

"Work? We love work." Scarlet sounded pleased. "Did you talk about dates?"

"He's flexible, so we can pick a date when the perfect venue is available. The more publicity, the better." It was so odd to be courting publicity at work and shrinking from it at home. "I need to go to the gym."

"Why? You're already perfect."

To work off some adrenaline so I don't burst into flames. "It helps give me energy. And the way business is booming I need all the energy I can get."

"Well, congratulations on roping the prince into a party.

Go pump some iron, lady, and I'll see you in the office tomorrow."

In the old days, oh, six months ago, before her life exploded, she would have gone for a quiet jog around leafy Georgetown and maybe down to the Capitol. Now that reporters sniffed around her heels, she had to work up a sweat in the privacy of a high-security gym next to well-toned congresswomen and senators, just to preserve some privacy. Wearing headphones and focused on their fitness goals, they left her in peace. Something she'd had very little of lately.

And now Simon Worth had decided to stay in D.C.

Three

How did a prince ask a girl on a date? The question kept Ariella awake late that night. The days of messengers delivering quill-penned invitations were over. Did His Majesty email it? Or was a discreet phone call possible in this age of rampant wiretapping?

She cursed herself for wondering. If Simon called her again it would be a simple business meeting to plan his party. If he even still intended to do the fund-raiser. He probably wouldn't want to see her again after she'd turned down his invitation to visit him in England. Which would be perfect, since the last thing she needed was more drama in her life.

But her question was answered when he showed up on her doorstep, totally undisguised and unannounced.

"Hi." She managed, after a moment of rather stunned silence. "Would you like to come in?"

"Thank you." His tall and broad form made her eighteenth-century doorway look small.

She glanced nervously around. Thank heaven she was a neat freak and had just put away her laundry. It was Saturday around noon and she'd been trying to decide whether to spend her afternoon looking at paintings in a museum or fondling interesting objects at a flea market. Since she hadn't made up her mind (frigid air conditioning versus sticky D.C. summer humidity) she was dressed in jeans and a spaghetti-strap tank top. Not exactly what you'd don if you expected a prince to stop by.

"Your house is lovely."

"Thanks. I only have the first floor. I rent it from the couple who own the upstairs. They have a separate entrance around the side. I do like it, though." She was babbling. He was only being polite. Her tiny and rather overstuffed space must have seemed quaint and eccentric to him. "Do sit down. How did you know I'd be here?"

"I didn't." He eased himself into her cream loveseat. "Do you live alone?"

"Yes. I keep such crazy hours and really need my sleep when I finally have time for it. I tried living with roommates but it never worked out for long."

"So all of these interesting things are yours?" He picked up a pocket-size nineteenth-century brass telescope she'd scored at an estate sale in Virginia.

"I'm afraid so. You can see I love to collect interesting trinkets."

He expertly opened the piece and trained it out the window, then glanced up and his eyes met hers. Her breath stuck at the bottom of her lungs for a moment. How did he have that effect on her? She dealt with celebrities and big shots all day long and had a strict policy of treating them like the ordinary people that they were, if you ignored all those extra zeros in their bank accounts. She'd worked with royals from Sweden, Monaco and Saudi Arabia, among others, and hadn't given a second thought to their supposedly blue blood. But somehow around Simon Worth she felt lightheaded and tongue tied as a naive schoolgirl.

"I can see you have good taste. I've grown up surrounded by fine things, and never had to exert myself to acquire any. It looks as if you've done the work of three hundred years of collectors." He picked up a hand-painted miniature of a lady and her poodle.

"Isn't she sweet? A client from England gave her to me to thank me for planning her wedding in Maryland. In a way I suppose I've stolen her from among your national treasures."

"Perhaps she's simply traveling for a while." His smile melted a little piece of her. "Objects might get restless, just as people do."

She laughed. "I sometimes wonder how they feel about being bought or sold or traded to a new person. I know that inanimate objects aren't supposed to have feelings, but they must carry some energy from the people and places they've been before."

"I know places can have their own spirit. My home at Whist Castle practically bustles with it." He leaned forward, his eyes sparkling. "If places can have a feeling, why not things as well?"

"I'm glad you don't think I'm a nut. I do enjoy seeking out little treasures. In fact I was thinking of ducking past any photographers and doing that this afternoon at the Eastern Market."

"Perhaps we could go together." He said it quite calmly, as if it wasn't the most outlandish idea she'd every heard.

"But if people see us together…they might talk."

"About what?" He leaned back, face calmly pleasant.

Suddenly she felt like an idiot for suggesting that people might gossip about a romance between them. Obviously that existed only in her own mind. What would a British royal be doing with her? "I'm being paranoid again. I probably think the press cares far more about me than they actually do."

"If anyone asks, we can tell them you're helping me source interesting items for a fund-raiser we're planning." He picked a pair of tiny silver sewing scissors and snipped the air with them.

"The outdoor concert?"

"A mad hatter's tea party, perhaps?" A cute dimple appeared in his left cheek. "People do expect us Brits to be eccentric, after all. You won't actually need a reasonable explanation."

"Well, in that case, let's go."

"Is there another way out of here?" He'd risen to his feet and offered his hand to her.

"You mean, besides the front door?"

He nodded. "I'm afraid I was spotted arriving here."

"The short guy with the ponytail?"

"The very same."

"Ugh. He's freelance and has sold pictures of me to at least three different papers. One was a picture of me carrying two grocery bags, and somehow he managed to bribe the cashier into handing over my receipt so everyone could learn what brand of aspirin I prefer. And there isn't another way out. I guess you'll have to stay here forever."

Her hand heated inside his as he helped her to her feet. He didn't look at all put out by either the photographer or the prospect of spending the rest of his life in Apt. 1A.

"I do hate to assist these lowlifes in their trade. We'll leave separately so there's no picture. I'll leave first in my car, you leave five minutes later and walk around the

block. I'll have a blue Mercedes meet you in front of the
Mixto restaurant."

"Goodness, I feel like I'm in a James Bond film." He
must have planned this. Which sent sparkles of excitement
and alarm coursing through her.

"Don't worry. I have years of experience in dodging
these leeches. I think of it as an entertaining challenge."

"I'm game. What should I bring?"

"Just yourself."

Simon left via the front door and she rushed to the window, where she saw him get into a waiting silver SUV,
which pulled away. She took a couple of minutes to fix her
hair and face, and put on a light blouse and some boots,
then she headed out in the opposite direction, toward the
tiny restaurant as if she was just on her way to the local
deli. She didn't cast a glance at the depressing figure in
his dull green jacket and faded black baseball hat, though
she felt his eyes trained on her.

Simon was right. As long as they weren't seen together,
there was no picture to sell. The whole world knew he
was in D.C. Everyone was already tired of pictures of her
leaving for work and coming back home again. No picture, no story.

A tiny ripple of triumph put a spring in her step as she
rounded the corner and spotted a blue Mercedes idling
double-parked halfway down the block. The car's rear
door opened and she saw Simon's reassuring face. Feeling like a ninja, she climbed in, and they cruised off down
the block. Her heart was pounding, and she wasn't sure
if it was because of all the subterfuge, or being so close
to Simon again.

"He didn't follow you."

"Nope. He rarely does. I think he's too lazy. Just snaps
a couple of pictures a day and hopes a story will break

so he can sell them. So far his biggest coup is the day I wore my Montana Grizzlies T-shirt. They plastered that picture all over the papers right as the story about my father was breaking, as if it was proof I was his daughter or something."

"Once you're in the public eye people read into your every move. You learn to laugh at it."

Up close like this she could see a slight haze of stubble on his jaw. She wondered what it would feel like against her cheek, and felt her breath quicken. She tugged her gaze out the window, where D.C. scrolled by. "We're going in the opposite direction from the market."

"My driver knows some antique shops in Maryland. We'll enjoy more privacy there." He leaned back against the seat, shirt stretching over his broad chest. "And I very much doubt any photographers will find us."

Was this a date? It certainly felt like one. There hadn't been any real mention of the event they were supposedly planning. And it wasn't exactly professional of him to show up on her doorstep without warning. "Do you whisk women off in cars on a regular basis?"

He shot her a sideways glance. "No, I don't."

Her chest swelled a little. So she was special? She wondered if he'd prolonged his trip to see more of her. Then chastised herself for having such a vain thought. She'd better steer this conversation in a business direction. "I told Scarlet about your plans for the fund-raiser and she's going to start work on finding the venue. How are your other fund-raising efforts going?"

"That's an abrupt change of subject." His tawny eyes glittered with humor. "And I'm forced to confess I haven't made much headway. Every time I try talking about education in Africa, people's eyes glaze over and they ask about my latest climbing expedition. I'm afraid I can never resist talking about climbing."

"You need to make your cause sexier." Uh-oh. Just saying the word caused the temperature in the car to rise a degree or two.

He cocked a brow. "Sexy? How do I do that?"

"You focus on the elements of your organization that make people feel good about themselves. For example, with breast cancer, pink ribbons make people think about triumph and recovery. That makes them want to get out their wallets a lot more than lectures about incredible new discoveries in small cell cancer treatments. For a party I'd have pink pearls and pink roses and pink champagne. They don't have anything at all to do with cancer, but they make people feel happy about embracing the cause."

Forehead furrowed, he looked intrigued. "So you think I need to rebrand my charity?"

"I don't really know enough about it. Do you have a brand or logo or imagery you use often?"

He made a wry expression. "Not at all. We simply print the name in blue on white paper. I'm beginning to see what you mean."

"So what excites you the most about what your organization does?"

He frowned for a moment and looked straight ahead, then turned to her. "Including people in the conversation about our future. Giving them access to technology that makes them part of our world and a way to be heard in it."

"That's sexy. And big technology companies are a nice target market for your fund-raising. You'd certainly be speaking their language. How about 'join the conversation' as your marketing ploy, so you're inviting everyone to be part of the future you imagine."

He stared at her. "I like the way your mind works."

She shrugged. "I brainstorm this kind of stuff all the time."

"I had no idea party planning was so involved. I thought it was all choosing napkins and printing invitations."

"That's the easy part. The hard part is making each event stand out from the thousands of others taking place during the year. In your case, people would expect a prince to have a very exclusive, private dinner, so an outdoor concert rather takes people by surprise. It also creates the sense of inclusion that your charity is all about. In addition to the event's raising money from ticket sales, it'll get people talking and that will generate additional donations and bring in people who want to help."

He still stared right at her, and she could almost hear his brain moving a million miles a minute. "Where have you been all my life?"

A smile crept across her mouth. "Read the papers. You can learn more about my past than I can even remember."

He laughed. "I know that feeling. I think we have a lot in common."

How could she feel so comfortable talking to this man from one of the great royal houses of Europe? Well, she'd never been too impressed by royalty. That probably helped in situations like this.

"That's probably why I've appeared in your life to help you cope with it."

"Destiny at work." She swallowed. Did she really believe that some mysterious workings of fate had brought her and Simon together?

No. They were simply going to spend a pleasant afternoon looking at antiques. They'd put together a fun concert that would get people talking about World Connect. Then he'd go back to England and she'd get on with whatever her life was going to be.

What about the chemistry crackling between them right now in the back of the car? What about the way her skin heated when he leaned toward her, or her stomach swirled with strange sensations when he fixed her with that thoughtful gaze?

She was going to ignore that. So was he. No one was going to do anything they might regret. They were both grownups and far too sensible for that.

What a relief.

The driver took them to a little town called Danes Mills, where he parked behind a quaint restaurant that reminded Ariella of a British pub. The entire main street appeared to be upscale antique shops, with maybe a gift shop or bookstore for variety. Simon helped her from the car while the driver held the door. It was all very formal and majestic and made her feel like a princess. Which she wasn't.

People did turn to look at them. She wasn't sure if she imagined the whispers. While she knew people thought she was pretty, she didn't have the kind of looks that demanded attention. In fact she considered herself a nondescript brunette, so she didn't usually have to worry about standing out from the crowd. People recognized Simon, though. He was tall and broad and attracted admiration without even trying. They'd probably stare at him even if he wasn't a well-known prince. Maybe they were turning to look at him for the same reasons she wanted to—because he was handsome and his smile could melt an iceberg.

In the first store they looked through some old paintings and drawings, all rather in need of restoration, and admired a painted cupboard. In the second, Ariella became entranced by a group of tiny snuff boxes. She loved to open them and find the tobacco smell still there, as if the owner had just finished the last pinch.

"Which is your favorite?"

"I'm not sure." She pressed a finger to her lips. "The silver one has such delicate engraving, and I love the colors on this enameled one. But I think I like this black one best." She picked up a shiny black box. She wasn't even sure what it was made from. Possibly something insubstantial like papier-mâché. It had a delicate painting of a girl standing under a tree that must have been painted with the world's tiniest brush.

He took it from her, which surprised her. She grew even more surprised when he handed it to the shop owner—who had to be roused from some old books he was sorting through—and paid for it. After the shopkeeper had wrapped it in tissue and deposited it in a tiny brown paper shopping bag, Simon handed it back to her. "For you."

She blinked. "I didn't mean for you to buy it."

"I know. I wanted to."

"I don't think a man has ever given me a snuff box before." She kept her voice hushed, not wanting to convey any impression of romance to the store owner.

"You can't accuse me of being clichéd, at least." That infectious smile again. She found her own mouth curving up. Surely there was no harm in the gift. It wasn't terribly expensive, just a sweet gesture. "I notice you like miniature paintings. I saw several at your flat." He opened the shop door and they stepped out into the sunlight.

"I do. A perfect world in microcosm. And just for one person at a time to look at and enjoy. Maybe it's the opposite of my parties where everyone must have a good time all at once."

"You keep giving me a new perspective on things I take for granted." He smiled. "Our driver, David, tells me there's a state park near here. What do you say we take a picnic lunch there?"

"That sounds great."

It was lucky she agreed because David had already been given orders somehow. The car was piled high with white deli bags and a newly bought cooler containing chilled drinks. She was so used to creating fairy-tale meals for other people that it was rather bizarre to have someone else pulling all the strings. All she had to do was enjoy.

David drove them into the park, past several battlefield sites, to the bank of a winding river. He spread a pretty French provincial patterned cloth—which must have been a rather expensive purchase back in Danes Mill—and unpacked the deli bags filled with gourmet salads.

Ariella settled onto the cloth and Simon poured her a sparkling glass of champagne. "I don't think I've ever been this pampered." They helped themselves to a warm tortellini salad and a crisp slaw of carrot and beetroot with a sesame seed dressing.

"You deserve it. You've been under a lot of pressure lately and it's time for you to let off some steam."

She sighed, and they sipped their champagne. Not surprisingly, it was very good. "Is your life like this every day?"

"If only." That intoxicating smile again. "My life is usually far more prosaic."

The driver had tactfully vanished, and they were all alone beside the rushing stream. Tiny yellow flowers bloomed along the banks, and the rich mossy smell of the trees and the soil soothed her frazzled nerves. "I used to wish my life would go back to normal, but if this is the new normal, I'm not complaining." She looked up at him and spoke with sudden conviction. "And I intend to meet both my birth parents." Her confidence had grown since she met Simon. "It's too big an opportunity to waste. Sure, I'm scared, but the potential reward is worth the risk."

"Fantastic. I'm glad you've come to that conclusion. I thought you would. Have you managed to make contact with your mother?"

"I wrote to her but I haven't heard back yet. It's so odd that I don't even know what she looks like. All I've seen is her high school yearbook photo from the year she got pregnant with me."

"What did she look like then?"

"Young, sweet, sort of shy. She had a terrible hairstyle. It was the 1980s after all."

He laughed. "I bet she's a lot more nervous than you are."

"She has good reason to be apprehensive. She's the only one who could be accused of doing anything wrong here. She says she didn't tell my father about me because she didn't want to prevent him from going off to college, but surely he could have made his own decisions about how to handle it. After all, if he can manage to become president of the United States, I think he could probably handle supporting a family while taking his classes."

"You're right. I'd be devastated if I got a girl pregnant and she didn't tell me."

Her eyes widened. Sometimes Simon was shockingly frank. He hadn't even looked up from his plate, and was busy munching on some arugula. "Is that something you have to worry about a lot? I mean, any child you had would be in line to the throne."

"Believe me, I've heard that over and over again since I was old enough to understand. My grandmother, the queen, would prefer that none of us date at all. If she had her own way we'd all be safely tucked away in arranged marriages by age twenty."

"Have they tried to pair you up with anyone?"

"Oh, it never stops." His eyes were smiling. "They're

constantly digging up blushing blue-blood virgins and inviting them to palace tea parties."

"But so far none of them has piqued your interest." She nibbled on a crisp green bean.

"Oh, several of them have piqued my interest." He chuckled. "But not in the way Grandmama was hoping, I'm afraid. And luckily, I haven't gotten any of them pregnant, either."

"You're shocking me."

"Why? You don't think a prince has feelings like any other man?"

"Well…" She bit her lip. "Of course I know you do, it's just…"

"You can't believe I'm talking about it out loud when I should be much more subtle and surreptitious?" He raised a brow. His dimple was showing. "My family hates how blunt I am. I can't stand beating around the bush. Heaven knows I do enough of it when I'm out in public, so in private I prefer to speak my mind. Don't be too shocked."

"I'll try not to be." She smiled. His candor was refreshing. He was so different from what she'd expected. It was disarming and intriguing and she had a hard time maintaining her own cool reserve around him.

"How did we start talking about me? I was asking about your mother. Didn't you say she lives in Ireland?"

"When she wrote to me there was an address on the inside of the letter. A post office box in Kilkenney, Ireland. She must have rented it so no one would find out where she lived. I haven't told anyone she wrote to me, except my closest friends. I told her I'd like to meet her and I'm willing to travel to Ireland if she needs me to."

"How will you do that without taking the international press corps with you?"

"I'm cunning when I need to be." She smiled mysteriously. "And it's always a good idea to do some location scouting for a big wedding, or something."

"Your profession lends itself to international travel. I'm forced by circumstance to do most of my travel in the British Commonwealth."

"The countries that were in the former empire?"

"Exactly. Lucky thing it was big and had so many interesting countries." He grinned, looking disarmingly boyish. "How did your mother end up in Ireland, anyway? I thought she was from Montana."

"I don't entirely know. I think she met an Irish man after she gave me up for adoption. Hopefully I'll find out the details once we meet."

"I'm sure she's missed you far more than you know."

She drew in a shaky breath. "I don't know. She might have other children. She didn't say. She didn't mention anything about wanting to meet me."

"She's probably nervous that you don't want to meet her. She did abandon you, after all."

"I told her in my letter that I have no hard feelings and that I had the best childhood anyone could want. I said it would mean so much to me if I could meet her."

"Has she responded?"

"Not yet." A sudden chill made her shiver. She put down her plate. "What if she doesn't?"

He smiled. "She will. I can feel it."

"Psychic, are you?" She sipped her champagne. The slight buzz it gave her was soothing, given the tense topic of conversation. "I wish I had your confidence."

"You do. You just don't know it yet." He sipped his champagne. "Let's see how cold this water is." He stood and walked to the bank, where the river rushed by only about a foot below. Before she had time to join him, he'd removed his shoes and socks, rolled up the leg of his dark slacks, and slid his feet into the water. "Cold."

"Is it really? It must be from an underground spring." The summer afternoon was downright balmy. Her own toes itched to dip into the sparkling depths. She sat on the bank next to him and slipped off her shoes. Her jeans were tight-fitting so she could barely roll them up at all, but she managed to get them above her ankles. Then she dangled her feet down the bank until the water lapped against her toes. "Ooh, that feels good."

Tentative, she slid her feet beneath the surface. The chill of the water contrasted with the warm throb of intimacy that pulsed between them, helped by the glass of champagne. Her shoulder bumped gently against his, then she felt his arm slide around her waist. It felt as natural as the cool clear water splashing against her ankles.

Now his torso almost touched hers, and they seemed to be growing closer by slow degrees. His rich masculine scent tugged at her senses. She could see the pale stubble on his chin, and the sparkle of light in his eyes—they were hazel up close—and then she couldn't see at all because her eyes shut and she found herself kissing him.

Four

The daylight dazzled unpleasantly as Simon opened his eyes. He'd had to tug himself away from kissing Ariella, and the taste of her lingered on his tongue, forbidden and delicious. She looked unbearably beautiful, sitting there on the bank, her eyes dark with desire and the forgotten cuffs of her jeans darkening in the water.

"We shouldn't have done that." Her voice was barely a whisper.

"I beg to differ." His entire body growled at him to do a lot more with this lovely woman. He let his hand wander into her long, dark hair. "Mostly because I don't think we had any choice."

"You always have a choice." One neat brow lifted slightly. He could feel her shrink back from him.

"Theoretically, I suppose. But some things are just irresistible." Her raspberry-tinted lips were among those things, and he lowered his lips toward them again. But this time she hesitated. "Simon, I really don't think this is sensible."

"Why not?"

"Uh…because your grandmother would be horrified."

"Nonsense." He stroked her hair. She stiffened slightly, as if she wanted to resist, but he saw his own desire reflected in her eyes. "I'm sure she'd adore you." He really didn't want to think about the queen right now. He didn't want to think about anyone but Ariella. He could deal with everyone else later.

Ariella shivered slightly, as anticipation rose in the air. If she didn't want to kiss him she could have leapt to her feet and darted back to the car. But she hadn't.

He waited for her to come to him, and she did. Her mouth rose to meet his and they sank deep into another sensual kiss. He was almost breathless when they finally broke again.

"Uh-oh." Her cheeks were flushed. "I couldn't help that kiss at all." She'd twisted into his embrace, and her nipples peaked against her T-shirt and the bra underneath it.

"See? Sometimes you just don't have a choice."

Desire made his thoughts spin. He certainly hadn't had enough champagne to feel this tipsy. He stroked the silky skin of her arm, wishing he could bare other parts of her. But he could still resist doing that—for now. "Sometimes you have to give in to forces more powerful than a mere human."

"You're not a mere human, you're a prince." She winked.

He loved how she seemed totally natural with him, not affected or intimidated at all. "Even royalty are subject to the whims of passion." He traced her cheekbone with his thumb. "Which can be quite inconvenient at times."

She glanced about nervously. "I hope there aren't any photographers hiding in the bushes."

"I've learned to go to places that would never occur to them. Why would a man with a large rural estate go to a popular state park?"

"Because it has this cool stream with yellow wildflowers growing along its banks." Her slender fingers touched the petals of a flower. How he'd like to feel them running over his skin, or through his hair.

"That is why I come, but they don't think like that. They expect me to go to expensive restaurants and exclusive gatherings. Of course I do that as well, it's my job, but I've become quite skilled at doing the unexpected when I'm off duty. I always have my driver study natural areas near wherever I'm traveling. A man can withstand a lot more dreary meetings around a conference table if he knows there's a bracing kayak trip waiting for him at the end of it."

"Very cunning, and keeps you fit, too."

"And sane. At least as sane as I'm going to be." He grinned. He didn't feel terribly sane right now. He wanted to do all kinds of things that weren't sensible at all, especially not when you did them with a girl who was already in the public eye and who didn't fit the queen's narrow ideas of what constituted a suitable consort.

But no one, including the queen, was going to keep him from bedding the lovely Ariella.

"I'd really better get back to D.C. I have a busy week to plan for."

Again he felt her pulling away from him. He stood and helped her to his feet. Landing a kiss on Ariella's lovely mouth was enough excitement for today. Their time together had only confirmed his intuition that she was no ordinary woman. He could pace himself and wait for the right moment to claim his prize.

"I need to do some planning myself. Now that I'm staying in D.C. a while longer I want to make sure I make the most of the opportunity." They walked back to the pretty clearing where they'd had their picnic. "I'd better think about who I want to wine and dine while I'm here—other than you, of course."

She bit her lip as they packed the remains of lunch back into the bags. He could see she still felt misgivings about their kiss. It was hard not to come on too strong with her when he wanted to throw her over his shoulder and take her back to his hotel.

Instead he helped her into the car and returned her discreetly to a location two blocks away from her apartment. From there she walked home alone, chin lifted in sweet defiance against anyone who wanted to know her business.

He sank back against the back seat of the car and let out a long breath. Ariella Winthrop. Something about her had grabbed him hard. He tried to distract himself by pulling his phone out of his pocket. He'd had it turned off all day. A message from his younger brother Henry seemed like the perfect diversion, so he punched his number.

"Are you really staying over there for another week?" His brother's incredulous voice made him smile.

"At least a week and with good reason."

"Let me guess, the reason has long legs and a toothy American smile."

Simon reached forward and closed the partition between him and the driver. "There's nothing toothy about her smile," he retorted, thinking about her lovely mouth.

"I knew it."

"You knew nothing of the sort. I'm here to raise public awareness of World Connect. I have big plans. We're going to hold an outdoor concert here in D.C."

"Nice. But let me guess—she's involved somehow."

"She might be." Was he really so predictable?

Henry laughed. "Don't let Grandma find out about it."

"Why not?" He bristled.

"She'd have a fit about you dating anyone who isn't marriage material. Remember that last lecture she gave you about it being time to settle down. She's got your wedding all planned and all you have to do is show up."

He growled. "I'm not marrying anyone."

"You'll have to sooner or later. You're next, big brother."

"Why don't you worry about your own love life, instead of mine? I suppose I'm lucky that the scandalous state of your affairs distracts attention from mine."

"That's why I need you to get married and draw the spotlight off me for a while." Henry had been photographed in compromising situations several times over the last year. "Why can't you make them all happy so I can keep on having fun?"

"That might actually be possible." He watched D.C. pass by his window. "I've met someone who could well be the one."

"You're not serious."

"Do I joke around?"

"Yes, often."

"Then you can just assume I'm jesting."

"An American girl?"

"The president's newly discovered daughter, Ariella, no less." He felt a bit sheepish using her media handle to describe her to his own brother. "She's quite something."

"Don't even think about it."

"I'm afraid it's gone well beyond thinking." He smiled as memories of their kiss heated his blood.

"Gran will need sedation. And can you imagine Uncle Derek's reaction?"

"I'll try not to." He shook his head. Their mother's brother took a keen interest in meddling in their affairs and throwing up obstacles at every turn. "If only he'd been born royal he wouldn't have to try so hard to be more royal than the rest of us."

"You do realize you can't marry an American."

"Why not? In the old days we nearly always married into royal families from other countries."

"Exactly. Married into royal families. You need a nice Swedish princess, or one from Monaco or Spain."

He shoved aside an annoying twinge of misgiving. "I'd say that the president's daughter is American royalty."

Henry laughed. "For four years, maybe eight, but I don't think our grandmother will see it that way."

"I'm sure she'll love Ariella once she meets her." Who wouldn't? And in his experience, people usually got over their prejudices once you gave them half a chance.

"Oh dear, you sound dangerously serious. And I know how bullheaded you are once you get going."

"I'm not bullheaded, I just do what I think is right."

Henry laughed. "So you do. I just hope poor Ariella knows what she's in for."

Ariella was attempting to butter toast while checking messages on her phone, when she saw seven messages in a row from Scarlet that must have come in while she was at the gym. She put down the butter knife and punched in Scarlet's number.

"You're not going to believe this." Scarlet was breathless with excitement.

"Try me." She could barely believe anything that happened to her lately. Every time she thought about that kiss, she was assaulted by a rush of starry-eyed excitement and a burst of salty regret. What had they started?

"We've been asked to put in a bid on the Duke of Buckingham's wedding. In England!"

"That's great." Her mind immediately started whirling with plans for a side-trip to Ireland to find her mother.

"Could you sound a bit more excited?"

"I am, really."

"You know how we're trying to branch out into Europe. This will be our fifth party over there. I'd say this is some kind of landmark. And now that you're intimate with royalty, we have an excellent chance of being chosen to plan the event."

"You're not going to say anything about me, are you?" Her adrenaline spiked.

"Why? Is there something going on that's secret?" Scarlet's voice grew hushed with anticipation.

Could she lie to Scarlet, her close friend and business partner? She sucked in a breath and braced herself. "I kissed him."

"Ohmygod. You kissed Prince Simon?"

The truth was out. She strode across her apartment, trying to stay calm. "I still can't believe it happened, but it did. Can I swear you to secrecy?"

"My lips are sealed. So you guys have a…a thing going?"

"I don't know what we have going, but I'm seeing him for dinner tomorrow." Already her heart fluttered with anticipation—and fear of where this would lead.

"You're dating a prince. Wow. It's a crying shame that I can't put out a PR release about it. Can you imagine how much we could raise our prices if people knew you were practically a princess?"

"Would you stop! I'm not practically anything, except late for work."

"You're totally going to London to pitch this."

"Fine. Can I eat my toast now and we'll talk when I come into the office?"

"Oh, okay. Make me wait for details. You're cruel like that. I'll see you in a few."

Ariella put the phone down and tried to distract herself by spreading some more butter. She only liked real butter but it was annoying to wait for it to melt enough to spread. She unscrewed the lid of her favorite organic apricot jam, and the phone rang again. What now? It wasn't even eight-fifteen in the morning yet.

She glanced at the number. Unavailable. Frowning, she picked up the phone. "Hello."

"Is that Ariella?" She didn't recognize the voice. It sounded very far away.

"This is Ariella."

"Oh, hello." The line crackled with static.

"Who's this?" She was growing impatient, trying to spread with one hand.

"It's your, it's…Eleanor. Eleanor Daly."

Her mother. Her breath caught in her throat and she dropped the knife with a clatter and gripped the phone tighter. "I'm so glad you called. Thank you so much for writing to me. You have no idea how much that letter meant." So many thoughts unfolded in her brain and she tried not to panic.

"The agency didn't think it was a good idea for me to contact you when you were a child. They wouldn't tell me who adopted you. I never stopped thinking about you. Never."

The emotion in her mother's voice made her chest constrict. "I've always wanted to meet you. Could we get together?" She spoke fast, afraid that at any minute the call would drop and she'd lose the fragile new connection.

"I live in Ireland."

Ariella's brain was racing, as she tried to mentally organize the long-awaited meeting with her birth mother. "I have to come to England soon for work. Would it be okay if I came to visit you in Ireland?" The words rushed out, and suddenly she was terrified Eleanor would say no.

Why did she think of her as Eleanor and not her mother? Of course she wasn't "Mom" to her. That title would always be held by the woman who'd raised her and who she still missed every day. But she wanted to meet Eleanor so much it was a dull ache inside her all the time now.

After a long pause, Eleanor spoke again. "I'm in a remote rural area. Perhaps I could come to England to visit you while you're there?"

"I'd like that very much." Exhilaration roared through her and her hands started shaking, causing her to press the phone against her ear. "I don't know the exact dates I'll be there yet. What works for you?"

"Oh, anything, really. I'm widowed now, and I do babysitting for income so I don't have any real commitments." Eleanor suddenly sounded more relaxed.

"I can't wait to meet you. It doesn't seem fair that I don't know what you look like. You can see pictures of me in the papers all the time."

She laughed. "I'm afraid I'm not very glamorous. I probably look like a typical Irish housewife. I've lived in Ireland since the year after I…had you. I haven't been back to the States since. I was trying so hard to run away from everything. From you and Ted and the mess I'd gotten myself into."

"I'm so glad you wrote to me."

"It was a hard letter to write. I knew I had to reach out

to you and I didn't know how. I was afraid. I am afraid. I know everyone thinks I made the wrong choices back then and I..." Her voice trailed off.

"You made the choices you had to make. No one blames you for them."

"There wasn't a day where I didn't think of you and wonder what you were doing right at that moment."

"I had a great childhood." She couldn't believe she was finally having this conversation she'd waited so long for.

"I'm so happy to hear that." She could hear tears in her mother's voice. "I did worry. I tried to imagine that you were being well taken care of and were happy."

"I could show you photos if you'd like. My dad was an avid photographer and there are really far too many of them." Then she wondered if she'd said the wrong thing. Would Eleanor find it painful to see all this evidence of someone else raising her child?

"I'd like that very much." Emotion heightened the pitch of her voice. "I've missed so much. I never did have another child. You're my only one."

She couldn't believe she was actually talking to her mother after all these years. So many questions flooded her mind. Things she'd always wanted to know. "Do you have brown hair?"

"I do, though I admit to coloring it now to cover some gray. And I can see you have my green eyes."

"Those are from you? People have always asked me about them. Green eyes are quite unusual. I wonder what other characteristics we share? Oh, I wish I could leave for the airport right now."

"I'm so glad I'll finally meet you after all these years. I do feel terrible guilt about what happened. That poor Ted never knew he had a beautiful daughter growing up all that time. I don't think I'll ever forgive myself for that. Have the two of you become close now?"

She hesitated. "Actually I haven't met him yet. Since he's the president he's surrounded by all sorts of high security and no one entirely believed the story that I'm his daughter until the DNA test results came out. I don't think the White House knows quite what to do with me."

She rambled on. "And I suppose he's busy running the country. And dealing with that mess in the Middle East. They're thinking of sending troops." Every time she watched the news now she felt each domestic and international event a bit more keenly, knowing that her own flesh and blood had to make decisions about how to handle each crisis.

"Oh, I just thought that since you were both in Washington…"

She shoved a hand through her hair and tried to keep her embarrassment out of her voice. "We're going to meet very soon. ANS is arranging a televised special and we're going to appear on camera together." She wanted to sound happy and excited, not terrified.

"You won't tell anyone that we're going to meet, though, right?" Eleanor's voice had shrunk again.

"I promise I won't tell a soul. Is it okay if I call you sometime?" She'd already scribbled down the number, afraid it might disappear into the recesses of her phone or get accidentally deleted.

"I'd like that very much."

They ended the phone call with much excitement about the planned meeting. Ariella then managed to wolf down the toast and dash to work before her first appointment, adrenaline pounding in her veins like a dangerous drug. The receptionist handed her a message that Francesca wanted to chat about the upcoming ANS special that would bring her together with her famous father.

"It's lucky I thrive on being busy," she muttered to herself, as she opened the door to her office. She had umpteen phone calls to make about events happening this week, and now her mind was being tugged between the prospect of meeting her mother, doing a TV show with her father and, of course, seeing Simon again. There was way too much going on for everything to work out smoothly. That was something she'd learned early on in her years as an event planner. Too many balls in the air meant broken pieces on the floor, and soon.

But which ball would crash first?

On the evening of her date with Simon she left work early so she'd have time for a shower. She was about to climb in and wash her hair when she remembered she'd run out of conditioner. Great. Frizzy hair for her dinner with a prince. She'd have to head to the deli around the corner and pick some up.

She tied up her hair and put on jeans and a jacket. There was no more running to the store in shorts and a tank top now that reporters lurked in every crevice.

She strode into the shop and picked up a bottle of some harmless-looking generic conditioner—the store didn't carry her rather esoteric favorite—and marched up to the counter, fishing in her pocket for cash. A magazine behind the counter caught her eye. *Royal Watch* was the title, emblazoned in yellow letters.

Simon's gorgeous face almost totally filled the front cover. The rest of it, unfortunately, was hogged by the shiny, overly made-up face of a young blonde woman pressing her cheek against his. A young woman who was most decidedly not Ariella Winthrop.

"Two ninety-nine." The cashier's voice tugged her back to the present.

She handed him a twenty. "And I'll take that magazine, too." Her voice came out hoarse. She pointed at *Royal Watch*. "Research for work." Because of course she was just buying it to see if there was any information about what the Duke of Buckingham might want for his wedding decorations. Yeah. That was it.

She hurried back to her apartment with the magazine rolled tightly. She certainly didn't need any press coverage of her buying *Royal Watch*. Once inside she locked the door and walked slowly to the kitchen counter, now almost afraid to look at the cover again. Was she jealous? She'd only just met Simon. He must have an entire history of romances that had nothing to do with his feelings for her.

She risked another glance at the girl on the cover. Blue eyes, heavily outlined with dark eyeliner. The text over the photo said *Prince Simon Engaged!*

She frowned. He couldn't be in love with someone else and kissing her—could he? She flipped to the "article," which consisted of two paragraphs accompanied by a lot more pictures. All the photos appeared to be from the same outdoor sporting event—some kind of horse race—with all the women in big hats.

The article said that Lady Sophia Alnwick and Prince Simon had told their closest friends of their planned engagement, and that the queen was thrilled to welcome her new daughter-in-law into the family.

How come she hadn't seen any of this in the more mainstream press? Prince Simon wasn't as much in the public eye as his older brother, who was heir to the throne, but the entertainment press still picked up on stories about him quite often. Could *Royal Watch* simply have made it up?

Apart from the cover picture where they appeared to be cheek to cheek, they didn't look that intimate. Still…

She showered and dressed with considerably less excitement and more trepidation than she'd been feeling before she saw *Royal Watch*. How could she bring this up without seeming like a jealous harpy? On the other hand, she certainly didn't want to kiss a man who was engaged—even unofficially—to another woman.

When Simon's driver opened the rear door of the car thirty minutes later, she was surprised to find it empty. Did she now expect one of the crowned heads of Europe to arrive in person to pick her up? She was definitely getting a big head.

The car slid through the more exclusive streets of the city. She had no idea where they were going, but somehow it seemed embarrassing to admit it to the driver, so she didn't ask. Before long, they pulled up in front of a classical façade. The driver opened the door and she stepped out. The building looked grand and impersonal, like an embassy or an exclusive law office. She walked up the front steps and a suited man opened the door and murmured "Good evening." Still no sign of Simon. If her life wasn't so unpredictable and over the top already she'd probably be growing alarmed by now.

"Ariella." His deep, smooth voice called from down a marbled hallway. Immediately her body heat rose.

He walked up to her and kissed her softly on the lips. *Who's Sophia Alnwick?* she wanted to ask, but now was not the time. Her mouth hummed under his kiss and she wanted it to deepen, but the man who'd opened the door must be nearby, and maybe others, too. She didn't want anyone to find out about their clandestine affair.

An affair? That sounded so…sexual. And it wasn't. At least not yet.

"What is this place?"

"An unofficial annex to the consulate. There's no one here in the evenings so I've requisitioned it so I could entertain you *at home,* so to speak. We'll just have to pretend we're at Whist Castle, since you won't do me the honor of visiting me at my real home."

His teasing hurt expression made her laugh. He always managed to diffuse any tension in the situation and make her feel like they were just two people who happened to get along well. "As it turns out, I might be planning a party in England soon."

He picked up her hand and kissed it, which made her fingers tingle with pleasure. "Then perhaps I'll have some beefeaters intercept you and whisk you up to Whist." His eyes glimmered with humor.

"You wouldn't."

"Wouldn't I?" One brow rose as if he was asking the question of himself. "You don't ever really know what you'll do in any given situation until you're faced with it. That's something I learned during my time in the military. You can only hope you'll do what you know is right."

"Speaking of which, are you engaged?" There, it was out. And ringing boldly through the marble-clad hallway. Any staff who were lingering in the corners had just seen them kiss, making the question really embarrassing.

"Engaged as in busy?" He gestured for her to enter a room.

Which she did, glad to get out of the echoing hallway. They were now in a large sitting room, with damask curtains and big armchairs. "Engaged as in betrothed." She managed to stay fairly calm while she waited for his response. Was he going to deny it?

"Most definitely not."

He did deny it. "I saw a cover story about it in a magazine in my local deli."

He didn't look the slightest bit flustered. "Do you believe everything you read in the papers?"

Her face heated slightly. "No. Especially not if it's written about me." She felt a smile creeping across her mouth. "I should have known it wasn't true."

"But you had to ask anyway." His gaze challenged her.

"Yes." She lifted her chin. "I don't kiss men who belong to someone else."

"I'm relieved to hear it. And I love the way you came right out and asked. I get so tired of people beating about the bush. You're a breath of fresh air."

"I'm not sure how fresh I am. I've had a rather long day. I just learned that the Saudi prince whose wedding we're planning for next month requires that the men and the women celebrate in different rooms."

"We princes can be quite high-maintenance." His cute dimple appeared. "Though that does rather seem like it would take the fun out of the occasion."

"So the queen isn't thrilled that you're to wed Sophia Alnwick, as the magazine proclaimed."

He shrugged. "I suspect the queen would be more than thrilled if I was to wed Sophia. I, on the other hand, feel differently."

She giggled. She loved his dry humor. "So the palace is trying to set you up with her because she's suitable royal bride material."

"Yup." He sighed. "Blood as blue as a robin's egg, pretty as an English rose and not terribly bright. All the makings of a royal bride."

"But not your cup of tea."

"I prefer women with keen intelligence, even if that

makes them more troublesome." A smile tugged at the corner of his mouth.

"I can't be that intelligent or I wouldn't be spending time with you when I'm trying to avoid media attention. I think you might be the most eligible bachelor in the known world."

"You'd think they could find something more compelling to write about. Global warming, for example."

"Nah. Too serious. Handsome princes are more fun to read about. Especially when they're kissing the wrong woman."

He'd closed the door and now stood in front of her. His expression was serious, brows lowered and eyes thoughtful. "I'd much rather be kissing the right woman."

Uh-oh. An inner warning signal flashed inside Ariella. *Getting in too deep.* His steady gaze held her like a vise. She could feel her breathing quicken and her body heat rise. Her mouth itched to kiss him and her fingers to sink into his shirt. Isn't that why she'd come here?

His gaze lowered to her lips, which quivered with awareness.

Where was this going? This was obviously some kind of vacation fling for Simon and he'd fly back to England and be dating English roses again before the end of the month. She didn't usually embark on any kind of relationship unless she saw some kind of future in it, which might explain why she was usually free to work events on Saturday nights.

She'd been jealous of some strange woman called Sophia whom she'd never even met. She was still jealous of her, truth be told, because the queen wanted her and Simon to be a couple.

What on earth did the Queen of England's opinion have to do with her love life?

Did she even have a love life?

Her thoughts ran in all directions like rats fleeing a sinking ship, but her body didn't move at all. Simon's face grew closer until his lips touched hers. A flash of desire rose through her and her eyes shut tight as they kissed. Sparkles flashed across her brain and danced in her fingers and toes as chemistry rushed between them.

What was happening to her? She was the sensible one who drove her wilder friends home from parties. She didn't get into scrapes with their celebrity guests or have skeletons tucked behind the coats in her closets. Well, not until it turned out that she was the president's unknown love child. Everything seemed to have spiraled downhill since then.

Or was it uphill?

Simon's hands fisted in her blouse as their kiss deepened. Her fingers roamed into his thick, short-cropped hair. The rough skin of his cheek and his simple masculine scent thickened the arousal building inside her. His erection had thickened to the point where she could now feel it pressing against her belly. A pulse of thick, complicated desire throbbed and urged her to tighten their embrace.

Until a knock on the door made them fly apart.

Flushed and breathless, she smoothed her blouse as Simon strode to the door. He pulled it open a few inches and murmured that he preferred not to be disturbed. The invisible person on the other side mentioned something about an urgent phone call from Her Majesty.

Simon turned to her. "I'm afraid I must take this call. I'll be back in a moment."

The door closed and she was left alone in the strange sitting room. For the first time she noticed the painting above the fireplace, a clipper ship sailing across a stormy sea, tossing on the waves. An expensive-looking collection of porcelain lined the top of the mantel. What was she doing in this strange room—some kind of official den—groping a man who might one day be King of England. Had she lost her mind?

The queen must be calling to remind Simon of his royal duties and to urge him to keep his hands off strange American women.

Simon's absence did little to diminish her state of arousal. She wanted to hold him again. To kiss him. To rip his clothes off and make hot crazy love with him on the pale pink striped brocade of the sofa. She shoved a hand through her hair, only to discover that it was tangled from his fingers. She was madly smoothing it when the door opened again and Simon reappeared.

"Now, where were we?" Amusement glimmered in his eyes, along with desire.

A flame leapt inside her. She didn't remember ever feeling an attraction this strong. Her whole body seemed to gravitate toward him. Even while her brain issued warnings about how this liaison had no future and would likely end in disaster, her fingers snuck around his collar and into the hair at the nape of his neck, as their lips played together.

"What are we doing?" she managed, when they both came up for air. Her head spun from the intensity of the kisses.

"I'm not entirely sure but I know I like it." He nibbled her earlobe gently, which made her shiver with pleasure.

"Don't you think we should both be sensible?" She inhaled the scent of his skin and her fingers pressed into the muscle of his back.

"What's sensible?" His eyes were closed and his lips trailed over her face. Her skin hummed under his touch, under his breath, making her long to be closer to him than ever.

"I'm not sure I know anymore." She exhaled, longing to let go of her doubts and lose herself in Simon. He projected such confidence and self-assurance it was hard not to simply do what he said. He must have been a very effective army officer. "But my life is very wacky right now and I'm afraid of making it worse."

He laid a line of kisses along her neck, which had a frightening effect on her libido. "Am I making it worse?"

"Absolutely," she breathed. "Don't stop."

He chuckled, then kissed her full and firm on the mouth, embracing her with a caress that mingled power and strength with the utmost tenderness. So many emotions and sensations roamed through her that she almost wanted to cry.

When they finally stopped kissing and pulled apart, a deep sadness fell over her. The tiny separation foreshadowed the time when they'd say goodbye for the last time, because this relationship—if it even was a relationship— had no future. "If we have to keep this a secret, then it must be wrong." Her voice sounded thin and sad.

He opened his eyes and looked right at her. "Then let's not keep it a secret."

Five

Ariella paced around her apartment. Her phone had been ringing off the hook all morning. She couldn't ignore it because any call could easily be from an important client, but she was getting quite cagey about screening callers. The *Examiner* had printed a series of pictures of herself and Simon strolling through Georgetown the previous afternoon, so one more cat was out of the bag. She glanced at the familiar number with more than a little trepidation.

"Hi, Francesca."

"Ariella, you keep knocking it right out of the park."

"I know you're not talking about my softball swing."

"No, I'm talking about your ability to garner amazing publicity for the upcoming TV special. Liam says it will have the highest ratings of any show this year."

"Oh, yes. That." She went between regretting ever agreeing to it, and wanting to hurry up and get it over with. "Is there ever going to be a confirmed date for the taping?"

"They're still trying to get a firm commitment from the White House. That's about as easy as booking a date for the outbreak of a war. He's hoping for next week or the week after though. How about bringing your new royal boyfriend?"

"No way." She shoved a hand through her hair. "Besides, he has to go back to England for a bit." Her gut clenched. He'd phoned her only half an hour ago to say he'd be flying back that afternoon on urgent family business. How long would he be gone for? He did live there after all. Maybe he wouldn't come back and she'd be left to mop up one more scandal all by herself.

"You're a very dark horse."

"I totally am not. I'm the same person I've always been. It's the rest of the world that's crazy. Simon's a sweet man who happens to have been born into a famous family."

"Just like you happen to have been born to one."

She hesitated. "I guess you're right. He's not at all like you'd expect. Very unpretentious and genuine."

"And dead sexy."

"Yes. That, too." He seemed to grow more handsome every time she saw him. Or was that just because she was falling in love with him?

Her thoughts screeched to a halt. She was absolutely not allowed to fall in love with anyone on such short notice. Love was a big, long, lifetime thing that had to be carefully planned so that no one's heart got broken. She and Simon both agreed they didn't know where their... thing was going, and that they'd take it one step at a time.

"Didn't you realize the photographers would see you together?"

They had. In fact the photo opportunity was planned. They wanted to get it over with so they could stop meeting only in dark private corners surrounded by armed guards.

"Photographers see everything I do lately. They're always lurking about somewhere." It was a relief to shed the cloak of secrecy, but also alarming to give people one more thing to gossip about.

"Well, I'm so impressed with how you seem to take everything in stride. Anyone would think you'd been born in the public eye and handling it all your life."

"I suppose I'm like a duck where everything looks calm and smooth above the water, but underneath I'm paddling like mad." She needed to get to the gym so she could run off some energy on a machine. Otherwise she might explode.

"No way you're a duck, Ari. You're a swan. A royal swan."

She paced back into the kitchen and poured herself a cool glass of water. "There's nothing royal about me. I hope Simon's family aren't having a cow now that the story's broken in the press over there."

"How could they possibly not like you?"

Simon flew into Cardiff so he could drive directly to Dysart Castle in the Welsh Marches. The estate was the seat of his uncle Derek, the Duke of Aylesbury. It was Derek who had insisted in the strongest terms that he return to England and confront the "noxious" rumors about his affair with an American commoner.

Derek strode into the drawing room in his shooting jacket shortly before the usual lunch hour. He was damp from the mist of rain and had probably been out killing things since dawn. "Ah, you're here."

Master of the bleeding obvious, as usual. "You said it was urgent."

Derek peered at him from beneath his bushy salt-and-pepper brows. "Her Majesty is beside herself at the ugly stories splashed all over yesterday's papers. Your visit to the States has obviously grown overextended if the American press has the time and energy to invent silly stories about you."

"It's not a story. Ariella and I have grown close." And he looked forward to growing a lot closer. It had taken all his self-control to stop at kissing her. He'd managed because he knew there was something special about her, and he didn't want to do anything to endanger their budding relationship.

"Well, you'd better grow distant, immediately. You're second in line to the throne, man. You can't kiss any girl with a pretty smile who happens to cross your path."

Simon stiffened. "Ariella is not just anyone. She's intelligent, charming and has more poise than most of us royals put together."

"Don't be ridiculous. She's American. You remember what happened last time one of our family got involved with an American. He gave up the throne of England! Madness." Derek shrugged out of his jacket and tossed it over a gilded chair. "Break it off with her immediately and pray that she doesn't make a big fuss in the media."

"Ariella would never do such a thing. And I most certainly am not going to break it off with her."

Derek's already bilious face reddened further. "I thought your irresponsible and reckless days were behind you. Your older brother is married to a delightful and entirely suitable woman. Look upon him as an example."

"I honor and respect my brother and look forward to saluting him as my monarch. I feel confident that he will enjoy Ariella's company as much as I do."

"Don't be ridiculous. And she's the daughter of the president. We have enough trouble negotiating the maelstrom of American politics without you allying yourself with the daughter of one party's leader."

"She has never even met her father and politics plays no role in our relationship."

Derek had poured himself a stiff whiskey and swigged it. It was doubtless his third or fourth of the day despite the early hour. "Never even met her own father? Oh, yes. She's some kind of unwanted bastard who was given up for adoption. Perfect royal bride material."

Simon wanted to remind his uncle of the many "royal bastards" who had contributed to the country over the centuries, but he restrained himself. "Ariella and I are both adults, and quite capable of managing our affairs with dignity. I don't need any warnings or lessons or instructions in how to behave." Derek's miserable wife, Mary, was a pale shadow of the pretty, bright girl she'd once been. If there was any dire warning on how not to operate a relationship, Derek was it.

"Listen, Simon. If you get into some embarrassing international scrape it will be bad for all of us. Monarchies are in a battle for survival in the twenty-first century. An affair with this girl is tantamount to abandoning your duties. Next thing we know you'll be moving abroad."

Simon's hackles rose. "I'll never leave England. I know my duty to my country as well as to my own conscience."

His uncle's beady eyes narrowed. "The way you're acting you may well be asked to leave."

"You'd have to boot me out of the family first."

The older man sipped his whiskey and studied a painting of dead pheasants, bound by the neck into a lifeless bouquet. "Nothing is impossible."

The early morning air in England smelled fabulously exciting to Ariella. Even the fume-choked atmosphere

around the taxi rank at Heathrow Airport. She had a roster of back to back appointments stretching over the next
four days. Most of them had to do with the Duke of Buckingham's extravagant wedding. She had scheduled meetings with florists, caterers, makers of the finest crystal
and porcelain for the handcrafted tableware, the list was
almost endless.

But one appointment loomed in her mind above all
the others. At three-forty-five on Wednesday—two days
away—Ariella would finally meet the woman who gave
birth to her twenty-eight years ago. Her heart pounded
whenever she thought about it. How odd that this stranger
had carried her in her belly for nine long months.

And of course Simon was here. She'd told him of her
visit but warned him that she was very busy. She was here
to work and just because she'd kissed a prince did not mean
she could abandon her career and throw caution to the
wind. Her friends at home had warned her that the British
press were far more aggressive—and often crueler—than
the press at home, so she should watch her step. Still, hopefully they could manage a meeting. Her skin tingled every
time she thought about him. What would her mother think?

The question made her laugh aloud. The mom who
raised her, the sensible Montana housewife, would probably be full of dire warnings, issued in the most kind and
heartfelt way. She'd have much preferred to see Ariella
with the owner of a solid car dealership in Billings, or
perhaps a kindly bank manager in Bozeman.

But now she had another mother to think about. What
would Eleanor think about her relationship with Simon?
She was obviously concerned about her own privacy
and shrank from the spotlight, so she wasn't likely to be
thrilled.

Ariella's phone vibrated and she checked the number.

Think of the devil. "Hi, Simon." She couldn't help smiling as she said his name.

"You must be on British soil." His deep voice sent a flood of warmth to her belly.

"I am. Traveling over it in a taxi, to be precise."

"Where are you staying?"

"The Drake. It's a small hotel near Mayfair."

"Perfect. Right near St. James's Palace, my haunt when I'm in town. I'll pick you up at seven."

Temptation clawed at her. But her sense of duty won out. "I wish I could, but I'm meeting a potential client to pitch the most magnificent wedding in history. It will probably go quite late."

"I suppose asking you to come over after dinner isn't appropriate."

She smiled. "No, I suppose not."

"Lunch tomorrow at Buckingham Palace. Come meet the queen. She's never in town for long so it's a great opportunity for you two to get to know each other."

Ariella clutched the phone in a panic. "Oh, gosh, I have appointments all day tomorrow."

"That's a shame because she's heading to Scotland in the afternoon. But there'll be other times to meet her."

"I'm sorry I can't make it." Was it rude to say you'd rather spend the night in a meat locker than brave a lunch with one of the world's longest-reigning monarchs? Of course if things persisted with Simon, she'd eventually have to meet Her Majesty, but right now everything was very new and tentative and she had a feeling that no one would be rolling out the red carpet for her at the palace.

Not that she wanted them to. She didn't know what she wanted. "I'd love to see you, really I would, but…"

"Dinner tomorrow. My driver will pick you up with exquisite discretion. No one will know you're with me."

"I can't. I have a dinner meeting."

"That won't take all night."

She swallowed, and attempted a laugh. "I need to sleep, too. I wish I had more time for…fun, but this is a business trip." A pause made her nervous. Was he offended? It certainly wasn't good for business to snub a prince. She didn't want to book anything for after her mom's visit, as she was hoping they'd hit it off and spend hours together. "My last appointment is Thursday afternoon at three and my flight isn't until the next morning."

"So you can squeeze dinner with me into your busy schedule on Thursday?" Was he teasing or mad?

"I could, if that works for you. Of course if you're too busy, I quite understand." London whipped by outside her window, as rows of identical suburban houses gave way to more office buildings and shops.

"I'd clear my schedule in a heartbeat for the mere chance of laying eyes on you."

Okay, now he was kidding. "I don't think that will be necessary. Let's make plans closer to Thursday, okay? I hope nothing crazy happens between now and then, but you never know." She could hardly believe she was telling a prince that she couldn't commit to anything firm.

"I'm penciling it in." She could hear the irony in his voice. "And call me at once if there's anything you need. Our entire nation is at your disposal."

"Thanks." She grinned. "Much appreciated."

She shook her head as she put her phone away. How had her life changed so much in six short months? There were even photographers at the airport, though she doubted they'd get much money for photos of her in jeans and with her hair in a messy bun, carrying her luggage to the taxi rank. There was so much to be excited about, sometimes it was hard to remember that she had plenty to be afraid of as well.

Meeting her reclusive mother, hopefully meeting her famous father and now a romance with a man who made her smile each time she thought of him. It was all just a little too fabulous. Rather like teetering on a tightrope between two skyscrapers. She had to keep her chin up, her eyes forward and put one foot in front of the other, and hopefully in another six months she'd be in an even better place, where everything wasn't quite so strange and precarious.

"You come from America?" The cab driver's loud Cockney voice jolted her from her thoughts. He didn't wait for an answer. "You 'eard about this girl who's supposed to be the daughter of your president?"

She froze. Did he recognize her? He looked in his side mirror and changed lanes. "I'm not sure who you mean."

"Pretty girl. Long brown 'air. Looks a bit like you." His eyes fixed on hers again in the mirror. She blinked. "Papers say she's 'avin' an affair with our Prince Simon. Some people have all the luck, don't they?"

"Oh, yes." She pretended to text on her phone, keeping her head down. Maybe he was fishing for information he could sell to the London tabloid that always had a barebreasted woman on page three. "Very lucky."

She kept her head down until they pulled up in front of her hotel. Mercifully there wasn't a photographer in sight and she checked in and changed, telling herself to be prepared for anything.

Frustration made Simon spring from his chair and pace across the room. How could Ariella be right here in his own country and too busy to see him? Their few days of separation had him in an agony of anticipation. Now he had to wait until Thursday to see her?

He called her on Monday night, hoping that her dinner meeting would be over and they could plan a moonlit tryst. No dice. She was still in consultation with a client, and she wouldn't even reveal the person's name. He rather suspected it was his schoolmate Toby Buckingham, and he tried calling him to intercept from another direction, but Toby didn't even answer.

On Tuesday morning he tried again, hoping for a quick tea, only to be politely brushed off. Restless as hell by Wednesday afternoon, he threw on a panama hat that covered his face and decided to stroll the short distance from St James's Palace to Buckingham Palace. Maybe he'd go for a ride on one of the queen's horses. He told his driver, who doubled as security, to head there without him so he could get some fresh air. David didn't make a fuss. He knew that nothing was likely to happen on the quiet streets between the two palaces, and Simon had his phone if needed.

He was walking briskly, trying to banish the vision of Ariella's intoxicating beauty from his mind, when a girl walking along the other side of the street, in the opposite direction, caught his eye.

She walked exactly like Ariella. Long-legged, and graceful as a gazelle, with the slightly loping stride of someone in a hurry. But this woman had shoulder-length blond hair. Large dark glasses hid her face. He turned and stared after her as she passed.

That was Ariella's walk. And those were her shoes. The sight of those simple black ballet flats she favored sent a jolt of adrenaline to his own feet. He turned, following her, still on the opposite side of the street.

Why would she be in disguise? The hair must be a wig. The neat black skirt did nothing to disguise the elegant swing of her hips. He'd recognize that walk anywhere.

Who was she hiding from? She had no reason to conceal her movements to plan the big wedding she was here to organize. She was used to photographers tracking her and mostly ignored them, as he'd witnessed on several occasions in D.C.

She was doing something that she didn't want anyone to know about. Including him.

She crossed the road to his side and he slowed his pace and hung back a little. Not that she even glanced at him. She was lost in a world of her own, barely noticing the other people on the pavement. She walked fast, but he had no trouble keeping up.

Why are you following her?

Because I want to know where she's going.

Something in his gut told him that this was wrong. She had a right to privacy. In fact they'd had several long discussions about how much they valued their right to privacy, which was often under siege. Somehow, that didn't stop him.

She turned left, down a small side road. She hesitated and pulled a phone out of her pocket, causing him to stop in his tracks. A man walking behind him bumped into him, and by the time he'd apologized she was walking again. Talking on the phone.

He couldn't hear what she was saying, but her singsong laugh was unmistakable. Which confirmed what he already knew. Ariella Winthrop was walking through Mayfair in disguise, and he was going to find out why.

Why hadn't she told him where she was going? Fresh from defending her to his suspicious family, he found doubts sneaking into his mind. He knew she wouldn't leak stories of their romance to the media. Would she? Not that there was anything to leak, though he intended to change that as soon as humanly possible.

Could it be something to do with her famous father? They hadn't spoken much about him. She seemed to find the subject awkward, considering that she'd never met him.

Or was there another man in her life? His mind and body recoiled from the idea and he didn't believe it for a moment. But where was she going?

She turned left and he hurried to keep up, in case she disappeared into one of the tall Edwardian buildings lining the street. She'd tucked her phone back into her purse and strode on, looking intently ahead. Then she stopped.

This time he glanced behind him before halting, to avoid a collision. She pulled out a piece of paper and glanced up at the plaque on the house. Then she climbed the steps, rang a bell, and entered through a pair of heavy wood doors.

He approached the building a full minute later and paused as discreetly as possible in front of the doorway. The Westchester Club. He had no idea what that was, only that he wanted to gain entry. He strolled to the end of the block, pretended to casually consult a No Parking sign and considered his options.

Ariella's heart pounded as she climbed into the elevator and pressed a button. It was the old-fashioned kind of elevator with the sliding iron gates, and hearing the porter slam them behind her didn't help her nerves. Her mother was waiting for her on the fifth floor.

Scarlet had suggested this private club as a venue. Rooms were available for rent only to the most exclusive groups, and Scarlet had called in a favor to secure one for this afternoon, since it was near Ariella's hotel so she could get there without attracting attention.

She pulled off the cheesy blond wig she'd bought to keep photographers off her scent, and loosed her hair from its bun. The elevator jerked to a halt on the fifth floor. She hauled back the iron gate and stepped out onto a polished wood floor. The hallway contained three tall doors, and she was wondering which one was number 503, when one of the doors opened.

"Ariella?" The tentative voice came from a slender, pretty woman with curly light brown hair.

"Yes?" There was a question in her voice, as if she wasn't quite sure who she was any more. She wanted to greet the woman as "Mom," but that seemed presumptuous. Her heart beat so fast she could hardly speak. "You must be Eleanor."

Eleanor's hands had risen to cover her mouth as tears welled in her big green eyes. Eyes almost exactly like her own. "You're so beautiful. Even more so than in the photos."

"You're sweet. And you look far too young to be the mother of a twenty-eight-year-old." She looked like she was still in her thirties, with smooth pale skin and a girlish figure.

"I am too young to be the mother of a twenty-eight-year-old." She shrugged and smiled. "That was the problem, really. I got pregnant when I was too young to be ready." Tears ran down her cheeks. "And I missed out on so much."

Eleanor seemed ready to lose it, and Ariella wanted to comfort her, but didn't know how. She ushered her back into the room, which was a large drawing room with several graciously upholstered sofas. "Shall we sit down?"

"Oh, yes." Eleanor pulled out a tissue and wiped her face. "I'm sorry I'm making such a fool of myself. It's just that…I've waited so long for this moment and I wasn't sure it would ever come."

"Me, too. I can hardly believe we're finally getting to meet." They sat next to each other on the plush sofa, and she took Eleanor's hands in her own and squeezed them. Her skin was cool and soft. Cold hands, warm heart. The cliché popped into her mind. "Thank you so much for coming to London to see me."

"It's my great pleasure. I'm too afraid to travel to the States. I feel like they'd know who I was when I go through airport security and there'd be a big to do." Eleanor had picked up an Irish lilt to her voice. "I'm very shy, really. That's one of the reasons why I knew I wouldn't be good for Ted. He was always so outgoing and friendly and loved to be around people."

Ariella realized that Ted was the man she still thought of as the president of the United States. "Was he your boyfriend?" She only knew what she'd read in the papers, and she knew from firsthand experience they weren't always a reliable source.

Eleanor sighed. "He was. We dated our junior and senior years in high school. I was so in love!" Her soft eyes looked distant. "Even then he had big plans and intended to go away to college. He dreamed of being a Rhodes Scholar and studying abroad, and then he wanted to join the Peace Corps and travel. He always had such grand ambitions."

"Well, he's achieved the highest office an American can attain."

Eleanor nodded. Her mouth tightened for a moment, her lip almost quivering. Ariella ached to put her arms around this delicate and nervous woman, but didn't want to frighten her. "I never did really understand what he saw in me. He said he found me very peaceful." Her eyes twinkled with the memory.

"I'm sure an energetic and outgoing man needs peace more than anyone."

She smiled at Ariella. "Maybe so. My husband, Greg, was a quiet man. Not as exciting as Ted but a good man who I shared a happy marriage with for twenty-three years. He died of a heart attack. Far too young, he was." Tears welled in her eyes again.

"I'm sorry. I would have liked to meet him."

Eleanor's gaze focused on her. "Did you tell me that you've never met Ted?"

Ariella swallowed and shook her head. "Not yet, but…" She paused. It sounded pathetic really. Embarrassing. How could they have gone all this time—nearly two months since the DNA test results were released—without any contact at all?

"I'm sure Ted wants to meet you. I know it in my heart." She squeezed Ariella's hands. "They must be keeping him from you. You must reach out to him."

"I've been talking to ANS about doing a taped reunion. It should take place soon."

"On television?" Eleanor's eyes widened into shock.

She nodded. "My friend Francesca's husband is president of the network. Apparently the White House is almost ready to agree to a date."

Eleanor winced. "A private meeting would be so much nicer."

"I know, but the president isn't a private person, really. Not to the point where I could call him up and introduce myself. Somehow it seemed more…doable."

"You're outgoing, too, aren't you?" She smiled slightly.

"I suppose I am. I plan parties for a living. I love getting people together and making it an occasion to remember."

She smiled again. "You must get that from Ted. You have his cheekbones, too. And that sparkle of determination he always had in his eye."

"I think you and I look alike, too." She drank in the precious sight of her birth mother's face. "Our faces are similar shapes, and we're both tall and slim."

"Will o' the Wisp, Ted used to call me. Said a strong breeze would blow me away one day. I suppose in a way he was right. It blew me over to Ireland and I didn't dare to look back."

"I'm sure he'd love to see you again."

Her eyes widened into a look of panic. "Oh, no. No. I'm sure he'd never forgive me for what I did. I thought it was for the best but looking back I can see that not telling him he had a child was a terrible thing to do. An act of cowardice. I won't forgive myself and I wouldn't expect him to, either."

Not knowing her famous father, Ariella wasn't really in a position to argue with her. "Why didn't you tell him?"

"I knew he'd do *the right thing*." She said it with mocking emphasis. "Not the right thing for him and the big career he'd dreamed of, but the right thing in the eyes of our parents and pastors and neighbors. He'd settle down in our small town in Montana and live a tiny fraction of the live he'd imagined, because he'd be forced to support a family instead of going off to the big college he'd won a scholarship to. I could never let him throw away his future like that."

"You could have let him make the decision himself."

"I know. Now I know that." Tears welled in her eyes again. "I didn't want him to grow to hate me so I did the one thing that should truly make him hate me. I gave away our child and never told him she existed." She broke down into sobs.

Unable to hold back any longer, Ariella wrapped her arms around Eleanor's slim shoulders and held her tight, her own tears falling. "Everything happens for a reason," she said softly. "Maybe we'll never even know the true reason, but I believe that all the same."

"You're a very clever girl. I can see that in your eyes."

Eleanor dabbed at her own eyes with a tissue. "You have your dad's keen intelligence. I bet you have a university degree, don't you?"

Ariella nodded. "In history, from Georgetown."

"It's such a coincidence that both you and Ted wound up living in Washington, D.C." She blew her nose.

"It is strange."

At that moment the door opened and their heads swung around. Ariella gasped when she saw Simon standing in the doorway.

Six

"Ariella." Simon had a hat clutched in his hand and a curiously intense expression on his face.

Eleanor gasped and brought her wet tissue to her face as if she wanted to hide behind it.

"What are you doing here?" Ariella's voice came out sounding stern.

"I…" He hesitated. A sheepish expression crossed his handsome features. "I confess that I saw you on the street and followed you."

"What?" Anger surged inside her, warring with the sharp sting of attraction. "What made you think you could follow me into a private meeting?"

He shrugged. "I'm embarrassed to say that I didn't examine my motives too closely." He looked at Eleanor, as if expecting an introduction.

"You need to leave." Ariella rose to her feet. She could feel Eleanor, desperate to preserve her privacy, shrinking back into the shell that she'd started to emerge from. "You may be a prince but that doesn't mean you can march in anywhere you feel like."

"You're absolutely right, of course. My sincerest apologies." He nodded and bowed to Eleanor, and started to back out the door.

"Wait!" She couldn't just let him go. Damn it. Angry as she was, she wanted to see him too badly. She turned to Eleanor. "This is my…boyfriend." She dared Simon to argue with her word choice. "Is it okay if I introduce you?"

Eleanor gulped, but nodded shyly.

"Simon Worth, this is Eleanor Daly. My mother." Her throat swelled with emotion as she said the word *mother*.

Eleanor stared. "*Prince* Simon Worth?"

Simon bowed. "At your service. It's an honor to meet you, Mrs. Daly." He swept forward, took her hand and shook it warmly, while she gazed at him in shock. "I know Ariella's been looking forward to this for a long time."

"Goodness." She stared from one of them to the other, as if she wasn't sure what was going to happen next.

A feeling shared by her daughter. "Simon encouraged me to meet you. I wasn't sure you'd want to."

"I'm so glad the two of you are finally getting together." Simon glowed with confidence and good cheer, as usual. "It seems a wonderful thing to come out of the wiretapping scandal."

Eleanor still looked shell-shocked. "I saw a headline about the two of you at the newsagent and I just assumed it was more made-up rubbish."

"Sometimes there's a grain of truth in the wild stories the press invent." Simon smiled. "I'm happy to confirm that this is one of them."

"So you two are actually…dating?" Eleanor stared from Simon to Ariella.

"We're not quite sure what we're doing." Ariella jumped in, not wanting Simon to be put on the spot. She couldn't even imagine how the royal family might be reacting to news of their romance. Simon hadn't mentioned the topic, which wasn't too encouraging. "We enjoy each other's company."

"Oh." Eleanor's brow furrowed with concern. Ariella got the sense that she'd love to issue some stern warnings, but was too polite. She probably wasn't happy that her newfound daughter was embarking on a relationship that wasn't likely to end in a glorious happy-ever-after.

Because really, did she expect Simon to marry her?

The whole idea was ridiculously premature. They hadn't even done more than kiss yet. She glanced at Simon, whose eyes met hers and sent a zap of heat straight to her core. It would have been so much easier if she could have avoided him. This week was hectic enough already.

"I'll leave the two of you in peace." Simon must have read her thoughts. He nodded nobly to Eleanor, and squeezed Ariella's hand, then turned and disappeared out the door. Ariella couldn't manage to think of anything polite to say, so they both stared after him in silence until the door closed behind him.

"Goodness." Eleanor looked dazed.

"Life has been pretty intense this year." They both sat back down on the sofa. "Sometimes I wonder what else could possibly happen."

"Don't tempt fate." Her mother patted her hand. "But I do hope you get to meet your father soon. I'm so proud of him for being elected president, and I know he's going to do a wonderful job running the country. He's off to a great start already. Almost makes me think I should move back."

Adrenaline surged through Ariella. "You should. It would be so wonderful to have you near. Come live in

D.C.! Georgetown, where I live, is quite peaceful really. Lots of trees and lovely old buildings."

"You make it sound very inviting. Perhaps I have been living in the back of beyond for too long. Hiding away, I suppose."

"You don't have to hide from anyone now."

Eleanor looked doubtful. "I don't think I could face all those reporters the way you and Ted have. I'd be tongue-tied and embarrass both of you."

"You couldn't possibly embarrass either of us. I bet it would be a huge relief to come forward and get it over with. Why don't you come back to the States with me at the end of the week? I'm leaving on Friday and I can probably get you a ticket on the same plane if I call in a favor or two."

Eleanor's hand stiffened. "I…I'm not ready for that." Once again she felt her mother shrinking away from her. "But I'd very much like to stay in touch with you by phone, and maybe I'll gradually pluck up the courage to at least come visit you there. And maybe take a trip up to Montana to see all the old friends I've avoided for so long. I never told a single soul there about my pregnancy and I'm sure they all wondered what happened when I just disappeared. I stayed in a special home for unwed mothers way outside of town until I was due, and then I took all my saved pennies and left for Chicago after the birth. I couldn't face any of them knowing I'd given away my own child. Ted's child. I met Greg there. He'd come from Ireland for the summer to work as a roofer and he swept me off my feet." Her sad eyes sparkled a little when she spoke about him. "With him I started a new chapter of my life. I never looked back. I felt that if I did I'd fall off some cliff and get swallowed by all the emotion I tried so hard not to feel during that time." Her pale eyes grew glassy with tears again.

"It's not good to avoid your true feelings. Sooner or later they'll come back to bite you. I learned that after my adoptive parents were killed. All that pain is scary, but once you come to terms with it you can move forward. Until then you're stuck in a place of fear." She squeezed her mother's hands, which had softened again.

"You're very wise, Ariella."

"I wish I was. I just try to handle one crisis at a time. In my job there's always another one coming so there's no point in getting ahead of yourself."

They laughed, and, taking a cue from the sudden intimacy, Ariella hugged her birth mother for the very first time.

Simon refused to let Ariella leave England without visiting his home. He promised that he wouldn't stalk her around London or corner her in private drawing rooms as long as she'd agree to postpone her return flight until the following Monday so she could spend the weekend with him at Whist Castle. He insisted that, in her line of work, staying at one of England's great country houses counted as research and client cultivation. After a little persuasion, and a conversation with her business partner, Scarlet, she agreed.

He had the staff prepare his mother's favorite bedroom for Ariella, ostensibly because it had such beautiful views over the lake, but mostly because it had a door connecting it with his own bedroom. It had taken all his gentlemanly self-control to keep all their activities above the neck so far, and he intended to steer them both into unexplored territory this weekend.

His driver brought Ariella up from London on Thursday evening. He had a full schedule of activities planned to keep her entertained and give her a slice of English country life, and he intended to introduce her to the family at a charity polo match taking place nearby on Sunday. This weekend would be an excellent taste of the pleasures and realities of life in the royal family.

The realities, of course, might scare her. There was no denying that his family had rather fixed ideas about whom he should marry. Someone British, with aristocratic heritage and a featureless past that could not draw comment in the press. Of course he'd informed them that he would marry for no reason other than love, but he wasn't entirely sure they'd listened. He'd been raised to believe that duty trumped all other considerations, including happiness. So far he'd managed to find his own happiness within the confines of his duty, creating opportunities where he saw them. There was no denying that choosing Ariella as his bride would likely draw censure and disapproval.

On the other hand there was no good reason for them to oppose her, and sooner or later they usually saw reason. He just hoped they wouldn't frighten her too badly.

He tested the handle on the connecting bedroom door, and pocketed the key. No sense filling his head with plans then finding himself locked out. His body throbbed with anticipation of being alone with Ariella. From the first moment he'd seen her, across the ballroom at that gala event, he'd had a powerful sense that she was the one. So far he'd managed to battle all the forces standing between them, and now he was within reach of holding her—naked— in his arms. The prospect heated his blood and fired his imagination.

He hovered at the front windows looking for the approaching car, fighting the urge to phone and see how far away she was, then practically ran down the stairs when it finally nosed up the drive. He couldn't remember being this eager to see anyone, ever.

Ariella looked radiant, as usual, in a simple black dress, with her long hair flowing over her shoulders. A smile spread across her pretty face as she saw him, and he felt his own face reflect it back. "Welcome to Whist Castle."

"It's every bit as beautiful as I'd imagined."

"I'm glad you think so, too, and you haven't even seen the grounds yet. Come in." He fought the urge to slip his arm around her waist, which took a great deal of self-control. "How did your meeting with your mother go?"

"It was amazing." He glanced at her and saw her smile. "I'd been so worried that she'd seem like a stranger, that maybe we wouldn't even recognize each other. But I felt an instant connection with her."

"That's fantastic. Do you think you'll see her again soon?"

She hesitated. "I don't know. I really hope so. She's still deathly afraid of publicity and the criticism she'll face for giving me up and not telling Ted Morrow about me. I got all carried away and started trying to convince her to move to D.C."

He laughed. "That sounds like the kind of thing I'd do."

"Too much, too soon?" She smiled. "And then I tried to talk her into visiting Montana with me. I hope I didn't scare her right away."

"I'm sure she's privately thrilled that you're so glad to meet her and that you want to spend more time with her."

"I hope so. I really liked her. I plan to call her regularly, and hopefully we'll build the relationship and take it from there."

Words to live by. He counseled himself to take the same course with Ariella. Just because he felt a deep conviction that they were meant to be together did not mean that she felt the same way. Gentle persuasion and thoughtfully paced seduction would be the sensible path for him to take, no matter how loudly his more primitive urges begged him to take her in his arms and kiss her hard on the mouth.

He showed her to her room, glancing at the door to his own, but not mentioning it. There would be time for that later. Then he took her on a brief tour of his favorite place in the world—the great hall that had once been a Saxon throne room, and had hosted many riotous dinner parties during his reign there. Then they walked to the oldest part of the building, which held the gallery of paintings collected over the centuries by his ancestors, which included works by Raphael, Titian, Rembrandt, Caravaggio and El Greco, among others.

Ariella was suitably poleaxed. "I think you have a better collection than most museums."

"I know. I do lend them out to museums from time to time so they're not entirely hidden away in my lair. I am lucky to have had ancestors with such good taste."

"Have you ever had your portrait painted?" She glanced up at a majestic Van Dyke portrait of a young Charles II.

"Never. They'd have to nail me down to keep me still enough."

"I think that's a shame. I'd love to be able to stare at a magnificent painting of you."

"Why, when you can eyeball the real thing?" They'd been unabashedly eyeing each other since she walked through the door. Their days apart had created sexual tension thick enough to fog windows.

"What kind of setting do you think would suit you?" She looked him up and down, as if wondering whether a landscape or interior might be better. His skin heated under his clothes as her green gaze drifted from his face, to his torso, and lower…

"Definitely the outdoors. Hanging off a mountain, maybe."

"That's a great idea. And these days they can snap a picture to work from so you only have to stay in the same place for a microsecond. Think of all those poor starving artists who would love to become the royal court painter. I think it's your duty to be a patron of the arts."

"I hadn't looked at it that way."

She swept down the hallway, and he hesitated for a moment to enjoy the swinging motion of her hips inside her fitted dress, before striding after her.

Simon's castle was very ancient, but with wear from centuries of loving use, it felt like a home rather than a monument. And Simon thought of everything to make her comfortable: tea and scones on the terrace overlooking a lake with water lilies in full bloom, an art collection that could make you weep with its magnificence and a sunlit bedroom with a view of the lake.

Still, she wasn't entirely relaxed. This weekend would undoubtedly take their relationship to a new level, one way or another. She was on his turf, at his mercy. She had no idea what he had planned for the weekend and he'd told her not to worry, she was in good hands. Which made her very nervous. She was used to being in charge and making plans and booking the entertainment. What if he decided to spring the queen on her as a surprise? With Simon around she knew she'd better be prepared for anything.

"I told the staff we'll fend for ourselves at dinner." Simon led her back from the art gallery into a sweeping living room with a high wooden ceiling. "I make a mean spag bol."

"Is that a British way of saying spaghetti bolognese?"

He winked. "And they say Americans don't bother to learn other languages."

He was actually going to cook? She'd tell her beating heart to be still if she thought it would do any good. Dressed in khakis and a white shirt, he looked classically handsome. And the ever present twinkle of mischief in his eyes always sent her pulse racing. "I'll have you know I speak Spanish and French, and I intend to study Chinese as soon as I can find the time."

He smiled. "I'm impressed. Of course I'd have expected no less of you. You're disturbingly perfect."

"I am not." She felt her face heat. Now he was making her blush? So much for her famous cool and poised demeanor. "I have many flaws."

"Name one. No, wait." He walked across the room to a wooden cabinet, then pulled out a bottle of wine. "I think we'll enjoy an excellent wine while we discuss your flaws." He uncorked the bottle with muscular ease, and poured the rich red wine into two glasses.

Her flaws? Was this like a job interview where she was supposed to have flaws like being too much of a perfectionist, or excessively punctual? Or could she be honest?

It's not like she was trying to get him to fall in love with her.

Their fingers touched as she took the glass from him, sending a jolt of warmth to her core. "One flaw. Hmm. I'm a terrible speller. I always have to get someone to re-read important documents. I'm quite capable of spelling my own name wrong."

"That's nothing. I'm dyslexic."

"Are you really? I had no idea."

"So you'll need a more impressive flaw than that, I'm afraid." They settled into a wide leather sofa. He peered at her as he sipped his wine. "A fatal flaw, perhaps. Or else I'll just keep insisting that you're perfect."

"I can be quite impatient."

"Nonsense. Look at how you've handled the press. Most

women would have had a tantrum or two by now. Next!"
His eyes sparkled.

"Hmm…" What could she say to shock him out of his
amused complacency? "I'm a reformed nymphomaniac."

His eyebrows rose slightly, but the rest of his expression
didn't change. "Not too reformed, I hope."

"You're terrible." She couldn't help laughing. "The truth
is I'm probably the opposite. Too uptight. Maybe that's
my flaw."

"That can be fixed." Heat flickered between them as
their eyes met in silence. A couple of buttons were open
at the neck of his shirt, revealing a tantalizing sliver of
rather tanned chest. His neck was thick and muscular, like
an athlete's, and she was pretty confident that the rest of
him would be, too.

He shifted closer to her on the sofa. Their thighs touched
and she wondered what he'd look like naked. Then she
wondered if she was going to find out tonight. Anxiety
crept through her, along with the steady pulse of desire.
Having sex with a prince wasn't something you could easily forget. Yet that's what she'd have to do, eventually, as
she was hardly going to become a member of the royal
family.

"Your brain is going a million miles an hour." His face
drew close to hers.

"There's another flaw. I think too much."

"No one's ever accused me of that. I'm known for acting first and thinking later." He grinned. She could smell
his intoxicating musky scent. "It's gotten me into some
scrapes over the years."

"And I have a feeling it's about to get you into another
one unless we put our wine down." Their lips were moving inexorably closer.

"You do think of everything." He took her glass and placed it on the floor next to his. "Now, where were we?"

She didn't have time to think of an answer, as his mouth closed over hers and his big arms wrapped around her. A sigh escaped her as she fell into his embrace. The days apart had been torture. Trying to stop herself from thinking about him, from wanting to see him. Then behaving appropriately in front of the drivers and the butler and all those other people constantly hovering around.

Now it was just her and Simon. Their kiss deepened and his tongue flicked against hers. The throb low in her belly grew more urgent, her nipples straining against the cups of her bra. But surely there was security or someone nearby? "Should we go somewhere more private?" she whispered. At night she was haunted by visions of photographers peeking in her windows, trailing her to the most mundane places and pouncing on her.

He didn't answer, but swept their glasses up and nodded for her to follow. They strode through the silent house. It wasn't dark outside. It stayed light until late in England in the summer, so it felt oddly like midafternoon though it must be at least eight. Why was she thinking about the time?

Because at this very moment she was about to climb into bed with a prince. At least she assumed it would be a bed. Knowing Simon she could well be wrong.

She followed him upstairs, and she felt a flush of relief when he turned into his own bedroom.

Condoms! Was now the right moment to mention the need for contraception? Or was that presumptuous? She took one look at the large bed. "Um, I have some condoms in my luggage."

He turned around with a smile. "Hmm. Maybe you

weren't lying about being a slightly reformed nympho-maniac."

"Or is it just that I'm annoyingly prepared for every-thing?"

"I suspect the latter. And don't worry, I have some spe-cially purchased for the occasion."

"How does a prince buy condoms? I mean, you can't wander into Boots the Chemist on your local high street and slam them down on the counter with a smile."

"Why not?" He pulled a packet of Trojans from an el-egant mahogany chest.

"Um, because everyone would know what you're up to."

"And they'd be jealous." He stepped toward her and stole her breath with a hot, urgent kiss. "But don't worry. My secretary purchases them in a cunningly anonymous fashion."

His fingers worked their way around the zipper on the side of her dress. Then he seemed stymied. Her breasts tingled at the thought of him touching them. "I have to lift it over my head," she rasped.

"No." He looked thoughtfully at the garment. "*I* have to lift it over your head." He lifted the hem and she held her breath and raised her arms as he pulled the dress up and off. With her dress crumpled like a tissue in his broad hands, he surveyed her—wordless—for a moment. She should feel self-conscious standing there in her bra and panties, but she didn't. Simon's desire was every bit as naked as her body.

She kicked off her shoes and tackled the buttons on his shirt, while he undid his belt and stepped out of his pants. Good grief. His chest was thick muscle, highlighted by a line of sun-bleached golden hair that pointed to the fierce erection seeking freedom from his conservative boxer shorts.

"Let me help you with that," she murmured, tugging the cotton down over his thighs. She realized too late that she was licking her lips. It had been a long time since she'd had sex and her entire body sizzled with anticipation. His legs were sturdy as the oak trees on his estate, with knees scarred by countless adventures, and she enjoyed the movement of his muscles as he stepped out of his underwear.

He unsnapped her bra before she had even stood up again, and her breasts pointed at him in accusation of arousing her past the point of decency.

At long last.

Together they pulled off her panties, then their bodies met, his erection fitting neatly against her belly. They breathed heavily, skin heating as they managed a very tentative kiss: a wisp of tongue, a graze of teeth, the tiniest, smooth, teasing and taunting until they couldn't stand it anymore. Then they fell onto the bed and Simon crawled over her, covering her with his body, with his kisses, tasting and testing her skin until she moaned with urgency.

He rolled on the condom and entered her carefully. Their eyes met for a moment, and the look of concern on his handsome face made her smile. She lifted her hips to welcome him and enjoyed his expression of rapture as his eyes slid closed and he sank deep inside her.

Pleasure coursed through her at the feel of his big, strong body wrapped around hers. She moved with him easily, enjoying sudden and intense relief from all the tension that had built between them in the short time they'd known each other.

"Ariella." He rasped her name with a hint of surprise, as if discovering it for the first time. Somehow it jerked her back to the reality of who she was. Ariella Winthrop, whose life had been turned upside down by the scandalous circumstances of her birth and now by a shocking international romance. Even as she writhed in Simon's arms she couldn't help wondering if this was all a crazy mistake. Would she wake up soaked in regret at compounding the madness that was her life lately?

If the press found out she and Simon had slept together they'd have a field day. They'd be clamoring for snapshots of the "royal smooch" or any casual indiscretion.

She'd let this whole thing spiral out of control. In D.C., she could have easily kept Simon at arm's length until he went back to Britain, instead of embarking on an ill-advised romance that would have people whispering and gossiping behind her back.

"Ariella." He said it again.

"Yes?" Was he asking a question?

"I just like saying it. Celebrating it. That we're here together at last."

She chuckled, then carefully maneuvered them until she was on top. "You're a hard man to resist." That was the truth. You couldn't say no to Simon. At least she couldn't.

She leaned forward to kiss him, then her hair trailed over his chest as she rose and moved over him. His eyes closed and his face wore an expression of sheer bliss as she rode him. His hands wandered over her chest, enjoying the curve of her breasts and circling her waist. Then he deftly changed positions again and took back the lead.

Thoughts slipped away as he drove her deep into a world where worries didn't exist. Nothing mattered but their two bodies, moving in sync, holding and clutching at each other, their breath mingling and their skin sticking together as they edged closer and closer to the inevitable climax.

Afterward they lay in each other's arms, as countless other couples must have done over the years in this same grand chamber. Dukes, princes and earls, wives, mistresses and probably a few comely servant girls as well.

"What are we doing?" She breathed into his ear. It wasn't the first time she'd voiced the thought aloud.

"We're in the throes of a passionate romance," he answered.

"You make things seem so simple."

"Usually they are simple, and people go out of their way to make them complicated."

"But how long can it go on for? You live here and I live in D.C. It's silly."

"It's wonderful." He stroked her hair, his eyes soft.

She exhaled slowly. "It is."

"So we need to enjoy our passionate romance one day at a time and see where it takes us."

"With the press breathing down our necks?"

He shrugged. "They'll do what they want to do, regardless of what we want or hope for. I try to ignore them in general. Unless I need some PR for World Connect. Then I'm all smiles and pithy sound bites." He grinned.

"I need to cultivate that attitude." She rested her head on his broad chest. "They're just doing their job. As you said before, they're not likely to leave me alone any time soon because of the president being my father, so I might as well get used to them."

"Good, because on Sunday we're going to a charity polo match and there will be plenty of press there." He had that mischievous look again.

"Uh-oh."

"It'll be fun. And you'll get to meet my family."

Anxiety spiked through her. "Your older brother and his wife?"

"They're away on a tour of Australia, but you'll meet

my grandmother and assorted cousins, aunts and uncles. And my younger brother will be there."

She swallowed, trying not to let her panic show. "Your grandmother...the queen?"

"Don't be intimidated. She looks fierce from a distance but up close she's very warm and easy to talk to."

She blew out a breath. "I hope I won't stutter like an idiot."

"You are the last person on earth to feel flummoxed in the presence of royalty. Especially since you're already sleeping with it."

She chuckled. "There is that." Then her gut churned. "Does the queen know? I mean, about us?"

"If she reads the papers she will." He stroked her cheek. "Don't worry. My family will love you. It will be fun."

Fun. Ariella very much doubted that it would be fun. Intimidating, alarming, fraught with potential pitfalls? Yes. Fun? Not so much.

Either way, in less than two days, she'd find out.

Seven

Ariella tried everything she could think of to get out of attending the polo match. The Duke of Buckingham had officially hired them for the wedding so she really should be in London scouting out suppliers for the party. But, yes, it would be a Sunday and in England most things were closed on Sunday. She should get back to the U.S. and… well, yes, it would still be Sunday.

So on Sunday morning she found herself combing her hair with shaking hands.

Simon opened the door dividing their rooms and looked in. He smiled when he saw her. "Just checking that you haven't climbed out the window."

"What if they all hate me?"

"They'll love you." His ebullient confidence did nothing to soothe her frazzled nerves.

"I don't know anything about polo."

"You don't need to. Clap when our team scores and you'll be good."

"What if a reporter asks probing questions?"

"They won't. It's a very exclusive event and there are unwritten rules that keep them at a respectful distance."

"What if I become hysterical and make a big scene?"

He grinned. "Then we'll call some nice men in white coats to come take you away. Would you like a glass of Pimm's to soothe your nerves?"

"No, thanks. I really don't like to drink before noon. Especially on Sunday. It affects my aim." She brandished her mascara wand.

"Quite understandable. I should probably warn you about my uncle Derek. He's likely to be three sheets to the wind by noon and isn't shy about expressing himself."

Uncle Derek? She'd never heard of him. Her confusion must have shown in her face.

"He's my mother's brother, so not royal by birth, but he's latched on to the family and is hanging on with a death grip. He tries to be more traditional than anyone so he's not likely to approve of me dating an American."

She sighed. "It's not like we're…serious." Was she trying to convince herself? Their weekend together had been so easy and fun. She and Simon really clicked. They could talk about anything. And the sex…

"Says who?" He sauntered into the room. "I can be very serious when the occasion calls for it." He walked up behind her where she stood at the mirror and slid his arms around her waist. His lips pressed hotly into her neck and sent heat plunging to her toes. "And I seriously like you."

She blinked, looking from her startled face to his relaxed one in the mirror. "I like you, too, but it is a strange situation, you have to admit."

"My entire life is a strange situation, by most measurable parameters." He nibbled on her ear, which made her gasp. "I don't let it bother me."

"I guess when you put it that way…" Her words trailed off as their eyes locked in the mirror. His managed to sparkle with amusement and desire at the same time. His hands roamed over her hips and belly, setting off tremors of desire. Last night's lovemaking still reverberated in her mind and body. If she could just get through this afternoon without any drama they'd be back in bed together, tonight. Their last night before her flight back to D.C. tomorrow.

Without making a decision to, she turned and kissed him, smudging her carefully applied makeup and gripping him in a forceful embrace. If this was all they ever had it would be well worth it. No regrets.

At least she hoped not.

"And this is my grandmother." Simon smiled encouragingly. People milled around them in the royal enclosure, laughing and clinking glasses. Photographers were at a discreet distance. Mallets thwacked against balls somewhere in the background.

The queen looked so tiny up close. Ariella began to curtsey, but the queen stuck out her hand, so she took it. Cool and soft, the fingers closed around hers with surprising strength. "A pleasure to meet you, Miss Winthrop. Simon tells me you've never been to a polo match before." Steel-blue eyes peered into her very core.

"No, this is my first."

"Simon also informs me that President Morrow is your father." The queen's cool grip trapped her hands.

"Um, yes." Did she realize they'd never met, or even spoken? "Rather a surprise to both of us."

"Surprises do keep life interesting, don't they?"

"They do indeed."

The queen bombarded her with information about the various polo ponies, their breeding and track records and finer qualities. She was clearly skilled at holding the entire conversation with little participation from others. Ariella decided she'd work on that skill herself. It seemed a safe way to keep conversations on the right track.

Simon smiled and nodded and generally seemed delighted at how things were progressing. Ariella smiled and nodded while thinking, *Omigosh, I'm chatting about horses with the queen. And I don't know anything about horses. And I'm sleeping with her grandson.*

She was definitely ready for a Pimm's by the time a new arrival interrupted their conversation to greet Her Majesty. Simon procured her a large glass of the tea-colored drink with its floating mix of strawberries, apples, orange and cucumber. She knew the sweet taste hid a base of gin, so she sipped it gingerly, not wanting to find herself giggling and falling over in her stilettos as some of the younger guests were already in danger of doing.

Simon's younger brother Henry was at the center of the group of more rambunctious partygoers, and Ariella felt a sense of apprehension as Simon led her over to meet him.

As tall as Simon, but with curlier hair and bright blue eyes, the youngest prince had a reputation as a hard-partying playboy.

"I see you convinced her to step into the fray." He fixed his eyes on hers as he kissed her hand, which felt very awkward in front of the gathered crowd of guests. Young girls, spilling out of their expensive dresses, stared at her with curiosity.

"My brother, Henry, Ariella Winthrop." Simon made the introduction.

"I think everyone in the developed world knows who

Ms. Winthrop is. And she's even lovelier than her photographs."

What did you say to a comment like that? "It's nice to meet you."

"But is it? You haven't known me long enough to be sure."

"Don't scare Ariella." Simon was smiling. "She's just heard the pedigrees of the entire equine half of the polo team from Gran."

"I hope you showed a suitable degree of fascination. Gran is very suspicious of anyone who doesn't share her passion for horses."

"I freely admit that I know almost nothing about horses."

"I thought Montana was cowboy country?" Henry was obviously enjoying this.

"Some parts of it are, but not where I lived."

"I think Ariella would make a marvelous cowgirl." Simon slid his arm around her waist. She tried to keep a straight face. Did he really want to do that in front of all these people? She felt eyes boring into her from all directions. "But I intend to make her fall in love with England."

Henry raised an eyebrow. "He must be serious. Usually he can't wait to get on a plane and go somewhere looking for adventure."

"Ariella has me thinking about adventures closer to home."

Ariella could hardly believe her ears. He was all but declaring himself. Maybe this was some kind of ongoing joke between him and his brother. She had no idea how to react. "I like England very much."

"Well, thank goodness for that. There's one thing I can't change about myself, and that's my homeland." Simon squeezed her gently, which sent a ripple of confused emotions through her.

"I'm not sure you can change all that much else, either." Henry teased Ariella. "He's very bullheaded and opinionated."

"I am not." Simon shoved him gently. Ariella could see the brothers had a friendly sparring relationship, but that they cared for each other deeply. As someone who'd never had a sibling to rib her, she found their closeness touching.

"Ariella came up with the idea for an outdoor concert to raise money and awareness for World Connect."

"I like." Henry grinned. "The lawns in front of the Washington Monument would be a great spot."

"I agree." Ariella smiled. "No harm in aiming high."

"Especially when your dad is the president." Henry winked. "We royals aren't averse to a little nepotism when the occasion calls for it. It's how we pass on the throne, after all."

Ariella's stomach clenched slightly. Everyone seemed to assume that she had a relationship with her father, when nothing could be further from the truth.

"Uh-oh, here comes trouble." Henry's nod made Simon turn.

"Too true. Let's head it off at the pass." He turned and led Ariella away from Henry and his gaggle of blushing admirers toward a tall man in baggy tweeds, approaching fast through the knots of glamorous polo-goers.

"Your uncle?" The man's bushy brows sank low over slitted dark eyes and his cheeks were the florid pink of a smacked behind.

"Good old Uncle Derek. Here to pour gasoline on untroubled waters."

Derek marched up to Simon and launched into a conversation about the polo team, totally ignoring her. She counted the burst blood vessels in his cheeks and wondered if he intended to simply pretend she didn't exist.

"Uncle Derek, do hold your fire a moment so I can introduce you to my honored guest, Miss Ariella Winthop. Ariella, this is my mother's brother, Derek, the Duke of Aylesbury."

"Just visiting England, are you?" His haughty voice grated on her ears.

"Yes, I'm going back tomorrow."

"Oh." He turned back to Simon and launched into a tirade about poor sportsmanship at his shooting club. Simon caught her eye as he nodded and yessed his uncle. Ariella sagged with relief when Derek finally finished his monologue and sauntered off.

"He's irritating but harmless. I try to ignore him." Simon's whispered words in her ear made her giggle. "One thing you learn to do as a royal is present a united front. We don't need the public to know that behind closed doors sometimes we drive each other insane."

"Quite understandable." She admired his ability to play the role he'd been born to. Such responsibility and the strict code of conduct would be too much for a lot of people she knew. It almost invited rebellion and debauchery, but Simon handled his unique life with ease and good humor.

Which only made her adore him more.

There was a brief commotion as one of the players fell off and, unable to support weight on an injured ankle, was helped to a medical tent.

"Simon, we need you!" Two of the other players beckoned from their horses. "Hugh couldn't come today and Rupert's still down with the flu so we're short. You know Dom would be happy for you to ride his horses."

Simon glanced at Ariella, then back at them. "I can't, I'm afraid. It would be rude to desert my guest."

"Oh, that's okay," she protested. "I'm sure I can take care of myself for a few minutes." The game had been going on forever, it seemed. It must be nearly over. "You go ahead." She knew his side was winning and she didn't want everyone blaming her if things went south because Simon couldn't leave her side.

"You're a brick." He kissed her cheek softly, which made her gasp and glance around as he jogged off to change.

Great. Now she was adrift in unfamiliar waters. And her glass of Pimm's was empty, mint leaves clinging limply to the remains of the ice cubes. She decided to go off in search of another, and hope someone scored the winning goal while she was at it.

"Ariella." A voice startled her as she headed down the side of a marquee. She turned to find Simon's uncle Derek right behind her. "A word, if you please."

Actually, I don't please. But she didn't dare say it. She paused, still half turned toward the drinks tent.

"Simon's young and impressionable." Those frighteningly large salt-and-pepper brows waggled up and down. "Enthusiastic and charming but not terribly bright, I'm afraid."

Her mouth fell open. "I find him highly intelligent."

"I'm sure you do." He swigged from a glass of clear liquid. "A coronet has that effect on women. The fact remains that a dalliance with you could destroy his future."

"I hardly think that…" She didn't know what she was about to say but it didn't matter because Derek blazed ahead.

"We all know what happened the last time a member of the British royal family lost his head over an American. He abandoned his country and his duty in the name of love. Not because he wanted to, but because he knew it was an *absolute requirement.*" His emphasis on the last two words was underscored with a hiss.

"Why?" Now she was curious to hear his answer.

"Because he knew she could not possibly fit in."

"I thought it was because the monarch can't marry a divorcée. For starters, Simon's not a monarch, or very likely to be one. And second, I'm not divorced." Her own boldness shocked her. Pimm's must be powerful stuff.

The monstrous brows shot up. "Times are different now, but not that different. Her Majesty holds very traditional views, and each of her grandchildren has been groomed from birth to follow a specific path. Simon will marry a member of the British nobility, and will raise his children here to be members of the British aristocracy. Lady Sophia Alnwick will be his future wife and the wedding invitations are all but printed. She'd be here with him today if she wasn't holding vigil at her esteemed father's deathbed. Within the next day or so she'll inherit all his lands and wealth and be the richest woman in England."

Ariella blinked. "I hardly think Simon needs to marry for money or prestige."

"Those two things are never a negative." Derek's beady black gaze chilled her. "You are a…a nobody. The illegitimate daughter of an American upstart who's clawed his way into a temporary position of power. Don't delude yourself that you can compete with the thousand-year history of the Alnwick family. Like his brother's, Simon's life path has been planned since birth. The estate he lives in, the so-called charity he's so enamored of, these are all part and parcel of his role. If you get your claws into him and cause him to do something foolish, he'll lose both of them."

"I don't believe you."

"No? The estate isn't his. It belongs to Her Majesty. That silly charity is funded almost entirely by the royal coffers. Simon's role in the family is a job like any other. His employment is contingent on Her Majesty's largesse, and can be rescinded at any time. Think about that when you kiss him."

He hissed the word *kiss,* and spittle formed on his bulbous lips. Then he turned and marched away. She wilted like the mint in her Pimm's. Was this true? Was Simon really a royal puppet whose strings could be cut at any time?

Part of her wanted to encourage him to tell them all to shove it and live his own life. Then she thought about how much he loved his home at Whist Castle. And how proud he was of the achievements of World Connect. Could she really be responsible for causing him to lose them both?

Her legs were shaking and her hand sweating around her glass. She hurried to the drinks tent and got another Pimm's, then walked around the perimeter of the royal enclosure, pretending to watch the match. She cheered wildly, heart pounding with pride and happiness, when Simon scored a goal. Then glanced around, wondering if she should have pretended more disinterest. He looked so dashing and handsome on top of the muscled bay horse, who listened to his every move and galloped for the ball as if its life depended on it.

"He's a fine player." The distinctive voice startled her.

"Yes, Your Majesty." The queen must have walked right up to her while her eyes were glued on Simon and she hadn't even noticed. Her attendants hovered at a discreet distance. "He obviously enjoys the game."

"Simon's been playing polo since he was about eleven. He'd already been riding for years at that point, of course. Do you ride?"

"No. I've never even sat on a horse. I suppose that seems

funny when I come from Montana, but we lived in town and I never had the chance."

"Ah. What did you do for entertainment in Montana?"

Ariella swallowed. This seemed dangerously personal. And she was to blame for bringing up her roots. "My dad used to take us to watch football games almost every weekend in season. And we went fishing at the lake."

"How nice." She didn't seem especially interested. And why should she be? "Do you plan to go back to Montana?"

"I have a business in Washington, D.C., so I'm not sure if I'll ever live in Montana again. Never say never, though."

"And when are you returning to Washington?" A hint of steel shimmered in her voice.

"Tomorrow, actually." Sadness mingled with relief. She'd have to leave Simon, but she wouldn't be stuck trying to make small talk with a monarch. "I was here on business. Simon's helped make it a wonderful trip."

She looked at the queen's face. She couldn't resist throwing in that last part.

"Simon tells me you're a party planner." The cool blue eyes had narrowed behind her glasses.

"Yes. I'm here to plan the Duke of Buckingham's wedding." She had no doubt the queen and the duke were old pals.

"How wonderful. Everyone's so happy to see him marrying Nicola at last. They've been chums almost since nursery school."

"I'll make sure it's an event to remember."

"I'm sure you will. Did Simon tell you he'll be getting married soon?"

She frowned. "What?"

The queen smiled sweetly. "A similar situation, really. A childhood friend who we all love. Perhaps he can get some wedding ideas from you."

Ariella's lung capacity seemed to shrink until she could hardly breathe. The queen was warning her off Simon. Telling her he was already spoken for and that she was not wanted on the voyage. A roar of clapping rose through the crowd and she joined in enthusiastically, though she wasn't even sure which team had scored a goal.

"I'm sure Simon's wedding will be an affair to remember," she managed at last.

"Indeed. Do have a good trip back to the States." The queen smiled thinly, then turned and walked slowly away.

Ariella felt like she'd just been slapped. She'd now been warned off Simon by two members of the royal family. They must feel quite threatened by her, which wasn't surprising given that Simon had allowed the press to get wind of their romance. Sophia Alnick was probably throwing a tantrum somewhere, too, if she was in on this whole aristocratic marriage scheme.

Standing there with her drink, she felt like a single tree in a tempest, while well-dressed people in big hats—she was hatless—swirled around her, going about their glamorous lives. Her role was to make those lives a little more glamorous by creating extravagant events for them, not to come play their own games with them. Clearly she was losing her grip on reality lately.

She counted the minutes until the match ended and Simon jumped down from his horse. He shared some congratulatory fist pumping with his teammates before jogging across the grass to her. "I hope everyone looked after you."

"Oh, yes."

He was even more handsome with his hair tousled and his chiseled face glowing with exertion. Shame he would never really be hers. "See? I told you they don't bite."

She didn't want to mention the tooth marks they'd left

on her psyche. Not while they were still here, at least. "I'm rather exhausted by all the excitement. Would it be okay if we left?" She certainly didn't want to find herself having to be polite to Uncle Derek, or even the queen, who'd practically shoved her toward her plane.

"Of course." He waved to a few people and escorted her to the car as if she really was the most important person there.

"Don't you need to say goodbye to the queen?" She didn't want to be blamed for him neglecting his royal duties.

"No worries. I'll be seeing her tomorrow after I take you to the airport."

"Oh." And why wouldn't he? She was his grandmother, after all. She probably wanted to go over wedding venue ideas, or discuss the ring he'd soon give to Sophia. Her heart sagged like a deflated balloon.

They talked about the game on the drive back to Whist Castle. Simon obviously loved his life here, surrounded by people who cared about him, and the excitement of his jet-set existence. He was born for it.

She wasn't.

They enjoyed a hearty dinner in the castle dining room, this time served by staff who were obviously trained to ignore the fact that he'd had a woman to stay for the weekend. They must know there was a connecting door between her room and Simon's, and she was pretty sure they knew she and Simon had been using it. It was embarrassing having so many people know her business. They'd all be whispering about her soon as Simon's last hurrah.

"You seem very thoughtful tonight." Simon spoke softly. They were still sitting at the dinner table, sipping coffee.

"Am I? I was just thinking about the Duke of Buckingham's wedding." There was some truth to it. This weekend had given her insight into the British upper crust that would help with the planning. "I hope I'm not being too dull."

"Impossible." His warm smile was so encouraging it almost melted her anxiety. "Let's go relax upstairs."

She gulped. How could she make love to him again, knowing that his family fully intended to keep them apart? "Okay." She'd always known this was never going to be a long-term thing. It was a crazy affair, something they'd both fallen into by accident.

He took her hand as they climbed the stairs, and the way he glanced at her sideways and squeezed her hand gently was so sweet and romantic, it stole her breath. Why did he have to be a prince? Why couldn't he have been a regular guy with an ordinary job and a house somewhere in the D.C. suburbs?

"You seem...worried." He closed the door to his room after they were both inside. The door to her own room was wide open. Apparently there was no pretense that they were sleeping apart.

"I am." It was hard not to be honest with him. He was such a straight shooter himself. "I'm going to miss you."

"Then we'll just have to make sure not to stay apart for too long." He gathered her in his arms and laid a warm kiss on her lips. Her anxiety started to unspool as she kissed him back.

"Yes." She said it but she didn't believe it. It would be better for both of them if they kissed and wandered back to their regular lives. Less media frenzy, less royal disapproval. Less fun.

Their kiss deepened until she had to come up for air. Simon's hands plucked at the zipper near her waist, and soon she was shimmying out of her dress and struggling with his belt and undressing him. Even though everyone in the outside world seemed to think he'd soon be marrying Lady Sophia, right now she knew he wasn't interested in anyone but her. Alone in this room they were two people who cared about each other. It felt so good to shrug out of the trappings of society and press her skin against his. His naked body was so sturdy and capable. She had no doubt he could leap tall buildings in a single bound if he wanted to. She felt so confident in his presence, like together they could accomplish anything. It would be hard to be back in her D.C. apartment, alone.

Simon nibbled her jaw and neck, his breath hot and urgent. "I don't know what I'm going to do without you."

So she wasn't the only one thinking it. They slipped under the bed clothes together. "You'll do what you did before you met me. You know, climb mountains, jump over waterfalls, that kind of thing."

"You're probably right. At least until my next trip to D.C." He maneuvered himself on top of her and his erection nudged her belly.

She inhaled a shaky breath. "Who knows what will happen between now and then?" No doubt the royals would warn him to stay away from her. If he had any sense, he'd probably listen. She'd be busy with her own dramas— meeting her father on national television, her frantic work schedule, dodging photographers.

"Let's not think about the future. We don't want to waste a single precious second of our last night together." Arousal thickened his voice. He raised his hips and entered her.

Desire and relief crashed through her as she felt him deep inside her. Sheer physical pleasure was a welcome change from all the thinking and plotting and scrambling she did during the day. Simon's powerful arms felt like the safest place to be in the whole world.

They moved together effortlessly, drawing to the brink of madness and back, as they tried to wring every last ounce of passion out of each other, only to find there was an inexhaustible well of it bubbling somewhere deep inside them.

When her orgasm came, Ariella wanted to cry. The feelings inside her were just too much. Desire and fear and pleasure and panic and wanting to stay right here in Simon's hot and hungry embrace until the world ended.

Simon gripped her tight, as if he was afraid she'd drift off into the night breeze. "Oh, Ariella," he whispered in her ear. She loved the way he said her name, with his formal sounding British accent and such conviction. She was sure no medieval knight ever serenaded his lady with such intensity.

She simply breathed, holding tight to the precious moments where she felt at peace, before she'd be spat back out into the world and have to fend for herself.

In the morning an alarm sounded, reminding them both that she had a plane to catch in a little over four hours. It was odd that you could be sleeping in a royal palace, with a prince, no less, then have to battle your way into coach and cram your bags into the overhead bin and hope your neighbor didn't drool on you while he slept.

She wanted to laugh, but nothing seemed too funny right now.

"Did you like my family?" Simon's odd question came out of nowhere.

It startled her into a fib. "They were very nice."

"Except Uncle Derek." His voice sounded curious.

"Yes, except him."

He sat up. "Did he say something to you?"

She hesitated for a moment. Why hadn't she told him about this already? She didn't want to spoil their last night together. And she knew it would upset him. "Kind of." Simon took her hand and peered into her face. She wanted to run from his thoughtful and caring expression, not hurt his feelings by telling him what his uncle had said to her. "I have to get ready."

"What did he say?"

"Oh, nothing really." She tried to get up, but he held her hand firm.

"I don't believe you. Come on, word for word or I'll have to start in with the medieval torture techniques." He acted like he was going to tickle her. But neither of them laughed.

"He said you're going to marry Sophia Alnwick soon."

"Which you already know is not true."

"And he reminded me of what happened the last time a British royal got involved with an American."

"You're hardly Wallace Simpson."

"I told him that. Not that it matters, anyway, since we're barely even dating. It was silly. I didn't think it was worth mentioning."

"Did anyone else say anything?"

"Not really. Though the queen did seem fairly interested in when I was going back to the States. I suspect they'll all be glad to see the back of me so you can go back to dating some nice, suitable English girls." She smiled and tried to sound jokey. That was what would happen after all.

But Simon's face was like stone. "I'll have a talk with them." He frowned. "I'm sorry they made you feel uncomfortable."

"I was fine, really. It was fun. I've never been to a polo match before and I loved watching you play."

"I shouldn't have left you alone. I'll sort them out."

"There's no need, really!" Her voice sounded too loud. Would they tell him what they'd told her? That he'd lose Whist Castle and his charity if he dared not to toe the royal party line? "I need to get dressed and throw my stuff back in my bag. And do you have the number for a taxi?"

"A taxi!" He wrapped his arms around her and hugged her tight. "There's no way anyone but me is driving you to that airport. And it'll be a miracle if I don't make you deliberately miss your plane."

"Then my partner, Scarlet, will kill me. She's been holding down the fort by herself all week."

"She can't kill you if she can't find you." He raised a brow and mischief twinkled in his eyes again.

"She can send out a hit man. They're good at tracking people. They can probably trace my cell phone."

"They'd have to get past the palace guards." He kissed her face and cheeks and lips. She shivered, hot pleasure rising inside her. "It can be handy living in a fortress."

"I see that." Her hands roamed over the muscle of his back. "I think I could get used to it." It was so easy to talk to him and tease him. He never made her feel like he was a prince and she was a commoner. With him she felt they were on the same team and could take on the world together.

The alarm sounded again. She pushed him back, very reluctantly, and leaped out of bed. "Duty calls."

"Being in the army I know all about that, so I suppose I'll have to go along with it."

They dressed and had a quick breakfast, then Simon drove her to Heathrow. They kissed in the car where no one could see, but he insisted on walking her into the terminal. She saw a photographer's flash out of the corner of her eye as they said a chaste goodbye.

Move along, she wanted to say. *There's nothing to see*

here. She felt numb as she checked her bag and moved through customs. Would he really come to D.C. to see her? Or would the queen and Uncle Derek make him give her up and turn his attention back to his royal duties?

Somehow she had to go from the most intense and wonderful romance of her life to…nothing. Maybe she'd never see him again except on the pages of a glossy magazine. She sank into her airplane seat feeling hollow and deflated.

Until she checked her phone and discovered that she was about to finally meet her famous father.

Eight

A brief text from Liam Crowe, the head of ANS, told her the taping was scheduled for Tuesday, only two days away, and everyone at the network was scrambling to pull it together. Ariella had barely arrived home and unpacked before Francesca, Liam's wife, came over to help her prep for the taping.

"It seems shallow to ask, but what do you think I should wear?" They both sat at her kitchen table, sipping herbal tea. Her nerves were firing like bullets. "I usually wear black but I've heard that doesn't look good on video. It disappears or something. I don't want it to vanish and leave me stark naked on national television."

Francesca's bold laugh filled the room. "It looks a bit flat, that's all. But colors do usually work better. Let's go look at your wardrobe."

They walked into the bedroom. Ariella opened her closet door sheepishly. The apartment was old, from an era when people had maybe five to ten outfits. Her collection of clothes looked ready to burst out and start running.

"How do you find anything in here?"

"My first boss used to have a sign on her desk that read, *'This is not a mess on my desk, it's a wilderness of free association.'* I took it as inspiration."

"It's a wilderness, all right." Still, Francesca dove boldly in and pulled out a knee-length red sheath. "Red portrays confidence."

"That I don't feel. I think I should go low-key."

"You? You're practically a princess. How about this royal blue?" She held up a matching top and skirt in an intense shade.

"I am sooo not practically a princess. Believe me. I was way out of my league with his family."

"You met the queen?" Francesca grabbed her arm.

She nodded. "We made small talk. It was scary." Ariella reached in for a quiet gray jacket and skirt. "How about this?"

"Way too mousy." Francesca shoved it back. "I can't believe you met the queen. I love her. She's so old-fashioned."

"Exactly. The kind of person who's horrified by the prospect of her grandson dating an Amerrrrican." She managed to roll her *R*s. Then sighed. "He's sweet but it's one of those things with no future."

"I'll have to read your tea leaves when we're done picking your outfit."

"Does that work when you're using a tea bag?"

"It does require more creativity, but I have plenty of that."

"Let's just stay focused on getting me through this taping in one piece. How about this lilac number?"

Francesca surveyed the dress. "Perfect. Fresh and young, yet sophisticated and worldly."

"I'm glad that's settled. Will I get to meet the pres— I mean, my father, before the taping starts?"

Francesca hesitated. "Liam and I did talk about that. He wants you to meet for the first time on air, for maximum dramatic impact. I told him this isn't a primetime special—well, it is—but it's your real life. If you don't like the idea of meeting him under the studio lights, I'll beg and plead until he gives in."

"Don't worry about it. I don't mind meeting him on camera. In a way it might help as I'll have to keep a lid on my emotions."

"Oh, don't do that. It's bad for ratings." Francesca winked.

"Liam would rather have me blubbering and calling him Daddy?"

"Absolutely."

She blew out a breath. "Yikes. That's not really me. I'm known for being calm under pressure. I'm afraid I won't give good TV."

"You just be yourself, and we'll let Liam worry about the ratings."

Ariella's usually calm demeanor was trembling. Her hands kept shaking as she tried to apply her mascara. Her lips quivered as she smoothed on her lipstick. Even her hair seemed jumpy. In seventeen minutes—not that she was counting—she'd be sitting on a sound stage with the man who shared half her DNA. She wasn't that nervous about the television cameras, or even the audience of millions that would supposedly be tuning in. She was nervous about what she'd see when she looked into Ted Morrow's face.

Would his expression encourage her to build a relationship that could shape the rest of her life? Or would he be wearing that mask of genial competence that had helped him clinch the election? She knew that mask. She wore it herself a lot. In fact, she planned on wearing it tonight.

She hoped that this meeting might be the start of a relationship between them, but she was keeping her hopes in check since he didn't know her well enough to trust her. He might not want to get close to anyone new. He was in a position of power and influence that made him strangely vulnerable. He probably didn't want to share intimacies and feelings with a stranger who might turn around and repeat them to the press, or even to her friends. Still, she knew she'd be disappointed if she didn't feel even a little bit closer to him after tonight.

"We're on in five!" The perky production assistant stuck her head around the corner. "Are you ready?"

"Ready as I'll ever be." She stood up on shaky legs and smoothed out the skirt of her lavender dress.

"You can come sit in the green room. The president is chatting with Liam so you won't meet him until we're on air."

"It's going to be totally live?" There'd been some back and forth about whether it would be taped and then edited, but the ANS producer had reassured her that if it was live she was actually more in control of the final output than if it ended up in the hands of directors and editors. Apparently live was also better for ratings.

"Yup. No delay. No one expects either of you to start cursing or doing anything else that needs to be tweaked before it goes out." The PA squeezed her arm. "You'll be great. Just remember not to talk too fast and try not to look at the cameras."

"Okay." She said it to reassure herself as much as the PA. What if she froze and couldn't speak? What if she passed out in a dead faint? Whatever happened would be seen live by millions of curious onlookers.

She followed the PA into the green room, which wasn't green at all but mostly gray and had two sofas and some chairs. A jug of water, glasses and a basket of muffins. She certainly didn't have any appetite. She sat on one of the sofas and smiled weakly.

The PA looked at a sheet of paper in her hand. "Barbara Carey will be going in first to introduce you, then the president will come in." Celebrity journalist Barbara Carey was known for her ability to make all her interviewees cry. They'd probably picked her just for that reason. No matter what happened, Ariella was sure she wouldn't cry. All she had to do was stay calm, be polite and survive the half-hour ordeal.

A light went on near the door marked Studio C. "Has the show started?"

"Yup, they're taping. Get ready." She ushered Ariella over to the door, and opened it quietly. The lights blinded her as she stepped onto a big sound stage with cameras on all sides. Barbara Carey was sitting in a set that looked a bit like a living room, with soft chairs and a potted plant. There was an empty chair on either side of her. In a few seconds she'd be sitting in one of those looking at her father.

Her heart clenched and unclenched and she tried to keep her breathing steady.

Barbara Carey's voice filled the air. "…a young woman who's been plucked out of obscurity and thrust onto the world stage by the startling revelation that her father is none other than the president of the United States. Ariella Winthrop." The PA had maneuvered her just outside the scene, so she plunged forward. Barbara stood and she shook her hand, then she sat in the seat indicated. Where was the president? She fought the urge to look around to see if he was standing offstage somewhere.

"Did you have any idea at all that your father was Ted Morrow?" Up close Ariella could see that Barbara Carey was wearing a tremendous amount of makeup, including long false eyelashes.

"Not until I read it in the papers like everyone else."

"Had your parents told you that you were adopted?" She leaned in, sincerity shining in her famous blue eyes.

"Oh, yes, I always knew that I was adopted. They told me my mother was unmarried and too young to provide for me and that she gave me up so that I could have a better life." Her thoughts strayed to Eleanor, so nervous and desperate to hide from the limelight. She'd rather die than be here on this stage.

"And did you ever hope to meet your birth parents?"

"I didn't." She frowned. People probably thought it shallow, but it was the truth. "I considered my adoptive parents to be my mother and father."

"But they died in a tragic accident. Surely you must have wondered about the man and woman that gave you life?"

"Maybe I didn't let myself wonder. I didn't want to try to replace my mother and father in any way." This was turning out to be more of an interview than she expected, and making her nervous. She wished they'd hurry up and bring Ted Morrow out. She probably wasn't giving them the emotional yearning they were hoping for. "But I'm glad of the opportunity to meet my father."

No one knew she'd already met her mother. She'd sworn to keep it a secret, and she'd stand by her promise.

"And you shall." Barbara Carey stood. "Let me introduce you to your father, President Ted Morrow."

A hush fell over the room as she rose to her feet, peering into the darkness just beyond the studio lights. The familiar face of the president emerged, tall, handsome,

smiling. He looked at her and their eyes met. Her breath
stuck in her lungs as he thrust out his hand and she took
it. His handshake was firm and warm and she hoped it
would go on forever. His eyes were so kind, and as she
looked into them she saw them brimming with emotion.
"Hello, Ariella. I'm very happy to meet you." His voice
was low and gruff.

Her heart beat faster and faster and her breathing grew
shallow. "I'm very pleased to meet you, too." The polite
words did nothing to express the deep well of emotion
suddenly rushing inside her.

His pale blue eyes locked with hers, and she could see
shadows of thoughts flickering behind them. "Oh, my."
His murmur almost seemed to have come from her own
mouth. Overwhelmed, their hands still clasped together,
they stared at each other for a long time that seemed ag-
onizingly short and then she felt his arms close around
her back.

The breath rushed from her lungs as she hugged him
back and held him with the force of twenty-eight years of
unexpressed longing. She could feel his chest heaving as
he held her tight. Tears fell from her eyes into the wool of
his suit and she couldn't stop them. It was too much. Feelings she'd never anticipated rocked her to her core. When
they finally parted she was blinking and pretty sure that
she wouldn't be able to talk if someone asked her a question. The president's—her father's—eyes were wet with
tears and his face still looked stunned.

He helped her to one of the seats, then took his place in
the other, on the opposite side of Barbara Carey, who tactfully remained silent, letting the moment speak for itself.
At last the interviewer drew in a breath. "It's been a long
time coming." She looked from one of them to the other.

Ariella's father—it didn't feel crazy to call him that

now, which didn't really make any sense, but then none of this did—stared straight at her. "I had no idea you existed." His voice was breathless, as if he was talking just to her, not to Barbara Carey, or the cameras, or the viewers.

"I know," she managed. She'd known he existed, of course, but not who he was.

"Your parents have obviously done a wonderful job of raising you. I've learned of all your accomplishments, and how well you've handled the avalanche of events these last few months."

She smiled. "Thanks."

"I should have met with you before now but I was foolish enough to take the advice of strategists who wanted to wait until we knew the truth from the DNA testing." His eyes softened. "I was a fool. I only have to look at you to know you're my daughter. And you have your mother's eyes."

Those same eyes filled with tears again, and she reached for one of the tissues from a box that had miraculously appeared on a small coffee table in front of them. Suddenly she could see herself in the jut of his cheekbone and the funny way he wrinkled his nose. They'd been living their lives often only a few buildings apart here in D.C. but might have never met.

"I suppose we have to be grateful for the nosey journalists who uncovered the truth." She said it to him, then turned to Barbara Carey. "Or we might have lived the rest of our lives without ever meeting."

"We have a lot of lost time to make up for." Ted Morrow leaned forward. "I'd like very much to get to know you."

"I'd like that, too." Her heart swelled until she thought it might burst. "I've been longing to meet you since I first learned you were my father. It's not easy getting an appointment with the president."

He shook his head. "I've been anxious to meet you, too. It's usually a mistake to let other people tell you how to run your life, and it's one I won't make again. I have a strange feeling we'll find we have a lot in common."

She smiled. "I've wondered about that. And I'd like to learn more about your life in Montana."

Something flickered across Ted Morrow's face. Maybe he was thinking back to his high school days, where he'd become involved with Eleanor. She wondered how he felt about being deceived for all these years. Would he forgive Eleanor for keeping her secret?

"I had a wonderful childhood in Montana. And I was very much in love with your mother." He spoke with force, eyes still shining with emotion. "It's been a strange journey since then, for sure. Who knows how different it would have been if she'd told me she was pregnant with you?"

"You might not be sitting here as president of the United States," suggested Barbara. "Your life might have taken a different course."

"I might have accepted the assistant manager position I was offered at Willey's Tool and Die." He chuckled. "They paid time and a half for weekends."

"But you had bigger dreams." Barbara tilted her head. "You'd just accepted a scholarship to attend Cornell University."

"I wanted to get out of my small pond and see if I could swim in a larger one." Then his eyes fixed on hers again. "I never intended to abandon Ellie."

Barbara Carey leaned toward him. "Ellie is Eleanor Albert, your high school sweetheart?"

"Yes. I wrote her letters and we'd made plans to spend the summer together." He frowned. "Then one day she stopped responding to my letters. She didn't answer the phone. Her mother hung up on me." He shook his head. "I guessed that she'd met someone else. I had no idea she'd been bundled out of town to hide a pregnancy."

"And you never saw her again." Barbara's famous voice added drama to the pronouncement.

He looked right at her. "Never. I've certainly thought about her over the years. Wondered where she was and hoped she was happy."

"But you never married anyone else."

"I guess I just never met anyone I loved as much as Ellie."

His usually granite-hard features were softened with emotion. Ariella's heart ached at the thought that Eleanor—Ellie—was out there and deathly afraid of him. Thinking he'd be angry and would hate her for her choice to keep her secret. She vowed that once she got to know him she'd convince Eleanor to meet him in person.

"Well, we have a surprise for you, President Morrow."

He lifted a brow. "I'm not sure how many more surprises I can take. It's been quite a year for them."

Barbara stood and peered off into the darkness beyond the studio lights, and both Ariella and her father instinctively stood as well. "It wasn't easy to convince her, but I'm happy to tell you that Eleanor is here with us tonight."

Ariella gasped. She tried to make out her mother's face but it was too hard to see. She glanced at Ted Morrow, but he simply looked shocked. At last she made out Liam Crowe, the head of ANS, walking toward them with Eleanor on his arm. Her hair was carefully coiffed, and she wore a simple burgundy dress, and looked young and pretty, and very, very nervous.

Her eyes were riveted on Ted Morrow like she'd seen a ghost.

"Ellie." The president breathed her name like a prayer. "It's really you."

Blinking, she walked into the glare of the lights. "Hello, Ted." Her voice was tiny, barely audible. He enveloped her in the same bear hug he'd greeted Ariella with, but there was something…tentative about the way he held her.

Stage hands quietly appeared with a chair for her to sit on, next to Ariella, who she greeted nervously.

Barbara leaned toward Ted. "I have to tell you that Eleanor approached us. She had heard of the special from Ariella, and she decided it was time to face you and tell her side of the story."

Ted stared at Eleanor in a daze as if he couldn't believe she was really here.

"Ariella and I met in London." She spoke quietly. "Meeting her meant so much to me. I don't suppose I realized how much I gave up until I saw her beautiful face and talked with her. After that I knew I had to face you again, too, Ted."

"I never knew what happened to you. I pestered your mother for years but she never told me. She said you'd gone to live abroad."

"It was true. I met my husband, married him and moved to Ireland all within a year of giving birth to Ariella. It seemed easier for everyone if I just disappeared."

"It wasn't easier for me," Ted protested. "Why didn't you tell me? You know I'd have married you."

She looked at him in silence, her lip trembling. "I knew that's what you'd do. That you'd give up your dreams to do the right thing. I couldn't let you do that."

"Ellie." Tears filled his eyes. "Maybe there were other things that were more important to me than building a big career."

"I'm so sorry." Eleanor's voice was higher. She was beginning to look as if she regretted coming. Ariella grabbed her hand and squeezed it. "Looking back I can see I made a terrible mistake. I was in a panic. My family said that the scandal of an unwed pregnancy would ruin your prospects. It was a different time. I was young and stupid and alone. I didn't know what to do and I followed bad advice."

"The important thing is that we're all here today." Ted Morrow's voice sounded presidential for the first time since he'd come on set. "We've all done things we'd do differently if we had the chance to do them over again. Instead of looking back and saying 'if only,' I suggest that we embrace the present."

"Well said," chimed in Barbara. "And we here at ANS are thrilled to be a part of bringing you all together again."

After the taping, they filed into the green room. Ariella felt shell-shocked. They'd all watched an edited montage of childhood photographs and background interviews and answered a few more questions. She was relieved it was over but also anxious to make sure she didn't miss the opportunity to get to know her father and mother better.

Ted and Eleanor stood together, awkwardly silent, staring at each other. She wondered if she should say something to break the ice, but then she wondered if it wasn't ice but something far warmer and maybe she should stay out of the way.

"You haven't changed at all." The president's usually commanding voice sounded gruff with emotion.

"You, either. Though the gray at your temples makes you look more distinguished." Eleanor's eyes sparkled. "I wasn't at all surprised to learn that you were running for president. I even obtained an absentee ballot for the first time so I could vote for you."

Ted laughed. "It was a close race. I'm glad of the help." He looked like he wanted to say so much more. He took her hands. "I know you did what you thought was best."

He spoke softly, as if they were all alone, though Ariella stood only a few feet away and production staff moved in the background.

"It doesn't seem that way now, but you know what they say about hindsight."

"I never loved anyone else." Ted's soft words shocked Ariella. She felt embarrassed to be eavesdropping, and wanted to disappear. But she knew how hard it was to engineer this meeting in the first place and who knew when she'd get another chance to spend time with her father. "I probably shouldn't tell you that. I know you were married."

"Greg was a good man." Ellie didn't seem so nervous and skittish anymore. Being in Ted's presence seemed to calm her. "He was always so kind to me and we shared a good life together, even though we were never blessed with children."

"I'm sorry to hear that he died."

"Yes, it was very sudden and unexpected." Their gazes were still locked on each other and they held hands as if afraid circumstances might suddenly tug them apart again.

It made her think of Simon. Circumstances certainly conspired to keep them apart. In fact it was odd that they'd ever met and managed to forge a few moments of intimacy. Some things just weren't meant to be. She was almost at peace about it. It had been a fun fling, a wonderful whirlwind romance, and now she needed to get back to her regular life—whatever regular was these days—and try to forget about him.

"Do you think we could…have dinner together?" Ted Morrow asked with a touchingly hopeful expression.

"I'd like that very much." Eleanor glowed. She looked so young and lovely standing there with Ted. Ariella would barely have recognized her as the white-lipped, anxious woman who'd met her in their secret London hiding place. "We have a lot to catch up on."

They both seemed to suddenly remember her. "You will join us, won't you?" Ted reached out and took Ariella's hand, so that they were all linked. "It would mean so much to me to finally get to know you after all these years."

"I'd be thrilled."

The dinner was very emotional. Their happiness at meeting was thickened with sadness at all the things they'd missed sharing together. Ariella arrived home feeling literally sick with exhaustion, emotional and physical. She'd had her phone turned off since before the taping, and when she finally turned it on she saw that Simon had left a message.

"Great news. I've managed to engineer a series of meetings in D.C. next week. I'd like to put in my application now to take you out for dinner on Tuesday. Call me."

Her heart constricted, partly with the familiar thrill of hearing his voice, and partly with the ugly knowledge that she needed to start weaning herself off him, not getting excited about dinners. Feeling dizzy, she lay down on her sofa, clutching the phone to her chest. She listened to another message from her partner, Scarlet, asking her to call and fill her in on the details. She decided that could wait until tomorrow because Scarlet had probably watched the taping like everyone else.

Her phone rang and she didn't have the energy to come up with a strategy, so she answered it. "Were you ever going to call me, or what?"

"Hi, Scarlet." Her voice sounded far away, like it belonged to someone else. "I'm wiped out."

"I bet you are. That was quite a live reunion. I do believe your parents are still madly in love with each other."

"Was that obvious on television, too? I felt like a third wheel."

"You don't sound good. Are you okay?"

"I'm feeling a little queasy. I'm probably dehydrated or something." They'd been out for a big fancy dinner but she'd found herself barely able to eat. "And I need a good night's sleep."

"All right then. Don't forget we have the Morelli meeting in the morning."

Ariella groaned. She'd totally forgotten they were meeting with the extended Morelli clan to plan a huge fiftieth wedding anniversary. "Ten o'clock, right."

"Call me if you're not up for it, okay? I can handle it."

"I'll be fine."

But she wasn't.

When her alarm went off at eight her comforter felt like a lead blanket. Her eyes didn't want to open. "Coffee. I need coffee," she tried to convince herself. But the moment she managed to get her feet on the floor, a wave of nausea hit her.

Her phone rang on the dresser on the far side of the room, and she leaped to her feet to go answer it. Or at least she tried, but her ankles didn't seem capable of holding weight so she found herself flopping back onto the bed, her breath coming in unsteady gasps.

After about five minutes of deep breathing she got the nausea under control, and managed to walk like a zombie to her phone. Scarlet had called again, so she dialed back without even listening to her message. "You know what you said about doing the meeting without me?"

"Not a problem. You sound terrible."

Her voice did sound rather raspy. "I must have come down with something. I'd better lie in bed for a bit."

"You stay right there and I'll keep you posted on everything that happens."

Ariella stayed in bed all morning. Every time she tried to do something useful the room started spinning or her stomach began to heave. She hadn't been sick in so long she'd forgotten how miserable it was. It was probably from all the stress and anxiety leading up to the TV special. She probably needed a day or two in bed to recover.

Not that she had time for that. She had phone calls to make, menus and décor to approve and clients to meet. But maybe she could lie down for a few minutes first.

Ariella awoke with a start to the sound of the doorbell. A quick glance at the clock revealed she'd been asleep for four hours. She staggered to the door and opened it.

Scarlet stood on the threshold with a concerned look in her face. "I brought some chicken soup." She thrust forward a container from the expensive bistro around the corner. "It has antibacterial properties."

"What if it's a virus?" Ariella couldn't resist teasing her.

"Ah, so you're not as sick as I thought. Let's put it in bowls anyway. I need to grab some lunch before I meet with the manager of that new venue near the river."

"I feel a lot better now. I think I've just been burning the candle too fast lately."

"And Prince Simon has been helping you do it." Scarlet lifted a brow. "But you had a few days to recover from your British romp before the taping."

"Not enough, I guess." She led Scarlet into the kitchen and pulled out two bowls and two spoons. "I usually fight everything off but maybe it's catching up with me. At least I made it through the televised reunion."

"What's he like?" Scarlet poured the soup into both bowls. "The president, I mean."

Ariella paused. "I liked him." She looked right at

Scarlet. "I mean, I liked him before, enough to vote for him—which is lucky, I guess—but he's very genuine and unpretentious in real life. You could tell he found the whole situation rather overwhelming, and that really touched me."

"I saw you guys both weeping."

"And I'd sworn I wouldn't do that." She grabbed a paper towel and wiped up some spilled drops of soup. "I can usually put a lid on any emotion."

"I know. I've seen you in action with the nuttiest clients and guests."

"But the whole thing blew me away. He's my father. We have the same genes. We probably have some of the same likes and dislikes, and he has the same funnily shaped earlobes as I do."

Scarlet peered at her earlobes. "Cool."

"It's frightening to think that I might never have met him. Simon was so right that this is a big life-changing opportunity for me."

"I hear ya. We can plan some White House parties now." Scarlet winked.

"You know what I mean. I have a new set of parents. They'll never replace my parents who raised me, of course, but we'll have new experiences together. We've already made plans to go up to his house in Maine for a few days in the fall."

"Without consulting me?" Scarlet put her hands on her hips in mock indignation. "Just because your daddy's the president and you're dating a prince doesn't mean we're not still partners."

They both laughed. Ariella shook her head. "What next?" A wave of nausea rolled through her. "I need to sit down."

Scarlet followed her into the living room, brow furrowed with concern. "Have some soup." She held out the bowl. "Have you eaten anything at all today?"

Ariella shook her head. Her throat slammed shut at the sight of the soup. "I have no appetite."

"Maybe you're pregnant." Scarlet smiled. She was kidding.

"Sure, if Simon and I had sex."

"You have though, haven't you?" She leaned in. "Even though you won't share the juicy details."

"Barely a week ago. I couldn't possibly be pregnant."

"It only takes one time. And my mom said she started feeling symptoms right away. She took a test and it was positive less than two weeks later."

"We used condoms." Ariella's nausea was getting worse. Scarlet was kidding, wasn't she?

"Don't they have a five percent failure rate?"

"What?" Her grip tightened on her unused spoon.

"That's why most people use something else as well. Still, you're probably not pregnant. You've had a lot on your plate." Scarlet leaned back into the armchair and spooned some soup into her mouth. "Don't worry about it."

Ariella stared at the bowl of soup Scarlet had placed on the coffee table. There was no way she could eat that. There was also no way she could be pregnant.

No. Way. It simply wasn't possible.

Was it?

Nine

Simon paused outside the building where his meeting was to take place and punched Ariella's number into his phone. She was proving very elusive since she'd gone home to D.C. If he were more sensitive he might think she was trying to avoid him. The phone rang, and he leapt to his feet when he heard her tentative, "Hello."

"How are you?" He managed not to ask where she'd been. Didn't want to seem too oppressive.

"Um, fine. How are you?" She sounded oddly formal.

"I'd be a lot better if you were here." He glanced around the busy London street. His imagination wanted to picture her darting along the pavement as she had been when he'd followed her on her secret assignation to meet her mother. "I can't wait to see you next week."

"Yeah." Her voice was barely audible. "Me, either."

"Are you okay?"

"I'm fine." The words shot into his ear so fast he almost jumped. "Great. Really busy with work. You know how it goes."

"Absolutely." There was so much he wanted to say to her but he knew now wasn't the right time. He'd probably come on too strong already, and he was pretty sure that introducing her to his family had been a tactical error. He'd been so sure they'd be bowled over by her charms like he was that he couldn't wait to get the introductions out of the way. Henry had been right. Poor Ariella. There was hardly anyone on earth who wasn't intimidated by the queen, and Uncle Derek was a force of nature akin to a sinkhole. He should have introduced her to one or two family members on a one-on-one basis and let her get to know them before plunging her into their midst. "I did rather shove you into the middle of things here. I could tell you were a bit dazed by your visit."

She laughed. "Was it that obvious? I was way out of my league."

"You were fantastic. I'm sure they'll adore you when they get to know you." He'd caught a lot of flack for bringing her to such a public event with no warning. Pictures of the pair of them had been all over the papers for the next week and there'd been a lot of flapping about suitable relationships and time to settle down and stop playing the field.

He tried to ignore the naysayers. You couldn't hold a sensible argument with fifteen hundred years of tradition so he'd learned to pick his battles and go about his business. If they wanted him to settle down, fine. But not with Sophia Alnwick. And if not her, then why not a fun, sexy, intelligent American girl? He generally preferred to just do stuff and explain it afterward, not get people all fired up over something that might not happen. "I can't wait to see you." Her face hovered in his mind all the time. He wished he could reach out and squeeze her. Traffic weaved along Regent Street in front of him, but time seemed to be standing still until he could see Ariella again.

"Me, neither." She didn't sound her usual self. Maybe she was in a room with other people, or rushing between appointments.

"I miss you."

"I miss you, too." For the first time she seemed to be speaking directly to him. "But I'm worried we're getting into something that's...too big."

He froze. "That's impossible." Then he realized that he was pushing things along the way he tended to, and he tried to rein himself back. "We're dating. That's a perfectly normal thing for two healthy adults to do, don't you think?"

"Well, yes, but...we're both in the public eye. And your family, I don't think they..."

"Don't you worry about what they think. Sometimes they need a little convincing but believe me, I have years of experience in that department."

"I don't want things to move too fast."

"I know. I've been telling myself to slow down. Sometimes I'm like a steam locomotive in motion, but I'm putting the brakes on, I promise you." He was running late for his meeting. "When I get to Washington, we'll do everything so slow it will be downright kinky." He glanced about, suddenly remembering he was in a public street.

She chuckled, but again, it wasn't her usual enthusiastic laugh. She must be getting cold feet now that they were apart. Which only made him more impatient to get there and warm them up for her.

"I've got a board meeting for UNICEF, so I have to go, but I'll talk to you soon," he said after a pause.

"Great. Thanks for calling." She sounded a bit like she couldn't wait to hang up. He was tempted to call her on it, then reminded himself not to be pushy.

"You're more than welcome." Telling her he loved her would be waaaay too much pressure, even if he was convinced it might be true. That could wait for a more intimate moment, preferably one where no one but Ariella was in earshot.

Ariella hung up the phone with her gut churning. In the last three days since Scarlet had planted the idea in her mind, she'd become more and more convinced that she was pregnant. She hadn't paid much attention to her menstrual cycle before, but based on the last period she could remember, she was due for another one, and it wasn't showing up.

Talking to Simon and trying to pretend everything was normal was agony. She could barely get words out of her mouth, let alone make polite conversation. How would his snooty family feel about the exciting surprise of an unplanned pregnancy? She'd bet that wouldn't go over too well.

If she was pregnant, of course. There was no way to be sure until she took a test. Scarlet had brought one over for her yesterday and told her to take it whenever she felt ready. It sat on the shelf in the bathroom, in its unopened white-and-pink box, mocking her.

Was she too chicken to find out the truth? Possibly. If she confirmed a pregnancy, she'd have to deal with how to tell people. Scarlet, for a start. She had enough money saved to take some time off work, but you didn't run a small business with someone then announce that you'd need a year of maternity leave. Then there was Simon....

She walked slowly into the bathroom and looked at the test. Picked up the box and read the directions. It sounded easy. Maybe she wasn't pregnant? Maybe the nausea was just from stress and exhaustion as she'd first suspected. Or maybe she'd eaten something funny.

Her nipples had become very sensitive, but that could happen when she was expecting her period. Same with the sudden swings of emotion that made her weep over television coverage of the fund drive at a local dog shelter. She could simply be losing her mind. People had cracked under less extreme circumstances than she'd found herself in lately.

Her stomach contracted as she picked up the box and ripped it open. She was a big girl and could handle the consequence of her choices. She'd willingly had sex with Simon, and sex could lead to pregnancy. Everyone knew that.

But for some reason it hadn't crossed her mind even once during those steamy nights in Simon's bed. In his castle.

Go on. Do it.

She picked up the stick and followed the directions, waiting the exact amount of time listed while watching the long hand of her watch. If she were pregnant, a line would appear. If she weren't the little circle would remain blank. She'd never wanted to see a blank space so much in her life. Her eyes started to play tricks on her during the agonizing wait, so she hid the stick under a tissue while the time was passing. When she reached the full five minutes she held her breath and lifted the tissue….

To see a thick pink line bisecting the white circle.

"Oh." She said the word aloud, and startled herself. Then she ran from the room as if she could run away from the whole situation. Which, of course, followed her. Apparently—and she still couldn't believe it—there was a baby growing inside her belly, right now. She glanced down at the waistband of her jeans. Her snug T-shirt sat against a totally flat stomach. Though of course at this stage the baby probably wasn't larger than her pinkie nail.

Suddenly she felt dizzy and plunged for the sofa. How could it all happen this fast? She'd slept with Simon for the first time less than two weeks ago and now her entire life was about to change forever. It didn't make sense.

She jumped out of her skin when the phone rang. A quick glance at the number revealed that it was Francesca. Normally she shared everything with her. She'd even taken her mother's very private letter to show Francesca when it had first arrived and she needed to share it with someone. But her friend was now madly in love with the head of the most powerful television in network in the country, and this was quite possibly the scoop of the century. What if Francesca tried to convince her to announce it on air? After meeting her father for the first time in front of the entire country, it seemed anything was possible and her own privacy, even her feelings, were of little importance.

She let the call go to voicemail, as guilt trickled through her. More secrets and subterfuge. She wouldn't tell Simon until he got here. It wasn't the kind of news you should break over the phone and she'd see him in a few days. She'd have to tell Scarlet right away, especially since the nausea came and went in waves and she wasn't sure how useful she'd be on the floor at events if she might have to rush to the ladies' every few minutes.

And then there were the reporters. The TV special had reignited interest and she'd had a harrowing couple of days trying to smile and answer journalists' questions every time she left the house. The creepy bearded guy who practically camped on her block had been joined by a few other camera-laden competitors, all vying for a money shot of her doing something newsworthy, like having a bad hair day. Maybe she could sneak away and run off to Ireland? It had worked for her mom, though of course she'd had her baby before she left.

The similarity in their circumstances smacked Ariella across the face. On instinct she picked up the phone and dialed the number of her mother's D.C. hotel room. Ted Morrow had persuaded Ellie to stay in D.C. at least until the end of the month, so they could all have a chance to get to know each other again. Ellie's now-familiar soft voice answered.

"It's Ariella." A strange wave of relief rushed through her, which was crazy as she'd barely met Ellie, but already she knew in her gut she had someone to confide in. "Something really strange has happened. Can I talk to you in person?"

"Of course, dear. Would you like me to come to your house?" Ellie had grown increasingly confident at navigating her way around D.C. despite an entourage of reporters.

"I'll come to your hotel if that's okay. I'll be there in twenty minutes."

Ellie glowed with warmth as she opened the door, and Ariella felt oddly relaxed in her presence despite her dramatic news. This one person would know exactly how she felt.

Ellie ushered Ariella into the large suite that ANS had reserved for her, and they sat on the sofa. "What's going on? You look white as a sheet."

"I'm pregnant."

Ellie drew in a breath. "Oh, no."

Ariella's throat closed. This was not exactly the comforting response she'd been hoping for. Though she had to admit it was her own initial reaction. "It's okay. I'm perfectly healthy and I'm in a pretty okay financial situation to have a baby." Now she was trying to soothe her mother, not the other way around. The irony of the situation made her want to laugh.

"Do you love him?" Ellie's question shocked her.

"I don't know. We've only been seeing each other a few weeks. It's Simon, who you met in London."

"Oh, dear." Ellie's face crumpled.

Ariella put a hand on her arm. "What's the matter?"

"I feel like history's repeating itself. Why couldn't you be pregnant by a nice ordinary man who could marry you and live a comfortable ordinary life?"

"Simon's surprisingly ordinary for a prince." She tried to smile. "Okay, maybe not ordinary but he's very warm and down to earth."

"But his family. Those royals are absolutely bound by tradition. That's why Prince Charles couldn't marry Camilla in the first place like he should have."

"He's married to her now, isn't he?"

"Yes, but." She sighed. "So much sadness happened in the meantime. I'm still not sure they're ready to welcome an American into the family."

"Me, either, to be quite honest." She lifted her brows. "I socialized with them at a polo match last weekend and I felt like any of them would have happily driven me to the airport right then and there."

Ellie stroked her hand and looked softly into her eyes. "So they're not going to be too happy about you having his baby."

Ariella's breathing was steadily becoming shallower. She stopped and drew in a deep draught of air. She certainly didn't need her baby to be deprived of oxygen at this crucial stage in his or her development.

She laughed.

"What?" Ellie's eyes widened. She was probably wondering if Ariella had lost her mind.

"I was thinking about my baby. I wonder if it will be a boy or a girl."

Ellie's eyes brightened. "I always knew I was having a

girl. I dreamed of little girl dresses and dolls and all kinds of frilly pink things over and over again."

"And you were right." Though Ellie had never had a chance to enjoy dressing her daughter in fluffy dresses or buying her Barbie dolls with extravagant wardrobes.

Ellie's blue eyes suddenly shone with tears. "You won't give the baby up, will you?"

"Not a chance of it. I'm lucky that I've had a good career for a few years now and I have some savings. I can work right through the pregnancy, and probably hire a nanny soon afterward and work from home a lot. It's very doable." She was trying to convince herself as much as her mother.

Ellie smiled through her sudden tears. "You're much more confident and capable than I was. That's a blessing." Then her face grew serious. "Have you told Simon yet?"

Ariella shook her head. "I haven't told anyone yet. You're the first."

Ellie gasped, and suddenly their arms were around each other. "That's a great honor."

"An honor?" Ariella buried her face in her mother's soft hair. "You were the first person I thought of when I needed to tell someone. I can't even begin to tell you how happy I am to have you back in my life."

"Back in your life?" Ellie pulled back a little. "They took you from me as soon as you were born. They never even let me see you." Her eyes still glittered with tears. "They said it was for the best, but even then I knew they were wrong."

"You took care of me for the nine months that I was growing inside you. During that time we formed a bond that could never be broken. Not really."

Ellie breathed in slowly. "I thought about you every day for all of those twenty-eight years."

"See? In a strange way we were always connected, and you came back into my life just when I need you the most."

Her chest heaved as she held her mother tight. It was going to be okay. But first she had to tell Simon.

Simon couldn't stop whistling. It was midmorning and he'd been floating on air ever since he got off the plane in D.C. the previous evening. He had some urgent business to attend to and now Ariella was on the top of his agenda. She had invited him to her apartment, and he took that as a very promising sign. She'd been cool on the phone lately—when he could even reach her. Suddenly she wanted to see him, and as soon as possible. Apparently meeting his family hadn't scared her off as much as he thought.

The sweet and gracious way Ariella had handled his large and intimidating family further confirmed that she was the perfect woman for him. He'd trusted his instincts when he first saw her across that crowded ballroom, and so far they had been dead-on. She was *the one they talked about,* who came along once in a lifetime. He felt it deep in his gut. Or was it his heart? His whole body sang with emotions that he'd only read about in books before. He didn't plan to waste his once-in-a-lifetime chance at happiness. Now all he had to do was convince Ariella herself that they were meant to be together.

His jacket pocket bulged slightly with the tooled leather box delivered just before he left. Nestled in white satin was the loveliest ring he'd ever seen. He had to admit he hadn't paid too much attention to engagement rings before, but once he'd decided to propose, he did extensive research among his female friends.

He made up the elaborate excuse that he might be interested in helping promote the sale of African diamonds to help his charity, and he wanted some feedback on designs. He wasn't entirely sure they fell for it, but he got a lot of great information anyway: not too bulky; flashy is fine but not for everyone; steer clear of color unless you know it's one she adores. There was a long list he'd carried in his mind to the jeweler.

With the help—and promised discretion—of the queen's appointed jeweler, he'd chosen a stunning, very pale pink diamond with a provenance dating back to the maharajas of India. Together they'd designed a setting of tiny diamonds and, since she always wore silver jewelry rather than gold, a simple platinum setting. The jeweler's workshop had put the ring together almost overnight and he was convinced that it was the perfect ring for Ariella and that she'd adore it.

If she'd agree to be his wife.

He wasn't nearly so confident about that part. Ariella wasn't the type to accept just because he was a prince—which was one of the many reasons he loved her. He'd missed her so much since she'd returned to D.C. Playing it cool and not bombarding her with phone calls had been torture. He ached to see her again. To put his arms around her and kiss her as if the world was ending. He'd never felt even a fraction of this passion for a woman before. He knew his intense feelings meant that Ariella was the only woman for him.

The car pulled up in front of Ariella's tidy Georgetown house and he got out. A sizzle of anticipation ran through him as he saw the lights were on in her first-floor apartment. He intended to build up to the proposal. He'd woo her and get the mood romantic before he plunged in with the question of a lifetime.

She'd had cold feet the last time he saw her. He'd be sure to warm them up and reassure her that even the most intractable members of his family would come to their senses. The monarchy hadn't survived for so many years by being inflexible. No one was going to force him out of the country or make him give up his position in the royal family because of whom he loved. Together they'd slowly but surely win them over and make them realize that an infusion of fresh energy from across the Atlantic was just what they all needed. He'd kiss her until she was weak in the knees and maybe even make love to her until they lay spent in each other's arms—then he'd ask her.

His driver handed him the big bunch of pink roses he'd ordered. No doubt any nearby photographers would have a field day, but soon enough they'd all be scribbling the story of their engagement so it didn't really matter what they were speculating. In fact he welcomed them heralding the happy news that he and Ariella would spend the rest of their lives together.

He climbed the steps to her building with glowing anticipation and rang the bell a little too long. The first sight of her face after a two-week absence almost made him shout. She was unquestionably the most beautiful woman on earth, with her long dark hair tumbling about her shoulders and those big, soulful eyes fixed right on him.

When he flung his arms around her, still clutching the roses in one fist, he noticed she seemed a little stiff. "It's so good to see you again."

"Yes." Her answer seemed a little less than enthusiastic.

"I brought you some roses. I thought they might remind you of our English rose gardens."

She smiled. "Your country does have the most beautiful gardens in the world."

They were talking about gardens? He was dying to propose to her and get it over with, as the suspense was killing him. But something wasn't right. She looked pale. "How are you?"

She ushered him into the apartment. Wordless, her shoulders slightly hunched, she seemed very tense. "Please sit down."

He frowned. "I feel like you're about to drop some kind of bombshell. I'm not going to fall down like an old granny."

That gentle smile hovered about her mouth again. "I'm sure you wouldn't, but just in case."

"You do have a bombshell to drop?" His mind ran through the possibilities. Her father had asked her to go live in the White House and forbidden her from dating? She couldn't take the press anymore and had decided to go underground? Aliens had invaded and...

"I'm pregnant."

Ten

Ariella watched as Simon's amused expression faded to a blank. "What?"

"I know it's hard to believe, but I took a test and it was positive."

"We didn't have sex until…two weeks ago. Is that even long enough to know you're pregnant?" He stared at her in astonishment and confusion.

"Apparently so." Did he think she was pregnant by someone else and had decided to pin the blame on him in the hope of a big royal payoff? Indignation stirred in her chest. "Don't worry, I don't expect anything of you. I know the timing is terrible and it's the last thing we expected, but it's happened and I intend to raise the baby. I'm financially well off, so you don't need to worry that I'll ask for money."

"That's the last thing I'm worried about." He blinked, staring at her. "We used a condom."

Apparently he still didn't believe it was possible. "It could have leaked or broken or who knows what. They're not very effective. At this point it doesn't really matter. I'm definitely pregnant." She'd done another two tests. Different brands, same result.

"Wow." He climbed to his feet and came toward her. "Congratulations."

She laughed. "You don't have to congratulate me. We both know it was a big accident."

"Still, it feels like an occasion for celebration." He reached into his pocket and pulled something out.

Oh, no. A leather box. Her heart seized as she realized what he was about to do. Could she refuse a proposal before it was even made?

He got onto one knee, confirming her worst fears. "Ariella." His eyes were smiling, which seemed downright strange under the circumstances. "Will you marry me?"

She bit her lip, hoping to hold back sudden and pointless tears that threatened. She couldn't seem to get words out so she simply shook her head.

He frowned. "You won't? Why not?" His sudden indignation would be funny if she didn't feel so sad. This must be one more sign that they weren't meant to be. It didn't seem to cross his mind that she might have her own opinion and it could be different from his. Probably being a prince trained you to think that everyone was on your side and wholeheartedly agreed with you.

"It would never work." Her voice came out broken and raspy. "Your family would be horrified. They made it abundantly clear that they intend for you to marry someone else."

"They'll get over it." His gaze turned steely.

"No they won't. I've seen enough press coverage of your family to know they're very set in their ways. I don't want to be the outcast and black sheep for the rest of my life. Nor do I want the queen to take away your beloved estate or kick you out of your charity. You've built a life that you love and marrying me would ruin everything, so it's not going to happen."

The truth of her words echoed inside her. She truly didn't want those things to happen, for Simon or for herself.

"Why are you talking about everyone else? I want to marry *you*. Now that you're pregnant there's all the more reason to do it, and soon." He was still on one knee in front of the sofa where she sat. The whole situation seemed ridiculous. Especially as his words were undermining her conviction. Could they really just forget about his family and the reporters and the British public and her presidential father and do what they wanted?

No. They couldn't. Life didn't work like that.

He smacked his head suddenly. "In all this talk about a baby and my family, I think I forgot to mention the most important thing." He took hold of her hands. "Which is that I love you. I never knew what love was until I met you. Every minute I'm not with you I'm wishing I was. When I am with you I don't want to leave. I want to spend the rest of my life with you, Ariella. I need to spend the rest of my life with you. I love you."

Her chest tightened as he tried to put such strong feelings into mere words and those words rocked her to her core. What hurt most was that she felt the same way. Since Simon came into her life nothing else seemed very important any more. But the truth was that the world was still out there, and hoping and dreaming wasn't enough to build a life on. "Love doesn't last forever. It's a brief flash of excitement and enthusiasm that brings people together. The rest of it is work. I know my parents—the ones who raised me—worked hard to keep their marriage strong in the face of all the tiresome details of life. My birth parents obviously couldn't manage to do that."

She frowned and stood up. She needed to put a little distance between them so she could think straight. It was hard to even speak with his big, masculine presence looming over her and his rich scent tugging at her senses. "There's a fierce attraction between us." She walked away from him, with her back turned. It was easier to speak when she couldn't see his bold, chiseled features. "It takes hold of me and makes me forget about everything else when I'm with you." Then she turned to face him. He'd risen to his feet and seemed to fill the space of her living room. "But that will fade. You were born with your whole life planned out for you. You're already married to your family and your country. You can't abandon them to marry someone who they disapprove of and who will never fit in. It was disastrous for your ancestor Edward VII and it would be disastrous for you." Tears fell down her cheeks and she couldn't stop them. "It's better for all of us if we break it off right now."

Simon exhaled loudly, like he'd been bottling up words and emotions inside him. "You're right. I am married to my family and my country and I'd never give them up. I know it's a lot to ask of you to embrace those things and love them as I do, but I am asking that." He strode toward her and took her hands. She wanted to pull away and attempt to keep some distance and objectivity, but he held them softly, but firmly, and she wasn't able to break free. "Marry me, Ariella."

Her gut churned. Her nerve endings cracked with an effusive "Yes!" but her brain issued loud warning signals. "I don't want you to marry me out of a sense of duty, because I'm pregnant."

"I'm not asking you because you're pregnant." Amusement sparkled in his eyes. "I bought the ring before I knew about the pregnancy. I was planning to build up to my proposal and do some romantic beating about the bush before springing the big question on you, but your surprise announcement made that seem superfluous. I want to marry you, pregnant or not, Ariella Winthrop, and I'm not leaving until you say yes."

"You're planning to bully me into it?" She stiffened. Sometimes his boundless enthusiasm and confidence were appealing, and sometimes it was a little scary.

He softened his grip on her hand. "No." He spoke softly. "There I go, running roughshod again. I apologize. I truly wish to embrace a lifetime of your moderating influence on my overly ebullient personality."

He said it so sweetly that her heart squeezed. She did believe him. "I don't think anyone could squash your bubble too much." She chuckled. It touched her deeply that he'd congratulated her on carrying their baby. For the first time it occurred to her that maybe he wanted to be congratulated, too. "I'm sure you're going to be a wonderful father, even if we aren't married."

"That's true, I will be." He hesitated. She could almost feel him bursting to insist that they would be married, but holding himself back, trying not to offend her.

"You're a wonderful man, Simon. I'm totally overwhelmed right now with all the publicity about my father, and my mother and the TV special. It's almost ridiculous that I met you at the same time. It would be crazy to leap into an unplanned marriage without thinking long and hard about the consequences. Perhaps at some time in the future we can discuss it again and...who knows?" She trailed off, running out of words. Part of her wanted to run screaming away from Simon and everyone else and hide from reality.

The rest of her wanted to rush to him and throw herself into his strong arms and let him take care of her the way he so confidently intended to.

"I'm not leaving, if that's what you were trying to hint at." That familiar gleam of humor shone in his eyes. "Me and my ring will sit quietly in the corner until you come to your senses."

"As if that was possible." She couldn't help smiling. "I doubt you could sit quietly anywhere for more than about three minutes."

"Three whole minutes?" He rubbed his mouth thoughtfully. "You could be right. In the meantime, you should be eating for two so I think we need to go out for a hearty lunch."

She laughed. "You're impossible."

"I'm all about making the impossible possible. They said I couldn't raft up the Zambezi or ascend the north face of Mount Everest. They laughed when I talked about internet access in the Masai Mara. I proved them all wrong. If they say an American isn't a suitable bride for a British prince, then I'll spend the rest of my life proving them wrong about that as well, and have fun doing it."

His passion made her heart swell. But he was talking as if she was just another mountain to climb. "You do make a compelling case for your own convictions, but you don't seem to be listening to me."

"How?" His look of confusion made her want to laugh again.

"I said I'm not ready to commit to anything right now. I've had the biggest shocks of my life these past few months and I barely know which end is up."

His expression grew serious. "Point taken. I'll stop pushing my agenda. Now, how about that lunch?"

"That, I'll agree to." And she let him take her hand and

help her up from the sofa. His skin sparked arousal as it touched hers. She hid a silent sigh from him. Why did her life have to be so complicated?

She frowned when Simon's driver pulled up in front of Talesin. The navy awnings created cool shade in front of one of the most exclusive restaurants in D.C. Unease trickled through her. "Are we eating here?"

"Their steaks are world famous. You need iron rich foods."

"Why does everything you say make me laugh?" Then she glanced about. "Did you know it's the president's favorite restaurant?" What if they ran into him here? She hadn't seen him since the dinner they'd shared after the taping, though he'd sent her several warm emails and they were talking about a weekend together at Camp David, the presidential retreat in Maryland.

"Is it really?" He helped her out of the car. "I've been meaning to eat here for ages."

"It's probably hard to get a table without a reservation." She remembered one tense afternoon of scrambling to book a room for an important client's dinner there.

He leaned in and whispered. "Not when you're a prince."

She chuckled. "Oh yes, I forgot about that."

"Welcome to Talesin, Your Highness." The imperious maître d' nodded and gestured warmly. "A table for two?"

"Thank you." Simon shot her an amused smile. "See what I mean?"

She arched a brow. "Don't get cocky."

"I'll do my best."

The maître d' led them through the main dining room and out onto a shady patio with a view over the river.

"Ariella." The now-familiar voice made her turn to find the president standing behind her.

"Oh, hello. How nice to see you." She felt a surge of panic. "Simon, this is President Morrow, my…my father. And this is Simon Worth." Should she have used the word *prince?* She hadn't researched the correct way to address him. Luckily, being Simon, he wasn't likely to mind.

Ted Morrow smiled at Simon. "Would you both do me the honor of joining me in my private dining room?"

"I… We…" She glanced at Simon.

"I suspect we'd be delighted." Simon glanced at her, a question in his eyes.

"Yes. Yes, we would." She swallowed. Simon *and* her father, the president? An odd nagging feeling suggested that this was a little too much of a coincidence.

They followed the president back inside the building through a doorway that led into a bright room with tall windows and elegant furnishings that were a mix of eighteenth century and modernist Italian design. The professional side of her brain wondered if it could be rented out for special occasions, while the personal side of her brain wondered what the heck they would talk about.

The restaurant's most trusted staff waited on them hand and foot, recommending dishes and bringing bottles of wine. She learned that the president had a policy of only drinking American wine, and it made her like him more, considering the other options that must be available in the White House cellars alone. She managed to refuse the wine by saying she didn't drink during the day, but the moment did serve as a reminder that there was a fourth person in the room—her unborn child. And Simon's unborn child. Ted Morrow's grandchild. Her whole life seemed like an elaborate spider web that kept expanding to encompass more of the people around her.

Simon kept the conversation going with easy banter about traveling and the parts of America that he hadn't seen yet but wanted to. Ariella was constantly amazed by how naturally he could talk to anyone. No doubt it was the chief requirement of his role in the royal family and if she were his boss she'd give him a raise. She'd actually started to relax by the time they finished their delicious appetizers and three gleaming steaks arrived, accompanied by mounds of fresh vegetables. Even her shaky pregnancy appetite felt revived by the sight.

"This is turning out to be the most extraordinary year of my life by quite a long way," said her father, after a pause while they all chewed their meals. "I thought last year with the run-up to the elections would be hard to beat, but it has been, and hands down. And the best thing of all has been learning that I have a beautiful daughter."

He gazed at her with such warmth that she felt emotion swell in her chest. "It does seem like a wonderful thing now that the media frenzy is dying down and we can finally get to know each other."

"And if the press hadn't found you, I might never have seen Ellie again. I had no idea she'd moved to Ireland, and if it wasn't for this whole brouhaha, she might never have come back to the States."

"I think she's considering moving back here for good."

He smiled. "I know. And she told me that the two of you are becoming close."

Ariella blanched. Ellie hadn't told him the secret of her pregnancy, had she? No. She knew her mother would never do that. She'd kept her own secrets for so long she could be trusted. Suddenly she hated herself for the subterfuge, but she knew it was too soon to tell anyone. At least until she and Simon had a few things figured out. "We are just getting to know each other but already she's becoming one of my favorite people on earth. I'm trying to convince her to stay in the D.C. area for now, so she we can all try to make up for lost time."

The president paused and took a sip of his white wine. "Making up for lost time is something that's been on my mind a lot." He put down his glass. "I loved your mother with all my heart, Ariella. I would never have let her go. She just didn't know that at the time. I was being a typical man and bottling up my emotions, trying to act cool."

Ariella glanced at Simon. He wouldn't do that. He was the last person to keep anything bottled up. It was one of the things she liked best about him. There were no guessing games with him. "Have you told her how you felt?"

"You'd better believe it." He smiled wistfully. "It was the first thing I did when we had a few moments alone. I apologized with all my heart for the fact that she felt so alone back then, and was forced into a choice she later regretted." He frowned and looked down at his glass, then looked up at her again. "I still love her, you know."

Ariella's eyes widened. She was mostly astonished that he was saying all this in front of Simon, who—as far as she knew—he'd only just met. "Have you told her that?"

"I most certainly have. I think she was astonished rather than delighted." He smiled. "We've been spending a lot of time together."

"That's wonderful." Her heart filled with gladness at the thought that her mother and father could rekindle their love after all these years. What a shame that they'd had twenty-eight years apart. "Is she the reason you never married?"

He nodded. "I tried to talk myself into loving other women, but when it came to the crunch none of them compared to my Ellie and I could never marry a woman I didn't feel wholeheartedly committed to."

"That's my opinion entirely." Simon chimed in. "I think

that choosing your mate is the most important decision you'll make in your entire life."

"Quite right, son. It's not a decision to be taken lightly." Her father looked at Ariella with a twinkle of amusement in his eye. "Which is what I told this young man when he demanded an audience with me to request your hand in marriage."

Ariella's jaw dropped. So they had met before. And this meeting was preplanned. Simon had been sneaking around behind her back. Indignation snapped inside her and she turned to Simon. "What were you thinking?"

"In our country, it's traditional to ask the father of an intended bride if he objects to the marriage. Given the sensitive circumstances of your father's position, I felt I should listen to any objections he might have."

The president laughed. "And you'd better believe I had them." He reached out and took Ariella's hand across the table. "I told him he'd better direct any important questions of that nature to the lady intended, not to me. Since I've been in your life for less than two weeks I don't feel I should have any say whatsoever over who you marry or don't marry." He squeezed her hand. "He's got a lot of chutzpah, I'll say that for him."

Simon smiled. "He told me to stop beating about the bush and go ask you. Which I did. So now I've asked both of you."

"Oh." Ariella's heart clenched as she realized the president was waiting to hear what answer she'd given Simon.

Ted Morrow looked at Simon. "Could I have a few moments alone with my daughter?"

"Certainly, sir." Simon rose from the table. He'd already finished his meal while they were talking. He smiled at Ariella. "I'll be on the balcony."

The door closed behind him, and Ariella frowned.

Should she tell her father she'd said no to him? Should she confess the truth about her pregnancy? It was all too much and her tired and emotional brain couldn't handle it.

"Well, isn't that something. I'm a guy from a small town in Montana and I just told a member of the British royal family to leave the room."

"And I'm a girl from a small town in Montana and I'm having lunch with the president of the United States."

He nodded and smiled, and his blue eyes sparkled. "I guess it proves we're all just people once you look past the pomp and circumstance." His expression grew serious. "Do you love him?"

She twisted her water glass in her hands. "I think I might."

"You don't sound too sure."

"We really…click. I guess that's the best way to put it. I have so much fun with him and I always feel relaxed in his company, which is really weird under the circumstances." She did not feel the need to mention the intense sexual attraction. "I like him very, very much. But the fact is, we only met a few weeks ago and they've been some of the craziest weeks of my life and I don't know what to think about anything anymore."

"Well, I'll give you a piece of advice that might be worth exactly what it'll cost you." He inhaled. "Don't wait around for the 'right time' when everything falls into place and feels perfect." He fixed his eyes on hers. "In my experience, which is considerable at this point, that time never comes."

She nodded slowly.

He leaned forward and took her hand again. His hands were big and warm and soft. "If you love this young man—and from what I see in your eyes, I think you do—don't blow the love of a lifetime because it doesn't fit your calendar. I went off to college naively assuming that Ellie and the whole life I had planned out with her would still be there when I got back." He shook his head. "Instead I got back to find that she'd left town and no one knew where she was. My entire future evaporated overnight just like that. Sure, I got the college education I wanted and then started the big career I'd always hoped for, but the soul of my life, the really important part, had got on a train one dark night and skipped town without me."

His eyes were now soft with tears. "I missed Ellie so much those first few years. Then I suppose I grew numb, or grew used to the dull ache of living without her. When I think of the memories we could have shared it infuriates me that I missed out on all that through my own stupid fault. I should have married her and taken her to college with me instead of stupidly insisting on waiting until the time was right. Yes, times would have been hard and we would have had to scrimp a bit, but we would have had each other, and that's the important thing. If you love this young man, then don't miss out on the opportunity of a lifetime." He squeezed her hand softly. "I don't want you to live to regret it like I did."

Ariella's chest was so tight she could hardly breathe. "I'm having his baby. I just found out this week." She had no idea how he'd react, but she knew she couldn't keep it to herself any longer.

His mouth made a funny movement, like he wanted to say something but was too choked up.

"I told Ellie a couple of days ago and she urged me not to hide it from Simon. I took her advice today. It almost feels like history is repeating itself, doesn't it?"

Her father shook his head. "No, Ariella. History isn't repeating itself because you and Simon are braver and stronger and maybe a little more bullheaded than Ellie and I were." He laughed. "Simon's quite a young man. I don't think you could go far wrong with him in your life."

She smiled. "I know. He's pretty amazing." Then she swallowed. "But then there's the rest of his family. And we'd have to live in England."

He shrugged. "England's just across the pond. A short plane flight. Simon told me he'd already introduced you to the whole family."

"Did he also tell you they were all trying to pack my bags and get me on the next flight back to D.C.?"

Ted frowned. "He didn't mention that part."

"He glosses over it like it's no big deal. He thinks they'd all come around. I'm not so sure."

"Well, I'm inclined to agree with Simon since he knows them better than you. And it probably doesn't hurt that your father is commander in chief of their largest ally." He winked.

She smiled, but then her stomach lurched as she remembered his uncle's cruel threats. "His uncle Derek warned me Simon could lose his estate and his charity if he doesn't follow the party line."

Ted laughed. "I wouldn't worry about that old coot. He has bigger problems to worry about than an American in the family. The CIA chief just informed me that he was involved in brokering an arms deal with a South American dictatorship."

"What?"

"Yup. I don't think he'll be hassling you too much after that scandal explodes in the press."

Ariella stared, speechless.

"Greed. That's what made him do it. Apparently he doesn't have the income of the rest of the bunch but he's trying to live like an emperor. The insecure ones are usually the meanest. That's what I've noticed."

"You've made me feel a lot better." She did feel like a weight had lifted. The queen had been stern, but not actually hostile. Derek was the only one who'd told her to get lost in no uncertain terms. And now he was going to be public enemy number one himself. She couldn't help smiling. "I think I can handle Uncle Derek."

"I suspect you can handle a lot more than one narrow-minded Limey, though I suppose I should stop calling them that if there's going to be one in the family. Shall we invite him back in for dessert?"

"Yes." She grinned. "Let's do that."

Ted opened the door to the balcony and called Simon back. He arrived with another woman on his arm—her mother.

Ariella gasped. "What kind of conspiracy is this?"

Ted Morrow kissed Ellie on both cheeks. "I asked Ellie to join us for coffee because I can't stand to be away from her for more than a few minutes."

Her mother was transformed from the pale and harried woman she'd first met in London. A soft jade-green dress hugged her girlish figure, and the light of passion shone in her green eyes. "And I feel the same way. It's embarrassing for someone my age." She blushed sweetly. Ted Morrow took her hand and led her to a chair right next to his. He seemed besotted with her. Ariella watched in astonishment.

"Did your father tell you how annoyed he was with me seeking his opinion before I asked for yours?" Simon slid his arm around her waist.

"Not really." Heat rose through her as she felt his body through their clothing. "He told me not to blow what might be the love of a lifetime."

"Excellent advice," Simon murmured. His breath stirred

the tiny hairs on her neck and sent shivers of desire running through her. "I hope you listened."

"I did. Did someone mention dessert?" She pulled away from him and reached for the hand-written dessert menu. It felt embarrassing to be romantic in front of her parents.

Though come to think of it, they were getting rather romantic themselves. Ted held Ellie's hands in his and they gazed into each other's eyes as if the rest of the world didn't exist.

"No, I don't believe anyone did mention dessert, but we don't want you starving, so let's get the trolley brought in." He smiled and looked at her belly.

Ariella's eyes widened. Then she realized that everyone in the room knew her secret, so it wasn't really a secret. "I am rather starving right now. Maybe there is something to the old wives' tales."

"Did you tell your dad whether you intend to marry me?"

"I did not." Ariella scanned the menu. Then she looked up, trying to keep her expression neutral while her heart swelled with emotion. "Though I'm pretty close to making up my mind."

"Torture is banned by the United Nations." Simon's imploring gaze made her want to laugh and touched her deeply at the same time.

She glanced at her parents, then tugged her eyes away quickly as they kissed each other softly on the lips, eyes closed in a rapture of togetherness. They'd lost twenty-eight years of happiness together, because they weren't ready to commit all those years ago. Because the timing wasn't right, they almost lost everything.

She drew in a long, slow breath, as conviction filled her heart, mind and lungs. "Yes, Simon Worth, I will marry you."

Epilogue

Three months later

Ariella woke up to the familiar sight of Simon's handsome face next to hers on the pillow in their shared bedroom in Whist Castle. He had scoffed at the notion that they should pretend to live apart until the wedding, and somehow the British public thought his honesty and disdain for tired etiquette was part of his charm. She'd been sharing his bed for a solid month now, since she'd finally packed up her D.C. apartment and her life in the States.

They hadn't told anyone about the baby yet. Somehow it made sense to keep the secret until after the ceremony, so the wedding preparations had to be rushed. She still wasn't showing, at least not in a way she couldn't pass off as the aftereffects of a large meal.

Their bodies were pressed together almost from chin to ankle. Somehow she always wound up on his side of the bed in the morning. It would be embarrassing if he didn't clearly enjoy it so much.

"Morning, gorgeous." Simon's husky voice sent a shiver of awareness through her.

"Same to you." Helicopters buzzed outside the windows, sending adrenaline streaking through her veins. "Is it really our wedding day or is this just a long, fantastical dream?"

"I'm not sure." He smiled, still resting on the pillow. "What do you think?"

She pretended to pinch herself. "I'm lying in a luxurious bed in a castle and getting ready to marry a prince. Sounds like a dream to me."

Simon leaned forward and planted a soft kiss on her lips. "How does that feel?" he murmured.

"Mmm. That feels real." Passion and warmth swelled in her chest and she slid her arms around him under the covers. "Breathtakingly real. But wait. You're not supposed to see me on my wedding day!" She pulled back, suddenly panicked. What else would she do wrong today?

Simon pulled her closer again. "There are some traditions best left by the wayside." He nuzzled her neck, which made her smile. "I'm probably not supposed to make love to you on the morning of your wedding, but luckily I have a rebellious streak."

"We can't. Can we?" Arousal trickled through her like music. "We have to get ready." She said it more as a question than a statement.

"We'll be ready when we need to. You're not planning this one, thank goodness."

She'd turned the reins of the wedding over to Scarlet and her new partner, and they'd done a spectacular job pulling together what promised to be the wedding of the century in less than three months. "It's hard for me not to worry about the details, though. What if the caterer can't get through the crowds to deliver the food?"

"Someone else's problem." He kissed her lips again.

Relaxation soaked through her veins. "You're very good at distracting me." She kissed him back, letting herself sink into his arms. Nothing ruffled Simon's feathers, at least not for long. He was so confident and capable that it was hard to be anxious around him.

His hands roamed over her chest, sparking trails of excitement, and she could feel his arousal thickening against her. "Uh-oh, are we really going to do this?"

"It's starting to look inevitable," he rasped.

"But we have a thousand guests coming. And our friends staying here at Whist are probably downstairs having breakfast right now."

"We'll see them soon enough."

He squeezed her backside, and she responded by pinching his gently, with a giggle. "You're a bad influence."

"I love you." He said it simply, and the truth of it punched her in the gut.

"I love you, too. I think I knew it from the first night I met you, which doesn't make any sense at all."

"Love isn't supposed to make sense." He smiled, looking into her eyes. "That's why it's so wonderful."

Her heart filled to overflowing. "If you weren't the most persistent and persuasive man on earth, I might never have dared to let myself fall in love with you."

"Tenacity has its virtues." He nibbled her earlobe, which made her gasp, then laugh. "Thank goodness I had your parents to help convince you to take a chance on me."

"And now they're getting married, too." She grinned, thinking about the rapturous looks Ellie and Ted always had on their faces when they were together. A president had never married while in office before, and the event,

planned for a month's time, was to be the American equiv-
alent of a royal wedding. She couldn't wait to be there and
watch them finally pledge their vows to each other after
so many wasted years.

A long steamy kiss sent blood racing through her veins
and arousal trickling to her fingers and toes, and other
parts.

"Come here, madam." Simon climbed over her, and slid
his fingers over her hot, ready sex.

"Yes, Your Majesty." Her back was already arching,
ready to receive him. Her fingers pushed into his thick hair
as he entered her, making her gasp with pleasure. Wedding
anxieties shriveled and floated up to the sky like embers
as they moved together under the soft covers, reveling in
each others' bodies. The sweet relief of their climax left
them relaxed and ready to face anything.

"I can't believe we get to do this whenever we want for
the rest of our lives," breathed Simon heavily, as they lay
spent, with their heads on the same pillow again. "I'm the
luckiest man on earth."

"We are lucky, aren't we? This year started out with all
the shocking press revelations that I was the president's
daughter, and spiraled out of control from there. I seem to
have landed in a very soft place."

"Are you trying to say my body is soft?" He poked her
gently.

"No one could accuse you of being soft. Well, except
your heart."

"Okay, that I'll admit to. I'm just glad I found the right
woman to give it to."

A knock on the door made them jump. "Sorry to disturb you," called a tentative voice. "But the dressmaker
requires your presence for an urgent fitting."

"Oh, dear," she whispered. "I think we'd better get up."

"If we must." He nuzzled her face. "The best part is that tonight we'll be right back here together."

The ceremony took place in the estate's thirteenth-century chapel. Since the chapel was only large enough to seat immediate family, Simon and Ariella's vows were simultaneously broadcast to the gathered crowd of guests on the estate lawns and an eager viewing audience on both sides of the Atlantic. When they were declared man and wife, the newest royal couple joined the guests outside on a glorious summer's day.

Scarlet had planned and executed the wedding with skill and courage worthy of a major battle. Tables and chairs were arrayed across the rolling lawns, each decorated with fresh flowers, and, in a green touch that Ariella especially loved, an assortment of beautiful tableware and linens borrowed and bought from collections, antique stores and markets, for a spontaneous yet luxurious, country garden picnic feel.

Given the estate's large size and the volume of the crowd, they decided that one band wasn't enough, so in addition to the traditional orchestra, they had an African ensemble, a bluegrass band and a group of singers from the Westminster Abbey boys' choir, who wandered the grounds serenading guests as they mingled on the lawns and nibbled delicacies at their tables.

Ariella saw Scarlet rearranging a Meissen jug full of roses, and hurried over to her. "Hey, lady, you're not supposed to be working today. You're here as a guest, remember?"

Scarlet spun around, red curls flying. "Old habits die hard, though the team we hired is doing a great job. I'm surprised you're not rearranging the glasses yourself."

"It's taking a lot of discipline." She grinned. "But I'm working hard to retrain myself."

"I'm still ticked off that you're leaving DC Affairs. You could have been our British office."

"I'll have my hands full arranging events for the palace."

"Lucky you." Scarlet sighed. "The most magnificent venues in England at your fingertips. And the most sought-after guests as your family. How did the queen feel about Simon choosing you as his bride?"

"I was very nervous about it but weirdly enough she was lovely to me from the first moment Simon told her he'd proposed to me. She said she could see how perfect I was for him and she welcomed me into the family. Probably the biggest surprise of my life. And with her on my side everyone else welcomed me, too. Simon's brothers are so sweet—it's like having brothers of my own."

"How did you talk them into letting you plan their parties?"

"I could see they needed someone with an imagination to take over. They were still throwing the same parties that seemed fun during post-war rationing. I told them I can provide ten times the flair for half the money, so they're letting me go wild. British people really know how to party when they get a chance."

"So I've noticed." Scarlet glanced around with a grin.

"And some of the Americans are getting crazy, too. I saw you and Daniel dancing like demons to the bluegrass a while ago."

"Daniel's definitely mined my fun-loving streak. Before, I always enjoyed watching other people have fun at events. Now I'm realizing how great it is to be one of them." She glanced up. "Cara's just as bad as me. She's only supposed to be managing PR for the event, but look, she's trying to retie the bow on that table skirt even though she's so pregnant she can barely bend." They hurried over to her. "Drop that bow or we'll send you on enforced maternity leave."

Cara had recently left the White House press office after she fell in love with a network news reporter, and now worked with DC Affairs. She had that famous maternal glow already, her eyes shining and her chestnut hair glowing. "I have more than a month left before I'm due. You should indulge me now as I may not be capable of anything once I'm only getting two hours of sleep a night."

Cara's husband, Max, appeared, glass of champagne in hand. "Max, darling." Ariella kissed his cheek. "You need to rein your wife in. She's trying to do everything again."

"I've talked to her about that and she's still unstoppable. She should never have agreed to work with DC Affairs. You and Scarlet are a bad influence."

"It must be killing you that ANS is getting the scoop on the wedding." Ariella and Simon had decided that ANS should have exclusive coverage of the wedding as a reward for Liam skillfully orchestrating her reunion with her parents. Until recently Max had been the popular anchor of a rival TV network and still worked for them behind the scenes.

"I'm over it. It's a nice change to be able to enjoy a royal wedding instead of barking about it while standing on a street corner somewhere. I notice Liam's busy dancing with Francsesca. Isn't he supposed to be manning the scoop of the century?"

"Nope." Ariella crossed her arms. "None of my friends is allowed to work today, by royal command. Anyone caught working will be thrown into a dungeon."

Max glanced up at the ivy-covered walls of Whist Castle. "Hmm, that sounds like an interesting experience. Maybe I could do a live feed—"

"Oh, stop." Ariella laughed. "Have you seen my husband? We've only been married forty minutes and I've already lost him."

Scarlet nodded toward the area near the champagne bar. "He's locked in conversation with my husband. I think Simon's trying to convince Daniel to expand his network into Africa." Daniel owned a social networking site that had helped spread the word about the concert for World Connect. "I still can't believe you guys managed to get Pitbull, Beyoncé and Jay-Z and Eric Clapton all on the same stage, and only two weeks before your wedding, no less."

"Uh, hello, don't forget Mick Jagger and Aretha Franklin." Ariella still glowed with pleasure at how incredible a success the concert had been.

"Seriously, you guys are a force to be reckoned with."

"The concert was for an awesome cause so it was easy to get people excited." She smiled. "I'm going to Africa with Simon next month to raise awareness of his projects there."

"Look out, Africa." Max grinned. "There's no question that you and Simon are the most popular couple in the whole world. I didn't think his older brother's romance could be outshone but you've proved me wrong."

"At least they don't seem to hate me." Ariella shrugged. "I wasn't at all sure how the British people would react. I can truly say they've welcomed me with open arms. Not that they had much choice with Simon around." From where they stood she could see the queen in apparently intent conversation with her father.

"How could the British people not love you?" Lucy had strolled up with her husband Hayden and his curious toddler. She was a former reporter for ANS where she and Hayden had discovered that her own stepfather, then head of the network, had approved the illegal phone tapping that had revealed Ariella's parentage. Lucy became friends with Scarlet and Ariella after hiring DC Affairs to arrange her own wedding. "I know Liam takes full credit for reuniting you with your dad, and for getting Ted and Eleanor back together."

"All of our ears are burning." Ted Morrow walked up behind Ariella with Eleanor on his arm. He looked both statesmanlike and warm at the same time, and Ellie looked radiant in a stunning Narciso Rodriguez dress Ariella had helped her choose.

Liam was hot on his heels. "I'm shamelessly trying to negotiate exclusive coverage of your father and mother's wedding. A president hasn't married in office since 1915."

Ted Morrow beamed. "I told this nice young man that I'm far too busy enjoying my daughter's wedding to think about my own just yet." He turned and kissed Ellie softly on the cheek. "Though we freely admit that it will happen this year." A big fat rock sparkled on Ellie's slim hand. "We have a few other things to do first. After this shindig winds down we're heading to Ireland to visit the village where my beautiful Ellie was hidden away for so long."

"They'll be really happy to meet Ted." Ellie gazed at him adoringly. "After my husband died five years ago, people started pestering me to date again, and I never wanted to. I seem to have changed my mind."

"Thanks to my efforts, of course." Liam beamed. "Everyone told me you'd never come on air for the reunion, even Ariella. But I've never been one to take no for an answer. If I had I wouldn't have won my own bride." He squeezed Francesca, who grinned. She wore a stunning ruched dress that made her look like an Italian bombshell. "She would have told me the stars weren't aligned right, or something. Speaking of stars, here comes Prince Charming."

Simon walked over and waved. "You all know my cousin Colin, right?" He gestured to the tall blond man walking next to him. "He's the diplomat who negotiated the privacy rights treaty that brought me to the U.S. in the first place."

"Where I found my wife, Rowena." Colin squeezed the pretty woman at his side.

Rowena waved hello. "I'm having the time of my life here in Colin's home country. Everyone's so sweet." She held the hand of her toddler son. Ariella had made sure that all children of the guests were invited as well. Who would want to go away for a weekend to a foreign country without their children?

"Ah, we're not always that sweet." Simon kissed Ariella on the cheek. "My wife can tell you that sometimes we're as stubborn as mules."

"I like to think of that as part of our charm." Colin smiled. "It certainly can be an advantage in foreign diplomacy."

They all laughed. Simon raised his glass. "I hope you'll all be regular guests here at Whist Castle. We intend to travel back to the States as often as possible so it's only fair that you all return the favor."

Ted Morrow lifted his glass. "I'll drink to that. As long as you don't start trying to tax our tea, we'll get along just fine."

"You Americans barely even drink tea," Simon protested. "One time I ordered tea in a D.C. restaurant and they brought me an ice cold glass of dishwater with a slice of lemon in it. Very uncivilized."

Ted chuckled. "We'll be sure to have some of that dark

witches' brew you British enjoy on hand when you and Ariella come to stay at the White House."

"Don't forget the biscuits," Simon teased. "And they're not the big puffy ones dripping with butter that you Americans eat, either."

"I know." Ted smiled. "They're what we call cookies. Since my beloved Ellie has now lived on both sides of the Atlantic, she's helping me navigate the language barrier. It's wonderful being part of a big, international family."

Ariella beamed with pride as her handsome husband wrapped his strong arm around her waist. In a few short months she'd gone from being a lonely orphan to finding herself at the center of a large and growing family, with two loving parents, a sexy and adorable husband and a network of friends stretching around the world. Could anyone be luckier?

"Three cheers for Their Royal Highness," chimed in Colin. They all lifted their glasses. "Hip, hip!" called Colin, and the crowd roared a deafening, "Hooray!"

Ariella laughed. It would take her a while to get used the sometimes antiquated customs in her newly adopted homeland.

"Hip, hip!" yelled Colin.

"Hooray!" roared the guests.

But she'd have fun doing it, and sharing her life with the most caring and loving man she'd ever met.

"Hip, hip!"

The cheers had spread through the crowd and the final "Hooray" boomed across the lawns like rolling thunder.

* * * * *

Look out for
Mills & Boon® TEMPTED™ 2-in-1s,
from September

*Fresh, contemporary romances
to tempt all lovers of
great stories*

A sneaky peek at next month...

Desire™

PASSIONATE AND DRAMATIC LOVE STORIES

My wish list for next month's titles...

In stores from 16th August 2013:

❏ Something about the Boss... – Yvonne Lindsay

& A Business Engagement – Merline Lovelace

❏ Conveniently His Princess – Olivia Gates

& The Nanny Trap – Cat Schield

❏ Canyon – Brenda Jackson

& Bringing Home the Bachelor
   – Sarah M. Anderson

2 stories in each book - only **£5.49!**

Available at WHSmith, Tesco, Asda, Eason, Amazon and Apple

Just can't wait?

0813/51

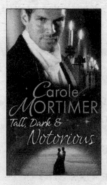
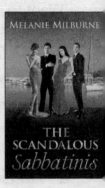

Join the Mills & Boon Book Club

Want to read more **Desire**™ books?
We're offering you **2 more** absolutely **FREE!**

We'll also treat you to these fabulous extras:

- 🌹 **Exclusive offers and much more!**

- 🌹 **FREE home delivery**

- 🌹 **FREE books and gifts with our special rewards scheme**

Get your free books now!

visit www.millsandboon.co.uk/bookclub
or call Customer Relations on 020 8288 2888

The World of Mills & Boon®

There's a Mills & Boon® series that's perfect for you. We publish ten series and, with new titles every month, you never have to wait long for your favourite to come along.

Blaze®
Scorching hot, sexy reads
4 new stories every month

By Request
Relive the romance with the best of the best
9 new stories every month

Cherish™
Romance to melt the heart every time
12 new stories every month

Desire™
Passionate and dramatic love stories
8 new stories every month

Lm 8/13